Praise for
THE 9TH MAN

"Berry and Blackwood keep the pot boiling vigorously until their final surprise.... My country, 'tis of thee, land of conspiracy."
—*Kirkus*

Praise for
THE LAST KINGDOM

"High-octane...A fun page-turner with historical elements."
—*Publishers Weekly*

"When readers crack open a new Malone adventure, it's like reuniting with an old friend. Another strong entry in a consistently fine series."
—*Booklist*

"What you'd expect if James Bond were an American who consulted with the CIA. Bring it on."
—*Kirkus*

"Berry once again proves that history matters, skillfully crafting a fictional story around historical truths."
—*Library Journal*

"What continues to amaze me about the Cotton Malone books is how Steve Berry can consistently find global stories about legendary loopholes or unwritten history that I am completely unaware of.... Berry is in very limited company when it comes to thrillers of this magnitude, which includes those written by the likes of Brad Meltzer, Brad Thor, and James Rollins. This series never disappoints!"
—BookReporter.com

THE
9TH
MAN

ALSO BY GRANT BLACKWOOD

NOVELS

THE 9TH MAN

STEVE BERRY
AND GRANT BLACKWOOD

GRAND
CENTRAL

New York Boston

Copyright © 2023 by Steve Berry

Cover design by Eric Fuentecilla
Cover photograph of Kennedy by Bettmann/Getty Images
Cover copyright © 2024 by Hachette Book Group, Inc.

Grand Central Publishing
Hachette Book Group
1290 Avenue of the Americas, New York, NY 10104
grandcentralpublishing.com
twitter.com/grandcentralpub

Originally published in hardcover and ebook by Grand Central Publishing in June 2023
First trade paperback edition: January 2024

Grand Central Publishing is a division of Hachette Book Group, Inc. The Grand Central Publishing name and logo is a trademark of Hachette Book Group, Inc.

The publisher is not responsible for websites (or their content) that are not owned by the publisher.

The Hachette Speakers Bureau provides a wide range of authors for speaking events. To find out more, go to hachettespeakersbureau.com or email HachetteSpeakers@hbgusa.com.

Grand Central Publishing books may be purchased in bulk for business, educational, or promotional use. For information, please contact your local bookseller or the Hachette Book Group Special Markets Department at special.markets@hbgusa.com.

Library of Congress Cataloging-in-Publication Data

Names: Berry, Steve, 1955– author. | Blackwood, Grant, author.
Title: The 9th man / Steve Berry and Grant Blackwood.
Other titles: Ninth man
Description: First edition. | New York : Grand Central Publishing, 2023.
Identifiers: LCCN 2022057906 | ISBN 9781538721070 (hardcover) | ISBN 9781538721063 (ebook)
Subjects: LCGFT: Thrillers (Fiction) | Novels.
Classification: LCC PS3602.E764 A614 2023 | DDC 813/.6—dc23/eng/20221212
LC record available at https://lccn.loc.gov/2022057906

ISBNs: 9781538721087 (trade paperback), 9781538721063 (ebook)

Printed in the United States of America

LSC-H

Printing 1, 2023

ACKNOWLEDGMENTS

Our sincere thanks to Ben Sevier, senior vice president and publisher of Grand Central. Also to Wes Miller, our editor, whom we've greatly enjoyed working with. Then to Tiffany Porcelli for her marketing expertise; Staci Burt, who handled publicity; all those who created the cover and made the interior of the book shine; and everyone in sales and production who made sure there was both a book and that it was widely available. Thank you, one and all.

A deep bow goes to Simon Lipskar and Dan Conaway, our agents and friends, who make everything possible.

Writing is usually a solitary endeavor. This book was a little different in that we each had to work with the other, as a team. Grant had done that before, cowriting with Tom Clancy, Clive Cussler, and James Rollins on full-length novels (scoring a #1 *New York Times* bestseller for *Dead or Alive* with Clancy). Steve had only done it with M. J. Rose on the Cassiopeia Vitt novellas. Thankfully, we get along great and the experience was wonderful. So much so that there will be two more Luke Daniels adventures coming.

But back to that solitary endeavor.

Let us tell you a story.

Vera Slonim married Vladimir Nabokov in 1925. He was a promising writer whose poetry she adored, the son of a well-known Russian politician. She was a Jewish lawyer's daughter. Both fled communist Russia, eventually settling in the United States.

Their union was special, one that annoyed Nabokov's relatives since he trusted Vera to do everything. She even wrote to publishers on his behalf and answered all of his calls and correspondence.

They kept a common diary in a single book. The Nabokovs always appeared in public together. When Vladimir taught at Cornell University, Vera sat beside him at all of his lectures. They were inseparable. Of course, gossip abounded. Some said Vera was really the writer, not the muse. This came from Vera always being seen behind the typewriter. In reality, Vladimir could write anywhere except sitting at a desk. He liked to say that *"the car is the only place in America where it's quiet."* Vera, who also was his driver, would take him deep into the woods and leave him alone to write.

Eventually, Vladimir Nabokov became noted for complex plots, clever wordplay, daring metaphors, and lyrical prose. He gained both fame and notoriety with his novel *Lolita* (1955). This, and his other books, particularly *Pale Fire* (1962), won him a place among the greatest novelists of the twentieth century.

But he always made one thing clear.

Without my wife, I would never write a single book.

If not for Vera, *Lolita* would have been destroyed, since she repeatedly saved the manuscript from the trash cans in which Vladimir would throw it. She was his inspiration, editor, and first reader. Every one of his books was dedicated to her. After his death she spent the rest of her life managing his estate, even at the age of eighty translating one of his works into Russian. As Vladimir Nabokov himself said he *would have been nowhere without her.*

We feel the same about our spouses, Julie and Elizabeth.

We count ourselves lucky to have them.

So this book is dedicated to them.

Martin Luther once said, *Let the wife make the husband glad to come home, and let him make her sorry to see him leave.*

Wise words.

And so true.

> For Steve, who pulled me from that chasm.
> I couldn't have made that climb on my own.

> —GB

For Julie and Elizabeth,
the most special of all.

Three may keep a secret, if two of them are dead.

—Benjamin Franklin

1.

LUKE DANIELS HAD ONLY ALLOWED ONE MAN TO EVER GET THE BEST of him. Harold Earl "Cotton" Malone. With an uppercut out of nowhere that had dropped him to the deck of a boat. At their first meeting. On the choppy waters of the Øresund, which separated the northern Danish island of Zealand from the southern Swedish province of Scania. Ordinarily, he would have responded with a swing of his own. But not that day.

"*Seems you got yourself a partner,*" Malone said to him. "*Me.*"

"*Do you have a pad and pen I could borrow so I can take notes on what I learn?*"

"*You always such a smart-ass?*"

"*You always so warm and friendly?*"

"*Somebody's got to see to it that Frat Boys, like you, don't get hurt,*" Malone said.

"*You don't have to worry about me, Pappy. I can take care of myself.*"

"*Thought I told you not to call me that.*"

"*Yeah. I heard you. And I gave you one free punch. There won't be any more freebies.*"

Malone's green eyes threw him a challenge that said it all.

Go for it.

But he'd let it go.

As introductions went, he'd had worse. Yet none had more profoundly affected his life than that one.

But enough musing.

Time to move.

He started to climb out of the rented Peugeot but stopped as

Malone's quiet, prudent voice, laced with a hint of a southern accent, whispered in his head. *Slow down. You don't know the area. Sit for a bit, get a feel for things.*

Haste makes for a wasted agent.

Good thing he'd taken those mental notes.

So he sat in the seat and scanned the darkened suburban street that stretched before him. Patience went against his grain. Army Rangers weren't sit-on-your-hands types. More direct action, and Luke had never rid himself of that bold audacity. He'd wanted to be in the military since he'd first noticed hair on his chin, and he'd accomplished that goal, skipping college, enlisting, then graduating from Ranger school. He served ten years with three tours in combat. Once out, he'd needed a job and the CIA had been his first choice. Having an uncle as the then-president of the United States should have been an asset. But he'd never once asked Danny Daniels for help.

Whatever he got, he wanted to earn.

And he found out that being recruited into the CIA's clandestine service was a smidge trickier than filling out an application. He'd made it past the initial interview but had been washed out after the next round. Then a call came from something called the Magellan Billet. Uncle Danny had put in a good word with Stephanie Nelle, who both created and headed the Justice Department's unsung special operations branch. But she'd been crystal-clear. No special treatment. No excuses. He had to earn his spot. Every step of the way.

And he had.

Handling assignments, as ordered.

The Billet now felt like home.

But this trip to Belgium wasn't official business.

No, this little foray was all personal.

Rue Emile Hecq stretched about half a mile on the outskirts of Genappe. The homes along its edges less suburban and more rustic, mostly two-story, white-stucco-and-brick A-frames, topped by traditional mansard roofs. The street was narrow, bordered by cobblestoned sidewalks and small, tidy front yards, each property separated by dense waist-high hedges. A lone streetlight, glowing amber in the night's mist, stood about a hundred feet away. Aside from his rental car there were no other parked vehicles.

He'd checked before arriving and learned online that Genappe was a town of about fifteen thousand whose only claim to fame was as the possible birthplace of a dude called Godfrey of Bouillon, the leader of the First Crusade. It also was only a ten-minute drive from the site of the Battle of Waterloo. That'd be something to see, as he loved military history. Read every book he could on the subject. Would there be time for a visit? That would depend on what he found inside the house two doors down on the opposite side of the road.

Six hours ago he'd received a text from a former acquaintance, Jillian Greenfield Stein. *Of the Pennsylvania Greenfields*, she liked to say with a smile, *not the Virginia ones. They're way too snobby.* Of course, she was not from money. Just a solid, middle-class upbringing in southern Pennsylvania. What she wasn't was emotional. All business in fact. Cool calm nerves flowing through a taut, fit body. Their exchange had been electronic and brief.

I've made a big mistake and need your help.

What kind of mistake?

The kind I can't take back and they may be coming for me.

Where are you?

Genappe. 18 Rue Emile Hecq.

I can be there in a few hours.

Thanks. God, what have I done, Luke?

That last comment compelled him to call her cell phone number. But all he heard was a voice-mail prompt. Two more calls achieved the same result. One thing seemed clear. She needed help. She'd done something, made a mistake, and was now worried *they* were coming for her.

He'd been cautious about his exchanges with her for two reasons. One, he had no way to know if Jillian was on the other end. Could be a trap. And two, no active intelligence officer ever gave away their current position haphazardly. *Stay in the wind*, Malone liked to say. Good advice. Thankfully, though, he'd been enjoying a little downtime in London after an assignment, before heading back to DC. So he'd managed to catch the first flight of the day from Heathrow to Brussels, where he'd rented a Peugeot for the fifteen-mile drive south to Genappe and the address Jillian had provided. Which he'd been watching for the past twenty minutes.

The porch light burned bright, but the front windows loomed dark.

God, what have I done, Luke?

"I've waited long enough, Pappy," he muttered.

And he reached for the door handle.

Suddenly a vehicle turned onto the street behind him, its headlights cutting a bright swath through the darkness. Instinctively, he aborted his exit and slid low in the seat, watching as a white Transit van motored to the curb fifty feet away and stopped.

At this hour?

That could not be good.

The rear doors swung open.

Nothing was visible in the van's darkened interior. Which made him wonder. Why no dome light? A figure emerged, swung the door partially closed, then crossed to the opposite sidewalk.

The man let out a soft whistle.

Not the casual, whistle-while-you-stroll type, more attention-getting.

After a few more paces the guy did it again.

Luke knew what was happening. He'd used the same tactic himself. Whistler was trolling for barks. A yapping dog could ruin even the best-planned operation. So draw them out beforehand. He wriggled further down and listened to the click of footsteps off the cobbles. Every few seconds came another whistle.

No dogs barked.

The footsteps halted.

The man had come to a stop at one of the tall hedgerows. A

hand was lifted to the mouth. A faint burst of static disturbed the silence, then the words, "All clear."

Another figure emerged from the back of the van, this one in a red ball cap and a matching T-shirt. Two more figures, each dressed in dark coveralls, emerged and trotted across the street in near-perfect synchronization.

Like friggin' ninjas.

They slipped through the hedges and sprinted toward Jillian's address, where the pair merged with the shadows along the side wall. Jillian's frantic texts had smacked of paranoia. But she'd been spot-on.

Someone *was* coming for her.

And here they were.

He counted four on the street. Add a driver in the van and that made five. Clearly, they were trained and surely armed. The odds were stacked. But the hard way was like candy to a Ranger.

Whistler motioned.

At the van, Red Cap started toward the house.

Luke reached up and disabled his car's dome light.

Whistler was walking faster now, hands moving. Luke saw the outline of a pistol with a sound suppressor, a big one too, roughly the size of a soda can. A rig like that was as close to silent as one could get. He kept his eyes fixed on Whistler and eased open the car door, slipping out without making a sound. He hunched over and backed up, creeping past the rear of the rental, swinging right and maneuvering behind his target. Whether the van's driver would see him and raise the alarm was hard to say. Didn't matter. He needed Whistler's gun to even up the odds. He hadn't brought his own weapon. Too many questions and lost time dealing with Customs.

He hastened his pace, trotting on flat feet, closing the gap.

Faster.

Almost there.

Now.

Whistler never saw Luke's roundhouse hook, which landed

squarely on the man's temple, knocking him unconscious. The form toppled into the hedge and settled with only his legs visible, which Luke quickly stuffed into the foliage. Then he retrieved the gun, checked the magazine, and, after a bit of groping in the dark, found the man's portable radio and earpiece, which he donned.

A voice was saying, calm and measured, "Preparing for entry."

Luke took this to mean he hadn't been spotted.

Perfect.

But that was about to change.

He eased forward along the hedge line, stopping at a waist-high brick wall, and peeked around the edge in time to see Red Cap unscrewing the front door's lightbulb, plunging the porch into darkness. The guy then knelt before the door and began working the lock. Luke saw the other two men, the ninjas, rounding the corner of the house. Stacking up for entry. Each carried a weapon.

This party was about to get serious.

He heard a soft *snick*, then the front door swung open. Red Cap gave his partners a hand signal and they slid along the wall toward the entrance.

Jillian needed an alert.

He raised the sound-suppressed pistol and fired two shots through the upstairs window. As expected, the report was nearly silent, but in the relative silence of the street the shattering of glass was jarring.

The Ninjas looked up and aimed their weapons.

A light popped on in another window.

Then immediately the panes went dark.

Atta girl.

Jillian was a former marine, a night fighter, skilled in combat. Turning on the light had been impulse, but dousing it came from training. The ninjas mounted the steps to the front door. Luke raised his gun, hopped the wall, and charged. The first man vanished through the door, but the second saw Luke and turned to face him, raising his gun.

Luke shot him twice in the chest.

The body dropped backward.

He adjusted his aim to cover the door, then darted for the dead ninja, snatching up the man's weapon and entering the house. Behind him, the van's door opened. Luke spun. The driver was coming around the hood with a weapon ready.

Luke fired.

Twenty yards, in the dark.

And missed.

The man, though, stumbled backward for cover and disappeared behind the van. From inside the house came a trio of muffled shots, followed by the loud crack of an unsuppressed weapon, a second shot, then a woman's voice.

"Don't move. Drop it."

Jillian.

Footsteps pounded on stairs.

More gunfire, the suppressed and non-suppressed reports overlapping one another.

This was turning into a full-on firefight.

He didn't give himself a chance to consider what awaited him past the front door, and burst through, the two guns up and tracking. A short hallway stretched before him, one doorway on the left, two on the right, a staircase at the end. A shadow figure appeared on the stairs. A muzzle flashed orange. The doorjamb beside Luke's head shattered with splinters. He ducked, rushed forward, and slipped through the first doorway as a second bullet punched the wall behind him.

Upstairs, the gunfire ceased.

"No, stay there. Behind my cover."

Jillian's voice again.

A lone, muffled shot pierced the darkness.

"Oh, God," Jillian screamed. "No. No."

He heard anguish in her voice.

What had happened?

He peeked around the corner.

The hallway and stairs were empty.

He sprinted forward, paused at the second doorway to clear it, then bounded up the stairs to the landing where the steps swung right and up to the next floor. Above, a sound-suppressed pistol opened fire with steady and paced shots. Suppression fire? Designed to keep the enemy's head down. In this case? The enemy was Jillian.

Above, he saw a balustrade and what looked like an open, loft-style space. Sprawled motionless beside the upper railing was Ball Cap.

That left only one of the ninjas.

Luke stuck the guns around the corner and fired twice with some suppression fire of his own. Then he charged up the stairs. Silhouetted by pale light leaking in from what looked like French doors the ninja hunched, half kneeling, obviously wounded.

The guy saw him and fired twice.

Luke dropped flat on the stairs, rolled right against the wall, then rose to his knees. As soon as his muzzle cleared the stair treads, he opened fire. The ninja dragged one leg behind him and shuffled toward the glass doors, which he opened. One of Luke's rounds caught the man in the back and he stumbled out onto a balcony where he pitched face-first over the railing. Luke was there a few seconds later and looked down. The ninja was crawling across the grass, dragging his grotesquely twisted legs behind him.

"Stop," Luke called out.

The ninja kept going.

He fired a shot just ahead of the man, who halted at the warning, tilting his head back and gazing up.

Two suppressed shots popped.

The ninja's body jerked, then collapsed to the grass motionless. A lone figure—the driver, he guessed—stood near the van, pistol aimed, after taking out his own. The man slipped into the van, powered the engine, and drove off. It took two precious seconds for Luke to register what he'd seen and get his mind back in the game. Problem solved. Still—

He stepped back through the open glass door and called, "Jillian."
No answer.

"It's Luke. Talk to me. They're all dead. It's just you and me."

In the distance he caught the warble of police sirens.

He checked to make sure Ball Cap was in fact dead then fled the loft, which was divided by a half wall into a reading nook beside the balcony door and a bedroom. Near the foot of the bed he found a large bloodstain and drag marks that led him to a closed door.

One more time. "Jillian, it's Luke. You in there?"

He placed himself to the left of the jamb, turned the knob, and shoved open the door. "Don't shoot, I'm coming in."

Through the door he found himself in a small bathroom.

On the tile floor lay an elderly man, dressed in pajamas, with a bullet hole through his head. Behind the body, white lace curtains billowed in an open window.

Jillian was gone.

2.

STARLINGS ISLAND, CHESAPEAKE BAY
12:30 A.M.

THOMAS HENRY ROWLAND STOOD, HANDS CLASPED BEHIND HIS BACK, and gazed out through the massive hurricane-proof windows that dominated the study's northwest wall. Wind and rain clawed at the glass, but the dimly lit room was silent save for the faint strains of Wagner's *Götterdämmerung*, spilling through ceiling speakers. He loved classical music, especially Wagner, whom he considered larger than life. For anyone else the opulent study, the grand bank of windows, the bronze bust of Friedrich Nietzsche resting on a lighted plinth, would all be affectation. But if anyone embodied Nietzsche's Übermensch, it was without question him. He lived by his own rules, his own morality, and maintained it with an iron, largely invisible, hand that only his enemies knew existed.

All part of being a professional fixer.

A man who could absolutely get things done.

Across the room stood Ateng Persik. Forty-two years old. Formerly a major in the Indonesian Army's elite KOPASSUS Red Beret Corps. A brutal lot. Their human rights violations were legendary, so bad that most foreign governments, including the United States, had stopped working with them. But for him they made for excellent employees. No consciences or morality to worry about. Six were currently on the payroll. For over a decade Persik, and the other five, had been his go-to team for excising the most difficult of problems.

Like the one in Belgium.

He and Persik had been waiting on a report, which had finally come a few minutes ago.

Persik ended the call and returned the phone to his suit jacket pocket. "The situation is contained. The primary is dead. The woman escaped."

Without turning from the darkened windows he said, "Explain."

"Someone ambushed the team. A man with obvious skill and training. He disrupted everything."

"Who just happened to be there?"

"Apparently so. He simply appeared and interjected himself. Four men are dead. The fifth, their driver, one of my team, managed to escape. It was him I was speaking with. Prior to leaving he heard on the comms that the primary was dead, the woman gone. The driver shot one of ours who'd been injured and another who was found unconscious in the hedges. So there are no loose ends."

"Quite industrious of him."

"As I said, he was one of mine and knew the parameters."

"No way to trace anything to your team?"

"None at all. I hired them freelance through intermediaries. My people are standing by, there, on the ground."

He wanted to know, "Will the police find anything of use at the scene?"

"None of the men carried identification. The weapons, clothing, and communications equipment are untraceable. Their finger-prints, faces, and DNA might appear in a criminal database, but nothing leads here. The van was stolen from a long-term parking garage in Nivelles."

He liked what he was hearing. Persik was meticulous, never taking anything for granted. Which was good, since luck was a fairy tale for the feebleminded. Unfortunately, the carnage in Belgium had been necessary. "And the woman? What's your plan for Jillian Stein?"

"We're working on that."

He needed to know. "Be more precise."

"She's not listed on the home's deed and she apparently has no ties to Genappe, but the Belgian authorities will connect her to the incident since her personal belongings are there. They'll determine she was a visitor in her grandfather's home and want to speak with her."

"Was any search made of the house?"

"No. Not possible. The local police are now there. We should assume the DGJ will be dispatched," Persik said, referring to the Belgian equivalent of the FBI. "Murders are rare for Belgium."

Rowland turned from the windows and tossed Persik a dead stare. "What's your point?"

The Indonesian shook his head. "No point. Just sharing infor-mation."

"You sound like you don't agree with what we did."

"I simply wonder about the risks."

"No need to trouble yourself with worry. What is the situation on the ground?"

"We are on the trail. I have local assets, men I've used before, who will find Ms. Stein, and we will search the house again."

"After the police?"

"That is unavoidable."

"Let us hope there is nothing there for them to find."

"I realize you want the rifle. I will get it for you."

"What do we know about this white knight that showed up?"

"Nothing at the moment, but I will remedy that."

"How?"

"I will handle it, like always."

"You do that."

He motioned that Persik should leave and his acolyte exited the study. He stayed at the window, watching the silent pulses of lightning as the storm swept northwest toward Washington, DC. Pocomoke Sound loomed invisible in the dark. There weren't many privately owned islands in Chesapeake Bay. Most of them were far out, without utilities, making construction difficult and expensive. Of the few near the mainland, only a handful were buildable. Starlings Island was one of those. Only about ninety acres of high land, most of the residents part-timers, enjoying unparalleled views of the bay in one direction and thousands of acres of pristine marsh in the other. Not him, though. This was his full-time home.

His refuge.

He pressed his fingertips to the window and closed his eyes, enjoying the feeling of the thunder rippling through the glass.

The eye of the storm.

Like him.

Chaos may rage all around, but his reputation was that of the unperturbed center of the hurricane. Only there could clear thinking prevail. But that ability had not matured overnight, nor had it been easily attained. And all because of one mistake.

A slight rap on the door broke the silence.

With a barely perceptible hiss the study's double doors opened and Jack Talley entered. Where Persik handled all of the covert off-the-books matters, Talley was the official head of security, a public face, out front, known to many. A former army captain, special forces, highly trained. He caught Talley's reflection as the man halted in the middle of the room and stood in silence, as if facing a general. Talley was tall, lean, with a broad nose, thin lips, and close-cropped black hair. Maybe fifty years old, Rowland had never really asked. The only blemish on the otherwise spit-and-polished façade? A limp in his right leg from a wound received in wartime, which had ended Talley's military career.

"How many of your core team do you trust without reservation?" he asked Talley, still gazing out the window.

"All of them."

He turned and faced his man. "Don't be obtuse."

"I wasn't trying to be. I meant it. There are seven that I'd stake my life on—and have many times in Iraq, Somalia, Afghanistan. We've been up to our knees in problems more times than I can count. They are the best."

"Families? Children?"

"Two of the men have those. The others are unattached."

Perfect. "Leave the two behind. Attachments are a weakness. Take your five and shadow Persik. He's headed for Belgium."

"I have a family."

"Yes, you do. But you're in charge and that makes you different."

A nod signaled understanding.

Talley had always been a man of few words.

"I'll advise you as things progress," he said. "But concentrate on Persik. Watch him. Until I say otherwise, if he blows his nose I want to know where he tossed the tissues. Be prepared to act, on my command."

"You have a particular concern with him?"

He realized that his request might raise some radar. After all, he'd never shown this level of distrust before. "I have a concern that he's not doing his job. That, I cannot tolerate."

Though he could not speak it, with this particular situation, if it wasn't handled properly, there could be dire consequences.

He pointed. "Can you handle that?"

Talley nodded, then turned and headed for the door.

"Jack," he said.

Talley stopped, turned, and faced him.

"Do this and there will be a larger-than-usual bonus this month that can help with those attachments of yours."

"I appreciate that. Consider it done."

3.

CHARLEROI, BELGIUM
7:20 A.M.

LUKE WHEELED THE PEUGEOT INTO A PARKING SPOT BEHIND THE Hotel De La Basse Sambre, allowed the tires to bump the curb, then shut off the ignition. He leaned his forehead against the steering wheel, then sat back. What had he managed to get himself into this time? One minute he was asleep in a London hotel room, the next he'd taken fire and eliminated the shooters.

Back in Genappe, as soon as he'd realized Jillian had disappeared into the night, he'd done the smart thing and wiped down the three guns, dropped them on the bathroom floor, then left the house as fast as his feet could carry him. Outside, he found the guy he'd coldcocked into the bushes with a hole in his head. That made two killed by their own. To the police any explanation he might have offered would have been pointless. He was a foreigner who, within minutes of arriving in their sleepy town, was found standing in a house full of dead people.

Oh, and by the way, I'm also an American intelligence operative.
Yeah, right.

That dog definitely wouldn't hunt.

Even if he managed to talk his way out of murder charges, whatever trouble was chasing Jillian might have caught up to her by then. Better to, as Malone would say, make like the wind and disappear. He wasn't even half a mile down Rue Emile Hecq when he heard the police cars screeching to a stop. By the time he reached Highway N5 the sirens were so loud it sounded like the mother of all carnivals had dropped from the sky and landed squarely in Genappe. In his rearview mirror blue lights pulsed in rhythm over the treetops.

Twenty minutes later he'd made it to the outskirts of Charleroi, an industrial city of two hundred thousand south of Genappe. Hard to know if any witnesses had jotted down his license plate. It was possible. But not likely. The houses back on Rue Emile Hecq were widely spread and screened by hedges so unless the shooting had prompted a neighbor to come outside and walk down the street, he was in the clear. True, taking the chance that he'd been seen was a big roll of the dice. But hell, wasn't everything? The army, combat, the Magellan Billet, the dozens of impossible scrapes he'd survived? So far the dice had been good to him. Of course, the older he got the more careful he'd become with his bets. Not circumspect, mind you, but clearly leaning that way.

Next step?

Find Jillian before the bad guys did.

First, though, he needed to become a little ghostly. True, his Magellan Billet–issued smartphone was state-of-the-art, operating off an isolated government server that was not subject to public access or scrutiny. Its incoming and outgoing transmissions were scrambled by a highly sophisticated program created especially for the Billet. And it was untrackable. About as private and secure as one could be on the open airways. One of the rules of Stephanie Nelle, his boss at the Magellan Billet, required that all field officers keep one on them at all times.

But this was not official business.

A quick Google search told him Belgium accommodated four primary cell phone carriers—Base, Orange, Proximus, and Telenet—all of which had retail stores in Charleroi. He noted the ones closest to him and their hours, then checked his watch. He had almost three hours to kill. Might as well get his head down while he could.

So he climbed out of the car and headed for the hotel lobby.

He found sleep elusive, so he stared at the ceiling. A whole mess of questions with no answers rifled through his brain. First, what could've spooked Jillian so badly that she left? The woman was no shrinking violet. In the history of the U.S. Marine Corps she was one of a handful of females who'd not only bested the grueling Infantry Officer Course, but gone on to serve as an 0302 platoon commander. Add to that three tours in Iraq and you had yourself a genuine American soldier. If Basra, al Kut, and al Anbar hadn't shaken her, what the hell had? Next, the dead man on Jillian's bathroom floor? Who was he? A hole to the head signaled execution. That meant personal. And what he'd heard her cry out. *No, stay there. Behind my cover.* Followed by a single shot. Then, *Oh, God. No. No.* That had sounded personal too. Third, what was Jillian doing in Genappe, Belgium, of all places? Not exactly a tourist hot spot. And then there was—

He stopped himself.

His thoughts were running wild.

Which is never good, Malone would say.

But there was something else gnawing at him.

This one was close to him.

Though he and Jillian had only been involved briefly, there was a not-so-small part of him that'd always wondered if she was the one who got away. She was a smart, sassy, brave woman who didn't mind using her femininity when necessary. He'd enjoyed their time together and had thought of her more than once over the past few years. Their communications had been sporadic, but steady. Two friends catching up every once in a while through texts and emails and an occasional call. Nothing in person, though.

So of all the people in the world she could have called, why him?

He forced his brain into neutral and closed his eyes.

Eventually, sleep came.

He was up and showered and at the hotel's breakfast bar by 9:20, where he was disappointed to discover Belgian waffles weren't exactly a thing in Belgium. But Liège waffles were, and there was plenty of hot coffee, toast, and marmalade. Ranger-rested from a quick snooze, his belly full, he left the hotel a few minutes before the nearest cell phone store opened at 10:00. The unit he bought was cheap and barely smart, its minutes expensive, but it would do the job. Back in his car, he punched in the number Jillian had used the night before and texted, It's Luke, call me.

Five minutes later his phone pinged. Prove it.

He thought for a moment then replied, You spilled bug juice on your IOC patch.

Bug juice was navy slang for the sugary drink served on ships. It came with no nutritional value whatsoever, but it tasted good and polished brass wonderfully. The day Jillian graduated from the Infantry Officer Course she'd spilled a glass of it on her brand-spanking-new IOC shoulder patch. Embarrassed, she'd told only Luke.

That tidbit should be enough identification.

But when five minutes passed without a reply he texted, Go silent on this number. Get yourself a prepaid cell and call me.

Another ten minutes went by then, okay.

An hour later his phone rang.

"Tell me it's a coincidence," Jillian immediately said.

"What are you talking about?"

"You, and that death squad, all showed up together."

"Not together. At the same time. There's a difference." He then

17

explained the sequence of events, starting with Whistler climbing out of the van and ending with the driver killing one of the intruders then fleeing.

"You didn't hear me calling your name?" he asked.

"As soon as I realized he was dead, I was out the window. I never heard you."

"Who's '*he*'?"

"My grandfather, Luke. They murdered my damn grandfather. Shot him in the head. He was dying of cancer and they just shot him."

He felt like he'd been punched in the stomach. Though he'd never met Benjamin Stein, he felt like he had from listening to her talk about him. When she was six Jillian's parents died in a car crash. Benji, as she called him, and his second wife, Karen, had raised her. He'd been military, so she became military. Luke had heard all of the Benji stories.

"I'm sorry, Jillian."

"Promise me you aren't part of this, Luke."

"Is that a serious question?" he asked.

"Promise me."

"Cross my heart. You texted, I came. Nothing more to it. And by the way, why contact me?"

"I decided to find the one person in this world I thought I could truly trust."

"So what's all this about? Who were those people? What do they want?"

"Question one, I have no idea. Questions two and three, it deals with my grandfather. I was researching something and must have triggered their interest. I think I got Benji killed, Luke."

"You don't know that. Where can we meet? We need to put our heads together."

Jillian replied, "I'm in—"

"Don't tell me where you are. Tell me where you want to meet. Pick the place and time. Somewhere public with lots of entrances and exits and a police presence."

"Give me five minutes."

It took two. Luke's phone pinged with a text.

Grand Place. Brussels. De Gulden Boot. 4:30 p.m.

4.

MARYLAND — 5:46 A.M.

JACK TALLEY FOUND HIS LUG BAG AT THE BACK OF THE CLOSET WHERE he kept it on ready. Cordura nylon. Fifty-five liters of storage space. Loaded with compartments, some even fleece-lined. Perfect for the most brutal of environments. Inside were all the essentials. Two Beretta M9s with extra magazines. A fixed-blade knife and multi-tool. An equipment web harness. $5,000 cash. False passport and identification linking him to the FBI, which made carrying weapons so much easier in Europe. Portable radio with headset. First-aid kit. A few calorie-dense rations. A flashlight. Thirty feet of paracord. Duct tape. Fire starter. And a compass.

How many times had he retrieved his go-bag over the past seven years?

Too many to count.

That was how long he'd been in Thomas Rowland's employ. At first, he'd been grateful for the job. His army career had come to an abrupt end with a bullet to the leg. It had taken three surgeries and months of physical therapy just to be able to stand again. Running? Out of the question. Walking with a limp? That had been his fate. And when he refused a desk assignment he'd been medically discharged and sent on his way without even a thank-you.

That sting still hurt.

Rowland had found him and offered a steady income with a generous salary. Both for his expertise and for discretion. Especially discretion. Thomas Rowland was, if nothing else, complex.

Jack had managed to learn a lot about him.

An only child with a loving, discontented mother, he grew up in Maryland horse country in a big house with few neighbors. His father, Charles Albert Rowland Jr., had been recruited into the OSS in its infancy, at the start of World War II, driven by both ambition and a sociopathic streak that made him perfect, after the war, to head the newly formed CIA's ugly-underbelly, paramilitary faction. Lots of assassinations, coups, murders, and bribery. Most of which failed to accomplish much more than cement Charlie Rowland's power.

On the home front his father was gone far more than there, appearing every so often and staying just long enough to stoke Thomas' own sociopathy. He did that with ridicule and by moving the goalposts, which steadily drifted farther away all through high school. His father pushed Thomas into Yale. Back in the early days of the CIA, Yale attendance was considered pro forma for any serious job consideration. Eventually, pleasing his father mattered less than following his own path, so he shied away from the CIA and found the Secret Service. In 1964 he finally surrendered and joined his father at Langley, determined to outshine him as an even uglier and crueler manipulator.

Which he accomplished.

No question.

Tom Rowland succeeded his father and headed up the CIA's special operations division for nearly three decades. Just a new fancy name for paramilitary missions. Along the way he managed to acquire and utilize the power of information. He took a lesson from J. Edgar Hoover, who was a close friend, and learned so much about so many. But unlike Hoover, whose files were all destroyed at his death, Rowland still possessed his. People in power had a tendency to do stupid things, which dug some fairly deep holes, and extricating themselves often proved difficult. Too many complications, too much exposure. That's where Rowland came in. His reward? A favor done was a favor owed. And Tom Rowland was an expert in accumulating favors.

To accomplish the task Rowland hired competent people and paid them well. For the first five years of his employment Jack had not minded the rule bending and breaking, reasoning that sometimes bad things happened to bad people. But when those bad things began to befall good people, he'd taken a second look. Even more troubling had been the realization that Tom Rowland was totally and completely amoral. The man had no conscience, nor any value system to violate. Literally anything and everything was on the table. Nothing was off limits. Not even murder. Jack, though, was not the same, and he'd come to realize that his narcissistic employer was a dangerous man.

But what was happening here seemed different.

Rowland had been sketchy with details.

Which was unusual.

And the distrust of Persik? That was new. And surprising. Always before, Persik had been given a wide latitude where no out-of-bounds markers existed. Too wide, in Jack's opinion. He'd never cared for Persik. Nothing more than a hired killer. But he'd kept his opinion to himself. Funny how money had a way of silencing one's own conscience.

"You look a million miles away."

He turned from the bed and saw his wife, Jill, at the bedroom door. They'd been married a long time. She'd been there with him through his entire army career. They had three children. Grown. Living their own lives. No grandchildren as yet, but they were hoping soon. The money he'd made over the past seven years had provided all of them a comfortable life. But that had come at a price.

"Just thinking about what I need to take with me," he said, lying.

"Where are you going?"

He smiled. "You know better."

With a wink she said, "Can't blame a girl for trying."

Long ago, back in the army, the rules had been established. No details on where, when, or why with regard to his work. Like the military, Rowland demanded total secrecy. No exceptions. Not ever.

"How long will you be gone?" she asked.

That question was allowed. Sometimes. "Hard to say. A few days at least. I'll check in when I can."

She entered the bedroom and came closer. "You look tired."

"I am. But duty calls."

Lately, he'd begun to make light more and more. A defensive mechanism? Probably. But he *was* tired.

Of everything.

She gently grasped his arm. "Will you at least try and sleep on the plane?"

"Did I say I was getting on a plane?"

She smiled. "No, you didn't. Do you want some breakfast before you go? Or maybe some peanut butter ice cream and Oreos?"

"The ice cream would be wonderful."

She kissed him on the cheek, then left the bedroom.

She was a good woman and he was lucky to have her. But more and more lately he'd wondered what she would think of him if she knew exactly what he did for a living. Where the money had come from. And all the people who'd been hurt or destroyed in the process. Rowland firmly believed that greed was a universal constant that cut across all races and cultures. It was what both created and solved problems. He'd resented Rowland's parting comment. A promise of a bonus, thinking that money would be a great motivator. Unfortunately, in the past, it had indeed been just that.

Not anymore.

He finished his survey of the bag, satisfied as to its contents. He was flying private on a NetJets Bombardier Global 5500, which could easily accommodate him and his team. They were scheduled to leave from Dulles in three hours, nonstop to Brussels. Cars would be waiting for them on the ground. Ateng Persik was a few hours ahead on another Bombardier.

He thought again about Rowland's sudden negativity on Persik. Which made him wonder.

Could this be the moment he'd been waiting for?

5.

LUKE WAS IMPRESSED.

Jillian had chosen their meeting location well.

Brussels' Grand Place, or Grote Markt, was a UNESCO World Heritage Site that began its life eight hundred years earlier as a common feature of most Belgian towns, a central location around which commerce and politics thrived.

The cobblestoned square, which Luke determined from Google Earth to be the size of two football fields, was flanked by opulent, spired guild halls, a town hall, and the King's House where the city's daily bread yield was once sold and traded. Today it served as the Brussels City Museum with its rooms partitioned into gift shops, chocolatiers, and restaurants. There was, Luke had noticed, even a Starbucks and a Hard Rock Cafe. While he had no problem with either business, their presence here left a sour taste in his mouth, like finding a Chuck E. Cheese beside the Victoria Memorial at Buckingham Palace.

He arrived shortly before 4:00 and spent twenty minutes getting a feel for the area. As best he could tell, vehicle traffic was prohibited within a hundred yards of the Grand Place including the alleys—seven of them—that fed directly into the square proper. He counted no less than five police cars roving the perimeter. At 4:00 on the dot he circled the Peugeot back to the public lot he'd spotted on Herb Market Street about a quarter mile away and parked.

He climbed out and texted Jillian.

Here. Same spot?

Her reply was immediate.

Y.

He found the De Gulden Boot, or Gold Boat, restaurant beside a Godiva chocolate shop in one of the guildhalls on the square's south side. Twenty euros to the hostess and he was shown to one of the red-and-green-umbrella tables outside. He perused the menu, then texted, Still partial to cappuccino? Though Jillian's forte had been combat, not intel work, she was a smart cookie and he hoped she was already watching from a distance. Over the past twelve hours the house she was staying in had been attacked, her grandfather had been murdered, and the man she'd called for help had come through her front door at the same time as the killers.

She had every right to be wary.

What or who was behind all this he did not know, but one thing was certain. They were shoulder-deep in a dangerous situation. Both of their heads had to be in the right place.

His burner phone trilled.

"Depends on the day," Jillian said when he answered. "Today feels like an espresso."

"Okay. This is your dance. What's the tune?"

"Were you followed?"

"If I was somebody got ahold of Harry Potter's invisibility cloak."

"Order a Donko's—"

"A what?"

"Just do it and sit for a bit," she said. "At 4:30—"

"Make it longer," he said. "If we've got company, they'll be more patient than that."

Open meeting locations like this could be double-edged swords, providing cover for both predator and prey. But he still liked them. He always found it amusing in movies and TV where the clandestine meetings occurred in some dark, secluded space. Talk about stupid. There was definitely safety in numbers.

"Quarter till, then," she said. "Meet outside the Belgian Brewers Museum."

"Don't tease me."

"It's a museum, Luke, not a pub. Directly across from you."

"Got it. If you spot anything that makes you froggy, go ahead and jump. Text me *abort*, clear the area, then contact me again when safe."

"Should I be nervous?"

"Until we know there's nothing to be nervous about, absolutely."

He passed the time people-watching and sipping what he judged the best cup of coffee he'd ever had. Donko's, it turned out, was a Belgian coffee company whose dark roast had won countless awards. The name was a bit off plumb, but a brew that good could've been named Pig Spit for all he cared.

At 4:45, having heard nothing from Jillian, he paid his bill, rose, and started across the square. Though it was a sunny, cloudless, barely spring day, tourist season wasn't yet in full swing. That meant foot traffic was light, perhaps a couple hundred people milling about in all directions. When he reached the museum's entrance Jillian texted Inside.

He climbed the steps and entered through a narrow door, paying the five-euro admission fee. Behind him Jillian said, "This brings back memories."

He turned to see her standing beside a postcard rack. "Memories of me taking you to places that don't serve beer?"

She smiled, "No, dummy, you and me on redneck dates."

On their first outing he'd taken her to the most dilapidated putt-putt course in the state of Hawaii. Most of the artificial turf fairways sprouted grass and mushrooms. And she'd beat him. Badly. They met during a joint army-marines RIMPAC exercise at Hawaii's Pohakuloa Training Area, a rough piece of forested real estate on a high volcanic plateau thirty miles west of Hilo. The monthlong exercise was an eight-hundred-person game of capture the flag involving laser-simulated small arms, mortars, and grenades. Each day they'd "fight" one another to digital death, and at night they'd retire to either Hilo or Waimea for a few hours of beer and bragging.

He and Jillian connected on that first night and had somehow started swapping worst-date stories, which quickly turned into the date-from-hell contest, which he'd won. Their attraction had been instantaneous and irresistible and they'd spent every available moment together. When the exercise ended, so had their romance, but not their friendship. That had endured. They'd kept in touch with the occasional *Hey, how are you doing?* text at holidays. Something was there between them. But not enough for either of them to acknowledge or abandon their careers for. Now here they were, as the song said, *Reunited and it feels so good.*

He gave her a big hug, which she returned, then whispered in her ear, "I'm sorry about Benji."

"Me too," she said, not letting go. "I'm sorry I dragged you into this."

"I'da been mad if you hadn't." He drew back, his hands still on her arms. "Are you hurt? There were a lotta bullets flying."

"A graze on my thigh, but it's fine. You?"

"Not a scratch."

"Good old Luke's Luck, right?"

He chuckled. "I chalk it up to unmatched skill and catlike—no, superhuman—reflexes."

"It's nice to see your ego remains at full strength." She grinned. "Follow me. I was wrong, by the way. They've got a beer tasting room here."

"Now we're talking. Lead on."

The museum itself was downstairs. In between exhibits, old oak casks, and copper machinery they found the tasting room, a small space of two-person standing tables lit by electric candle sconces. They ordered the standard tasters selection. The waitress deposited a tray of shot glasses on the table, then disappeared. He sampled a sip of an amber ale, then said, "So how did all this start? What do you know?"

"I brought it down on me and Benji," she said, anguish in her voice. "I sent an email I shouldn't have."

"To who?"

"I don't know."

Odd. "What did you say in the email?"

"It was a request for information. Then seven words that most likely started the ball rolling. *Tell me what you know about Kronos.*"

6.

LUKE WAS PUZZLED AND CONFUSED.

"What's Kronos?" he asked her.

"I have no idea. But, apparently, it's code for 'come kill me.' "

And her eyes began to moisten at the bad memories.

He hadn't seen her in several years, but little had changed. Still curvy and incredibly fit. Her hair remained the darkest black and shiny, like a raven's feathers, but a little longer and fuller than before, down to her shoulders. She was about his age, early thirties, her face full of memorable features, especially the eyes, a pale, lovely green. Best, though, had been her confidence. Never any sign of misgiving, nervousness, or uncertainty. Always decisive and determined, which he'd really liked. He also noticed that little had changed in the fashion department. Her wardrobe outside of a military uniform was always black, white, gray. No other colors. Never. Ever. From their intermittent communications he knew she'd served five years, then did not re-up. Last he recalled she was working for a private security firm somewhere on the East Coast.

Now here they were.

"You couldn't have known any of what would happen," he said to her. "Let's back up. When and where did you first hear the word Kronos?"

"From Benji."

"Why do you call him that?"

"A habit from childhood. He was my grandfather, not my father, so I shortened his first name. The nickname stuck."

He smiled.

"He was career army," she said. "Thirty-five years. His last posting was to the International Military Staff at NATO Headquarters in Brussels. He loved it here so, when he retired, he bought the house in Genappe. His second wife, Karen, died a couple of years ago, so I moved here six months back to be with him, after he was diagnosed with terminal cancer. Last month his doctor recommended a care facility, but he was having none of that. He wanted to die at home with me. A nurse came a few times a week, but I handled most of his care. A few weeks ago the pain became so bad the doctor started morphine, which sent him off to la-la land. He started talking about Kronos. Disjointed stuff. Stream of consciousness. Babbling. But not all incoherent."

"About anything in particular?" he asked.

She gave a frustrated shake of her head. "He kept talking about a secret he'd discovered. It would change everything. He said that over and over. The weight of it, and how it had to be exposed."

Her pain was obvious. She'd had a tough time.

"Until a few weeks ago I thought my grandfather was the

happiest, most contented person I knew. But that was all a façade."

Not surprising. Everybody had secrets.

Even old soldiers dying with cancer.

"Last week he let slip something about a lockbox. Eventually I found it. One of those fireproof document-sized models tucked into the floorboards under the bed."

"Where is it now?"

"Still there, I hope."

So did he.

"The worse the pain got, the more he talked," she said. "He was never lucid enough to fully explain anything. Just nipped around the edges. Kronos. Secrets. Need to do the right thing. Luke, whatever this is, it destroyed him. He was top of his class at West Point, a decorated combat vet, brave, brilliant, dedicated. Everything it took to make general, he had it. But he retired out as a full bird colonel, one step below brigadier general. It hurts me to say this, but his career was never what it should have been."

"And you think this Kronos business is the cause?"

"Without a doubt. He said as much during his ramblings. *Kronos will hurt us all.* A couple of nights ago it all got to be too much. He's lying there dying before my eyes. I was angry, sad, and frustrated. So I found that lockbox, opened it, and started rifling through the contents."

"Which were?"

"Not all that much. But I did find an invoice and a key, along with an email address on a scrap of paper with the word Kronos. I thought maybe at the other end was someone who could make sense of this for me, so I sent the email, explained who I was and what was happening, then asked, *Tell me what you know about Kronos.* Thirty-six hours later those guys show up at my door."

"When you called me, you said people were coming."

"By the time I sent the Kronos email I'd been awake for more than a day. My mind was spinning. I told Benji what I'd done, and he went ballistic. I'd never seen him that way. He seemed to grab hold of his senses and kept telling me to run while there was still time, that I had no idea what I'd done. *They're coming for us both.* That's what he said. He told me to leave and get far away. But I couldn't do that. I couldn't leave him." She paused. "That's when I contacted you. Luke, I got him killed. I lost my head—something I never do—and now he's dead. I'll never forgive myself."

"Those men killed him. Not you."

"I know that. But I'm going to find out the what and why and who. I'm going to do that. I swear to God I will. Then I'm going to kill whoever is behind this. With your help, I hope. So don't tell me to sit this out and you'll handle it. We clear?"

"Crystal, ma'am," he said, with a smile.

Truth was, not only did she deserve to be in on the hunt, he welcomed the partnership. But bravado aside, he knew that his training had cautioned him to be patient and make sure he hadn't been walking into a trap. Had he hesitated too long in the car? Had that gotten Benji killed? Hard to say. But he definitely crashed someone else's party. At the moment, though, working together was their best chance of not only making sense of this mystery, but surviving it as well.

He needed to know, "What happened in the house?"

"I actually fell asleep, which has been hard to do lately. Of course, I've been wearing my clothes to bed ever since Benji went freaky on me. I was lying there when glass broke in another room and brought me awake."

"That would be me," he said. "I thought an alert was in order."

"It worked. I switched on a light, then realized that was stupid. Been a while since I was in combat. That's when I heard people in the house. I had one of Benji's pistols on the nightstand, so I used it. But they got to him. Shot him right in the head."

"By the time I made it upstairs you were gone."

"I grabbed my wallet and passport and went out the window. I had no idea you were there."

"The gun?"

"The magazine was empty. I tossed it in a dumpster."

She leaned over and gently placed her hand over his. Soft. Tender. Unexpected.

"Luke," she said in a hushed tone, staring into his eyes, "someone's interested in us. At your seven by the hops display."

He was a little disappointed that this was all for show, but he kept up the performance and smiled back at her. "Describe him."

"Asian. Bald, late twenties, green leather jacket."

He squeezed her hand in another display of affection. "How sure are you?"

"Enough that it would be my final answer on *Who Wants to Be a Millionaire*."

Good enough for him. And he realized he'd broken a cardinal rule and failed to check earlier if the museum had a back exit. "Keep looking. Where there's one there's usually another."

She chuckled at him and pointed, conveying that he'd said something funny. "Got him. Roughly the same description, but taller and wearing a light-blue hoodie. He just sat at a table to your five."

A waitress walked by and he caught her attention and asked loud enough to be heard, "Restrooms, please?"

The woman pointed deeper into the museum, toward a collection of tall bronze vats and crisscrossed piping.

"*Dank je.*" To Jillian he said in a low voice, "If there's an emergency exit it's probably by the restrooms."

"What's the plan?"

He kept up the acting, his words not matching his actions as he leaned in close to her. "Gotta assume they're armed. There was no metal detector when we came in. If they open fire in here there'll be a lot of collateral damage. Let's take a walk."

He too was baffled by the question he'd seen in her eyes.

How had they found her?

They stood and casually headed into the museum, becoming

engrossed in a brochure Luke snatched from a display, making a show of wandering the exhibits while slowly winding their way toward the rear of the building. Once sure their pursuers had fallen in behind, Luke led her into a warren of copper vats. Ahead, the restroom sign directed patrons to the left down a short hall. A green-on-white pictograph for the emergency exit pointed straight ahead. He was counting on the privacy of the restrooms to allow him to spring a trap.

"Hopefully they'll split up," he said. "One for each of us. Take yours out as fast as you can."

"You sound excited. You have a strange idea of fun."

"You don't know the half of it."

They turned down the hall.

The women's restroom was first on the left, the men's second. Luke pushed open the door. The men's room was empty save for an elderly man washing his hands. Luke walked to one of the urinals and positioned himself appropriately. The man at the sink left, passing the two Asians on the way in.

Okay, he got them both.

And they wasted no time.

While one stood guard at the door, the other in the green leather jacket stepped up behind Luke.

"Don't make this harder than it has to be," the guy said in lightly accented English.

He glanced over his shoulder and smiled. "My doctor tells me I'm awful young for prostate issues, yet here I am."

The guy tossed him a curious look.

"You go ahead," Luke said. "I'll be here awhile."

"Funny man. Come with us."

"It's these damn pills, they don't do a thing," Luke droned on, accentuating his frustration with a rap on the wall.

"I said come on."

He spun and slammed his fist into the man's nose. Blood gushed out. The guy stumbled backward from the blow. Luke then drove a knee into the belly. With a guttural *umph*, the man collapsed, stunned, unable to recover. The other man reached beneath his jacket, surely for a weapon.

The door burst open.

Jillian kicked the guy in the back of the knee.

Something cracked.

She spun on her heel and punched again, the aim and ferocity designed to dislocate a shoulder. The man let out a muffled scream that Luke silenced with a hook to the jaw, sending him motionless to the floor.

"Aren't you the tough one?" Jillian said.

"You don't know the half of it." He frisked both attackers and found two 9mms, a pair of cell phones, and a car key fob.

"See if the coast is clear," he said.

She did so, saying from the door, "We're good."

He powered down the cell phones, then handed them to Jillian. No sense leaving any means of communication for these guys to use. He kept the guns. Then he dragged the shorter man's body toward the door. "We're going out the emergency exit. When the alarm goes off, don't look back and don't run. Hopefully our casualty here will be the center of attention."

She led the way as Luke hauled the man down the hallway into the open where he'd be unmissable by anyone responding to the alarm. He then hit the crash bar and shoved open the emergency exit door.

Nothing happened.

They started walking.

The door eased closed.

Jillian said, "What are the odds—"

The alarm went off, the whoop, whoop, whoop loud even through the closed door. They hustled forward into a ravine-like courtyard. On either side, three- and four-story building façades rose to form a rectangle of blue sky. Straight ahead, some fifty feet away, was a black steel door that had no knob.

No way out.

The alarm went silent.

"That was fast," he said.

He spotted a wheeled garbage bin against a nearby wall and together they dragged it, screeching and rumbling, until the museum's exit door was blocked.

They'd been in the courtyard less than sixty seconds, fifty seconds too long for his tastes. If more of their pursuers showed up, they were easy prey here, trapped in the courtyard. His sharp eyes surveyed every square inch.

Then, he saw it. In a far corner.

"There," he said, pointing.

A small tunnel behind an iron grille.

They ran to it, pushing through a thicket of weedy bushes that had shoved their way up through cracks in the concrete. Set into the wall was a waist-high gate secured by a rusty latch and padlock. Through the bars was a darkened tunnel about two feet square, its floor damp with moisture.

"Drainage for this courtyard," he said. "Otherwise, it'd be a swimming pool."

"To where?"

He had no idea. Definitely underground, though.

The museum's emergency door banged against the side of the garbage bin. Police? Or more hostiles? Either one was bad.

"Welcome to the frying pan," he said. "We need to go."

Jillian bent over, retrieved a chunk of loose stone from the ground, and tossed it to him. Half a dozen blows was all it took to break the latch. Luke tugged at the gate, which didn't budge. He whacked at the hinges with the stone, showering the ground with powdered rust until Jillian was able to wrench the gate open.

"After you," he said.

"You sure?"

"Not really. But we have no choice."

He handed her one of the 9mms, then she crawled inside.

He followed.

7.

Luke used his full body weight and managed to return the gate to its original position, or at least he hoped close enough to pass a cursory inspection. The problem was he had to enter the tunnel feetfirst, lying on his belly, in order to make that happen. Now, backward, he wiggled his way forward, following Jillian. The confines were tight. No question. Luckily, claustrophobia had never been a problem for him. They'd covered roughly twenty feet when he heard the garbage bin's steel wheels rumbling on the concrete behind them.

"They're out," he whispered.

"Any idea where we're headed?" she asked.

"Nope. But wherever it is, we need to get there in a hurry."

The tunnel canted downward, which helped his efforts, dropping them below street level. After another twenty feet or so the path emptied into a larger underground reservoir with brick walls about five feet high and three feet wide, their ankles in a few inches of brackish water.

"Drainage system," he said. "At least it's not a sewer."

Back the way they came, he heard a shout.

He retrieved the gun from his waist, ejecting the magazine and finding it full, fourteen rounds, plus one in the chamber. He also had the magazine from the other gun he'd obtained back in Genappe.

Good.

He snapped it back into place.

"You keep going. First turnoff you find, even if it's a bump in the wall, flatten yourself into it. Chances are good we've got some rounds headed our way. If you find an exit to the street, take it. Walk, don't run. We'll meet up later."

"I don't want to do that, Luke."

He realized she was no damsel in distress but still, "We don't always get what we want."

"I know what you're doing, trying to slow 'em down. But—"

"This is what I do," he said. "I'm trained for it."

He'd shared with her in past communications that he worked for the Magellan Billet, which may have been another reason why she'd called him.

"Look," he said, "we have a better chance separated. Now would you please go."

She didn't keep arguing and, instead, headed off down the channel of water into the darkness, using her phone light to guide her. He crept back to the tunnel through which they'd come and saw a man-shaped figure crouched before the bars, fifty feet away, in the light of day. But it was still hard to tell who it was. For all he knew the figure was a cop or another first responder, and he didn't want to shoot either. From their vantage point this was a black pit.

Had he been spotted?

The figure was joined by a second man and together they tugged at the gate, which gave way. A third man appeared and shoved a gun into the opening. Luke pulled back to the side of the tunnel just as a round snapped past his ear and gouged the brick wall behind him.

That was rude.

He swung back around, placed the shooter square in his gunsights, and squeezed the trigger. The man let out a yelp, then crumbled away.

The other two scrambled out of the line of fire.

No point hanging around.

He turned and hustled forward, hunched over in the pitch dark, trying not to make noise in the water. His foot caught a raised cobblestone and he pitched forward, catching himself on the side walls.

Careful now.

More rounds came from above, ricocheting off the brick walls, hurtling in every direction. One zipped past his head, then another.

The shots stopped for a moment.

He knew what that meant.

They'd cleared the way and now were coming down his way.

He heard splashes behind him.

A light clicked on.

He dropped into the water and rolled onto his back, aimed between his feet, and squeezed off half a dozen rounds. Did he hit anything? Hard to say. But the light beam found the floor, dulled by the water.

He stayed low and crawled ahead.

"Here," a hushed voice said in the darkness.

A light came on, filtered by something. He saw Jillian, her hand over the phone light, motioning for him to come quick. He scampered ahead, escaping the water and entering a niche in the brick wall. She angled the phone light upward and he craned his neck to see a ten-foot ladder bolted into the wall that led to a closed wooden hatch.

"Have you tried that door?" he asked.

"It's not locked, but something heavy is sitting on it."

"Every few seconds send a shot down the tunnel. I don't know if I got them or not."

"We're sure they're not cops?"

"They're angry and trigger-happy. That's good enough for me. Stall them."

He scaled the ladder and pressed his ear to the hatch. All was silent on the other side. Jillian kept firing periodically.

Then stopped.

"The gun's dry," she said. "They're still there. At least two, maybe more."

He coiled his legs on the ladder, planted his shoulder to the hatch, and stood up, straining until he heard something topple over.

The hatch burst open.

"Got it," he called to Jillian.

She climbed up and he helped her emerge, then he slammed the hatch shut behind them. They were in a triangular-shaped storage room, perhaps twenty feet to a side, with one exit and no windows. A basement? Rough-hewn shelves bearing sacks of flour, rice, and millet lined the walls. A shabby recliner and side table had been blocking the hatch. Together they replaced them, then piled several of the heavy sacks on top for added measure.

Outside, police sirens wailed. For the moment they were safe, and he was glad for it. One look at Jillian's face told him she felt the same.

"That was interesting," he said.

"To say the least."

He liked her coolness in a crisis. It was something that could not be taught. You were either born with it, or not.

Both of them were wet.

Him particularly.

He still had his 9mm. She'd tossed hers.

"Now what?" she asked.

The sound of feet clanking on ladder rungs filtered through the floorboards. The pile of bags shifted slightly from movement below. He drew a finger to his lips signaling quiet.

"*Politie*," a hushed voice said from below.

Police. But they were no salvation.

The bags bulged upward again, held there for a few moments, then went slack. Feet clanked back down the ladder.

In his ear Jillian whispered, "We need to go. I doubt they are the give-up type."

He agreed, and headed for the open doorway.

A wooden stairway led up.

He climbed to a closed door, which he eased open into a small commercial kitchen. No lights on and no one in sight. Two windows opened out, which he ignored. Instead, he headed for the other open portal. A quick peek revealed a small bakery with glass cases. All dark. Empty. No lights or people. This place was closed. The front windows were wide and opened to the street with a single exit. Through the glass he spotted more police cars on the street, each of the uniforms sporting an automatic rifle.

He retreated back into the kitchen and faced Jillian. "If I were a betting man, I'd say they're gearing up for a house-to-house, trying to figure out where that hatch below us is located. We need to get moving. I saw another doorway on the other side of the bakery. Seems our only choice. Stay low and use the counters for protection."

He led the way out and crouched down, scampering across the bakery behind the counters. They made it to the other side and through the second open doorway. Another set of wooden risers led up. They climbed to a second floor and a locked door. One more set of stairs led up to the third floor, which opened into a small furnished apartment.

His senses went to red alert, especially since the door had been unlocked.

Anybody home?

It soon became clear that the place was unoccupied.

He crept to one of the windows and peered out. The view overlooked a valley of gabled rooftops that dived into their building one story below. The evening sun cast much of the slate shingles in shadow. He spotted no access to ground level. But to the side of the window, just around the corner, he caught the outline of a tangle of pipes that led downward. Below he heard a crashing sound, followed by a commanding voice calling out in Dutch.

Jillian whispered a translation. "He's saying, 'Armed police, if anyone is in here, make yourself known.'"

Apparently someone had done the math quick and found where the hatch was located.

Time's up.

He stuffed the gun at his waist and quietly opened the window. "Climb down, using the pipes at the corner, to the roof next door."

Jillian didn't hesitate and squeezed through the window, reaching around and grabbing the pipe, then planting her feet on the outer wall and shimmying down. He followed and was halfway to her when he heard *"Politie"* from the other side of the window. Below, Jillian had already dropped to the roof next door. He mouthed, *Hide,* and she scurried to a chimney and disappeared on the other side. He could do nothing but hang in place around the corner, hoping the lengthening shadows were cover enough. He changed his position to the pipe farthest from the edge to conceal his grip from any prying eyes. Jillian signaled to him from her hiding spot that someone was at the window. He risked a quick peek and saw a forehead and a police garrison cap. He gritted his teeth and tightened his fingers, the heel of his boots knocking against the wall.

Stay still. Don't move.

He could manage a few more seconds, but no more.

"Politie," the officer called.

He closed his eyes and held his breath.

Finally, the window screeched shut.

Jillian tossed him a thumbs-up.

He hustled down to the roof and landed, working the pain out of his hands, and together they crouched against the exterior wall.

"Look for a way down," he said. "Step carefully. We don't know what's below us."

Though only about a hundred feet across, the rooftop was multi-gabled, like a mountain range. They quietly navigated the peaks and valleys. Then, deep in shadow along the roof's east side he found a gap between the buildings barely wider than his shoulders, wires and conduits festooning the walls. Every few feet linesman's pegs jutted from the stone.

"What is it?" she asked, peering downward.

"Architectural glitch, probably. Looks like they turned it into a cable run for these buildings."

Again, with no hesitation, she dropped herself into the gap and began picking her way down the wall. He followed and soon they were on the ground in a dark narrow alley. Drooping cables lent the passageway a jungle-like feel. He oriented himself, then headed away from the bakery toward the square's south side.

They reached an intersection.

To the right was a dead end. To the left, fifty feet away, they could see people milling about the square. He continued straight. The next intersection was a mirror image of the last. He turned right. Ten minutes later they were clear of the square and all the excitement.

"What now?" she asked.

"We go get Benji's lockbox."

8.

LUKE DROVE, KEEPING TO THE SPEED LIMIT, DRAWING NO ATTENTION to them. They'd backtracked their way to his rental car, then made their way out of Brussels. The return to Genappe had taken a little over an hour, during which their wet clothes dried. Their conversation had centered on the men in the museum. Who sent them? Why? And how had they found them? Unfortunately, there were no answers. They simply had too little information to make any meaningful assessment. Clearly, though, Jillian's inquiries had started something into action. By the time they reached Genappe his watch read 7:30 P.M. and the spring evening was rapidly evolving into night.

"Turn right," she said. "Lights off."

He did as directed.

The gently sloped lane was bordered by grassy drainage ditches. Dirt and small gravel crunched under the tires until Jillian finally said, "Turn here."

He guided the car into a driveway that ended before a farmhouse.

"I know the owners," she said. "They're gone for a few weeks." She turned in her seat and pointed through the rear window. "That's our backyard, to the left of that big chestnut."

They'd not approached the house from Rue Emile Hecq on the off chance that the police, or someone else, were watching. Instead, Jillian had brought them around to its rear and a street over. Behind a tall privacy fence the house was a dark form against an even darker sky. He was about to ask about neighborhood dogs, but caught himself. Whistler had already covered that point. They were taking a risk returning. Getting arrested topped the list. Plus, there was no guarantee the lockbox hadn't already been discovered, either by their pursuers or by the authorities. If so, he might have to make a call to Stephanie Nelle, asking her to intervene. But he preferred not to do that. The house was the scene of a mass murder. If the police thought something of investigative value was there, they'd tear it down to the studs. But maybe the obvious had caused them to be a little careless. It would not be the first time.

"I assume you won't allow me to handle this," he said to her. "And you wait here."

"Not a chance."

She was out of the car and marching off before he could protest. He jogged to catch up. "All I'm saying is, one of us should stay here and keep watch."

"I nominate you."

And she kept walking.

He shrugged and headed after her.

They crossed the road down into one of the ditches then hopped a wire fence into a small treed meadow of wildflowers wet from an earlier rain. After a few steps their pant legs were saturated again. They reached the privacy fence, which stood slightly taller than

Luke. On tiptoes, he peered over. All of the house windows were dark. Nothing moved save the fluttering blue-and-white tape the police had strung through the bushes down each side.

"Don't they guard crime scenes here?" he asked her.

"They're probably out front."

"Okay, up you go."

He made a stirrup with his hands but she said, "There's an easier way."

She led him down the fence to a section of loose boards. With a bit of waggling she removed two and created a gap through which they entered. On the other side they crouched behind a lilac bush.

"I noticed that needed repair a couple of weeks ago."

"Wait here a second," he told her. "I need to check out the front."

He picked his way through the yard, down the side of the house, until he reached a corner. No police in sight. But there was a car parked about fifty yards away with no one inside. His *something's off* radar blared an alert. Both from the car and from the nearby streetlight, which was dark and unlit, unlike last night, its glass panes shattered. He still carried the 9mm taken off the guys in Brussels. He withdrew the weapon from his waist, kept low, and made his way through the ever-thickening shadows to the car.

Empty.

But the engine hood was still warm.

Which meant they weren't alone.

He circled back to her and recounted what he'd seen.

She asked, "You think they're inside waiting?"

He nodded. "Could be a two-birds-with-one-stone situation. Let you lead them to the good stuff, then they take it and kill us. How did you get to Brussels?"

"Bus. Cash ticket, no ID required."

"When we talked yesterday morning, were you already at Grand Place?" She nodded. "And you pulled the battery on your phone?"

"Not until you told me to get the burner. What's going on, Luke?"

The phone? Possibly. But there was a better explanation. "I made a mistake. I should have seen it. They must have planted a GPS tracker on my rental car last night. It's the only thing that makes sense."

"Why would they?"

"In case I got away. Which I did."

"Which means they know we're here."

He thought for a moment. "What's the fastest you can run a mile?"

"Personal best is a five-twenty in a sixty-pound ruck. What have you got in mind?"

He kept his attention on the darkened house. "As far as they're concerned, where the car goes, we go. We passed a diner about a mile back."

He saw she understood.

"Give me the keys."

He handed them over.

"Be right back."

She crawled through the fence and disappeared.

He sat in the dark and kept watch on the house.

Nothing stirred.

What would his daddy say now? He'd been born and raised in a small Tennessee town where his father and uncle were both known commodities, particularly his uncle, who served in various local political offices, then as governor before becoming president. He had three brothers. Matthew, Mark, and John. He'd completed the evangelists, the names coming from his mother who remained, to this day, deeply religious. His father? Not so much, but he faithfully attended church every Sunday until the day he died—which, ironically, had been on Sunday.

Cancer.

Fatal. Fast.

He and his three brothers had been there for every moment

of those final days. His mother took the loss hard. They'd been married a long time. Her husband was everything to her, and then, suddenly, he was gone.

That's why he called her every Sunday.

Never missed.

Even when on assignment.

It might be late at night her time when he had the chance, but he called. His father always said that the smartest thing he ever did was marry her, proclaiming that *even the blind-eyed biscuit thrower occasionally hits the target.*

He'd never forget his last conversation with his father.

"I'm going to die later today or tomorrow. I'm done. I can feel it. But I have to say this to you. I want you make something of your life. Okay? Something good. You choose what works. Doesn't matter. But whatever it is, make the most of it."

He could still feel the gentle grip of his father's sweaty palm as they shook hands for the last time. And he'd known exactly what his dad had meant. School had never interested Luke, his grades barely passing. College was not in his future. So he'd enlisted right out of high school and enrolled for Ranger training. Sixty-one of the hardest days of his life. Not for the weak or fainthearted—that's what it said right in the handbook. Kind of an understatement, considering the failure rate was way over 50 percent. But he'd passed. Eventually, he'd been deployed to some of the hottest spots on the planet and received multiple commendations. Then he was chosen to work for the Magellan Billet where he'd been involved in more high-stakes action.

He was thirty-one years old and the loss of his dad still hurt. What was the saying? *Real men don't cry.* Bullshit. Real men bawled their eyes out, as he and his brothers had when they watched the man they idolized take his last breath.

Perhaps that was why he'd grown fond of Cotton Malone.

The two men were a lot alike. No bullshit. To the point. And 99 percent of the time they were right. Luke was lucky to have met Malone, though he'd never let Pappy know that. No need really. That was another thing about Malone and his father. Both knew the obvious. No need to say it too.

Fifteen minutes later Jillian came trotting back.

In between breaths she said, "It's parked at the diner. We're having a late supper."

He liked it.

"Okay, let's go ruin their surprise."

9.

Luke kept pace with Jillian across the backyard to a padlocked cellar door. She'd led the way since her firsthand knowledge was invaluable. She groped around in the dark and finally grabbed a nearby rock, giving it a sharp twist and revealing a hidden key compartment. Ten seconds later they were through the cellar door and down the steps without a sound. The air was damp and cool and smelled of mothballs. They stood in silence a few moments so their eyes could adjust.

He held the 9mm.

"Take point," he whispered in her ear.

She knew the house and had cleared her fair share of buildings overseas.

He'd watch her back.

"If we get a chance to take a prisoner, do it," he said. "We need an info dump. Bad."

He knew that instruction wasn't going to go over well.

She'd watched the man who'd raised her be murdered. And while the men who'd actually killed Benji were dead, those who'd ordered the attack weren't. She wanted her pound of flesh.

"We need some answers," he whispered.

She gritted her teeth. "I can't promise anything."

He did not like the sound of that.

She took the lead as they crossed the darkened basement to a set of stairs leading up into the house. Using hand signals she told him, *They're noisy. Step where I step.*

They climbed without making a sound, staying, he noticed, to the risers' outer edges. At the top she signaled to stop.

A creak of wood past the closed door broke the silence.

Then a faint scuff of a shoe.

She whispered in his ear, "Kitchen's through this door. We swing right, then another right, and we're in the hallway. The stairs up to the bedrooms will be on our left."

He nodded, recalling that part of the house from the previous night, only in reverse order.

She eased open the door and they slipped inside, cleared the kitchen, then turned down the hallway. At the stairs Jillian peeled off and pressed herself against the wall. Luke kept going, checking the room on his right before veering left.

First space empty.

At the second, a figure emerged. Fast.

But not unexpected.

Luke reacted instantly, lashing out with the butt of his gun and popping the man behind the ear. The body went immediately limp and he caught it under the arms to prevent a thud. But the deadweight dropped him to his knees with the body draped across his thighs.

Jillian hadn't moved.

She gave him a nod.

He disentangled himself from the limp form and finished clearing the last room. All good to their sides and flank. Back in the hall he stacked up behind her, then placed a hand on her shoulder signaling he was ready to proceed.

Up the stairs they went.

At the landing she made the turn and continued toward the loft. He stopped halfway up with his head level with the upper floor, staring through the spindles. He motioned that she should proceed on and he'd cover her. She nodded and continued up the stairs and into a bedroom directly across from his position, a narrow hall running perpendicular in between. He noticed some gray plastic bins stacked a little way down emblazoned with the words GENAPPE POLITIE. The police had been busy accumulating evidence, but obviously had not finished yet. A night-light burned in the loft and cast enough of a glow for him to see Jillian sweep the bedroom for any hostiles. He'd sent her in reasoning that whoever was here was expecting her, not him. He stayed on the steps, peering through the spindles, eyes keeping watch ahead and below.

"If you move, I will shoot you," a disembodied male voice said.

Jillian froze.

"Say yes if you understand," the voice commanded.

Luke zeroed in. The voice was coming from under the bed.

"I understand," she said.

"Turn to face the bathroom."

"Okay, relax," she said. "I'm unarmed."

The narration was for the moron under the bed's benefit, but she did as instructed.

"Stay still," the man said.

He heard a rustling sound and saw the man worm his way out from under the bed, standing about six feet behind Jillian, a gun trained on her. Close enough that he couldn't miss, but beyond her arm's reach. Luke saw the guy was Caucasian, his English faintly accented.

Israeli?

"Please, please, don't kill me," she said, feigning fear. "All I want is a box of my grandfather's army medals so he can be buried in them. The police refused, so here I am, like a thief in his house, come to get them."

Perfect. Keep him guessing.

"You came to retrieve some medals?"

"Just let me get them and I'll go."

"You're Jillian Stein," he said.

"How do you know my name?"

"Did your grandfather have a safe place to keep things. Old things. Like those medals you're talking about. Or maybe a rifle?"

Rifle? That came out of nowhere.

"What kind of rifle?" she asked.

Good question.

"An old one. Did he keep an old rifle?"

"He did have a hiding place. I know exactly where it is."

"Show me."

He wondered where she was headed, but stayed out of sight and allowed things to play out. *Turn on the vacuum cleaner*, Malone would say. *Suck in more than ever goes out.*

She stepped to the bed and shoved it to one side. It stammered across the hardwood. She knelt down and removed a knife from her pant pocket. She opened the blade and jabbed the tip into the floor where it stuck, allowing her to use it as a handle to lift out two planks. The guy with the gun stood to one side, weapon aimed, watching. She reached into the exposed cavity and removed a metal box about eighteen inches long and six inches wide, which she laid on the floor. Apparently the police had yet to fully search and find that hiding spot. She was probably banking that it would attract the guy's attention.

And it did.

"Move away from it," the man said.

She hesitated, standing.

"I said move away."

A click broke the silence.

The hammer of the guy's gun snapping into place.

Jillian slowly stood.

"Over there," he ordered.

And she approached the outer wall. The guy grabbed a pillow from the bed. The gun he held had no sound suppressor attached, so this fellow was apparently concerned about noise. He swung around, his back to Luke, and now stood between him and Jillian.

"No rifle?" the guy asked.

"Unless it's in miniature. That's the only hiding place I know."

"Too bad for you."

"How about a couple of answers before you shoot me?" she said, unfazed. "Who sent those men last night to kill my grandfather?"

"No idea, lady. That was somebody else."

"Okay, who sent you?"

He chuckled. "People interested in your grandfather."

"Did my email draw you, and them, here?"

"I don't know anything about that. But that box there will bring me ten thousand euros. An old rifle? That would have been more."

"What's so special about an old rifle?"

"I have no idea. People like me are not told the details."

"Just the what, who, and how much you'll earn?"

"Something like that. Are we done with the questions?"

"Just one more."

It happened fast.

She spun on one foot and kicked the guy hard, square in the chest. The blow sent him staggering out the doorway toward the railing and spindles, arms flailing, trying to regain balance and re-aim the weapon. But Jillian advanced with another kick that sent him off his feet and through the railing, in the air, over Luke's head. The body thudded solid into the stairs, then slid down to ground level.

"Really?" he asked. "You were doing so good."

"He was going to shoot me."

"Like I was going to let that happen."

"He got on my nerves. Cocky-ass bastard. He didn't know spit."

Luke descended and checked for a pulse. Faint. But there.

"You okay?" he asked her.

"Peachy. He sounded Middle Eastern."

"Israeli, I think. Hired muscle. Any idea what he was talking about with the rifle?"

"Not a clue. Benji owned a few handguns, but no rifles."

He hated to leave something like that hanging, so he filed it away in the get-to-that-later box.

They needed to leave.

"Get that lockbox and let's go."

10.

LUKE RAN THROUGH A QUICK SITUATION ASSESSMENT.

They were still alive, they had Benji's lockbox and two fresh 9mms taken from the guys inside Benji's house, they'd removed the GPS tracker on the rented Peugeot, which he'd been right about, and, knock on wood, they were finally free of pursuers. Better still, despite both the Genappe shooting and the Brussels incident getting media coverage, neither he nor Jillian had been mentioned as either suspects or witnesses. No one, though, should ever push their luck, so he decided to put some distance between them and the ugly events of the past few hours. Find a place to regroup. A change of scenery. Jillian had suggested Bruges, on Belgium's North Sea coast, so off they went, arriving a little after 10:00 P.M. After some tooling around he spotted a hotel that struck his fancy.

The Relais Bourgondisch Cruyce sat just off Bruges' old town center overlooking a canal intersection and the old market square. The façade was half timbered and distinctly Gothic with narrow, sharply pitched roofs and gabled windows. Water seemed everywhere, with canals weaving paths through the city. Once inside their room they each had a shower followed by a brief debate over which came first, nap or dinner. They decided on the former and fell asleep. He didn't wake up until around midnight. Opening his eyes he saw the light was on and that Jillian had the contents of Benji's lockbox spread across the floor, studying everything. He rid the sleep from his brain and sat down on the floor beside her.

"Where's that email address you sent the Kronos message to?" he asked.

She handed over a small scrap of paper. "That's what I found."

Written in block letters was HARVEST~SUN~RIVER17@BTCMOD.COM.

Along with the word KRONOS.

"I searched it out," she said. "It's a Googlewhack."

That was a new one. "You're going to have to translate."

"You really do lead a sheltered life," she said. "Googlewhack is an obscure nerd game. The objective is to come up with a Google search that returns only one result. That email address returned zero results, so it would be a super Googlewhack."

"Is that important?"

She shrugged. "Maybe not. But it is damn interesting."

He was not all that computer-literate. He could make do, but he was no tech specialist. Luckily, the Magellan Billet employed several experts on twenty-four-hour call. "I know someone who might be able to make some sense of this."

The Magellan Billet's tech support was first-rate. Problem here? This was not official business and Stephanie Nelle had a strict rule about misusing resources. Everything had to be on deck, ready to go at all times, to support the assets in the field.

No freelancing. But one particular specialist had taken a shine to him.

"Trustworthy?" she asked.

"Impeccable." He checked his watch. Midnight in Belgium was 6:00 P.M., dinnertime, in West Virginia. He knew the number having called it several times before, and he dialed it on his secure Magellan Billet phone.

Marcia Pooler answered on the second ring.

He tapped SPEAKER.

"Miss Marcia, it's Luke Daniels."

"Little Lukey, haven't heard from you in a while."

"I know. I should have checked in."

"If you don't call your friends often enough, they forget who y'are."

"I'm real sorry about that, ma'am. I'll do better, I promise."

"So to what do I owe the pleasure? Are you callin' to finally admit my apple cobbler's better than your mama's."

"And cross her? No thank you." Though Marcia did make a super cobbler. "I'm hoping you can help me with a computer issue." He paused. "Off the books."

As prodigies went, Marcia Pooler was a late bloomer. She'd gone decades without the faintest notions about random access memory or what a dual core processor did. And then on a lark, she'd signed up for a computer literacy class at her local community college hoping to expand her horizons. By the second session she was obsessed. Fortunately, her instructor had been not only a patient soul, but also a retired Defense Department tech manager who lived and breathed the digital world.

In short order Marcia was all over cyber mumbo jumbo like pan gravy coated country-fried steak. Computers and their software underpinnings just made sense to her. Code sang songs she readily understood. Eventually, her skills developed to the point that her professor helped secure freelancing work for Apple, Deutsche Telekom, Raytheon, even the Department of Defense. Three years ago the Magellan Billet became a client.

Now, at age sixty-eight, Marcia Pooler, grandmother and *Wheel of Fortune* fanatic, was a certified IT specialist with a high security clearance. She'd helped him before with a favor, so he was hoping she would again now.

"Oh, little Lukey, you do love to push the envelope," she said. "But I can keep a secret, if you can."

Which meant they were now in don't-ask-don't-tell territory with Stephanie Nelle.

"I've got an email address that's giving me trouble," he said. "Can I give it to you?"

And he read off the odd combination of letters and symbols.

"Got it," she said.

"It's a Googlewhack."

"I had no idea you were so computer-savvy."

"I'm not. But that's what I was told. In fact, it may be a super Googlewhack. I'm looking for everything you can give me on it. Especially, who owns it."

"Anything for you, darlin'. How do I find you?"

"I'm on my Billet phone."

"Speaking of that, have you called your mama?"

"Last Sunday, like always."

"Good boy. Give me a few hours."

He ended the call.

"She sounds like a character," Jillian said.

"She lives on a goat farm and raises alpacas. I've been there. Her brain's wired differently from the rest of us. She's a friggin' genius. Have you found anything useful?"

"A lot of diary entries from Benji's time serving in Europe. Things he saw. People he met. I saw them the first time I was in this box. Like he was going to write a book or something. He seems to have been keeping notes for decades, but there are large time gaps. Then there's this."

And she pointed to an invoice with a key taped to it. "This is what I told you about. It's for unit 214 at something called Fetschenhof Stockag. In Michelau, Luxembourg."

"Let's see what we can learn." And he started a search on his phone. "It's a self-storage company twenty-five miles north of Luxembourg City."

"The invoice is dated ten months ago," she said. "He paid a year's rent in advance."

"Did your grandfather ever mention Luxembourg? Or Michelau?"

She shook her head. "Not a word during his ramblings."

"Obviously, there are things he considered important enough to keep locked up far away from his house."

"Like a rifle?"

He nodded.

He knew her mind was also working. Why else would she be awake in the middle of the night pondering over things her grandfather had so deliberately hidden away? Things that might have led to the old man being killed before the cancer had done its worst. Which begged a question. Why kill Benji? He was going to die anyway. Whoever ordered that hit had gone to a lot of trouble. Which could only have happened for one reason. He, she, or they were afraid the old man would reveal something before he died.

But what?

"If we leave early in the morning, we can be there by noon," he said. "Luxembourg is not that far away. What do you say? Road trip?"

11.

STARLINGS ISLAND, MARYLAND
WEDNESDAY — MARCH 25 — 5:30 A.M.

TOM ROWLAND WAS ENJOYING A BREAKFAST OF POACHED EGGS AND blue crab cakes, the shellfish caught yesterday out in the Bay. His chef had worked for him a long time and knew exactly how he preferred his food without an array of overpowering salt, pepper, or spices. Just plain and simple, he liked to say. He lived alone, having never married, which had spawned repeated rumors about his sexuality that he did nothing to dissuade.

Keep them guessing.

His motto.

"Sir, Mr. Persik is on the phone," his chamberlain said.

The third call since midnight.

He laid down his fork and napkin and stood from the table. Inside his study, with the door closed, he sat at his desk and lifted the receiver for the landline. He listened as Persik explained what happened a few hours ago at Benjamin Stein's house.

"The men I hired," Persik said, "are low-level earners for the Harpaz crime family, an Israeli gang trying to make inroads in Brussels. The job was unsanctioned by their bosses. Our only connection to them is a call forwarding exchange that no longer exists. They were to be paid after the job, in cash. If they located the rifle a bonus was mentioned. The good news is that with this latest incident at Stein's house no police were involved and the two men, though injured, are gone from the country. Given what a spectacle the previous Genappe incident has become, even if caught, the Belgian DGJ will be only too happy to seize the organized crime angle."

A valid point. He knew the Israelis were looking for a way to tighten the screws on the Harpaz bosses in Tel Aviv, and the

Belgians had been begging for intelligence on local ISIS cells. One hand washed the other. Still—

"Major, this is the second time you've failed in as many days."

"I still have eyes on Jillian Stein."

"You should have led with that."

"I decided to deliver the bad news first."

He allowed the impertinence to pass considering what was at stake. "Tell me."

And he listened. When Persik finished he said, "Excellent work. How long until we have the situation contained?"

"A matter of hours."

"I'm glad to hear that." Now was not the time for negativity. "Forget about Genappe. It doesn't concern us any longer. Focus on Stein's granddaughter. Whatever brought her back to that house is now in her possession. The rifle, Major. Focus on that."

"I'm leading the team personally for the intercept."

"Find that rifle. Get. It. Done."

He ended the connection and stepped away from the desk.

Everything was proceeding ahead.

Daylight was flooding the Chesapeake. Another day. Another opportunity. That had always been how he lived his life. But now, approaching ninety-three years old, his time was coming to an end. Thankfully, he enjoyed a robust constitution with few to no physical afflictions. That good health had been aided by a life of nonsmoking, smart eating, and limited alcohol. Long lives ran in his family. His father lived to be ninety-one, his grandfather to nearly a hundred.

But they'd spawned heirs.

Sadly his wealth, and all of the favors and promises he'd amassed, would die with him. No one would carry on after he was gone. No heirs. No assigns nor designees. It would all just end, with his fortune going to the Smithsonian Institution. He'd always loved that place. One condition of the multimillion-dollar gift was that something prominent bear his name. What? Didn't matter. Just as long as something did. He liked the idea of that.

The THOMAS HENRY ROWLAND EXHIBITION HALL.

Some would be glad to see him go, their debts remaining unpaid. Others would mourn, wanting favors previously given repaid. Of course, he wasn't dead. Not yet. And this was all about what would survive death.

His legacy.

How he would be remembered.

And that was important.

Talley had already reported in, so little of what Persik had said was news to him. Talley and his team were on the ground, landing in Belgium hours ago, already acting on information Persik had provided earlier on a rental car the white knight in Genappe had utilized, one they'd managed to electronically tag the night before. That's how Persik knew Jillian Stein and her savior had met in Brussels, then returned to her grandfather's house. They also had a license plate, which led to the rental company, which led to a name.

Luke Daniels.

Whom Talley knew.

"Special forces is a relatively small community. He and I crossed paths. Daniels was an Army Ranger. A damn good one, too."

"You said 'was.' What is he now?"

"To the best of my knowledge, a private citizen."

"Who shows up out of the blue. What might be his interest in this?"

"Unknown, at this time," Talley said.

"Find out...discreetly."

"I shall. Sir, I should say, whatever his reason for being there, Daniels is a—"

"Speed bump. Flatten him out."

He'd sent the second team to Belgium to provide him with choices.

Just in case. Thank God.

He stepped back to the desk.

And called Talley.

12.

Luke slowed the Peugeot as they approached the border between Belgium and Luxembourg. The crossing itself was notional rather than physical, an invisible line down the center of Martelange's main thoroughfare that magically shifted into Martelange-Rombach in Luxembourg. Residents could, in theory, buy a cup of coffee in Belgium, then cross the street for a croissant in Luxembourg. Usually, it was a nonexistent line. But today there was a line of cars being held up by guards checking each vehicle.

"Should we worry about that?" Jillian asked.

"Doubt it," he said, but he wasn't as confident as he tried to sound.

Based on media reports their involvement in Genappe and Brussels appeared to have gone unnoticed, but police often withheld critical details from the media. If that was the case here, and they were identified, there'd be no way they would be allowed to cross into Luxembourg. On the other hand the police could have just as easily nabbed them when he traded rental vehicles back in Bruges for another Peugeot. Yet nothing occurred.

Which seemed both good and bad.

"Both Belgium and Luxembourg are EU members. The borders are essentially open," he said. "But they're still sovereign nations. If they want to check vehicles, they can. Usually, they do it for training rookie border guards."

"That's real comforting, Lukey."

He smiled at her use of Marcia's euphemism. Whom he'd not heard from. Memo to himself. Call her.

He guided the Peugeot in between a line of wheeled barricades then coasted to a stop behind a red VW coupe, which the guards waved through with only a cursory glance into the back seat. Luke pulled forward. One of the guards halted him with a raised palm.

"I'm not liking this," Jillian muttered.

"Just keep smiling," he said.

He lowered his window.

"*Paspoort, alstublieft,*" the stone-faced guard said.

Luke handed over his blue American passport through the window.

"The purpose of your visit?"

"Bit of sightseeing. Larochette, then Bourscheid Castle."

"And you are?" the guard asked Jillian.

"The girlfriend. Dragged along to see another damn castle."

The guard smiled. "Do you have a passport?"

"I do, but not with me. I didn't know it would be needed. I'm American too."

"One moment," the guard said. "Please put your vehicle in park."

Passport in hand, the guard walked around the Peugeot's hood to his partner. They began a huddled conversation.

"Luke, that second guard photographed our license plate."

"Standard practice. Forms to fill out, boxes to tick. This one will come up as a rental. Nothing more."

He hoped he sounded more confident than he felt. This scrutiny was a bit above and beyond. He'd already mapped out an escape route ahead with the Peugeot. But there'd be damage. No question. Bloodshed? Maybe not. Neither guard toted a weapon. But he and Jillian were armed with the pistols from yesterday.

Finally, the uniformed man returned to Luke's window.

"Mr. Daniels, that is your name, yes?"

"So my mama tells me."

The guard's face remained stoic. "Please be aware your passport expires in seven months. If you plan to stay either in Belgium or Luxembourg, I suggest you contact the nearest U.S. embassy."

"Thank you, I'll do that."

"Enjoy your stay."

He rolled up his window and drove on.

"You think we're good?" Jillian asked.

"We can only hope."

Another hour's worth of driving south brought them to the outskirts of Luxembourg City. With them came rain. Clouds had been building for the past forty-five minutes and now, as the city's skyline came into view, rain began stippling the windshield. The wipers came on and thump-swished over the glass in a soothing rhythm.

Luke had visited Luxembourg City once before on assignment. From a population standpoint it wasn't a large place, about 130,000 people, many of whom were high-income expatriates from around the world there to take advantage of loose financial laws and loads of privacy. The city's layout was intricate, spread across rolling lush hills and astride the confluence of two grand rivers. It felt more like an intertwined series of medieval villages connected by fortification walls, arches, elevated winding roads, and exquisite stonework bridges. It served as one of the de facto capitals of the European Union, along with Brussels, Frankfurt, and Strasbourg, hosting several EU agencies and governing bodies.

Jillian lowered her window and sampled the outside air. "Is there a better smell in the world than spring rain?"

"Not that I've found. Though freshly mowed grass is a close runner-up."

He could see she was bothered, and her quiet for the past half hour only confirmed something was on her mind.

"What is it?" he asked.

She faced him. "Who said there was anything?"

"Your silence."

She smiled and raised the window. "If I hadn't dug around, he'd still be alive."

"Until the cancer killed him. At this point, we don't know anything. Let's focus on what's in front of us and not speculate on what might have been."

While it seemed likely her email query about Kronos had triggered the attack on Benji's home, he suspected this ball had started rolling a long time ago.

The rifle.

That had seemed important to the Israeli last night.

A rifle Benjamin Stein supposedly possessed.

Whether intentionally or through happenstance, Stein had gotten himself mixed up in something bad and the consequences had finally landed on his doorstep. Had Jillian pointed the way? Maybe. Which was probably why guilt was getting the best of her.

So he tried to take her mind off it and asked, "Do you know our route?"

She found her phone and checked the map app. For the next ten minutes she guided him through the city center before directing him to turn onto the 53A toward the outskirts of town.

"You do know that coming through Luxembourg City wasn't the fastest route," she said, tracing a fingertip over her phone's screen. "We could've bypassed the city altogether."

"Twists and turns make it easier to spot anybody tailing us."

She turned and stared out the back window. "Is there?"

"Not that I've noticed. And I've been looking."

"I was hoping for a resounding no."

He smiled. "No such thing."

"You really are getting into this spy business, aren't you?"

He agreed with Malone. They weren't spies. They were intelligence officers. Field agents. Eyes and ears on the ground. There to investigate, analyze, and report. Only if a field officer began to operate clandestinely with the enemy, interacting, subject to arrest, detention, even torture or death, did they become a spy.

"I think I found something I'm pretty good at," he said.

"That's really good to hear."

He liked that she cared. Was he still attracted to her? Who wouldn't be? She was smart, assured, and beautiful. Did he have feelings toward her? That was harder to answer. All he knew for sure was that he wanted her to be happy.

He glanced her way. "How about you? Have you found something you're good at?"

She shook her head. "Still searching."

Luxembourg City disappeared into the rearview mirror and the road gradually steepened as they climbed into more rugged terrain penetrated with deep, narrow valleys hemmed in by thick forests. Twenty minutes later they reached the small town of Ettelbruck, then turned north into the Portes des Ardennes. A few minutes later a sign for Michelau appeared.

"I did a quick count," she said. "Between Luxembourg City and Ettelbruck there were three self-storage companies. Yet Benji chose one way out here in the middle of nowhere."

"Maybe for the same reason we took that indirect route. Avoiding prying eyes."

Half a mile east of the road they found the Fetschenhof Stockag storage facility tucked up against a forested hillside behind a large expanse of ramshackle warehouses. The weed-strewn asphalt and graffiti-plastered façades told him the compound was not well maintained. Among the fourteen warehouses he counted he saw only a handful of unbroken windows. Apparently, this was the spot for teenage vandalism. He pulled to a stop beside a pole-mounted keypad and rolling security gate topped with barbed wire. A touch of modernity in an otherwise neglected place.

"Do we have a code?" he asked. "Seems to be four digits."

"Try five-nine-two-four."

He punched in the number. In red letters the screen flashed Incorrect pin.

"Sorry," she said. "Swap the last two digits."

He tried again. The screen flashed green and the gate began rolling aside. "What was it?"

"The last four digits of Benji's army service number before they changed over to using socials. It was his password for everything."

"I like it. Easy to remember. But hard to guess."

Beat the hell out of those suggested passwords every computer program around today liked to offer. A confusing and impossible-to-remember mix of letters, numbers, and symbols that no one in their right mind would choose.

"Okay, we're looking for unit 214," she said.

He drove through the gate, deeper into the warren of connected storage units, which varied in size from a walk-in closet to a two-car garage. Jillian spotted 214. He stopped the car beside a white corrugated aluminum door and they both climbed out into the cool, damp late-morning.

"A little brisk," she said, zipping up her jacket.

The rain had chilled the air enough that they could see their breath. The wind had picked up, sending bits of trash skittering across the asphalt. All was quiet save for the ticking of the Peugeot's resting engine and the patter of rain on the aluminum roofs. Unit 214 was one of the larger spaces.

They approached the padlocked door.

"Pretty damn big," he said. "He must have a lot of stuff."

"Here goes nothing," she said.

The key fit perfectly and the lock snapped open.

"It's oiled," she said. "And the thing looks relatively new."

That it did.

Together, they lifted the door up on its rollers. Inside measured about twenty feet square and was empty save for three white cardboard banker's boxes stacked against the back wall.

"A bit underwhelming," she said.

"What were you expecting?"

"Not this."

"Even the smallest of boxes can contain the greatest of secrets."

She tilted her head at him. "Who said that?"

"Me. Just now. You're welcome to use it anytime."

She tossed him an exasperated smile. "Anyone ever mention you're a bit of smart-ass?"

"All the time."

They stepped inside and approached the stack.

Luke heard a faint, intermittent clicking and froze.

So did Jillian.

"What the hell?" she muttered.

He turned, realizing the sound was coming from beside the door and up, near the ceiling, where a shoebox, sealed with black duct tape, hung half suspended by a wire.

Jillian said, "You don't think it's a—"

"If it was, we'd already be dead." Another thought popped into his head. "I thought you said your grandfather wasn't tech-savvy."

"He wasn't."

"You still have that knife from last night?"

He'd left his in London along with his Beretta.

She fished it from her back pocket and handed it to him. He walked over and reached up, cutting the wire and freeing the shoebox. The sound he'd heard was coming from within. He scored the tape, keeping the box shut, and lifted off the lid. Inside, nestled in form-cut foam, rested a cell phone attached to an external power pack.

"So the door opens," he said, "which upends the shoebox, which sets off the phone's accelerometer, which then wakes up and calls. Problem is the battery is nearly dead. Not enough power to trigger the phone. Only enough to trip the switch on and off."

He yanked the wires from the battery pack.

The clicking stopped.

"That lock being relatively new and oiled and this burglar alarm shows this was an important place. I assume your grandfather wasn't able to travel?"

"Not in the six months I was there. He could barely walk."

"So he wasn't able to maintain this place. That had to be a problem for him. Seems your grandfather was full of surprises."

His tone was lighthearted, but Jillian's frown only deepened. "Why would he do all this?"

He turned his attention to the cache.

"Let's find out."

13.

LUKE DECIDED SINCE THEY WERE ALONE AND THINGS WERE QUIET, A cursory search of each box seemed in order. Two contained what looked like photographs, souvenirs, knickknacks, and military keepsakes. Personal mementos. The third box contained only a military rucksack. One of the smaller models. Nylon. ACU camo-colored, camouflaged exterior. He'd worn one for years. He opened the top flap and saw it was empty.

Odd.

Wedged behind the boxes, though, lying against the outer wall was a long, black Pelican case with a thick Lexan exterior, heavy-duty hinges, and three reinforced clasps, the middle of which had a keyhole.

He tried the center clasp. Locked. "I'll need your knife."

She handed over the blade and he used it to work the lock open. He then flipped up the remaining two buckles and lifted the lid. Inside was a rectangle of white canvas tarp. Jillian carefully folded back the layers until what lay beneath was laid bare.

A rifle.

Lo and behold. In the flesh.

He immediately recognized the weapon as a military-style semi-automatic rifle, which was surprising enough, but it was the packaging that really piqued his attention. From buttstock to muzzle tip the weapon was vacuum-sealed in clear, heavy-duty polyurethane. A few inches beyond the muzzle, where the bag's end had been sealed, was a strip of red duct tape on which something was scribbled, but the ink had faded to a blur.

"What is this?" she said, leaning closer.

"Benji was preserving evidence," he said.

"The question is, of what? And why?

He examined the rifle closer. "This is a Colt AR-15. It's essentially a civilian version of the M16. It's old, that's for sure. First or second generation. We're talking late 1950s to early to mid-1960s."

"Is there a serial number? Check the receiver."

He zeroed in for a closer look through the plastic, not touching or disturbing anything. "It's gone."

"At least we found it," she said. "Now what?"

"Let's get out of here and we'll figure it out."

Jillian rewrapped the gun. Together, they carried the three boxes out and slid them, along with the rifle in its case, into the Peugeot's cargo area. They climbed in and started back toward the main entrance. As they rounded the last corner and the security gate came into view, he slammed on the brakes. A hundred yards beyond the security gate, outside the perimeter fence, a pair of black Renault sedans were parked, blocking the road. A lone man in a dark-blue suit exited one of the cars, strode around the hood, and faced them, empty hands at his side. He was medium in height, with swarthy skin, Asian features, and short dark hair.

"Looks like an invitation," Luke said.

"Or a trap. How did they find us?"

He had a few ideas on that one. None of which mattered at the moment.

"We can't stay behind this gate forever. Might as well see what he wants. What's your effective range with one of those nines?"

"Forty yards. Ninety percent center-of-mass hits."

She added a sweet, but brittle smile. He knew it well. Her game face.

But no use kidding each other.

This was serious.

He shifted the Peugeot into gear and approached the gate, which rolled open, then he drove past. He closed the distance to the Renaults until about fifty yards separated them.

He reached for the door handle. "Stay inside, unless you have to shoot."

"If I do, you stay out of my line of fire."

"If I go down, drive like hell—"

"Get real. I'd no sooner leave you than you'd leave me."

Good to hear.

He lowered the windows so she could hear, then climbed out.

"Hey," she said. "Don't get killed."

Seemed like a good thing to keep in mind.

He walked halfway to the Renaults and stopped. The man strode forward until ten feet separated them. Luke noticed a Bluetooth headset jutting from the man's right ear. People were in contact with one another. One of the Renault's rear doors opened. A thin, bald man emerged but remained behind the open door, hands out of sight.

Not good.

"You are Luke Daniels?"

Double not good. He wondered what else this guy knew.

"What do I call you?" he asked.

"Ateng Persik."

"You here on your own or on behalf of others?"

"Let's leave that one for later."

"I'd be grateful if your friend back there would put his hands where I can see them."

"You're quite polite."

"I was raised right."

"What if I don't want to do that?"

He lifted his right hand and motioned. Behind him he heard the car door open. He didn't need to look back. He knew Jillian was out, her gun aimed and ready.

"I have a shooter of my own," he said.

"That you do."

Without turning his head Persik barked something in another language. The man back at the car raised his hands and draped them over the door's upper jamb.

"Happy now?" Persik asked.

"Getting there. Open your jacket for me."

Persik did as ordered. Luke saw no weapons.

"What about your shooter?" Persik asked.

He motioned again and heard the car door shut behind him. "Now that we've come to know one another, what can I do for you?"

"First, I assume it was you who intervened at the Genappe house the other night?"

"Why do you ask?"

"I lost some good men."

"You and I have different definitions of 'good.' They executed an old man."

"Simply business," Persik said.

"What could he have possibly done to deserve that?"

Persik gave a slight shake of his head. "Doesn't matter anymore. I would like the items you just removed from that storage facility."

"And why would I give those to you?"

"It will allow you to remain alive."

He chuckled. "Lying is a terrible way to start a new friendship. I've got a counteroffer. We keep what belongs to us, and you tell us who you're working for."

"And why would I agree to something so absurd?"

"Because you're outgunned."

Playing poker had been a contact sport with the Rangers, serving as a mix of stress relief, entertainment, and competition. Stories of the games were legendary. He'd earned the nickname Bird Dog because of his ability to always remember a route to anywhere, no matter how convoluted the terrain. But he'd also been tagged Oscar for his command performances bluffing at poker.

"You didn't think I came alone?" he asked. "Since you know my name you surely know my training. See that ridge behind me? Past the storage facilities?"

Persik's eyes flicked over Luke's shoulder. "I see it."

"That's what we call a superior firing position. Always secure the high ground."

Persik chuckled. "You're bluffing."

"Fair enough. Let's find out." He retrieved the burner phone from his pocket, tapped the keyboard a few times, brought it to his right ear, and faced Persik. "Have Baldy back there draw his weapon, and let's see what happens."

They stared at each other for a long ten seconds.

"How about this," Luke said. "You call the shot."

"Pardon?"

"You choose into which of his eyes the bullet goes. Left or right. Or, since you caught me in a good mood, we could do an ear. It's your call. And, for fun, whatever you call, the shot might come to your man back there or to you. I'm going to let my shooter decide who he plugs. Surprises are fun."

Persik did not respond. Again, his eyes shifted from Luke's face to the ridgeline then back again. "I don't believe you."

"Have it your way." He raised his index finger, then murmured into the phone, "You heard what I said. Single shot, right eye. Send it—"

"Stop," Persik cried out.

He raised his fist. "Hold on target."

"I see no reason for bloodshed," Persik said. "My orders are to take whatever you have, then kill you. However, my employer trusts my judgment. So give us what you have and I'll convince him you're no threat and should be left alone."

Another lie, and not a convincing one either. Still, it was bait too good to refuse for stalling. "I have your word?"

"Soldier-to-soldier."

"Where did you serve?"

"A major in Indonesia's KOPASSUS Red Beret Corps."

He feigned being impressed. "Those guys are legendary. Drinking snake blood, rolling in glass, breaking bricks with their heads, walking on fire. Is all that true?"

"Every word."

They were also regarded as some of the most ruthless and lawless security forces in the world with a litany of human rights violations, including torture and mass murder. Good to know who he was dealing with.

Which only increased his concern.

"Okay, solider to solider, you've got yourself a deal. Which my sniper will make sure you keep." He gestured with the phone. "He can hear every word we're saying. Benjamin Stein kept a storage locker here. We were hoping there'd be something inside that'd help explain who and why someone wanted him dead."

"What did you find?"

"A cardboard box."

"You have it?" Persik asked. "In the car?"

"We do. It's full of documents." A lie, but he needed to keep this guy talking. "By the way, how did you find us?"

"We tracked your car. Obviously, you found our tag and disabled it. But we still traced the car to Bruges and learned you traded it for the Peugeot. Five hundred euros to one of the employees at the rental agency gained access to the rental car's internal tracker. All of the companies have those today."

"How fortunate for you. And here you are. Johnny-on-the-spot. In Luxembourg."

Persik said nothing.

"Wait here," he said.

And he walked back to the Peugeot, passing Jillian, who kept her eye on Persik and the cars behind him. He opened the cargo hatch and stuck his head inside.

"What's going on?" she asked.

"We're making a trade." He grabbed the empty box that had held the rucksack. "I give them a cardboard box full of nothing, and we do our best to rain down enough hell that we can get away."

"You do realize you're bluffing with not even a pair of twos. Sniper on the hill?"

"That's why they called me Oscar. Where's the other nine?"

"On the back seat."

He stretched in, retrieved it, then stuffed the gun at the base of his spine.

"Your new friend's lips are moving," she said, referring to Persik.

"Bluetooth headset. Probably explaining to his buddies in the car, or elsewhere, what happens next."

"Care to tell me?"

"My bluff bought us a little wiggle room, but there's no two ways about it. They want to take what we have and kill us. And we are seriously outgunned."

"I don't like either one of those."

"Then let's change the outcome."

"You're annoyingly optimistic."

"My former commanding officer said the same thing."

He quickly told her what he had in mind.

"You'll be in the open without cover," she said when he finished.

"Hopefully for only a few seconds. Remember, pedal to the metal. Don't slow down. We only get one chance at this."

14.

LUKE SET THE EMPTY CARDBOARD BOX ON THE GROUND, CLOSED THE hatch, then picked the box back up with his best this-is-really-heavy pantomime. He stepped out from behind the Peugeot and headed toward where Persik was standing, still feigning that the box had weight. No one had moved in his brief absence, which was promising. As was the fact there'd been no mention of the rifle or other boxes. Apparently, they hadn't been under surveillance inside the fence line. Behind him, Jillian had surely switched seats, now behind the wheel. He stopped ten feet before Persik and set the box on the ground. Persik stepped forward. Luke placed his foot on the box lid and raised a halting hand. "Let's talk ground rules."

Persik stopped. "You're testing my patience."

He removed the phone and displayed it. "I'm going back to our vehicle. You're going to stand perfectly still until we drive away. Once we're gone, the box is yours. Agreed?"

Persik nodded.

"My backup on the ridge will have you in his sights until we're gone. We understand each other?"

"You won't see us again."

Yeah, right.

He removed his boot from the box top, then placed it against the side, suddenly lift-kicking it toward Persik. At the same time he drew the 9mm. His timing was perfect, but so were Persik's reflexes. He stopped the box midair then launched it back at Luke.

And charged.

Luke spun on his heel, sidestepping Persik's tackle by inches.

Not his first rodeo.

He slipped his left arm over Persik's shoulder, grasped the chin, and wrenched the neck, yanking him close. He shoved the barrel of his gun into Persik's ear and angled their bodies to face the two Renault sedans.

All the doors were open.

Six men were out, automatic rifles aimed at Luke.

He learned long ago that few survived first contact with the enemy. Things changed. Like a bold charge from Persik. On the plus side Jillian, having realized their original plan had derailed, had held her fire.

Thank goodness.

He shifted most of his body so he was hidden behind Persik. "You broke our deal. My feelings are hurt."

"You can't win this."

Baldy sidestepped away from the car, trying to improve his firing angle on Luke.

"He takes another step and you go down."

"You have no sniper," Persik spit out.

A shot rang out from behind him. The round skipped off the pavement within inches of Baldy. Jillian had fired, announcing her presence.

"I may not need one," Luke said. "Tell him to get back."

Persik shouted something. Baldy froze.

He realized the only thing keeping those six men from opening fire was the fact that their boss was in dire jeopardy. Obviously, there was loyalty there. Good. He'd exploit that.

"Everyone lowers their weapons," he told Persik, "and Baldy goes back to the car."

He knew better than to demand more. Men like this didn't self-disarm. Plus, the longer he kept this going the greater his chance of making a mistake.

Persik barked out the order.

"No way," Luke said. "English. Tell them in English."

To make his point he jammed the gun harder into the ear and cocked the hammer. No matter how tough you were, that sound always brought anxiety. Just a twitch of the finger away from death.

"Lower the guns," Persik said.

"To the ground," Luke added.

They did. In unison. He assumed this was a tight-knit group. More important, they were leader-focused, not mission-focused. Otherwise, they wouldn't have hesitated to sacrifice Persik. Perfect. That he could work with.

Once Baldy was back behind the door, he told Persik, "We're leaving now."

"With me as your hostage?"

He'd considered the possibility, but wrangling this guy would be a fox-in-the-henhouse-on-steroids complication he couldn't afford.

He and Persik walked forward in lockstep until they were twenty feet from the Renaults. "You guys get back in your cars, and stay there until we leave."

"We won't stop coming after you," Persik said. "You have no idea who you're dealing with."

"Care to enlighten me?"

"It's not too late. You can live through this, both of you."

"I plan on it. Tell Baldy to bring you his cell phone. In English."

Persik gave the order.

Without hesitation Baldy complied.

"Put it in my right hand," he commanded.

Persik handed the phone over. He grabbed it with his right hand, but kept his grip on Persik's neck. The gun remained cocked at the ear. Baldy retreated.

"We'll be in touch," Luke said.

"Once you leave here, there will be no deals. No mercy."

"We'll see about that. You've gone to a lot of trouble to get what we have. Tell your boss he can still have it, but it'll be on my terms. I have the rifle. You can find me on that cell phone I just took."

Luke glanced over his shoulder and caught Jillian's attention. She cranked the engine, then eased forward until the passenger door was even with him.

"Change of plans?" she said through the open window.

"Ms. Stein," Persik said. "You need to—"

"Shut up," Luke said.

The six other men remained inside the two Renaults.

"Anyone gets out, they die," Luke said. "My man on the ridge is watching." He shoved Persik forward. "Hands on your head. Plant your butt on the hood."

Persik strode back to his car, then turned to face Luke.

"Last chance," Persik said.

Luke fired two rounds, one each into a front tire of the Renaults.

The gun's magazine emptied after the second shot and the slide locked open.

Persik noticed too.

"Crap," he muttered, before opening the passenger-side door and leaping in. "Go. Now."

The Peugeot surged forward, heading for the gap between the Renaults. He saw Jillian's 9mm lying in her lap. He grabbed it and whirled around, seeing through the rear window as Persik's men leaped from the cars and leveled their weapons.

He sent three rounds their way out the open passenger window.

Which caused them to duck for cover.

"Get down," he yelled.

Muzzles flashed orange.

The Peugeot's rear window shattered. A bullet punched into the headrest beside his face. White foamlike confetti spewed into the air. They came to a curve, which she navigated crouched low in the seat. Jillian jerked the wheel back straight and kept accelerating. They were now out of the line of fire.

Ahead, a black sedan appeared.

And sped straight toward them.

15.

LUKE REALIZED THAT THE CAR COMING AT THEM WAS MOST LIKELY Persik's backup team. No wonder he'd been so accommodating. Back to that out-of-the-fire-and-into-the-frying-pan thing. But since he was making things up as they went, mistakes were unavoidable. Like running out of ammunition in front of the guy you're trying to bluff. He shoved the doubts aside. There'd be enough time to beat up on himself later. Right now he and Jillian needed to survive the next few minutes.

"Pedal to the metal," he told her.

She jerked the wheel, skidding the Peugeot around the sedan, which did a 180 behind them and began pursuit. To their left, a chain-link fence ran parallel to their route. More of the warehouse acreage. The black sedan following them matched their speed, pulling alongside. The sedan's rear passenger-side window descended, revealing a gun barrel.

"Tap the brake," he said, "then swerve left, accelerate, and straighten out."

She did exactly as instructed, slamming the Peugeot into the sedan's side doors, forcing it to sheer away.

"Again, but gun the engine."

She performed the maneuver a second time, this time maintaining contact and using the Peugeot's power to drive the sedan sideways, its tires smoking over the cracked asphalt. The driver lost control and the car spun off the road in a cloud of dust. She slammed the accelerator to the floorboard and they sped away.

"I'm not a damn race car driver," she said. "This is not comfortable to me."

Their speed kept increasing.

"Let me take over," he said to her.

He wiggled left and she squirmed over him, her foot momentarily leaving the accelerator, her hands replaced by his on the steering wheel. Luke settled into the seat and pressed the accelerator, speeding them back up.

"We've got new trouble," she said, glancing back. "And coming fast."

He saw it too in his rearview mirror.

The black sedan. Back from the dead.

To their right the chain-link fence was converging into a corner. He tapped the brake, slowing for the turn in the road, which allowed the sedan to close the gap until it was five feet off his bumper. The spinout had clearly gotten the driver's blood boiling. Good. He was now driving angry, not smart.

"Seatbelt on?" Luke asked as he quickly buckled his own.

"Go for it."

He stood on the brakes. The sedan slammed into their rear bumper. Luke accelerated again and cast a glance at the rearview mirror. The sedan's windshield was bloated by white airbags. He tapped the brakes, bled off some speed, and readied for another turn.

Out of the corner of his eye he saw a blur of white.

Jillian saw it too. "Do they have an army?"

He was wondering the same thing.

Luke looked left and registered a white Volvo speeding toward them. He then glanced in the side mirror and saw a pair of men climbing from the stalled black sedan, their guns already coming up.

He made a snap decision.

Time for some hill and dale.

"Hold tight," he told her.

He whipped the wheel hard right. The Peugeot's tail snapped around, tires stuttering sideways before he accelerated and straightened out. Ahead, a hundred feet away and closing fast, was the fence.

"You might want to duck," he told her.

"You sure about this?"

"I'm sure we're out of options. Get your knife out and be ready."

She did so. "What's this for?"

"You'll see."

The fence loomed through the front windshield. He aimed the hood at what he guessed was the softest part of the span then glanced at the speedometer.

Eighty kilometers per hour.

Should be enough.

Please be enough.

He knew that fences were all different and seldom did they react to a collision as Hollywood portrayed, lying flat the instant a bumper touched them. More often they bulged outward, if only for a split second, before turning into a tangle of steel netting and sheered-off aluminum poles that whipped about like javelins.

They left the road and hit the fence at the midpoint between a pair of poles. For one breathless instant the fence held, bulged, then snapped. The Peugeot's airbags exploded, driving Luke's head backward. Something slammed against the roof, then raked down the car's side with a screech. He heard a metallic chattering sound and knew part of the fence had snagged on the Peugeot's undercarriage. He returned his hands to the wheel, steering blindly.

"You okay?"

Her arm appeared before his face. She plunged the knife into the airbag and ripped sideways, then again. With a *whoosh* the bag deflated. He shoved the material aside and blinked his eyes clear in time to jerk the wheel. The Peugeot glanced off a tree, slewed sideways, hit another tree broadside, then slid down a short slope.

The car lurched to a stop.

Its wheels spun, sending up a rooster tail of leaves and dirt. He lowered his window and leaned out. A section of fencing had snarled around the tree trunk. Luke shifted into reverse, then accelerated.

The fencing held.

"Sit tight," he said.

He slammed the gearshift into park, climbed out, and scrambled up the slope until he could see over the crest. Persik's men, now numbering four, were gathered about the gap in the fence. Mangled metal had rebounded and formed a barrier that had prevented them from driving through. One of them had a phone pressed to his ear. Probably requesting guidance. The others were clearing the obstacles. He slid back down the hill, then lay on his back and shimmied beneath the Peugeot, groping about until he found where a strand of fencing was hooked to the gas tank bracket. He freed it and returned to the driver's seat.

"Are they still there?" asked Jillian.

He nodded. "They'll be through shortly."

He shifted the Peugeot into drive and began easing them farther down the slope using taps on the brake and the accelerator to navigate through the ever-thickening trees. The afternoon sun was dimmed by the leafy canopy.

A jangling filled the air.

From his pocket.

Baldy's phone. He handed her the unit. "Put him on speaker."

"You have nowhere to go," Persik said. "Come back and our deal still stands."

"Liar, liar, pants on fire. You said no mercy."

He was ad-libbing, since he had no intention of going back. But the longer he kept Persik talking the more distance he could place between them, which in turn translated into a larger search area.

"We'd want more conditions to guarantee our safety," he said. "You may not like them."

"Try me."

He paused. "Give me ten minutes. I'll call you back."

Jillian ended the call.

"Pull the battery."

"For a moment there I thought you were really making a deal."

"Not unless we want to die today."

They drove for another ten minutes through the trees, but with each foot forward the foliage grew more tightly packed until he decided this was the end of the line. "We're on foot from here. Let's grab the rifle. The rest stays here. You okay with that?"

"I'm not in a sentimental mood."

They retrieved the rifle case.

"It won't take them long to track us to here," he said, sliding the remaining 9mm tight at his waist. "We left a fairly easy trail to follow, and they can still track this car. So we need to get lost."

And they headed off into the woods.

16.

A QUICK CHECK ON THE MAPS APP OF HIS PHONE TOLD LUKE THAT they were hiking through what was known as the Oesling, the Luxembourgish name for this section of the Ardennes mountain range which stretched through Belgium and Luxembourg then into Germany and France. Plenty of wild, old-growth forest with undulating, ankle-snapping terrain consisting of decomposed foliage and layer upon layer of fallen trees. In places, it was less forest and more a warren of grottos and vegetation tunnels. At best, he and Jillian could cover a mile or so every hour. Come nightfall they'd be lucky to do a quarter of that distance.

It would be worse, though, for whoever Persik sent in. While they'd probably have little trouble picking up the trail, their subsequent movements would have to be coordinated and meticulous, lest they walk right past a hiding spot or stumble into an ambush. He considered sending Jillian ahead, then lying in wait and picking off their pursuers one by one. It appealed to the Ranger in him. Fight on the terrain of your choosing. At a time of your choosing. Take every advantage and make the enemy pay for it. Beyond the question of whether he could pull it off alone, armed only with four rounds from Jillian's pistol, there was something more important at stake. First, getting her to safety. Then, second, finding out what deadly secret Benjamin Stein had been keeping.

For an hour they picked their way deeper and higher into the forest, he in the lead, Jillian following with the rifle case in one hand.

In the distance came a warbling sound.

He froze and lowered into a crouch. Jillian followed suit.

That was no bird, and he saw she agreed.

They waited.

Thirty seconds passed.

Then the squelch of a radio and a tinny voice back from the direction they'd come. That suddenly cut off. As though silenced by a mute button?

"How far away do you think?" Jillian whispered.

"A few hundred yards. Let's keep moving. They're catching up faster than I thought."

He realized that in a forest this thick twilight would come well before sunset, but he was still surprised when darkness began to fall like a curtain. The surrealness was compounded by slivers of bright sky that peeked in through the tall boughs. He stopped walking and together they crouched behind a tree. No sign or sound of Persik's men for the past thirty minutes.

Had they lost them?

They kept going until he saw an anomaly for the wilderness. A shrine. Erected in a small clearing encircled by trees. A building about eight feet square, formed from rough lumber that was badly in need of paint. The door was intact on its rusted hinges and creaked open. Inside was plain. Just a crucifix, a small altar, and room for a few to kneel together before it. Whitewashed stucco walls had seasoned to a creamy gray, the wood for the altar and floor bleached out with age. Only a faded painting of Christ and bits of colored glass in the small side windows relieved the monochromatic look.

"Nobody has been here for a while," Jillian said.

They needed to shed the rifle and case. If they were caught, it might be their only bargaining chip. He looked around. No hiding places here, except for the altar. He knelt down and examined the cabinet-like structure. Maybe four feet wide, that much and a little more high, and about a foot thick. Made from planks nailed together. One side was solid, but the other not so much. Two of the boards were loose. He managed to free them both on their nails and saw that the altar was hollow inside. A tight fit, but enough room. Jillian handed him the case, which he slipped inside.

He replaced the boards and pounded them into place with a closed fist. He felt better with that secreted away.

The rifle should be safe.

"We need to keep going."

Twenty minutes later he heard a new sound. Faint at first, but growing in volume. He peered upward through the trees, squinting at the bright sky, and listened to the basso overlapping chop of rotors. A sound he'd heard many times overseas.

A helicopter.

The volume increased until the helo closed the distance and passed directly overhead, then faded, heading west.

"He's low," he said. "And flying dark."

"You don't think—"

As if in answer to her question, the chopper swung around and returned, hovering nearly above them. Through the canopy Luke saw what looked like a boom silhouetted against the sky.

"That's a FLIR," she said, referring to forward-looking infrared radar.

"These guys are well equipped."

Bullets rained down.

They both sought cover behind a thick trunk.

To whoever was wielding that rifle he and Jillian were easy targets, negative-image monochrome silhouettes set against the dark forest floor, the weapons coupled to the thermal imaging. On the upside, NV optics didn't wield the same penetration power as infrared.

Which offered them an opportunity.

"Get ready to move." He peeked around the tree and received another near-miss bullet. "He's still in the same place, but that won't last long. He'll be guiding the others toward us. Let's go."

He kept the tree between them and the chopper, crouched down, moving forward with Jillian close behind. He spotted a narrow game trail, slithered under a fallen tree, then turned left along its length. Sure, he should be concerned for snakes, but the bullets from above seemed a far greater threat. He rolled right, scrambling, then started sliding downward. Branches and leaves slashed his face. He spread his legs to slow his descent. Jillian bumped into him. Tangled together they lurched to a stop and the bottom of the slope, inside a tunnel of sorts, a tangle of fallen trees and crisscrossed branches that blocked out the sky. Above, the helicopter was circling as the shooter tried to reacquire them.

In the distance came a shout, then another.

Over here. This way.

Bad guys were converging from every direction. Not an unfamiliar feeling, like an old friend you don't especially like but can't seem to shake. Especially when you know you're outnumbered and the cavalry ain't coming.

But he wasn't caught.

Not yet.

What was the Ranger way?

When in doubt, act.

17.

LUKE CRAWLED FORWARD, LETTING THE SLOPE TAKE HIM DEEPER INTO the makeshift vegetation tunnel, which was roomy. He lifted his hand and felt the curve of a tree trunk. He reached back, grabbed Jillian's arm, and dragged her closer.

"Through there. Go as far as you can."

"They're right on top of us," she whispered.

"I know. Crawl through."

She wriggled through the gap ahead and disappeared.

Behind them at the mouth of the tunnel a voice called, "Over here."

He froze, then gripped the pistol, flattened himself on his spine, and stayed still. A flashlight beam panned down the slope.

"I'm going in," a male voice called out.

The beam advanced, widened, then grew brighter. Slowly Luke eased the pistol up and aimed between his legs. His heart pounded. He sucked a breath, held it, then slowly let it out. His pulse slowed. Overhead, the thump of the helicopter's rotors intensified. Surely circling. Hunting for movement. Were he and Jillian deep enough to make the radar useless? Was the brush thick enough? Up the tunnel, the flashlight beam appeared over the crest. It moved down the slope, gliding toward him. He readied himself, settling the pistol's sight on the figure behind the beam. The light skimmed over his head, then stopped. It returned and paused. He gently tightened his index finger, eliminating the trigger tension, readying for a quick shot.

Milliseconds counted here.

A radio chirped and the man said, "Nothing down here."

The flashlight retreated over the crest and back up the tunnel.

He wriggled himself sideways and crawled into a bough-covered cave-like cavity. He and Jillian lay shoulder-to-shoulder, staring upward. Boots clomped on the logs above. A flashlight beam pierced the branches above Luke's head, casting moving shadows. When the footsteps faded he whispered to her, "Looks like they're headin' out. They may think we're still ahead of them. Let's get moving before they decide to double back."

"And the helicopter?"

"We have to risk it." He found his phone and used the maps app again. "If we get separated we'll meet, here, in Burden. It's not far. There'll probably be a bus station. Stay off the roads and—"

"How about this, Ranger. Shut up with that nonsense, and we don't get separated, we stay together."

"Yes, ma'am."

"Good answer."

"But if we somehow do get separated—"

"I've got it. Let's go. You're on point this time."

He smiled. Once a marine, always a marine. "Hooah."

They found their way out of the tunneled foliage. Then, in single file, picked their way west, following the undulating contours of the land and stopping every twenty paces to look and listen. Occasionally, they heard a burst of radio static in the distance as Persik's men moved north. He hadn't heard the helicopter for several minutes. They'd covered what he guessed was half the distance to Burden when the ground began sloping downward. Jillian, walking ten feet to his right, suddenly motioned for quiet and crouched down.

He did the same.

She signaled, *Movement.*

He followed her gaze and saw the faint profile of a man leaning against a tree, blocking their route. They must be closer to Burden than he realized. Persik had dispatched a sentry. He gestured that they should separate, pincer around the guy, and regroup on the other side.

She nodded and crept away.

He did the same, shifting left to gain distance between himself and the sentry. A rocky ridge halted his progress. It rose a few feet higher than he was tall and ran east-west, the outcrop covered in vines and lichen. Climbable but not quietly, so he turned west and began following the ridgeline down the ever-steepening slope.

Below he heard the fast gurgling of water.

A creek? River?

Suddenly, ten paces before him a figure hopped off the ledge and landed on his boots with a soft thump, an automatic rifle slung across his chest.

Luke froze.

The man faced away and hadn't seen him, but that would last

only a few seconds. He raised his pistol, then decided against it. The shot would draw everyone within half a mile. He adjusted his grip so the pistol could serve as a bludgeon.

And quickly advanced.

The man spun.

Change of plan.

Luke dropped the 9mm and rushed him. But even as they collided the man was stepping backward, lifting his weapon. The rifle fired, rounds whizzing off into the air, making lots of noise. Luke wrapped the guy in a bear hug, keeping the gun pointed up. The momentum of his impact sent them stumbling off the path, the man trying to stay on his feet, Luke trying to drive him to the ground. He slammed his forehead into the man's nose. The guy grunted, stunned. He repeated the headbutt. The man's legs buckled and together they tumbled down the steep slope, picking up speed as they bounced over tree roots and ricocheted off trunks.

Then he felt himself free-falling.

Through the air.

Huh?

With the other guy still in his grasp.

An electric jolt of cold jarred his senses as he hit water.

Hard.

Immediately, a strong current dragged them along a rock-strewn bottom. The man thrashed and clawed. Luke released him, switched his grip to the rifle, and twisted hard to reverse the barrel and shove it into the guy's belly. His finger found the trigger. Though the shot was mostly muffled by the rush of the water, the man's shocked expression told him the bullets had struck home.

Blood began to tint the water.

Luke slammed against a boulder.

Which hurt.

He rolled himself toward what he guessed was the riverbank, trying to find a handhold. He groped until gripping an exposed root. Then clung on hard. Which stopped his forward progress. The man's limp body swept past and into the main current, along with the rifle, both disappearing away, while Luke clutched the root against the flow. He needed to get out of the water. So he hauled himself up using the roots and grabbed a foothold, climbing onto the bank. He sat for a moment and savored a few breaths. Thank goodness the river was deep or he would not have survived the fall off the cliff, and his gun was gone.

Where was Jillian?

This definitely qualified as separated, so he needed to head for the rendezvous point. Above him, higher up the embankment, tires squealed on pavement.

Which grabbed his attention.

About thirty feet of trees and foliage led up to what was apparently a road. He sought cover behind thick clumps of brush. A car door opened, then slammed shut. A figure appeared at the top of the ridge.

"You see any way across?" he heard someone call out. "To the other side?"

"No," came the reply.

"Find one, I'm going to walk the road."

"I got one of them," a new voice shouted. "I got her."

Oh, crap.

Jillian.

He started climbing.

18.

LUKE FORCED HIMSELF TO PAUSE AND TAKE STOCK. BLINDLY RUSHING to Jillian's aid could worsen the situation. Still, waiting went against his every instinct. What would Malone say? Focus. Make a plan. Act on it.

Good advice.

He was uninjured. Amazingly. Which went into the plus column. So he carefully made his way up the wooded bank and saw there was indeed a road and a parked vehicle. Along with another Asian man holding a radio.

"I'm here. Nothing yet. Still looking." A pause. Someone was speaking through the earpiece. "Where are you taking her?" Another pause. "Okay, send me the airfield's GPS coordinates. I'll head that way shortly."

The guy walked off in the opposite direction.

The chop of helicopter rotors returned, filling the afternoon air. He craned his neck until he pinpointed the sound. The helo from earlier streaked by in the distance, heading northwest. He watched until its navigation lights disappeared over the trees. He completed the crawl up the slope until he was a few feet from the shoulder berm.

He paused to listen.

Where are you, pal?

He did a half push-up so he could see over the top. A Range Rover, its exhaust steaming in the cool air, idled in park ten feet away. He glanced left, saw nothing, then looked right. Twenty feet away, his back toward Luke, a man walked the shoulder, studying the foliage down the slope toward the river. Crouching, he crested the berm and scuttled behind the Range Rover.

Thirty seconds passed.

Footsteps crunched on loose gravel.

Closer. Keep coming.

The man appeared around the corner of the vehicle.

Luke sprang and wrapped his right arm around the guy's neck, then clamped his left hand on in a tight vise. He closed the windpipe and kept the pressure until the body went limp. Not enough to kill. No need.

He released his grip and helped the limp form down to the asphalt. Then he caught the guy's collar and dragged him toward the vehicle. A quick frisking turned up a passport, a cell phone, a set of four zip-tie cuffs, a sound-suppressed semi-automatic pistol, and two spare magazines. He used two of the cuffs to hog-tie the arms and legs, then opened the Range Rover's rear hatch and wrestled the guy inside.

"Hey, Galang, did you see anything?"

Luke almost turned, but caught himself. The new guy was approaching and had mistaken him for a cohort, the vehicle between them providing some cover. He waited until he judged the man was almost on top of him, then spun and raised the pistol. The man skidded to a stop, but his right hand, holding a pistol, started to rise.

"That would be really stupid," Luke said.

The man froze.

"Drop. The. Gun."

"Relax," the man said. "I'll put it down."

Had he not made himself clear? He told the guy to drop it, not place it. Slowly, eyes fixed on Luke, the man crouched, extending the pistol down toward the pavement. The body language spoke volumes. This fool was going to be a hero.

"Don't do it," he warned.

The pistol touched the ground.

"See," the man said, "no problem."

The hand jerked and regripped the gun. The arm angled upward.

Luke shot him twice in the chest.

The guy toppled backward, not moving.

He hated when people were stupid.

He scanned the road for a full minute to ensure reinforcements weren't coming, then searched the dead man, finding another cell phone, the pistol and two more spare magazines, and more zip cuffs. All of which he pocketed before rolling the body down the bank into the river.

He climbed into the Range Rover's driver's seat and scrolled through Galang's phone until he found the most recent text message, a thumbnail of a map with a red pin in its center. He tapped it to bring up the full image. The red pin sat in what looked like a patch of forest about halfway between him and the town of Ringel, seven kilometers away as the crow flew. Northwest. He saw no markings that indicated an airfield at the location. Didn't matter. *Where are you taking her? Okay, send me the airfield's GPS coordinates.*

This had to be the place.

He climbed out and hauled the unconscious Galang back out of the vehicle, leaving him bound on the side of the road.

No need for any passengers.

Then he hopped back inside and sped off.

He drove for ten minutes, then turned onto a winding, two-lane road until he reached a T-intersection. A sign pointing to the left read RINGEL 3 KM. Across the road ran another fence and more forest. He turned left toward Ringel. He needed to reach Jillian before Persik began any painful interrogation. His heart raced, each beat like the ticking of a clock's second hand.

Get there. Fast. Find a way.

With one eye on the road he scanned the fence line through the open passenger window. He'd covered half the distance to Ringel when he spotted a set of double fence posts spanning a dirt tract.

A gate.

He stopped in front, stepped out, and walked over.

The right-hand fence post was bound to its neighbor by a pair of nails and a loop of bailing wire. He used the butt of his pistol and bent one of the nails until the loop spun free. He dragged the post across the tract, tossed it aside, then returned to the Range Rover and drove through.

The tract led deeper into the forest. After a few hundred yards the trees began thinning and he spotted the helicopter, engine off, rotors still.

Okay. One question answered.

If Persik planned to take Jillian elsewhere they would already be gone.

Out the car window something caught his eye. At the edge of the tract stood a crumbling, overgrown stone plinth. A steel post jutted from it. A matching plinth sat across the road. Another gate? No. Something older. No longer in use.

He eased off the road into the trees, parked, then climbed out.

He made his way toward the structure and decided it had indeed once been a gate. What was this place? He crept closer and parted an overgrowth of weeds at the plinth's base. Eroded by time and weather, a symbol was barely discernible.

But he recognized it.

A *Balkenkreuz.*

The German cross.

Now he knew. This was an abandoned World War II Luftwaffe base. The Germans had built them all over Belgium and Luxembourg, using them as fighter stations and emergency night landings for bombers. Most of them were grass runways, and this was no exception, the only concrete a small amount in and around two metal hangars that were in surprisingly good shape. The perimeter fence had likewise looked relatively recent so he assumed this whole place was now privately owned and maintained. Nothing other than the faded cross on the plinth reflected this place's checkered past. Nazi Germany's occupation was surely something most Luxembourgers preferred to forget.

He checked his gear.

He had the two pistols he'd acquired and four spare magazines. Maybe fifty rounds of ammunition. But Persik had more men, more bullets, and a defensive superiority with the hangars. A firefight could get both him and Jillian killed.

Best option?

Don't get shot.

19.

LUKE HAD NO IDEA OF THE BASE'S ORIGINAL SIZE. ONLY TWO buildings had survived the intervening eighty years, along with a reinforced concrete hangar whose open side was bracketed by a chest-high revetment, which he assumed had served as a half door / blast shield for the hangar's interior. Attached to the right side of the hangar was a boxlike concrete structure with a flat roof. Probably once an office of sorts. Nature had done its best to try to reclaim both the hangars and the clearing with shrubs and stunted trees. What little of the original concrete surface Luke could see was either eroded or strewn with faded graffiti.

He spotted two more Range Rovers parked head-on to the revetment. Neither of the vehicles appeared to be running. The helicopter rested quiet and empty. Galang's phone vibrated in his pocket.

He checked.

A text message.

ETA to airfield?

They were looking for their compatriot. He found the other phone he'd lifted and saw the same query. A thought occurred to him. If Persik hadn't noticed Galang's and his partner's absence, their silence could lead to a check on their status.

He sprinted back in a half crouch toward the Range Rover. Just as he arrived, a figure exited the hangar, hesitated a moment, then started walking toward the vehicle. Apparently, they'd already decided on a check and, lo and behold, the Range Rover was here. The guy was armed with another automatic rifle. Luke dropped to his belly and rolled underneath the vehicle. The man stopped ten feet from the front bumper, surely wondering what the vehicle was doing here. Luke could only see him from the shins down.

"Galang, you there? Rimba?"

Luke heard the rifle being raised as the man walked to the driver's door, opened it, and looked inside. When he saw it vacant he stepped to the rear hatch. Luke let him pass, then rolled out behind him and kicked the man's knees out from under him. The body dropped and Luke cradled the head, slamming it hard against the side panel, knocking the guy unconscious.

The pop of head to metal had been loud.

He waited a moment to see if it had been heard.

All quiet.

He repeated the frisking process, found a similar array of stuff, then zip-cuffed the man and shoved him in the cargo area. He scrolled through the text messages on the man's phone until he found Persik's number. He typed, They just arrived. Engine overheated. No sign of Daniels.

A reply came a moment later.

The three of you secure the perimeter.

He allowed himself a half smile. So far, so good.

But whatever he was going to do, it had to be now.

He returned to the edge of the clearing and picked his way through the trees until he drew even with the helicopter, which he used as cover to reach the hangar's attached concrete structure.

Quickly, he snapped a photo with his phone of the chopper's ID numbers.

The office door was missing, so he easily slipped inside and stood in the darkness until his eyes adjusted. Save for a few rickety lawn chairs and a scattering of trash, the room was empty. It stank of mildew. To his left was a closed door that led, he assumed, into the hangar. He had only one advantage. Surprise. No, he had something else. Knowledge, or at least the appearance of it. So negotiate. Swap himself for Jillian. Then use the rifle to bargain.

He realized that he and Jillian were leaks that Persik needed to plug. This realization brought him full circle back to the only course open. Go in with as much firepower as he could muster, try to take out or scatter as many of Persik's men as possible, and hopefully escape with Jillian in the chaos. The odds against a favorable outcome were steep, but it was still preferable to allowing Persik to simply call the shots.

So do it, Ranger.

One of the phones he'd taken vibrated with an incoming text. He checked the screen. No words. Just an image. Jillian's face with the tip of a knife hovering a hair's breadth from her eye. Persik knew. How?

He texted back, You have my attention.

Give yourself up. You have thirty seconds or she goes blind.

Dammit. He was out of cards to play. He texted back, I'm coming out.

Make sure your hands are empty.

He dropped both guns and spare magazines. Then, after a few moments' thought, he turned the knob and swung open the door. Hands raised, he stepped across the threshold. On either side of the door a pair of men stepped forward and shoved him to the ground. His hands were zip-cuffed and he was yanked back to his feet. Persik appeared and walked over, stopping when they were nose-to-nose.

"You killed my men?" Persik said.

"Just two of 'em. The other two are trussed up."

To the nearest minion Persik ordered, "Go find them."

The man jogged away.

Luke was curious. "What gave me away?"

"Instinct," Persik said.

"Luke, is that you?"

Jillian. Calling out from somewhere deeper in the hangar.

"It's me," he said back. "Unfortunately, I'm a little tied up at the moment."

"Join the club."

He smiled. She was a tough one.

He lowered his voice to a whisper and said to Persik, "I'm going to ask you to do me a favor."

"You have no leverage, Mr. Daniels."

"Soldier-to-soldier. Like before. But this time for real."

Persik stared into his eyes, then nodded. "Ask."

"Let her go. She doesn't know anything about this. Somebody killed her grandfather and she was trying to figure out who, that's all. I'm a government intelligence officer and I know a lot. You let her go and I'll work with you."

"That's a chance I cannot take. But you already know that. So ask your real favor, Mr. Daniels."

He stayed silent.

"Let me guess," Persik said. "When the time comes, you want her to go quickly, correct?"

He nodded. "I mean it. She doesn't know anything. Don't put her through this. Once she's gone you can take your time with me, if that's your thing."

"I don't have a *thing*. I have a mission. And there are consequences for every choice," Persik said. "Choices you made."

That there were. He could have turned away and left at any time. Hell, he had no idea what this was about beyond helping a friend. Malone would definitely give him some crap for being so uninformed.

"Come here," he said. "I need to tell you something. Between you and me."

Persik hesitated, then drew closer. Luke leaned in like he was about to whisper, then headbutted the idiot square in the brow, driving Persik back in stunned pain.

"You son of a—"

Persik charged and landed a fist into Luke's jaw. He'd expected retaliation, but it still hurt. As did the second punch into his gut. But he'd managed to tighten his abs in anticipation.

"You both are going to die real slow," Persik spit out, rubbing his forehead.

"Where I come from we have a saying. The hen shouldn't cackle before she lays the egg."

Persik stayed back, out of range. "Where did you put the contents of Stein's storage locker? And I'm not talking about what you left behind in the car. We found that junk. What else was there?"

"Who says there was anything else?" he tried.

"You fought awful hard for nothing."

Good point. "We FedExed it to CIA headquarters."

Persik chuckled. "If only you knew the irony in that smart-ass comment."

Interesting. A clue as to who was pulling the strings?

The man Persik had dispatched to check on the others returned and whispered to his boss. Then Persik asked, "Where are the two men you killed?"

"Assuming they didn't get hung up on rocks, they're probably halfway to Luxembourg City by now."

Persik gestured to the guards. "We'll start on him first. Maybe watching the process will make Ms. Stein more cooperative."

20.

LUKE WAS LED AROUND THE REAR OF A PARKED RANGE ROVER INSIDE the hangar. Light bled in through a series of windows high on the walls filtered by the dirt and grime on the panes. Propped between a pair of crates was a thick board. Several five-gallon buckets of water and a towel sat on the floor. Now he knew what Persik had meant by *process*. His stomach rose into his throat. He'd seen this kind of crap before in Afghanistan inside locales that weren't listed on maps. Places people and governments never talked about.

Waterboarding.

Just friggin' great.

Before the practice was banned Luke had undergone a milder version of it during Ranger SERE training. Survival Evasion Resistance Escape. The four basics that every soldier had hammered into their head. Which had included being strapped to a board, his face covered by a tautly drawn towel, while water was poured down his gullet. While it lasted a mere sixty seconds, the experience had pushed him close to the breaking point. Its terror bypassed toughness of character, strength of body, and dedication of mind, and latched onto the most primitive part of the brain that will do anything to survive.

Anything.

He supposed it was a favorite tactic around the world for its simplicity. Not much was needed in the way of tools to cause someone an enormous amount of agony. He saw Jillian, on the ground, her hands zip-cuffed to the Range Rover's bumper. She struggled to rise. One of Persik's men planted a boot to her ribs and shoved her down.

That made five men inside the hangar.

He saw no sign of the rifle case, which suggested it was still safe in their hiding place. Which Persik apparently did not know. Why else would either of them still be alive?

"You hurt?" he asked Jillian.

She shook her head. "You?"

"Couldn't be better. Whatever they ask, just tell the truth."

"You're not serious."

"Just do it. It's not worth lying."

"Good advice," Persik said. "Before we get started, do either of you want to tell me exactly what you found in that storage locker?"

"A bunch of old papers," Luke said, keeping to the lie.

"Relating to what?"

"We didn't have time to read them."

"Where are they now?"

"They were in my backpack I had. I lost it in the river. If you want to go look for it, we'll stay right here. Cross my heart."

"Ms. Stein, anything to add?" Persik asked.

"It was just papers."

"What kind of papers?"

"I have no idea. We were a little busy trying to not get killed."

"There was nothing else in the locker?"

She shook her head. "Not a thing."

"What do you know about Kronos?" Persik asked her.

"It's just a word my grandfather kept mentioning. He was on heavy pain meds so—" Jillian said.

"You used it in the email you sent."

"I was just trying to find out what the word meant. I had no idea and still don't."

Luke liked what she was doing. Keep him talking.

"I don't know what Kronos is, or what it means, or even who I sent the email to," Jillian said. "That's the truth."

Persik considered this for a few moments. "We'll see."

Luke cleared his throat and continued the lie. "About that backpack."

Persik turned to him. "Go on."

"It's water-resistant. If you're quick, those papers might still be salvageable."

"And where should we start looking?"

"Where I went into the water. Not far from where Galang's Range Rover was parked on the side of the road. Take me there and I'll show you."

"Perhaps later." Persik nodded at Luke's guards. "Strap him down. Let's get started."

He was shuffle-marched to the board and laid flat. One of the men produced a roll of duct tape and looped it six times around Luke's chest before spiraling it down his legs to his ankles, which got another six loops.

"The towel," Persik ordered.

One of the men dunked the towel in the nearest bucket, then unfurled it and handed one end to his partner. Together they laid the sopping mass over Luke's face and drew the ends taut. Immediately he felt a familiar panic explode in his chest.

"Wait," Jillian called out. "There was something else in the locker."

"Tell me."

"First, take off that towel."

It was lifted from Luke's face. He let out the breath he was holding.

"A rifle," she said. "An old one."

That magic word again. Which had an effect on Persik. The Indonesian was definitely interested. "I'm listening."

"It'd been there a long time," Jillian said. "It was carefully wrapped. Obviously important to my grandfather."

"What kind of rifle?"

"Like you don't know," Luke said.

Persik turned toward him. "For this to be your ticket off that board, I need to know what kind of rifle."

"A Colt AR-15. First or second generation."

He wanted to see what reaction the truth would bring.

But nothing was offered, only Persik asking, "Where is it now?"

"It's back where you caught me," Jillian said. "I hid it in some tree roots. You won't find it on your own."

"Anything else?"

"That's all I know," she said.

"I don't believe you." Persik motioned to the guards. "Continue."

"If you do this, I won't help you," she made clear.

"I'm going to drown Mr. Daniels until he's almost dead. And I'm going to keep doing it over and over and over until it's your turn. By the time I'm done, neither of you will have a secret left in your head."

"I swear to God," Jillian said. "You'll get nothing from me."

The towel was draped back over his face.

Everything went dark.

He kept telling himself, keep your head, snatch breaths when you can. Unless they killed him while he was still strapped to the board, there'd come a moment when they'd move him to make way for Jillian. Meager as it would be, that could be his chance.

A phone jangled.

"Hold there," Persik ordered his men, then took the call. After a few moments of listening, he said, "I've got them both here." Another pause. "I've just started." More listening. "How far out are you? Okay, we'll stand by." The call ended. "Remove the towel."

The guards complied.

Luke blinked his eyes clear.

"Just a delay, Mr. Daniels," Persik said. "Don't get your hopes up."

A few minutes passed and, from outside, came the revving of an engine. Tires skidded on dirt, followed by a door opening and shutting. A sole man entered the hangar. Tall and broad-shouldered with close-cropped black hair, he walked straight to Persik with a slight limp. The man gave Luke, then Jillian, a once-over.

"Is this them?" the newcomer asked. "They don't look like much."

"Why were you sent? I have things in hand."

"Tell me the situation."

Persik recounted all that he knew. When finished, he said, "I believe Mr. Daniels is lying, so I was about to persuade him to be more truthful."

"He's a former Army Ranger. That might prove tough."

"We always have Ms. Stein."

"True."

The tall man drew a sound-suppressed weapon and shot Persik twice, then spun and dropped Luke's two guards. Persik's remaining two men, standing near Jillian, were cut down before they had a chance to find their weapons. Each shot was delivered with expert precision. Finally, the prostrate men were finished off with a single round to the skull.

The tall man walked over to Luke and stared down at him. "You order a pizza?"

21.

THE WITHERING GUNFIRE CEASED FOR A MOMENT.

In the silence Jack Talley could hear shouts in Pashto or Dari echoing down the slope. He knew what the lull meant. The Al Qaeda forces that had had them pinned down for the last seventeen hours were prepping for yet another charge in the hope of overrunning the Delta Force's already tenuous position on the ridge's steep backslope. He knew that AQ soldiers liked to get in close and finish off foes with knives and hatchets.

Old school.

Once bad guys made it inside your wire, ejecting them became almost impossible. And he'd already counted eight of his own wounded, combat-incapable. So far the Deltas had driven back nine charges. The ground between them and the AQ forces was littered with corpses, some of them half buried in the snow with only faces, or extended arms or bent legs, visible.

This wasn't the first time he'd found himself at the jagged end of bad intelligence, but this was the first time it had gotten his men killed. Intelligence hiccups were common, but usually restricted to minor details like structure layouts and whether a target was currently in the area. This time, intel had underestimated enemy forces by a factor of ten. Instead of thirty AQ, over three hundred had bivouacked in the Afghan valley to ride out the storm.

"More massing on the eastern outcrop, boss," one of his sergeants from the rock alcove nearby called out.

Their position was less than fifty meters wide and a hundred meters long, a stretch of barren ground with a waist-high shelf of rock facing the enemy and a thousand-foot precipice on the back side to which Talley had almost lost two of his troopers unsuccessfully attempting to find a route of retreat.

None existed.

They were stuck here.

And were probably going to die. Their ammunition was nearly gone, and once the guns ran dry that was all she wrote.

Except for the hand-to-hand that would surely come from the enemy.

"They've definitely got reserves filtering in from somewhere," one of his men said.

By Talley's count his sixteen remaining Deltas had killed or wounded nearly ninety bad guys but still they kept coming, surely force-marching their way through the blizzard and up the mountain from Celam Kae, three kilometers away. He estimated enemy strength at battalion-sized, perhaps five hundred men. Clearly they weren't happy the Deltas had managed to snatch Nizar Tawfiq, AQ's regional commander, right from under their noses. While part of the operation had gone flawlessly, a barking dog during their exfiltration had given them away.

"Gimme an ammo count, Bobby," he said.

"On it."

"Any word on the Chinooks?"

"Still socked in. Pilots want to come, but command's saying no."

Four times Kabul had dispatched Chinook helicopters to pull them off the ridge and four times the blizzard had driven them back. Resupply had been only partially successful. Most of it had slid off the ridge and into the valley below. They were out of food and water and down to the dregs of their medical supplies and ammunition. And now with night only an hour away the Chinooks would be grounded until morning. He and his Deltas wouldn't be here to rescue by then.

He wanted to know, "How's our guest?"

"Sleeping like a baby."

Upon grabbing Nizar Tawfiq from his house, they'd sedated him for transport. It wasn't so much that these AQ soldiers wanted Tawfiq back as they didn't want him in American hands. The man would be an intel gold mine.

"They're shifting one of their DShKs," Talley heard over his radio.

"Heads down," Talley called out. "Incoming."

Two of the Russian .50-caliber machine guns had been chipping away at their already thin cover for the past six hours. Now they were trying again to drive the Deltas from cover or force them to give up.

Neither was going to happen.

Men like those under Talley's command neither wavered nor surrendered.

Moments later the machine guns opened up. Rounds slammed into the outcrop above Talley's head, sending rocky shrapnel whizzing over their encampment. This was heavier, he noted, preparatory fire for another charge. The AQ forces weren't going to risk their quarry slipping away under the cover of darkness.

"OP coming in," he heard over his radio.

Talley had dispatched a single soldier to an observation post in the no-man's-land between them and the enemy. Now he was coming back.

"Give him covering fire," he ordered.

Despite the incoming .50-caliber barrage, Talley's men rose and returned fire, picking off exposed AQ soldiers and driving others to cover as their OP sprinted back to the command post. The enemy had more guns and ammunition but were no match for the accuracy of Talley's troopers who were one-shot, one-kill trained. The OP baseball slid over the rock shelf and landed in a heap in the snow. Talley grabbed the guy's collar and dragged him to cover.

Panting, the man said, "They're not messing around this time, boss. I estimate 150 massing."

"Trading bodies for ground," Talley said. "All Deltas, they're coming hard this time. Get ready to go hands-on."

"About time," came a reply.

"Damn straight," someone added.

"Here they come."

Talley radioed, "As soon as the fifties go quiet, start dropping bodies. Make 'em pay for every inch."

Shouts could be heard up the slope as the AQ soldiers ramped themselves up for the charge. It was an unnerving animal-like sound, indecipherable, guttural.

The .50-caliber machine guns stopped.

Talley peeked his head up.

The AQ soldiers were moving down the slope at a sprint, so thick they were shoulder-to-shoulder and backed by multiple lines.

"Open fire," he shouted.

Across the front M4s began popping. Their lone machine gun, an M249 SAW, started chugging, mowing down groups of front-line soldiers. The ones behind didn't hesitate, leaping over their fallen comrades as they closed the gap to Talley's line.

This was it. The end.

Hell, you can't live forever.

Geysers of snow erupted amid the enemy lines. Then Talley heard it, the familiar whump of mortars somewhere to their rear. The rounds, fused to detonate ten feet off the ground, walked down the enemy front, scything through bodies and dropping eight or ten soldiers at a time.

Sixty-millimeter mortars.

Several firing in unified volleys. In less than a minute a third of the charging enemy were gone, either dead or writhing in the snow, trying to crawl back up the slope.

"Pour it on," Talley ordered. "We've got friendlies at our six."

Heartened now, the Deltas concentrated their fire on what few AQ soldiers were still charging. These too began dropping. The charge hesitated, then broke apart. In Pashto, Talley heard calls of retreat.

From his rear, Talley heard, "Rangers coming in."

Damn straight. Welcome to the party.

Through the swirling snow a dozen figures emerged, then more on top of that, some making their way to where the wounded were collected. Most assumed positions at the rock ledge beside Talley's Delta Force.

"Who's in command?" one of the Rangers called.

"Here. Jack Talley."

The Ranger knelt beside him. "You ordered a pizza?"

Talley laughed. "That's us."

"Sorry we're late. We had a bit of a hike."

"How many are you?"

"Depleted platoon. About forty."

"Where the hell did you come from?"

"There's a narrow path on the back side. Chinook managed to drop us in the draw down below. It's waiting, if you're ready to move."

He didn't have to be told twice.

"We'll get your wounded stabilized, then head out," the Ranger said. "How many bad guys out front?"

"At least two hundred."

"We'll see about discouraging them. Mortars up. SAWs up," the Ranger called.

"Pretty happy to see you guys," he said. "Our shelf life was another hour, no more."

"Can't have that, can we?"

"What's your name?" he asked the Ranger.

"Luke Daniels."

22.

LUKE LEARNED A LONG TIME AGO THAT THE OLD ADAGE WAS TRUE.

Never, ever look a gift horse in the mouth.

"Good thing you got here," he said. "Our shelf life was another hour, no more."

"I see you do remember."

"Hard to forget Captain Jack Talley."

Talley drew a knife off his belt, leaned over, and began slicing the tape securing Luke to the board. He then cut the zip ties binding his wrists. Luke stood and removed the rest of the tape as Talley freed Jillian from the bumper. He also used the moment of distraction to scoop up a cell phone that had slipped from Persik's jacket when he collapsed to the floor, quickly pocketing the unit.

Another gift horse.

"Where do you know this guy from?" Jillian asked.

"Celam Kae, Hill 19," Talley said.

Luke had not heard that location in many years. "Six days in November, Bravo Squadron. Delta Force went in with twenty-four and came out with—"

"Sixteen," Talley said. "It would have been a lot less if you guys hadn't shown up."

He told her what happened.

Credible intelligence placed a high-level Al Qaeda commander in a compound near Celam Kae. Talley's assault troop from Delta Force's Bravo Squadron hiked up into the mountains along the Afghanistan-Pakistan border for what was to be a quick snatch-and-grab. Instead, Bravo found itself ambushed by a mixed force of Al Qaeda and Taliban fighters. Trapped in a hastily fortified position on Hill 19 and cut off from reinforcements by a brutal winter storm, Talley and his team were facing annihilation until a squad of Rangers managed to fight its way up the north-east slope of Hill 19 and rescued the besieged Deltas. They then conducted a fighting retreat to a helicopter extraction zone twelve kilometers away.

"And you were wounded," Luke said. "In the firefight."

Talley nodded. "Lost my spleen and almost my leg. But I'm still alive and walking thanks to you."

"Not just me. We lost three of our own," Luke said. "What's this about?"

"I believe it's called returning the favor."

"The men you just killed knew you," Jillian said. "Did you have anything to do with my grandfather's murder?"

"That operation was already under way when I found out about it."

"You didn't answer my question."

Talley glanced at Luke. "She's spicy."

"A marine. Best you answer her, and quick-like."

"No, Ms. Stein, I had nothing to do with the death of your grandfather."

"But you work with these men?" Jillian asked.

Talley nodded.

"Give us the name of your boss," she demanded.

"If you knew what you were saying, you wouldn't ask for it."

"Try me."

Luke cupped her elbow and whispered in her ear, "Take a breath."

"I don't want to take a breath."

"Pick your battles," he said. "He saved our asses. Let's hear him out."

That did the trick. She nodded and backed away, not looking happy.

Luke asked, "Why is Benjamin Stein dead?"

"That's above my pay grade."

"You're good with the non-answers."

"Comes with the job."

"You do what Persik does—or did?"

"Not so much anymore, but at one time, yes, I was like him."

He was puzzled. "How? Why this path?"

"After I recovered from Celam Kae, I couldn't pass the physical. They offered me a desk job. Supervisory, with advance planning. I lost eight of my guys on that damn hill. Eight Delta troops the army spent millions of dollars training. They needed somebody to blame. It was never official, of course, but the message was clear. Screw up and you ride a desk for eternity. I didn't screw up. The intel was awful. Of course, they're not going to admit to that. So they blamed me. I told them to shove it, took my honorable discharge, my 'didn't-get-killed' medals, and left."

The tone of Talley's words was offhanded, casual, but this guy was angry and bitter, even years after the incident. Honestly, Luke couldn't blame him for that. "What did you do? Put an ad in the paper offering your services?"

"Something like that. You know how it is. Special operations is a small community. Somebody always knows somebody else. A month after I left, I got a call. I took the meeting and here I am."

"Mercenary murderer," Jillian snapped.

He could see that comment stung. Jack Talley was a certified American hero. He'd stood his ground in the face of a superior opposing force, knowing he'd probably die. But he hadn't. Which sometimes was the hero's curse.

"I had a family to support, Ms. Stein. And I had limited capabilities for doing that."

"I had a grandfather."

"I told you, I had nothing to do with his death."

"But you're not going to do anything about it either, are you?"

"I just did."

Luke decided to try another tack. "If you could've stopped it, would you have?"

"It doesn't work like that."

"How does it work?"

"I get my orders and I'm expected to perform. I'm paid well for that service. So was Persik. But he, along with the rest of his KOPASSUS Red Beret Corps, were mercenary murderers. Let's just say I had my fill of him and them."

Which seemed accurate. Talley had shot those men without a moment's hesitation. Exactly as he'd been trained to do.

"Before you got here," Luke said, "Persik mentioned something about consequences for failure. Is that what you're talking about?"

"More or less. Who I work for...you don't get to resign. You die in the position."

"But the money's just too good, right?" Jillian asked.

"My wife and children want for nothing and never will. College, retirement, house with no mortgage, all of it. They're set for life."

"But at what cost?" Luke asked.

"You married? Got kids?"

He shook his head.

"If you did, would there be anything you wouldn't do for them?"

He decided to not fall into the moral trap. "Here's what I know. *De Opresso Liber.*" The Army Special Forces motto. To Free the Oppressed.

"Don't do that," Talley said.

"*I pledge to uphold the honor and integrity of their legacy, in all that I am—in all that I do.*" He knew reciting part of the special forces' creed was a gut punch for Talley, but the man needed reminding. It was the pledge by which they all lived, retired or not. "*I will not fail those with whom I serve. I will not bring shame upon myself or Special Forces.* Did you forget all that when you were discharged?"

"I didn't come here for a lecture."

"Hardest thing of all is doing the right thing when no one's looking."

"I know. I just did it."

He wondered what was happening here. Talley came in firing. He'd definitely come on a mission. And it wasn't to save the guy who saved his ass all those years ago. But he still needed to know—

"Who do you work for?"

"Like I'm going to tell you that."

"Then at least tell us what this is all about," Jillian said. "Why'd your boss want Benji dead? And now us?"

Talley did not immediately reply and Luke could see he was struggling.

"Why is that so hard a question?" she pressed.

"I don't know why your grandfather was killed, and that's the God's honest truth."

Jillian was about to say something, but Luke cut her off with a raise of his hand and tried, "Does this involve an old rifle?"

Talley did not reply, but the look in the older man's eyes provided the answer.

Yes, it did.

Talley shook his head. "I've said too much already. Listen, as it stands, I'm not even sure I can sell this."

He understood. "That we turned the tables on Persik and killed them all? By the time you got here we were gone."

"It's a tall order. Persik and his men were highly trained and ruthless."

"But a little too trusting of a co-worker, right?" Jillian said.

"Something like that."

"So what's going on here?" he asked Talley.

"I'm giving you a head start. And a warning. If you persist with this, everything will be thrown at you, and we possess nearly bottomless resources. Which will all be pointed straight at you. Let this go. Leave it alone. Let me handle it."

Okay, he got it. Whoever was in command had a long reach. But—

"I have resources too," Luke said.

"I know. But this doesn't involve the Magellan Billet."

Good to know he was not a stranger to this man. Which meant he'd been identified *before* Talley arrived.

"Tell me a name and I might be able to solve your problems. I have the U.S. government behind me."

Talley chuckled. "You're so damn naive. This is different. Keep on and everything will be on the line, including your lives. That includes the people you love. Nothing is off limits to the person I work for."

"Like my grandfather," Jillian said.

"Precisely."

Time to make things clear. "I'm not backing off."

"Neither am I," Jillian added.

"Haven't either one of you heard a word I've said?"

"We heard you," Luke said. "But we have a job to do."

"You do realize that if I hadn't shown up you'd both be dead, covered in a lye slurry and buried under those trees out there."

"I get that," Luke said.

"Okay," Talley said. "So we're clear, you and I are even now. The debt is paid. You need to leave and get going, wherever it is you're going. Do your job, and I'll do mine. Our paths are almost certainly going to cross again, and soon. Count on that. And when that happens, Ranger, things will be different."

23.

Talley watched as Luke Daniels and Jillian Stein fled the hangar and headed back to the Range Rover parked beyond the old fence line. Taking that vehicle would be consistent with the report he would make to Tom Rowland. Contact was made with Persik. Daniels and Stein's capture had been completed. Interrogation was about to begin. Talley traveled to the rendezvous point alone in Luxembourg to observe. Upon arrival he found Persik and his men all dead, Daniels and Stein gone. Hopefully, with no one left alive to contradict any of those details, Rowland would accept them. His employer had never had reason to question anything he'd done before and, with Rowland's patience with Persik apparently at an end, the entire scenario was both plausible and believable.

His team was waiting in Luxembourg City. He'd summon them shortly. The land around him belonged to Rowland through a series of shell corporations, bought long ago and occasionally used by the CIA as a Central European staging area. It once served the Nazis, now it served a modern-day manipulator.

Thomas Rowland.

He'd never heard of the man prior to the call that came a month or so after his military discharge. He'd traveled to Maryland, then by boat onto the Chesapeake Bay and Starlings Island. The man waiting for him had been well into his eighties, the features then, and now, belonging to age. A pale aquiline face, gaunt cheeks, coarsened hair, veined hands, frail with an expressionless quality about him, impassible as a statue.

He'd also learned about Thomas Rowland's professional life.

His thirty years at the CIA had been served heading up covert paramilitary units. All ex-military personnel and veterans of special operations like the Green Berets, Marine Force Recon, Army Rangers, Navy SEALs, and Delta Force. They worked exclusively on foreign soil, trained in sabotage, personnel and material recovery, kidnapping, bomb damage assessment, hostage rescue, and counterterrorism. Skills Rowland had also put to use in his side venture.

Problem solver.

People of power and influence had a way of attracting trouble. It came in all forms, from the petty, to the obscene, to the embarrassing, to the criminal. Lawyers were sometimes useless, so Rowland filled a void and provided a service that eliminated problems. In return? Certainly money. Rowland was extremely wealthy. But more often than not, favors were the currency of choice.

A favor done is a favor returned.

Rowland's motto.

Talley walked back inside the hangar.

The bodies bled out on the cracked concrete. He was glad Persik was dead. Good riddance. Rowland had more and more in recent years come to rely on Persik, the methods they employed both violent and amoral. Nothing seemed off limits. Daniels was right. *I will not fail those with whom I serve. I will not bring shame upon myself or Special Forces.* But he had. Much shame, in fact. All done for money.

No murders, though.

Until today.

But he considered what had just happened more righteous justice than a criminal act. Of course, he'd definitely coerced, blackmailed, threatened, and terrorized people. He'd many times told himself that the victims of his abuse were no innocents. Which was true. But that didn't excuse it. He hadn't killed anyone in a long time, and when he had it had been in combat. Not inside an abandoned hangar in ice-cold blood. What had he become? What would his children think of him?

What would his wife think?

She adored him, as he did her. Thankfully, she knew little to nothing as to what he did for a living. Only that he worked for Rowland, heading up his personal security staff, a job that required lots of time and travel. He'd seen the way Jill had started looking at him. Not the same as in years past. More puzzlement. Questioning. Wondering. Did she still love him? Of course. No question. But was it the same? No. He wanted his life back. His conscience. Along with his self-respect.

And what he'd just done was a start to regaining those.

Thomas Rowland was ninety-two years old and just as dangerous and deadly as he'd been decades ago. Perhaps even more so since the man had absolutely nothing to lose. Or maybe he did. A man of that age and reputation feared only one thing. A taint on his legacy. Rowland sometimes spoke of that. Enough that Talley had come to view it as a weakness. The only one he'd ever observed in the man. There was no wife, no children, no other close family. Only a precious reputation. Sure, death was coming soon enough. But a part of him did not want Rowland to die unpunished. He deserved some pain and misery. But this had to be done carefully. He'd meant what he'd said to Daniels. Families and loved ones were always in play, and his own were no exception. If Rowland sniffed even the slightest hint of betrayal or treachery, others would be hired to wreak havoc on the Talley household. Nothing would be off limits. He'd seen Persik dish out cruelty. Though dead, there were plenty more greedy men with no morals to hire in his place.

So far, though, so good.

He found his cell phone and dialed one of his men, explaining what he'd found in the hangar. "I need you to get here and clean up."

That meant not a usable trace of what happened would be left, and the remains of Persik and his men would go the way of Jimmy Hoffa.

"Make sure the bodies are sanitized. Total evidential black hole—tattoos, dental, clothing, labels. You know the drill."

He ended the call.

The course ahead was now irreversible.

We have a job to do. That's what Daniels had said.

He had a job to do as well.

Rowland would want retribution. His narcissism would not allow anything less. He'd be ordered to hunt down Luke Daniels and Jillian Stein and extract revenge. Along the way he would also have to retrieve what Benjamin Stein had secreted away. A rifle. That's what Rowland had told him there was to find. An old Colt AR-15. Daniels had made a point to mention one, and he'd made a point not to react. If Daniels had it, and Rowland wanted it, then so much the better. Another part of the special forces creed came to mind. *I serve quietly, not seeking recognition or accolades. My goal is to succeed in my mission and live to succeed again.*

Damn right.

Especially that *live to succeed again* part.

Luke Daniels would never give up.

And he was counting on just that.

24.

LUKE DROVE THE RANGE ROVER AND CROSSED THE BORDER FROM Luxembourg into Belgium. Traffic was light for a late afternoon. They'd fled the hangar and used one of Persik's vehicles to speed away. Not the best choice. The only choice. He'd also retrieved the two pistols and spare magazines he'd dropped in the hangar. Jillian remained irritated, unsure of Jack Talley, lumping him in with all of the other undesirables. He hadn't said much, just listened, trying to make his own assessments. But he'd definitely made a decision.

"We're going back to Genappe."

She tossed him a puzzled look. "For what?"

"There's a lot more to Benji than you knew. All the time you lived with him he played at being a Luddite. We now know that's not true. He either rigged, or had rigged, that early warning system back at the storage locker. Then there's the hermetically sealed rifle. You don't see that every day. He was keeping a big secret."

"Are you suggesting he did something wrong?"

"I don't know. And neither do you."

"He was a good man, Luke."

"I know that. Not a doubt in my mind. But delirium brings everything out of the well, to the top. Benji never let something go. And that rifle may be the key to it all."

"You think it's safe where we left it?"

A good question. "Better there than with us. Luckily, Persik and his men are dead, so there's no one to steer Talley back into those woods. What we need to be sure about is that there's nothing left to find in Benji's house." He added what he hoped was a disarming smile. "Heck, third time's the charm, right?"

"Third time could be jail."

"Not the way we're going to do it."

"I'm listening."

He kept speeding down the highway. "First thing we do is ditch this vehicle. We then take a bus to Genappe and walk to Benji's house. We see the crime scene tape and call the police. We've been on a mini vacation to Brussels, Luxembourg, and Bruges and just returned."

"Would they not already have searched the house? What's to say there's anything left for us to find?"

"That lockbox was still there. I have faith in Benji's tradecraft. There may be more things hidden. Worst case, we have a murder investigation hanging over our heads. The police surely know about you by now."

"That's a risky game you're playing, Ranger."

"They're going to connect you to the house and then start looking for you. We don't need the press or attention. The sooner we get ahead of this, the better. We can be there in two hours."

She took a full minute to digest his plan then said, "You believe Talley?"

"About the threat, or all of it?"

"Both."

"Absolutely. Save one thing. His boss will want our asses. No matter what."

And he'd already done the math. Their odds of winning a fight against Talley's mystery puppet master were not good. The question was, did they fight like lambs or lions? He knew his choice.

"Here's the thing about untouchable types," he said. "A man older and wiser than me once said, Cocky asses get complacent and complacency is—"

"Vulnerability," she said.

"I see you heard the same advice."

"I've missed you, Luke Daniels. We had quite the time in Hawaii. A shame neither one of us followed up on that."

"Where'd that come from?"

"It just needed to be said."

"It's never too late, you know."

She chuckled. "No, it never is."

They spent the entirety of the drive north, toward Genappe, rehearsing their stories, making sure they matched in the right places and were appropriately fuzzy in others. Surely the two men from last night were long gone. The second-floor railing was definitely destroyed, but there was nothing connecting them to that. To explain away any physical evidence, like hair and finger-prints, was easy for Jillian. His would come from the fact he'd stayed in the house before on a visit, all before any trouble started. As alibis went they weren't perfect but solid enough if they could hold their ground.

Which should get the cops off their asses.

Outside Charleroi they found a rural back road and abandoned the Range Rover. They then walked a couple of miles to a small commercial center and a clothing store where they paid cash for new outfits before trashing their old ones. The bus ride to Genappe took another thirty minutes, the walk to Benji's house ten more.

It was a little after 6:00 P.M. when the show began.

Panicked, Jillian ran to a neighbor's house and in broken Dutch begged to know what had happened at her grandfather's house. The police were called and in short order six cars arrived, lights blazing, sirens blaring. Luke and Jillian were promptly whisked away to headquarters, immediately separated, and, for the next three hours interrogated by a string of federal police investigators who expertly played good cop / bad cop, sympathetic cop / enraged cop. The same questions were asked in a variety of ways, details probed, re-probed, and challenged. Finally, a little past nine, after signing statements, they were released and given condolences and offers of help if required. Stein's house had indeed been searched, they were told, and the crime scene technicians were done. Remnants of the murders remained, they were told, so Jillian needed to be prepared for what awaited her should she choose to go home. A police car drove them there.

Once it disappeared around the corner, he said, "Was it bad for you?"

"I held. You?"

"I think we're okay. Any mention of what happened here last night?"

She shook her head.

"Then they have no idea about last night."

Interesting.

"For safety's sake, we keep playing our roles," he said. "Tomorrow morning you'll call the lead investigator and ask permission to leave town. You just can't stay here. It's too emotional."

"That's not a stretch for me."

"I know. Make sure he knows you're asking permission. Tell him you want to be kept informed about the investigation. You want Benji's killers caught."

"Again, all true."

"Come on, let's go see what we can find."

25.

LUKE HAD ONCE WANTED TO BE A POLICEMAN. HE'D THOUGHT IT THE perfect way to serve. But that was a teenager's dream. The older he got the less appealing the job seemed. So he'd opted for the army and the Rangers, then the Magellan Billet. Which seemed a cross between the police and Rangers.

In a loose sort of way.

Being at a crime scene, one he helped create, he felt like a cop searching for evidence. For the next three hours, save half an hour to eat two delivered pizzas, they turned Benji's home upside down, starting in the basement and finishing in the upstairs bathroom, where Jillian had made her escape two nights ago.

And found nothing.

All over the house bright-yellow adhesive arrows showed every bullet strike in the walls. As advertised, no effort had been made to clean up bloodstains. Standing in the middle of the bedroom, Jillian slowly turned a circle as though the room had somehow become foreign to her.

"It's strange being here now," she said.

"How much time did he have left?"

"The doctor told me last week, maybe three months. No more."

"Whatever he knew, somebody wanted to make sure he told no one during that time. Otherwise, you just wait out the cancer."

"I agree."

She kept studying the room.

"What is it?" Luke asked.

"Something's off."

"Like what?"

"This," she said, pointing to the lamp on the bedside table, lying on its side, the shade askew. "Several times in his delirium Benji mentioned peonies. It was strange. I just ignored it. I thought he meant the flower, but could he have meant this."

The vase-like lamp, about six inches wide, was painted a dark green, the exterior covered in peonies, the deeply lobed leaves in varying shades of white and yellow.

"He never used this lamp," she said. "He said it was too bright. The last time I turned it on, he barked at me."

She lifted the lamp and removed the shade, then the finial.

"What are you noticing?" he asked.

"Not what I'm noticing. What he said."

He was listening.

"*People might see.* That's what he said when I switched it on. He said it more than once. I never thought much of it, just part of the morphine, until now."

She turned the lamp over. Nothing there. At the top, an octagonal-shaped nut below the bulb held the mount in place.

"Shake it," he said.

She did. No sound or movement. Then he noticed something near the nut. Scratch marks in the glass.

"You see those," he said.

"I do. Strange place for them. And they're circular."

Like the nut had been repeatedly unscrewed.

"Can't hurt to look."

She cradled the base with her left arm and gripped the silver nut between her thumb and first finger. Which turned. Easily. She unscrewed the nut from the threaded post. Beneath it was a silver cap that topped the painted glass pedestal. She lifted the cap away revealing a hollow interior filled with a towel. He reached in and carefully removed the tan-colored terry cloth. What remained inside were two pieces of curled white paper.

"Clever boy," he murmured.

On the sheet appeared a drawing.

"What is it?" she asked.

"Not sure. A symbol, map, code?"

On the other sheet were blocks of random numbers, above each, either a single letter or a word.

"Did Benji have a code or shorthand he used?"

Lots of military folks did.

"Not that I know of," she said.

"This is a key to a code," he said.

Together they scanned the two sheets looking for any clue as to their meaning or purpose. On the drawing, there was nothing save the four symbols in each corner, an arrow with 6r? before it, and some letters, M, E, H.

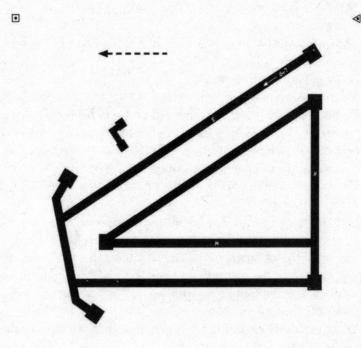

"Let's search this place again," she said. "If Benji got this past the police, who knows what else there might be."

Two hours of careful probing found nothing.

It was a little after 2:00 A.M. when they finished.

"So we have it all," she said. "Unless he had other off-site hiding places."

"Which we'll never find. Let's pack up and get ready to hit the road. First, though, lemme touch base with Marcia."

He dialed her number.

She answered on the first ring. "Do you have something for me?"

"On that email address, nothing yet. Whoever created it knew their business. It's fairly untraceable. But I haven't given up."

"Keep at it. One more thing, if you're game."

"Hit me."

"A helicopter tail number. I need to know who it belongs to, origin, destination, all that."

"Easy peasy, lemon squeezy."

"I'll text you a photo."

He hung up and found the other cell phone in his pocket. "And we have this. When Talley shot Persik, it dropped to the floor. I managed to snag it without him seeing."

"You continue to impress me, Daniels."

"Hold off on singing my praises. It's password-protected. I need to get it to Marcia."

"And that tail number. The helo from the air base?"

"Someone surely flew it back to its point of origin. Assuming Talley ain't flying commercial, and assuming he was keen on reporting back to his boss, maybe he took a private jet out of the same place. It's a long shot, but with any luck we can narrow down the mystery boss's home base."

"That's a lot of ifs, but it'd give us more than we have at the moment. What now?"

"We're out of leads, until we hear back from West Virginia."

His phone rang. Marcia.

Damn. Was she listening to him?

He answered. "You miss me already?"

"As much as the day is long. I have info on that tail number. Like I said, easy peasy. Poorly protected databases, and all that. That particular bird is a lease from Francorchamps Heliport outside Verviers. It belongs to a company called Zolder Exclusive Flights. They cater to luxury clientele, most of them uber-wealthy F1 Grand Prix fanatics. You want me to do a sneak 'n' peek into their network?"

"Hold on." To Jillian, he whispered, "How far to Verviers?"

"Ninety minutes, give or take."

He said to Marcia, "Leave it to us. We've got targets on our backs. Best we stay on the move."

26.

STARLINGS ISLAND, CHESAPEAKE BAY

ROWLAND LISTENED AS THE REPORT WAS MADE.

"What do you mean they're gone," he said into the phone.

"When I arrived at the site, Persik and his men were dead, all from close-quarters gunfire," Jack Talley said. "Daniels and Stein were not there and one of our vehicles was gone."

"How many were dead?"

"Five. The hangar was set up for interrogation. But somehow Daniels and the woman turned the tables."

"How is that possible? The major was well trained."

"Daniels is better. I explained this already. I warned you not to underestimate him."

"Don't lecture me."

"I'm not. Just pointing out facts. I apologize if I offended."

"What about Persik's other men? His team was bigger than four."

"We found one unconscious and tied up. Persik told me that two more were killed and dumped in the river. Their bodies have not turned up yet."

"Forget them. What else?"

"As I said, one of Persik's vehicles was gone. Daniels most likely took it. I've reported it stolen so the police will be on the lookout for it."

"And the items found in the storage unit?"

"No sign of any of it."

He paused to think, choosing his words with care. "Is Daniels vulnerable to compromise? Can he be leveraged?"

"Doubtful. When I knew him, he was a stand-up guy."

"Is that respect I hear in your voice?"

"For service to this country, yes. But nothing more."

"Everyone has a price. Find his."

"I think that'll be a dead end."

"Which leaves us with limited options," he said. So he gave his usual command, "I want to know who he loves. His family, friends, anyone and everyone. Same with Stein's granddaughter. Find out what will hurt them most."

"I'll start assembling information," Talley said. "But first I have a few other routes I want to try."

"Please explain."

"I might know where they're headed next."

"I was hoping you were ahead of them. Will that destination offer them anything?"

"No. I've seen to it. But it could provide us with an opportunity."

"Sounds promising. Keep me informed."

He ended the call.

This nightmare might soon be over. No longer were things spiraling out of control. Instead, he'd turned lemons into lemonade.

And was now on the verge of sealing this ever-expanding leak in the dam.

27.

THURSDAY — MARCH 26

LUKE AND JILLIAN LEFT GENAPPE A LITTLE AFTER DAWN ON A BUS that took them about a hundred miles east. They arrived in Francorchamps around 7:00 A.M., a rural area of Belgium surrounded by an array of small storefront shops. Its big claim to fame was the motor-racing Circuit de Spa-Francorchamps. Seven kilometers of twisting track that tested some of the finest Formula One cars in the world. Luke loved Formula One motor racing. True, the individual behind the wheel controlled everything, but no matter how good a driver you were you could not win without a team. A lot like the Rangers.

And the Magellan Billet.

The heliport sat just outside of town, not far from the race-track. Despite its high-end reputation the facility was small and unassuming. A single, whitewashed building and three hangars, all behind a tall chain-link fence. One gate led in, and was open. They stepped through, and followed a short gravel path to an acre-sized grass clearing at whose center sat three empty concrete pads, each emblazoned with the traditional *H*. If the helo Persik had used to hunt them was here it was likely in one of the hangars. The back side of the property was encircled by a fence and tall hedges. They hunkered down at the corner of the office building, watching and listening until satisfied no one was about. He saw no cameras. Both of them were armed with the guns from the hangar.

"Which first, hangars or the office?" she asked.

"Office. Even if the helo is here, it won't give us anything useful."

They crept along the back side of the building until they reached a door. He checked for signs of an alarm system, found nothing, then had Jillian do the same. Two pair of eyes were always better than one.

She shook her head.

Nothing.

As expected they found the door locked. Lacking any tools to pick it, he decided on blunt force. A nearby softball-sized stone worked perfectly to knock the knob off the door. He nudged the metal panel open a few inches with the toe of his boot, then led Jillian across the grass clearing where they huddled in the shadows along the fence.

"What are we doing?" she asked.

"Waiting to see if we'll get a party crasher. If we missed an alarm or camera, or the noise woke somebody, we'll know shortly."

Ten minutes passed.

All quiet.

"I hate this," she murmured. "The anticipation."

"Patience, marine."

He gave it another five minutes.

Still quiet.

They returned to the back door and entered.

He shut the door behind them.

"Check those filing cabinets," he said. "Use your sleeve when you touch things. No prints. I'll see about the computer."

Using a pencil from a nearby cup as a makeshift finger, he powered up the desktop and waited for the login menu to appear.

None did.

"Hallelujah," he muttered.

No password.

He started punching keys, starting with a search for the helicopter's tail number.

Jillian appeared over his shoulder. "The files are just personnel records, maintenance reports, and advertising documents. No rental records. Have you got anything?"

"We're about to find out."

A phone vibrated.

Which startled him.

His was on silent.

He fished the unit from his pocket and saw it was Persik's that had come alive. "I didn't pull the battery, 'cause nobody knows I have it."

The screen read Access 4792 then 5214.

"I don't like this," Jillian said.

He punched in the code pair and the main screen appeared.

Then a ding from a text.

Take the call, Luke.

A moment later the phone rang.

"Don't," she said.

"We have no choice."

He answered on speaker.

"Now do you get it?" Talley said. "You got to keep that phone because I wanted you to have it. You took it, just like I knew you would, just like I knew you clocked that helo's tail number."

"So what's this lesson I'm supposed to learn?"

"That I'll always be a step ahead of you. I knew you'd run the tail numbers. It was the only viable lead you had. But that computer you're on will get you nowhere. Same with the files. Everything's been wiped. And that helo's at the bottom of the North Sea."

He came alert. They were being watched.

Be cool.

"Okay." He sucked a breath. "What happens next?"

"You walk to the window."

"No, thanks," he said.

"If I wanted you dead, it would already be done. Walk to the window."

He did so.

"Raise your hand and hold up any number of fingers you want."

He held up four.

Talley said, "Four fingers, left hand. I say the word and a bullet goes in your forehead."

"I tried that one on Persik."

"But I'm not bluffing. My man watched you walk in. Watched you crouch by the corner of the office. Watched you break off that doorknob. When you hunkered down by the back fence and waited, he was within twenty feet of you."

"Okay, I get it. You're a badass."

"So are you."

There had to be more to this. Talley was indeed a step ahead of them. And true, if he wanted them dead then dead they would be. No. This was something else entirely.

"Get to the point," he said to Talley.

"On Persik's phone you'll find a name and address for a guy

named Simmons. It's who Persik was going to visit after he finished with you."

"Is he connected to Benji?"

"Absolutely. If I were a betting man, I would say I'll be sent to the address on Persik's phone next as well."

He was curious. "Your boss isn't concerned about us?"

"I reported that you'd be dead within forty-eight hours."

"Good to know." But something was bugging him. "Why are you sticking your neck out like this?"

"Contrary to what you might think, I am an American soldier. There's still honor and integrity left in me. My employer, on the other hand, is dangerous and has to be stopped. Many have tried. All have failed. But I have something they never had." Talley paused. "You."

And there was also something else.

He saw it in Jillian's eyes.

Talley did not know what they had found at Benji's house. Or maybe he didn't care and wanted them to keep going.

"Do your thing, Ranger," Talley said. "Save the day. Just like you did at Celam Kae."

They left the office and walked to town, where they caught a bus back to Liège. As Talley had said, there was a name and address on Persik's phone and Jillian copied down the details. Luke then tossed the phone away, no longer wanting Talley to find them so easily. The time was approaching noon so they found a small diner where they were the only customers. The waitress brought a carafe of coffee, took their orders, then disappeared into the back.

"That was a bit spooky back there," Jillian said. "Talley seems to be using you."

"The question is, for what? Everybody likes to think they know how they'd react in worst-case situations. But until it happens, it's all guesswork."

"Are you speaking from experience?"

"I've done some things."

"In Afghanistan?"

"There, and elsewhere. But I've never been in Talley's shoes."

To date, the only folks he'd ever placed in his gunsights had been trying to kill either him or someone else who didn't deserve it. All those kills were in-the-moment-with-no-choice scenarios. In that he'd been lucky. Never had he pulled the trigger in cold blood. But that didn't mean he was incapable.

Only hesitant.

He found his phone and did a quick search on the name and address. "Ray Simmons lives in Cameron Parish, Louisiana. It's in the southwest corner of the state, about fifteen miles inland from the Gulf of Mexico. According to Google, it's the most rural parish in Louisiana. No major cities, twelve hundred square miles, and only seven thousand people. Mostly bayou and alligators, which, according to one site, outnumber people five to one."

"Sounds like a wonderful place."

He caught her sarcasm. "You don't like alligators?"

"I have the greatest respect for a forty-million-year-old killing machine that's more dinosaur than lizard."

He kept scrolling. "Hackberry's population is about a thousand. Apparently, it got hit hard by Hurricanes Rita and Ike and never fully bounced back. The question is, what do Benjamin Stein, retired U.S. Army colonel living in Belgium, and Ray Simmons, resident of a remote part of Louisiana, have in common?"

"There's only one way to find out."

He agreed.

But first there was something he had to do.

28.

LUKE HAD FINALLY MADE THE CALL TO STEPHANIE NELLE. HE'D TAKEN to heart the warning of Talley's boss's reach, thinking that might extend to U.S. Customs and Border Protection. If so, that person might know when and where their international flight would touch down. On the chance that Talley was leading him back to the United States and a trap, he decided to use the resources available to him. So he called Stephanie and explained everything.

"*And the reason you're still on this?*" she asked. "*Besides the obvious, a former girlfriend.*"

"*An old man is dead.*"

"*I get that. Which is why we have police departments.*"

"*Something's happening here. I've got a feeling.*"

"*You've been listening to Cotton way too much.*"

"*Pappy makes sense. Most of the time.*"

"*Unfortunately, he does. Sit tight and I'll be back to you.*"

Two hours later Stephanie made contact.

"*I checked out Jack Talley, retired U.S. Army,*" she said. "*He works for Thomas Rowland.*"

"*Is that important?*" he asked.

"*Important enough that this has now become official Magellan Billet business. Rowland is bad news, with a capital B.*"

And she'd provided him with some quick background on Rowland, enough that he got the picture. Now he understood Persik's sarcasm—*If only you knew the irony in that smart-ass comment*—when he'd mentioned the CIA.

"*If we can take Rowland down,*" she said to him, "*that would be a public service.*"

"*Sounds like you know the guy.*"

"All too well. Let's just say I owe him. Tell me what you need."

He did, and they both agreed that he should continue to work off the grid since, as she explained, Rowland's reach was enormous. Better to keep this between the two of them with direct contact only. She did manage to get him a car that was delivered to the diner in Liège.

He'd intended on driving back to Luxembourg and hiking to the shrine in the woods for the rifle.

"No need," Stephanie told him. *"I've already made a call to Copenhagen. Cotton is on his way to get it. He'll make sure it stays safe."*

"While he's at it," Luke said, *"could he retrieve Benji's personal stuff from the car I wrecked. Jillian should have that."*

"I'll have it done."

They decided flying commercial would be the fastest way back home, and Stephanie booked them two seats on a flight out of Brussels to JFK, then on to Nashville. She'd even splurged on business class—*so you can rest*—which meant this must be serious. The Magellan Billet's per diems and expense account rules were not usually on the generous side.

"What's the plan?" Jillian asked as they left Customs at Nashville International Airport.

He led her through the terminal and outside to a part of the airport where private planes were accommodated. His watch read 10:45 A.M. He headed for the hangar Stephanie had noted. Waiting for them was a Justice Department Learjet.

"I see there are advantages in being a government operative," she said.

"That there are."

"But you realize Talley could be waiting for us in Louisiana."

"I certainly hope so."

Five hours later, shortly after 4:00 P.M. Central Time, they reached the outskirts of Cameron Parish, then the town of Hackberry an hour later. A Ford Bronco had been waiting for them when they landed at another rural airport west of New Orleans, two Magellan Billet Berettas with spare magazines in the glove compartment.

Stephanie rarely missed a beat.

Hackberry was small and, as advertised, cast an air of vacancy. But the streets were clean, the storefronts well tended, and most of the stilt-raised homes looked relatively new, probably rebuilds following the devastation two hurricanes wreaked. Plenty of marsh grass, live oaks, moss, and water, from brackish inlets to serpentine bayous to lakes miles across. It seemed more an archipelago than dry land. The address for Ray Simmons took them to a ramshackle saltbox building across from a Circle A gas station. The sign above the door read, KEN'S CONVENIENCE.

They stepped inside.

A bell tinkled and the screen door banged shut behind them. An industrial-sized ceiling fan churned the humid air. From the chain that controlled its speed a purple-and-gold LSU Fighting Tigers key fob dangled. A woman with a red bouffant hairstyle rose from her stool behind the counter and gave them a curt nod.

Luke grabbed a pair of soft drinks from the cooler and walked up. "Mornin'."

He added one of his trademark smiles.

"And to you," she said, with a grin.

He was back in his element. A country boy come home to the country. Like a hog in mud. Usually, he'd work her a bit, soften her up, but they were racing the clock. "We're looking for a friend of mine. An old army buddy. Ray Simmons."

"That'll be $2.50."

He paid her. "He gave me this address."

"That so?"

"Is he around?"

"Not here. This is a, what do you call it—mail drop. Unofficial, of course."

Jillian asked, "Does he live nearby?"

"Depends on your definition of *nearby*. A few miles, give or take."

"Can you give us directions?"

"Can't get there by car. Swamp boat only."

"Swamp boat?" Jillian asked.

"You know, fan boat. Might be able to get my boy to take you. Cost you, though."

"Fine by us," he said.

The woman disappeared through a curtain in an archway behind the counter. They enjoyed their drinks. She returned five minutes later. "Elijah will take you." She found a pad from under the counter and drew them a map. "Our place is 'bout three miles at the end of Maggie Herbert Road. Right next to the solid waste place. Small dock, yellow boat. Can't miss it."

"Thanks. Now?"

"Give him twenty minutes. And that'll be fifty dollars."

He happily laid a crisp U. S. Grant on the counter. "One of my favorite presidents."

"Mine too," she said, scooping up the bill.

"One more thing. You have a small plastic bag I could buy off of you?"

"Not buy, but I'll give you one."

"Deal."

Outside, he folded the two pages they'd found in the lamp and slipped them into the resealable bag. Safe and sound. Way too much water here for loose paper.

They drove around for ten minutes.

Besides a few curious, strangers-in-town glances he saw nothing that suggested they'd been tailed. The woman's map was spot-on and they had no trouble finding the dock. Beside it a black-on-yellow sign read SABINE NATIONAL WILDLIFE REFUGE.

A fan boat bobbed beside the dock. Waiting for them was a really tall bearded man in a red T-shirt, gray cargo shorts, and calf-high rubber boots.

"You Elijah?" Luke called as they climbed from the car.

Half expecting the son to share his mama's taciturnity, he

was surprised when the man broke into a broad grin. "I'm him. Howdy, folks. Looking for a ride to Ray's, I hear."

"If it's no trouble."

"Not a bit. Did Mother talk to you about—"

He realized that Mother had taken him for a ride on the money train, milking an extra fifty out of him. That was okay. Money might not buy happiness, but it sure did open up your choices. "Will a hundred do for your time and gas?"

"Plenty generous. You two ever ride in a fan boat before?"

"Actually, I have," Luke said.

"Never," Jillian added.

"You'll be fine. Just buckle up. The front seats get a little bumpy. And damp."

29.

LUKE CLIMBED ABOARD LAST AND SETTLED NEXT TO JILLIAN IN ONE of the two pedestal seats at the bow. They buckled belts across their laps.

"We look to be alone," he whispered to her.

"I agree. Nothing piqued my interest."

They were both concerned about Talley.

With good reason.

Benji's drawing and the other sheet rested safe in his pocket, sealed in plastic. For safety's sake, back in Belgium he'd imaged both and texted them to Stephanie.

Elijah climbed up onto the elevated driver's seat behind them.

"It's about six miles. Forty minutes or so. Gotta go slow on account of the gators. This time of year they spend a lot of time on the surface gettin' warmed up. It was extra cold this winter. Don't want to run over 'em."

After a few coughs the engine turned over and the forty-eight-inch-wide fan started turning. Elijah eased away from the dock and began expertly picking his way through the inlet, tweaking the throttle on the straightaways and drifting into the curves until they reached open water. In the distance a cluster of pink, wide-winged birds banked over the surface and disappeared past the trees.

"Are those flamingos?" Jillian asked. "They're beautiful."

"Some kind of spoonbill, I think," Luke said.

"Roseate spoonbill," Elijah said. "Used to be endangered. Coming back strong now."

"You've been doing this awhile?" Luke called out over his shoulder, trying to get the guy talking.

No reply.

He turned.

Elijah's face had changed. Gone was the casual smile, replaced by hard-set eyes and a tense jawline, the fist on the rudder stick bone-white.

He leaned closer to Jillian and murmured, "Trouble."

He lifted the tail of his shirt and tucked it behind the Beretta at his waist, ready for quicker access. Jillian did the same. They kept their backs to Elijah.

"What is it?" she asked.

"Not sure yet. Something's up with our driver."

The boat's engine faded to idle, then sputtered and stopped.

Elijah called out, "Gator on the bow. Best let him scoot outta the way."

Luke scanned the water ahead, but saw nothing. With his right hand he gripped the butt of the Beretta and placed his left thumb on the seatbelt's release button. Ready.

Elijah said, "You best let me see your hands, if you like how your head sits on your shoulders."

The request was followed by the distinctive mechanical racking of a pump shotgun. They raised their arms.

"Unbuckle yourselves then turn around, straddle them seats, and drape your arms over the backrests."

They did as ordered.

Elijah's shotgun was leveled at their chests. At this range the blast would send them both into the water where the alligators would finish them off.

"Tour's over, I'm guessing?" Luke said.

"Permanent-like, if I don't get answers. First, toss those pistols down at my feet. Easy, now, two fingers."

"Who says we're armed?" Luke asked.

"I do."

He decided not to press the point. Gently, they each drew a Beretta from their waist and dropped them onto the boat's deck. The aluminum hull let out a muffled gong.

"What're your names?" Elijah asked.

"I'm Luke. This is Jillian."

"What's your business with Ray Simmons?"

"We have no idea. Never met the man."

Elijah offered them a puzzled look. "That's honest, if a little odd. Tell me more."

"Somebody murdered my grandfather," Jillian said. "We think Ray might know why."

"Murdered, ya say? By who?"

"No clue," Luke said. "We know it wasn't Ray, so we've got no quarrel with him. He's just our only lead."

While that wasn't technically true, it seemed that recounting the saga of mercenaries, manhunts, and waterboarding that had led them here would do more harm than good. So he tried, "Ray seemed important to her grandfather, so here we are."

"So you ain't cops? Feds?"

"Neither," Luke said, lying. "What are you? Simmons's social secretary?"

"Somethin' like that. We take care of our own here."

"Does Ray have a lot of strangers come looking for him?"

"You're full of questions."

"So my mama tells me."

"Your accent...Tennessee?"

He nodded. "East, in the Smokies."

"Pretty country."

"I have a proposition, if you're inclined."

"I'm listening," Elijah said.

"I'm guessing either you or your mama called Ray Simmons while we waited at the counter. If he wasn't curious about us, you would've sent us packing."

"Maybe we just decided it'd be easier if you were cinder-blocked to the bottom of this lake."

"If that was the case, we wouldn't be talking now. Would we?"

Elijah shrugged, then raised the shotgun a couple of inches so Luke was staring straight down the muzzle. "You said you have a proposition. Get to it."

"Call Ray and let us make our case."

Elijah thought for a moment and then, careful to keep the shotgun steady, removed a satellite phone and dialed a number.

"Yeah, I got 'em here. Okay, hang on. What's your granddaddy's name?"

"Benjamin Stein."

Elijah repeated the name into the phone, listened, then extended the unit toward Jillian. "Say everything you know about your granddaddy's time in the army."

She spent the next two minutes talking about Benji's career, from postings he'd held, to stories he'd shared, to commendations he'd received, to friends he'd made and lost along the way. "That's all I can remember right now. Until he was diagnosed with cancer, we didn't spend much time with each other in recent years."

She handed the phone back to Elijah, who listened a bit then asked Jillian, "You said he was murdered."

"He had terminal cancer, but people came and shot him dead."

Elijah listened again to the phone, then disconnected. "He'll see you. Same rule applies, mind you. Get frisky and you're gator bait."

An hour passed before the airboat's engine throttled down.

With the scraping of aluminum on sand, the boat lurched to a stop. Luke checked his watch. 6:20 P.M. Twilight in the bayou had arrived. The bow rested on a spit of land surrounded by hardwoods bearded with moss. Before them a narrow game trail snaked into the foliage.

"Follow the trail until you hear otherwise," Elijah said, tossing Jillian a palm-sized portable radio. "Don't ask questions, just do what you're told."

He hopped off the bow. Jillian followed.

"Do we need to worry about gators?" he asked.

"Not if you stay on the trail. And don't step on a nest."

"I'm gonna want our guns back."

"Later," Elijah said. "Maybe."

"I'd prefer now."

In response, Elijah lifted the shotgun from his lap and cradled it in his elbow. "Start walkin'."

No choice.

Off they went.

Ten feet down the trail they lost sight of Elijah and the boat. The width of the path varied little, which told him it was a game trail. Save for the hum of insects and the occasional splash of water all was silent. Occasionally the flutter of wings overhead could be heard, but the canopy was so thick he could make out only shadows. They'd covered half a mile when a voice suddenly said, "Hold there."

Not from someone nearby.

Instead, from a speaker.

Female.

They stopped walking.

"Take three paces back, face left, and say cheese."

They complied.

Even with his expert eyes Luke didn't immediately see the camouflaged game camera affixed to a nearby tree trunk. He did catch a faint glint as the shutter snapped.

The voice said, "Walk on."

Definitely coming from the camera, which had an audio function.

For thirty minutes they followed the trail deeper into the swamp. While Luke didn't have his tried-and-true Ranger pace beads, he knew from the length of his step and by keeping count in increments of ten they were nearly two miles from where Elijah had dropped them off.

He stopped and raised his hands in the air, then called out, "You're good, but I spotted you thirty meters back."

Behind them a voice said, "Forty meters, but who's counting? You can turn around and lower your hands."

No speaker this time.

They turned and he found himself standing before a woman in her mid-thirties, lean, with ash-colored curly hair and a face full of life and candor. She wore blue jean shorts to her knees, a light blue polo shirt, and boots. A bowie knife hung from her belt, and she cradled a shotgun, aimed right at them.

"I was navy," she said. "We didn't do all that much ground tracking. So I'm not that good."

"I was marine," Jillian noted. "He was a Ranger."

The weapon was lowered. "Elijah said you were good folks. He can tell."

Glad they passed muster.

"And you are?" Luke asked.

"Sue Simmons. My granddad was Ray."

"We came to see him," he said.

"And that's another thing. You don't know and that makes a difference."

"Don't know what?" Jillian asked.

"Ray killed himself 'bout a month ago."

30.

Luke assumed the rear guard as Sue led them another half mile into the swamp, until it gave way to drier land, thicker foliage, and towering trees. Finally they stepped into a clearing at whose center sat a two-story cabin that looked like it'd been airlifted from a Hollywood soundstage. It was, Luke decided, the epitome of ramshackle with mismatched plank siding, a roof that was half-thatch, half-asphalt shingle, and eaves dripping with moss. It had clearly been there awhile. Faintly, he heard the hum of a generator and spotted a satellite dish.

"Home sweet home," Sue announced.

A portly corgi lounging on the porch trotted over to Sue, who provided a welcomed neck scratching.

"This is Crusoe," Sue said. "Crusoe, meet Luke and Jillian."

Tail wagging, the dog gave each of them a thorough sniffing before wandering off.

"As in Robinson Crusoe?" he asked.

"That's the one. After Hurricane Ike I found him washed up on shore, half dead. The name seemed to fit. You two hungry? No doubt you're thirsty."

"Both," Jillian said.

"Come on in. Shoes off, if you please."

They mounted the porch.

Sue opened the door and stepped aside for them to pass. A wave of cool air washed over him. If the exterior was quintessential bayou cabin, the interior was its antithesis, complete with wood walls stained a golden brown, a sectional sofa and plush recliners arranged around an open-hearth fireplace, and gleaming hardwood floors. A pair of floor-to-ceiling built-in shelves brimming with books and knickknacks flanked the fireplace. Across the room was a compact kitchen with modern appliances in brushed nickel.

"It's beautiful," he said.

"Thank you kindly. Ray loved the privacy of living in the boonies, but he also loved his creature comforts."

"You lived here with him?" asked Jillian.

"No, but I visited a lot. Now it's mine."

They both removed their shoes and settled onto the leather sofa while Sue prepared two glasses of ice-cold lemonade.

Jillian downed half of hers in one gulp. "Best thing ever. Thank you."

Sue sat down opposite them. "I was sorry to hear about your grandfather, Miss Stein."

"Call me Jillian. And thanks. Did Ray ever talk about him?"

Sue nodded. "Enough that it was clear they were friends. How exactly, I don't know."

He said, "I have to say, after the welcome Elijah gave us you're not what we expected."

"I'm sorry about that. This close to Papa killing himself, and you not knowing he was dead, I wasn't sure what to think."

"No offense, but your accent isn't as—"

"Thick as everyone else's? I moved away when I was eighteen. Spent my time in the navy, then lived in California before coming back. I lost the drawl somewhere along the way. So tell me about what happened to Mr. Stein."

Jillian recounted the night of the attack but, to Luke's relief, went no further with any details about the rifle and what they found in the lamp. His gut told him Sue was genuine, and no threat, but it was always good to be careful.

"What happened to Ray?" Jillian asked.

"About a month ago he called and asked me to come out, then left a note on the door apologizing. Crusoe led me to him. He'd put a pistol to his head, but did it outside so as not to mess the place up. That was like him."

"I'm so sorry," Jillian said.

"It's awful. The worst." And he meant it.

Sue stood, opened one of the kitchen drawers, then handed him a piece of paper.

I'm so sorry but everything eventually catches up, no matter how hard you try and avoid it.
I love you

"He left that for me," Sue said. "Ray was beloved around here. People would do anything for him. Being his granddaughter I guess that extended to me too. That's how Elijah knew to call me when you showed up at Ken's. We look after each other. But Papa had a lot of baggage that he kept to himself. People around here never knew, but he was mighty troubled. Like he said, it eventually caught up to him."

"You know about that baggage?" he asked.

She nodded. "He had a lot of guilt about my grandmother. He was selfish with her. Treated her badly at times. Took advantage of her. And she died too early for him to make amends."

He decided to let that topic go. For now. "I saw the game cameras on the trail coming in. With audio. That's high tech. Did he have any other surveillance equipment?"

"Lots. He never explained why and I never asked. There are motion sensors and cameras all over. You couldn't get within a hundred feet of this place without him knowing about it. But that was most likely the law enforcement and paranoia in him. Ray always thought people were out to get him."

And maybe with good reason, considering what happened to Benji. From Talley they knew that Ray Simmons and Benji were connected, which Sue just confirmed. How? Hard to say. Plus Stephanie had discovered a new player. So he had to ask, "Did your grandfather ever mention the name Thomas Rowland?"

Sue shook her head.

"Or Kronos?" Jillian added.

"Not a word." She paused. "Ray liked to keep a lot to himself.

Suppose that was the FBI in him. But there were some odd emails."

"Are they still on his computer?" Jillian asked.

"I have no idea. But I do know the password."

Sue walked over to a laptop resting atop a small desk. She tapped the keyboard and pointed at the screen. "They're still here."

He and Jillian joined her and they scanned the emails.

All of them were encoded with a series of random numbers. No words anywhere. Just numbers.

"Look at the addresses," Jillian said.

There were emails to Oceanus at river~sun18@btcmod.com from an address noted as sun~river19@btcmod.com. And many back. But none to or from harvest~sun~river17@btcmod.com, which had brought all the trouble onto Jillian.

"Notice the change in tags and numbers for each e-mail," he said.

Sun and river were flipped out in the first position and the numbers altered between 18 and 19, depending on the sender.

Not a thing though to or from harvest.

"The addresses are similar to the Kronos one," he said. "That's not a coincidence. My guess. Ray Simmons was sun. Benjamin Stein river."

He focused on the last one, sent by Simmons to Benji over a month ago. "Look at the date," he said to Sue. "How is that date in relationship to your grandfather's death?"

"The day before."

He studied the screen.

```
2456-1253-0989-9737-1130-5492-5942-7073-2187-
9713-5329-8437-0539-3402-3537-7024-8007-4418-
5418-4223-4164-0539-8299-2343-3665-7728-4576-
2832-2390-8322-8748-9708-1508
```

He worked his phone and learned that, "In Greek mythology Kronos was identified with the harvest, Hyperion with the sun, and Oceanus a river."

"Code names?" Jillian said.

"Clearly. But there's nothing here about Kronos. No emails in or out."

"I agree," Jillian said. "That's odd."

His mind was working. "We need to find out if these coded emails are to and from Benji. I think I know how we can make sense of these numbers."

And he saw she knew exactly what he meant.

31.

BEFORE HE MADE THE NEXT MOVE, LUKE TRIED TO FIND OUT WHAT HE could about Ray Simmons. It might be helpful to understand the personality involved. Especially one who'd taken his own life. So he asked Sue questions.

Ray had been born and raised in Tulsa, Oklahoma. His father, a police officer, was shot twice in the line of duty, so he discouraged his son from signing up for the force. Ray worshiped his dad so he listened and chose another path. Four years of pre-law at college, then on to the University of Chicago Law School, where he befriended another student, his future wife, Maureen. He proposed at their graduation after-party, embedding the ring in a copy of *Commentaries on the Laws of England* by Sir William Blackstone.

They were married a few days after they each passed the Illinois bar exam. Ray, having had enough of Oklahoma, followed Maureen back to her hometown of Lafayette, Louisiana. Less than a week after arriving an agent from the New Orleans FBI field office knocked on his door. Ray's name had been passed on by one of his professors at law school, who considered him a prime candidate. By then his father had died so he took the meeting, agreed to attend the training academy, and was eventually sworn in as a special agent.

His wife, though wanting to start a law practice in her hometown, was an old-school southern girl devoted to her husband. So she gave up her ambitions and followed Ray to his various postings, as he rose through the ranks. He logged twenty-two years chasing bank robbers and white-collar criminals before retiring. He, Maureen, and their only son returned to Hackberry, where Maureen's family owned a house. The idea was to finally settle down for their golden years. A chance for him to make up to her for all the years of sacrifice. But Maureen died. Breast cancer. Sudden and fast. Ray took it hard. He harbored a lot of guilt on his career coming first. Maureen never complained, but he knew that she'd wanted to be a lawyer, and never had the chance. A year after she died, he sold the house in Hackberry and retreated into the bayou, where he'd lived for the past thirty-four years.

"My dad," Sue said, "is a city boy. He lives in Los Angeles and cares little for the bayou. He came back here for the funeral, then left quick."

"And you?" Jillian asked.

"I love it here, and Papa liked having me around."

He'd noticed something earlier when he surveyed the house, learning the lay of the land. Two bookcases stood just past the kitchen, the sagging wooden shelves filled with volumes on one subject.

JFK's assassination.

Hardcover, softcover, and paperbacks in all shapes and sizes by a multitude of authors, each one surely offering its own spin and interpretation as to what happened in Dallas on November 22, 1963. All in stark contrast with Benji's house where there'd been nothing on the subject.

"Was Ray into the Kennedy assassination?" he asked.

"Heavens, yes," Sue said. "He read a lot of books on the subject and even had a part in the later investigation."

He listened as she explained that in 1967 at a Maryland ballistics laboratory, CBS News commissioned eleven volunteer marksmen, who, unlike Oswald, had prior experience with a properly sighted 6.5mm Carcano rifle, the one used to kill Kennedy. Despite their skill and expertise, and the lack of pressure from their shots not being actual murder attempts, only one of the eleven shooters was able to score three hits of the target.

Ray Simmons.

"Papa was there for the FBI and hit the three targets without the gun jamming. For the others, there was a lot of jamming."

He knew why.

Ticking off high-powered rifle shots with an old weapon like that generated a lot of heat, which tended to lessen its effectiveness. During World War II and Korea rifle jamming was common. Yet Oswald, who fired his three shots in a matter of seconds, had not experienced that. Which conspiratorialists had long seized upon.

"How was he chosen?" Jillian asked.

"He'd been involved with testing on Oswald's actual rifle," Sue said. "He was working with the FBI in 1963 and was known as a good shot. He told me all about it. Several times."

Luke smiled. "And you listened as a good granddaughter does?"

Sue nodded. "Absolutely. It was not long after November 22 that the FBI ran tests on the rifle. He was the one who fired it. Let me show you something."

She sat at the computer and worked the keyboard, finding a file she opened. Luke studied the screen and saw it was a copy of an official FBI document stamped DECLASSIFIED.

"This is the findings from what he did in '63," she said.

He and Jillian read.

Based on test firings, FBI firearms experts have concluded that the 6.5×52mm Carcano Model 38 infantry carbine with a telescopic sight is an accurate weapon. The targets we fired show that. From 15 yards, all three bullets in a test firing landed approximately 2½ inches high and 1 inch to the right, in the area about the size of a dime. At 100 yards the test shots landed 2½ to 5 inches high, within a 3-to-5-inch circle. The scope's high variation would actually work in the shooter's favor. With a target moving away from the shooter no lead correction would have been necessary to follow the target. But the rifle could not be perfectly sighted using the scope without installing two metal shims (small metal plates), which were not present when the rifle arrived for testing, and were never found. There was also a rather severe scrape on the scope tube indicating that the sight could have been bent or damaged. It was impossible to tell when the defect occurred before the FBI received the rifle and scope on November 27, 1963.

"Ray was the one who made the test shots?" he asked.

Sue nodded. "He knew a lot about guns and rifles, and was really proud to have been a part of that. He was fascinated by the assassination the rest of his life."

He checked his watch. 8:20 P.M.

Crusoe suddenly sprang alert just before two double knocks came at the front door. Sue calmed the dog down and opened the door, first checking outside from one of the windows.

He heard Elijah outside, asking if everything was okay.

"All is good," Sue said. "Thanks, Big E."

"You want me to stick around?" Elijah asked.

"Nah, we're getting along fine. I've got my quads, if we need to leave. Talk soon."

Sue stepped back to the den and handed over their guns. "Elijah thought you might want these back."

"Never leave home without them," he said, adding a smile and placing the Berettas off to one side, but within easy reach.

Time to deal with those emails.

He found the ziplock bag and removed the sheet with numbers and letters they'd found in Benji's lamp, the four number blocks similar to the ones in Ray's email, except that on the page from the lamp, above each block was either a single letter or a word.

"It's called a private key, onetime pad," he said. "A tried-and-true way of encoding and decoding transmitted messages. Absolutely unbreakable unless you have the key." He pointed. "Which we do. These number-letter substitutions you see here. Benji had one. I'm guessing Ray had one around here somewhere too."

"Seems like a lot of trouble," Sue said.

"Not considering the response to my Kronos email," Jillian said.

He agreed. "A code would also be a way to make sure Ray and Benji knew they were talking to each other, not some ruse by a third party. It's built-in security."

"Let's solve it," Sue said, excitement in her voice.

He smiled. "We can't solve them all right now, but we can do the last one. I counted. There are forty-four number blocks in Ray's email. Let's divide them up, make the substitutions, then put the pieces together."

It only took them about ten minutes to convert the random numbers into organized letters that formed words. When finished the email read

> Old friend, my time is over. I've decided to go be with Maureen and tell her I'm sorry. She was always there for me. I was never there for her. I know your time is also short, so take care. Maybe I'll see you there too. Hopefully our friend will make it all worth it. I know we found the truth.

He glanced at Sue.

Her hands were shivering, eyes brimming with tears.

Jillian was upset too. "Your grandfather killed himself. It's horrible. But I got mine killed."

"What're you talking about?" Sue asked.

She explained, starting with Benji's deathbed narcotics-induced ramblings and ending with her desperate and impulsive sending of the Kronos email. "I was exhausted, sad, angry, looking for answers. Benji was consumed by something, almost more so than he was by the cancer. I wanted to know what and why."

"How could you have known?" Sue asked. "I would have done the same thing."

He liked her decisive practicality. No crying over spilt milk for her. Forward. Full steam ahead. He stood and walked to one of the windows, gazing out as night claimed the swamp.

"You think Talley's out there?" Jillian asked.

"Who's that?" Sue asked.

"Old friend, new enemy," he said. "He works for a man named Thomas Rowland, the man who sent those men after Benji. Code name Kronos, we think." He was curious. "Did Ray's death get any media coverage?"

"Locally, yes. The whole parish turned out for the funeral."

"So Rowland could know that Ray is gone," Jillian said.

He nodded. "No need to send Talley, except if there's something here, hidden, that Ray was safeguarding."

He saw Jillian understood.

Perhaps something similar, like the rifle from the case that Benji had hidden away.

"Sue, do you have any idea about Ray's connection to Benji? Where they met or how? They seem to be old friends. Both men obsessed with something."

"I have no idea," Sue said. "Papa never said anything on that, just that he had a friend in Belgium."

"Was he a secretive man?" Jillian asked.

"He was the king of secrets. He worked for the FBI into his fifties, until their mandatory retirement age. After Nana died, he was elected here to the local police jury. One of five commissioners who govern the parish. He served for nearly thirty years and took care of a lot of people. Ray was Cameron Parish's goodfather, like the godfather, selfless down to his bones. There wasn't an ounce of malice in the man. But deep down he was troubled."

Obviously.

"He drank a little too much too," Sue said. "Especially these past ten years. Looking back on it, I should have gotten him help. An empty bourbon bottle was found beside his body. Some fortification, I assume."

"How old was Ray?" Julian asked.

"Ninety-four when he pulled the trigger."

The dog lay still on the floor, resting.

"Did he have a safe?" Jillian asked. "Or a special hiding place?"

A good question.

"He had a safe. It's upstairs, but I don't have the combination. I was going to get it opened."

"With a locksmith?" Jillian asked.

Sue shook her head. "Not exactly."

32.

LUKE WASN'T A FAN OF EXPLOSIVES, HAVING DEALT WITH HIS FAIR share of IEDs in Afghanistan. But getting into Ray Simmons's safe was crucial. Blowing things up, Sue explained, had been a childhood hobby. In the navy, she'd risen to an Explosive Ordnance Disposal Technician, Petty Officer 2nd Class before she cycled out after six years. He knew all about EOD techs, considered part of special ops. Not SEALs. Next tier down. But they worked closely together. Training after boot camp started with open-water diving school, followed by explosives and weapons training, then parachute jumps. Nothing about that job for the faint at heart.

Only the best of the best.

She'd continued the interest after her discharge. With Ray's permission, she'd moved all of her supplies to a shed at the back corner of the property where she liked to tinker, far enough away that any accidents would not take out the main house.

"I wouldn't have pegged you for explosives," Luke said, as Sue led them to the shed.

They were toting Ray's two-hundred-pound safe among the three of them.

"It's not so much the blowing things up I like. It's the chemistry. That's my degree from LSU. I like the precision of the work. It's satisfying to get a charge exactly right, so it does what you want it to. That's what I do. I work for construction companies handling demolitions."

When they were fifty feet from the shed Sue said, "This'll work, let's put it down here."

They deposited the safe onto the grass. Darkness had arrived and they were working without the benefit of much light. With Crusoe sniffing along, Sue spent several minutes examining the safe's exterior, peering at the hinges, the combination keypad, and all six sides. A flashlight provided illumination. She tapped the black steel here and there before rising to her feet. "I've got some homemade plastique that—"

"As in C-4?" Jillian said.

"My version of it. I tweaked the chemical combination a bit. It packs less of a punch, but it's much more malleable. Great for when you prefer your explosions gentler and kinder."

"What do you do with the stuff?"

"It's great for scaring away the gators."

Sue disappeared into the shed and reemerged with three

pencil-sized strips of homemade plastique and three detonators that looked like pop-up turkey thermometers. Luke held the flashlight while she tucked one charge each around the safe's hinges and the third into the seam around the locking mechanism.

Finally, she inserted the detonators.

"This should be enough to get the job done. We'll have sixty seconds. Walk, don't run, away. You don't want to stumble and fall in the dark. You ready?"

He and Jillian nodded.

"Here we go."

Sue activated the detonators.

They started retreating.

"Crusoe, come," Sue said.

They made it about a hundred feet away before a muffled thump erupted from the safe as the plastique exploded, the force enough for the safe to tumble forward in a cloud of pale-gray smoke, coming to rest with its front side down.

"I actually thought that would have more punch," Sue said.

They walked back and, together, Luke and Jillian rolled the safe over. The scorched, but otherwise unscathed door fell away.

"Okay, like the Monkees sang, I'm a believer," he said. "You know your stuff."

Inside was a single nylon bag, rectangular in shape and large enough to hold legal-sized documents.

"That's it?" Sue said.

"Seems that way."

They carried the bag inside the house. Like the safe, the pouch was nearly empty. Just three pages. One was another sheet with numbers and letters, similar to Benji's. The other key, just as Luke had surmised, which Simmons had used to decode Benji's messages. Identical to the page they already possessed from Benji. The other two pages were graph paper, covered in what looked like formulas, numbers, and symbols.

"Variables and Discrepancies?" Jillian asked. "What is this?"

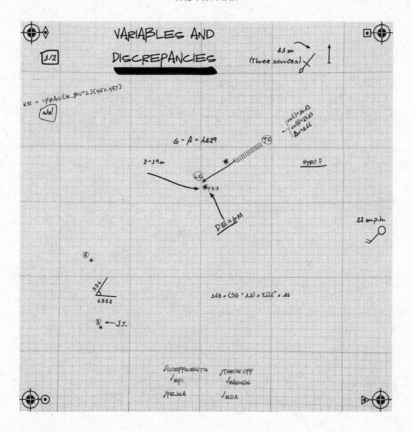

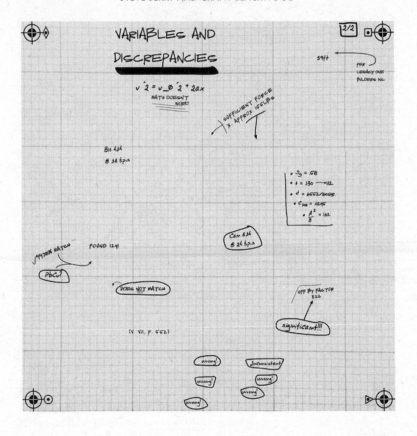

"Any of this look familiar or mean anything?" he asked Sue.

She shook her head.

"Look in the upper right-hand corner," Jillian said. "It says one of two, then two of two. These are a matched set."

He agreed.

"What's it all mean?" Sue asked.

He smiled. "That is the question of the night."

33.

Talley studied the iPad's screen, watching the drone's video feed. They'd sent it into the swamp of Cameron Parish to the coordinates of Ray Simmons's former residence. With Persik gone, as expected, Rowland had ordered him to Louisiana.

"Burn it all to the ground," Rowland said. *"All of it. Nothing should remain."*

Purposefully, he'd been vague when reporting about the fate of Luke Daniels and Jillian Stein, assuring Rowland that the forty-eight hours had not yet expired.

"It will happen," he assured Rowland.

Darkness was here. The drone was capable of night flight and high altitude where it could hover in silence, equipped with high-res nighttime vision. They'd watched as Daniels and Stein's granddaughter, along with Simmons's granddaughter, had explosively opened a safe, removed a bag of some sort, then retired back to the house.

"Bring the drone in," he ordered the operator.

His team had traveled with him from Belgium. They'd only been a few hours behind Daniels. A NetJets charter had delivered them to New Orleans, then they'd driven west to Cameron Parish.

A couple of months back he'd read an article about dealing with manipulative or narcissistic people. Of course, the best option was to stop all contact and get as far away as possible. But what if that wasn't doable? Not everyone could escape a toxic relationship. The article noted that, if you couldn't leave, then set boundaries. Become disengaged and unresponsive. Try to make the manipulator lose interest in you. How? Avoid eye contact. Maintain a flat tone in communications. Respond with simple answers like *yes, no,* or *I didn't know that.* Visualize yourself as a gray rock. Become an immovable, impenetrable force, disinterested.

But there were dangers.

Unresponsiveness could aggravate the narcissist because they would not be getting the reaction they were accustomed to. They could feel their power slipping, or their control waning, which could lead to unpredictable behavior.

Best advice?

Don't defend, engage, explain, or personalize. He tacked on a fifth piece of advice to what the article had said.

And destroy them.

Definitely.

Which was what he planned to do.

His men were ready.

Of course, they knew nothing about what he had in mind. They were simply following his orders, as they had for a long time. Their loyalty was entirely to him, as not one of them had ever laid eyes on Thomas Rowland. Hopefully, nothing he planned would spill over onto them or their families. What was the saying? If you come to kill the king, make damn sure you kill the king. For the alternative was something unthinkable.

Especially with Tom Rowland involved.

He left the pilot to deal with the drone and walked over to his men.

"Load up," he told them. "We're going in."

34.

Luke had to admit, Sue Simmons could cook. She'd made a feast of bayou dishes. Andouille, jambalaya, gumbo, finishing it all off with praline brownies and what she called Cajun coffee. Finely ground Colombian beans, a couple of teaspoons of dark molasses, a splash of rum, and a sprinkle of nutmeg.

Heaven.

He and Jillian both were hungry and starting to fight jet lag. Luckily, they were both familiar with the malady and knew how to deal with it.

A little decompression felt good.

Especially considering what was coming. He had no doubt Talley would come. And soon. Surely once darkness had settled in. Or at least that's the play he'd make if the roles were reversed.

Sue and Jillian's lives seemed to overlap. In an eerie way. Their grandfathers had both died suddenly and violently, taking to the grave a shared something. Compounding their grief, they'd been left a legacy that neither asked for nor understood. Even worse, whatever Benji and Ray had been involved with seemed to now be visited upon their descendants. Jillian was all in. No question. But he'd given Sue the option of leaving and letting them handle what might come before morning. Their hostess declined saying she'd never run from a fight in her life and wasn't about to start now.

Around 10:00 p.m. Sue wandered upstairs with Crusoe on her heels, a shotgun in her hand.

Jillian curled up on the couch. "I'm going to rest my eyes for a few minutes."

The two Berettas lay on the coffee table.

Luke was counting on the fact that the property was wired to give them some advance warning. So he made himself a second cup of Cajun coffee then returned to the three pages they'd amassed. Lots of formulas and equations. Variables and Discrepancies. Benjamin Stein and Ray Simmons were investigating something. What had Ray written? *Hopefully our friend will make it all worth it. I know we found the truth.* That seemed to indicate there was someone else involved. One thing was certain. They'd taken great pains to keep the nature of whoever that was and what they were working on private.

The rifle from Benji's storage unit still bothered him. Stephanie had reported Malone retrieved both it and the other materials from the car. They were all currently on their way to Washington by a special flight. It was equally strange that Simmons would keep only the three sheets of paper in a locked safe. None of them were self-explanatory or made much sense. So why secrete them? After the lamp in Benji's bedroom he decided on a more thorough inspection. The safe itself had been empty, save for the nylon bag. He examined the bag's exterior. Blue, puffy to the touch signifying padding between the inner and outer layers. He squeezed all around and felt nothing unusual. The bottom had a base, a couple of inches wide and about a foot and a half long, that allowed the bag to stand upright.

He squeezed that too.

Pliable.

Except for one end, where he felt something solid inside the seams among the padding. Round. Maybe three inches long.

He walked into the kitchen and found a steak knife, which he used to make an incision in the nylon and freed the object.

A small plastic vial.

Like what pills came in from the drugstore.

Sealed at the top with tape and filled with cotton. Embedded within the cotton he saw a flash drive.

He smiled. The hits just kept on coming.

He heard a faint beeping from upstairs.

"We've got company," Sue called down.

He quickly folded the pages back up and stuffed them into the ziplock. He then slid the vial with the drive into his pocket and shook Jillian awake.

"Showtime."

She came alert and they both grabbed a Beretta then headed upstairs. Sue was ensconced before a laptop, Crusoe at her feet. He came close and saw a topographic map with the house and surrounding area on the screen.

"Those red dots are—"

"Surveillance camera triggers." He counted four, which meant men were approaching the house from the south. "See if you can catch one."

Sue brought up the camera program, then scrolled through the multiple images until finally they spotted a shadowed figure frozen in mid-step. Then another crouching by a tree. And a third prone in the grass.

He recalled their arrival. "How many of these cameras have two-way audio?"

Sue pointed at the screen. "That one, that one, and that one. What do they want?"

"Our asses," he said, not mentioning what was in his pocket. "You two get moving, like we discussed. I'm gonna see if I can slow them down."

35.

LUKE WAITED UNTIL HE HEARD THE BACK DOOR CLOSE BEFORE returning his focus to the laptop. He clicked on one of the audio cameras then nestled his Beretta near the laptop's microphone and racked the slide. To anyone near the camera, that familiar sound would stop them in their tracks.

He chose another camera and barked out, "Over here."

He clicked on a third camera and shouted, "Talley."

One more for good measure. He returned to the first camera and said, "Did you miss me?"

That should generate some confusion with noise coming from several directions. He raced down the stairs and left out the back door. Jillian and Sue, who had Crusoe tucked under one arm, were waiting near the shed.

"With any luck I've bought time," he said. "Show us those quads you mentioned earlier."

They headed for the garage, about fifty yards behind the house. He quietly swung open the big door, revealing a pair of black quads sitting side by side.

"You take one and head north," he told Sue. "Make your way to town and disappear. Use the locals for protection."

He was guessing Talley's priorities were first, finding any pertinent writings and/or evidence, and second killing him and Jillian.

Hopefully, in that order.

"Why north?" asked Sue. "East is—"

"The cameras that got triggered were to the south. They're coming in from the water the way we did earlier. It'll be easier for you and Crusoe to get through to the north. And you know the way. They don't."

They'd discussed this over dinner and laid out the plan, just in case Talley decided tonight was the night.

"Give me the lay of the land again," he said to Sue.

"At the tree line you'll find a path that Ray cut. It leads straight to a dock where he keeps his swamp boat."

"How far?" Jillian asked.

"About half a mile," Sue said. "Take the boat, follow the buoys out of the inlet, then west until you hit a headland. Straight on until you're on Five Lakes. Watch yourselves, the mangrove gets gnarly in there. Make your way to the north shore until you reach a canal. Follow that north three miles until you find a gravel road. Head east. It'll lead you to the north side of Hackberry. Find Spencer Marina and ask for Laird. Use my name. He'll help."

"Got it," he said. "Sorry we brought this down on you. Lie low until we reach out. We'll call Ken's and ask for Robbie."

"As in Crusoe?"

"That's how you'll know it's us. If you've got problems on your end, use the phrase—" He thought for a moment. "*It's a bit sweltry for my taste.* We'll know to stay away. Everybody good to go?"

They nodded.

He took a moment to listen and watch for signs of Talley's men. Nothing. But they surely knew how, as he did, to pass silently over any terrain.

Time to move.

"Sue, push yours for a hundred yards before starting the engine," he whispered. "We're going out fast and hard. That'll draw them to us."

Sue nodded and left with the dog in tow.

He gave her a solid minute head start, then he and Jillian mounted the other quad. He started the engine, doused the headlights, then gunned the throttle, lurching forward, leaving a rooster tail of dirt in his wake. He steered left along the cabin's rear wall, hoping it would give them cover until the quad reached full speed. They burst from behind the corner of the cabin. From their left came a sprinting figure. Luke saw him at the last second, palmed the Beretta, fired once, and kept driving.

"Is he down?" he sked Jillian.

"He was, but he's getting up. Hobbling, though."

"Hold tight."

He switched on the headlights and hunched over the handlebars, bringing the quad up to full speed. Behind them came the crack of a rifle, then another, then two more joined in. The distinctive snap of close-in bullets erupted around them. One whipped past his elbow and shattered the speedometer.

"Give them something to think about," he said to her.

"They're out of range," she said.

"They don't know that."

She sent off a trio of shots.

While unlikely to hit anyone, multiple rounds of incoming fire tended to send folks scrambling for cover. The return fire slackened for a few seconds, then increased. He concentrated on the road, easing the quad through the trail's twists and turns. Insects peppered his face.

"You smell that?" she called out. "We're leaking gas."

He glanced over his shoulder. Fuel gushed from the underside of the quad. He torqued the throttle, but the engine was already dying. The best he could hope for was to put as much distance between them and Talley's men as he could before the quad ground to a halt. They covered another fifty yards before the engine sputtered and died.

"End of the road," he said.

They both climbed off.

"Keep running," he told her. "It's only a quarter mile to the boat. Get it prepped. I'll be along shortly."

She didn't argue and hustled off.

The marine in her understood.

They were conducting a fighting retreat.

36.

LUKE SPRINTED TO THE NEAREST OAK TREE AND DROPPED FLAT BEHIND it. He drew a few calming breaths to lower his heart rate then turned his attention to the most important thing first.

A safe exit.

His attackers carried assault rifles and he was already within their range. When the shooting started he would need cover, if he hoped to make it out. So he scoped out his best route to the boat, then peeked around the tree and began scanning for movement.

There'd be a pattern.

His enemy would be leapfrogging from tree to tree, advancing, until they found his position. Suppressing and covering fire would follow while they moved to flank him. If he lingered too long, he'd get caught in the pincer.

"This isn't the Afghan highlands," Talley called out from the darkness.

No, it wasn't. At least they'd come his way, which meant Sue had probably escaped. He spotted a figure about a hundred yards out, advancing parallel to the path. He then saw a second shadow on the opposite side.

"Come out, hands up, and I won't shoot you," Talley said.

He wondered if all the bravado was merely for his team's bene- fit. When he came to kill Persik and the others Talley came alone. Tonight, he'd brought the whole traveling road show.

So where was this headed?

He allowed Talley's point men to cover another twenty yards, then aimed the Beretta's muzzle at the ground, so his body would shield the flash, and pulled the trigger. That moment of distraction allowed him to spring to his feet and, using the big live oaks as cover, he ran until he reached the thicker brush, where he stopped to see whether his handiwork had paid off. While the gun's report would be a beacon to Talley's men, the lack of a muzzle flash would leave them stuck with a broader search area. A rifle cracked. Then another. A third. All single shots. Reconnaissance by fire. Talley was hoping to provoke him into giving away his position.

Not today, pal.

He carefully picked his way through the brush, playing out in his mind Talley's next moves. By now they'd be clearing the area where Luke had fired the shot. Then they'd be on his tail. He'd been quietly snapping off branches and trampling foliage as he made his way northeast away from the boat dock. When he'd covered what he hoped was enough distance, he turned west and this time left no trail. Fifteen minutes later he emerged back onto the quad path and jogged to the dock.

Jillian was nowhere in sight.

Crap.

"Over here," came her whispered voice, and she emerged from the foliage beside the dock. "We've got half a tank of gas."

"You take the bow. Stay low. Keep watch ahead. Make any shots count."

She smiled. "Remember who you're talking to."

She took her place and Luke climbed up to the driver's seat. He turned the ignition key. The engine caught immediately and growled to life. He allowed the fan blade to spin up to full speed then eased the rudder stick forward. Mimicking Elijah's driving style he goosed and glided the boat down the inlet, following the buoys on their zigzag course toward the main channel where the inlet widened. As they passed the last buoy, Jillian's clinched fist shot up.

He throttled back and shut off the engine.

She glanced over her shoulder and pointed at her eyes, then toward the main channel followed by a gesture he took for *boat*. Talley had covered his bases. He'd left some men in reserve on the water.

No shocker there.

He followed Jillian's outstretched finger. Though the sky was overcast, the obscured moon shone full and bright. He glimpsed the barest outline of another boat skimming across the mouth of the inlet. He couldn't see how many were aboard. He gestured to her, *How many?*

She shrugged.

The boat disappeared from view.

A moment later an engine revved and it reappeared, heading in the opposite direction. They were trolling, guessing where their target might reappear, trying to be at the right place at the right time. He gestured to Jillian his general plan.

She nodded.

He waited until the other boat made its next turn, then spun the rudder west—the direction they needed to go.

The other boat disappeared from view.

He started the engine and shoved the rudder forward. They exited the canal doing about thirty miles per hour. He jerked the rudder hard right, nearly laying the hull on its side, then straightened out. Dead ahead, not a hundred feet off their bow, was the other boat.

Muzzles flashed orange in the darkness.

Jillian stayed low and returned fire.

He felt mighty exposed in the raised seat.

Too late, boys. You're done.

He gained more speed, rapidly eating up the distance. The other boat veered left, but Luke was already on them. Darkness made aiming tough and him coming straight at them had to be unnerving. At the last moment he tweaked the rudder and glanced the bow off their fan shroud. Jillian added rounds that sent the occupants downward. Bullets snapped behind them, but there was another noise, the staccato grinding of steel on steel. He'd knocked their fan blade out of kilter, rendering it useless.

"Nice move," she called out.

They were moving fast, now beyond rifle range.

The gunfire faded, then stopped.

A couple of minutes later they reached a headland, just as Sue had directed. He rounded it, then steered northwest. They skimmed over the smooth surface like a thrown flat stone. Off their port bow the moon's glow was a rippling shaft of milky light.

"Trouble," Jillian shouted. "Right side."

He glanced that way in time to see an outboard V-hull speedboat bearing down on them.

He turned, trying to get clear, but not fast enough.

37.

LUKE SHOUTED FOR JILLIAN TO MOVE.

And she dove toward the stern.

The speedboat slammed into their bow, spinning their boat across the surface and graphically demonstrating the dangers of a flat bottom. Luke throttled back and tried to keep them afloat. But there'd been damage to the old hull, lots of it, and water flooded in.

They stopped moving.

Jillian lay curled at the base of his seat, hanging on.

"You okay?" he asked.

"That was different."

To their right the speedboat was making a wide U-turn.

About to return.

"We can't outrun or avoid them," he said. "Into the water."

"What about gators?"

"One hundred percent chance of getting shot. Alligator? Less than that."

"Good point."

She dove over the side. The hull was half full, the boat listing heavily right.

"Move away," he said.

She started swimming.

He leaned over, grabbed the port gunwale, and threw himself backward. Combined with the canting weight of the engine, the momentum was enough to capsize the boat. He plunged beneath the water, groped until he felt fingers grasp his own, and pulled Jillian toward him. Together, they surfaced in a narrow air pocket in the upturned boat's stern. Pitch black. He could feel Jillian's breath on his cheek. He heard the drone of the V-hull's engine coming closer.

"You do know that this hull isn't thick enough," she said. "Their rounds will punch right through."

"I know. We're not sticking around. That boat came from an inlet nearby off to our right. Can't be far. We dive and keep going. Crawl along the bottom, if that's what it takes to stay submerged. When you hit dry land do whatever it takes to stay hidden. Wait for an hour after they leave. We'll meet in Hackberry."

"What about the gato—"

A bullet punched through the hull, revealing a dot of pale light. A second hole appeared a foot to their left.

"Time's up," he said. "Big breath."

They dove.

Almost immediately Luke lost sight of her in the dark water. What little light the moon offered was swallowed just a few feet down. So fine was the silt bottom that the water had turned to an impenetrable murk. His outstretched hands touched mud. He started kicking toward what he hoped was the inlet. In the absolute darkness there seemed to be no up or down, left or right.

Just forward.

He stopped swimming and listened. The V-hull was headed his way. He rolled onto his back in time to see it pass overhead.

Spotlights pierced the water from above.

The boat moved on.

He kept going and did his best to focus on keeping hold of the bottom rather than on what else might be down there. Jillian was right to be concerned about gators. This was their home. The burning in his lungs became unbearable.

He kicked off the bottom.

When his head broke the surface he snatched a lungful of air, took a quick bearing on the inlet, and dove again. He repeated this pattern, crawl-swimming along the bottom, surfacing for another gulp of oxygen, submerging again. On his third breach he caught a glint of light off to his right. The V-hull was circling, its spotlight reflecting off the surface.

A rifle cracked.

"Bubbles. There," somebody shouted off in the distance.

A pair of rifles opened fire. The water's surface boiled with rounds. Jillian.

He had to do something. So he shouted, "Hey, over here."

And waved his arms.

The spotlight swung around and pinned him in its beam.

The V-hull turned and headed in his direction. He ducked under with a pike dive and paddled hard for the bottom. He heard a string of muffled rifle cracks. Like tiny javelins, bullets appeared on either side of him. He felt a sting to his right calf. He turned left and kicked harder. The pitch and volume of the boat's prop filled his ears. More gunfire came, increasing to a crescendo before abruptly stopping.

The boat sped away.

Was Jillian returning the favor?

Drawing them away?

After two more surface-breathe-dive repetitions he felt his belly scrape sand. He crawled forward until he was half out of the water and looked left.

The boat had come ashore fifty yards away. One of Talley's men was wrapping the bowline around a mangrove root. Two more hopped from the bow and the three disappeared into the trees.

He lay still in the dark.

Unseen.

He was about to head out when something caught his attention. Ten feet away. The black form of a gator resting on the sand, just out of the water. Thankfully the reptile paid him no attention, hopefully resting with a full stomach.

He rose ever so slowly and crept away.

38.

LUKE REALIZED HE HELD AN ADVANTAGE OF SOUND OVER THE MEN from the boat. Or so he hoped. Talley's men were moving together, or at least they would be for a while, so their passage through the foliage would be noisy. Hard not to be in this thick mess. Plus, they'd be in a hurry. Talley would want quick results. He and Jillian could wait them out. Hopefully she was thinking the same. So he advanced with exaggerated slowness, picking his way inland, the idea to follow the general course of the inlet.

"Hold it right there," a voice said from behind.

He froze.

Crap.

"You move, I'll put one in your head."

He hadn't seen that one coming. "I'm not moving."

"Slowly, hands up, then down on your belly, arms outstretched."

That he did not want to do. Especially with the gator not all that far away at the water's edge.

He took a moment to gauge his chances.

The guy had appeared from nowhere and gotten lucky, allowing himself to get too close, probably within a couple of barrel lengths of Luke's back judging by the voice. Once he had Luke prone, reinforcements would be called and the odds were only going to worsen. The Beretta was a no-go. Drawing it would take too many steps.

So don't think about it.

He spun on his heel, pushed off, and whipped his arm up and around. His elbow smacked into the gun barrel, shoving it aside. He wrapped his fist around the front sight post and gave the weapon a jerk. The man stumbled forward, but recovered immediately, releasing one hand off the rifle and lashing out with a tight hook that caught Luke in the temple.

His eyesight sparkled.

Legs went rubbery.

He tipped sideways, but told himself to not let go of the barrel.

The man twisted the gun and smacked Luke in the chin with the butt. He tasted blood and countered by shoving the sight post into the side of the man's neck, which caused a gasp of pain.

But the guy recovered.

And advanced.

He caught movement from behind the guy.

Another of Talley's men?

No. Black, elongated, lumbering along close to the ground.

The damn gator. Coming their way. Maybe his belly wasn't full. All the commotion had attracted interest.

His heart filled his throat.

No telling where this was headed.

He front-kicked the guy in the chest. The man stumbled backward, his feet slipping on the muddy soil, but was able to check his retreat and regain balance, still holding the weapon, which he began to bring level for firing. The alligator sprang from behind, jaws open, snapping shut on the man's right leg. Luke heard the crunch of bone. The man managed half a scream, and then the alligator was sliding backward, dragging his prey with him. The guy fought, trying to free himself, attempting to swing the rifle around for a shot to kill the gator. But the alligator kept retreating, taking his meal into the water with a death roll.

Then the guy was gone.

Luke's heart thudded in his chest.

That was no way to go. Who was the man? Probably a fellow veteran, now working for the highest bidder. No matter how you cut it, there was no feeling good about any of it. Except that he was still alive and kicking.

He shook himself back to reality and realized the shot would bring others. He snatched up the man's fallen rifle. Things had changed. He was now well armed. Should he set an ambush for Talley's other men? Keep them away from Jillian. No. Not smart, no matter how much he wanted to do it.

He could hear Malone in his head.

"You're not a Ranger anymore. You're an intelligence officer and your job is to stay faithful to the three L's. Look, learn, listen. Let the bad guys tire themselves out. You live to report another day."

Damn right.

He headed out, found a clump of dense brush, hunkered down, and concentrated on his breathing while he waited. He hoped Jillian was doing the same. Time passed slowly, most of it in silence except for the near-constant buzzing of insects and the croaking of frogs. Gnats and mosquitoes found their way into his ears, nose, and eyes. He forced his mind elsewhere and breathed through it telling himself that this too would pass. Occasionally he'd hear the distant cracking of branches as Talley's men continued the hunt.

An hour of waiting ended with the roar of an outboard engine, which faded away on the water. He crawled from his hiding place. To his right the eastern horizon was pink with the rising sun.

He oriented himself north and started walking. The terrain was flat and mostly dry, but thick with foliage. His route repeatedly snaked northeast then northwest. He kept going, steadily covering the miles until finally around midmorning he stumbled onto the gravel road Sue had mentioned.

He started jogging.

After four miles he came to a stop sign and an asphalt road. A figure rose from the grass beside the sign. Jillian. He was glad to see her.

"What took you so long?" she asked.

"I fell asleep."

"Yeah, right."

"How long have you been here?" he asked.

"No more than half an hour. Your leg's bloody."

He glanced down at his calf. "Flesh wound. Let's find this marina Sue mentioned. I've had enough swamp for a lifetime."

39.

ROWLAND SAT ON THE TERRACE, HIS LAP DRAPED BY A WOOL BLANKET, and admired the waters of the Chesapeake Bay. He liked what the author James Michener wrote. *The bay is like a beautiful woman. There's no humiliation from which she cannot recover.*

How poetic and apt.

The day was cloudy and cool. Though spring had arrived a week ago no warmth had followed the change of season. He wondered how many more springs by the water he'd be allowed to enjoy. Hopefully a few, as it was one of the great joys of his life.

The terrace doors opened and his chamberlain stepped out.

"Sir, you have a visitor."

Really? That was unusual. No one came to see him unless invited. And he'd extended no invitations for today. On a week-end? His thoughts were entirely with Jack Talley and all that was happening in Europe and Louisiana. He wanted no interruptions. "Tell whoever it is that—"

"You tell me, Tom," a new voice said from the terrace doors.

Female. Familiar. And not appreciated.

"You were told to wait at the front door," the chamberlain said.

"I'm not good at following orders. Am I, Tom?"

"Leave us," he said to the chamberlain, who vanished back into the house.

And he faced Stephanie Nelle.

She was a petite woman, in her sixties, and a little testy about her age. Justice Department personnel records, he'd been told, contained only a winking N/A in the space reserved for date of birth. Her blond hair was streaked with waves of silver and her pale-blue eyes offered both the compassionate look of a liberal and the fiery glint of a prosecutor. Which had long made her politically appealing to both sides of the aisle. Two presidents had tried to make her attorney general, but she'd turned both offers down. One attorney general lobbied hard to fire her—especially after she was enlisted by the FBI to investigate him—but the White House at the time nixed the idea since, among other things, Nelle was regarded as scrupulously honest and they didn't want the flak.

Recently, she'd run afoul of the current president, Warner Fox, to the point that both she and the Magellan Billet seemed on their last leg. He'd actually encouraged both actions since he'd earned Warner Fox's ear years before the man had managed to be elected president. He'd been unapologetic in saying both Nelle and the Billet were anachronisms that no longer were needed. Stephanie had created the unit within the Justice Department and had run it from day one. It was the only branch of the American intelligence community Rowland had not been able to successfully infiltrate. Nothing and no one from there had ever been of any assistance. So Stephanie being here, unannounced, on a Saturday morning meant only one thing.

Trouble.

With a capital T.

"We need to speak," she said. "Face-to-face."

"Then, by all means, sit. Talk."

She stood before him. "I don't like you. I've never cared for you. There is something inherently dishonest about you. I'm sure you feel the same about me, since one, I have never had any need for your services, and two, you have nothing on me through which to blackmail or coerce me."

"Everyone has secrets," he said. "We just have not fully fleshed out yours. There's been no need."

"And President Fox? Was there a need there? I know you were involved in what happened to me."

He smiled. "You did that all by yourself, with no help from anyone."

"And I resolved the matter, all by myself too."

"You did manage to wiggle your way off that hook. Congratulations."

"You must be in great turmoil," she said. "Here, in the twilight of your life, facing such a personal dilemma."

"I was not aware I was in conflict."

"I'm not one of your lackeys, nor one of those corrupt or weak individuals who need you to fix something for them. I have an asset in the field, right now, under fire from your man Jack Talley."

He kept his composure frozen, revealing nothing. The situation had just gestated from bad to worse. Luke Daniels was Magellan Billet? He'd not, as yet, made any calls regarding Daniels, as Talley had said he'd be dead shortly. No inquiries meant no trail back to him. Just let the problem be handled at a distance without comment.

A mistake on his part.

Obviously.

"Benjamin Stein and Ray Simmons," she said. "Both dead. One by your hand, the other by his own."

"And these men are?"

"Problems that you eliminated."

"What a fertile imagination you possess."

"I don't read much fiction. I prefer nonfiction. Reality."

"What is this about?" he asked.

"Your demise."

"You seem excited at the prospect."

"Nothing could please me more."

"Why are you here?"

"To tell you that, this time, you will lose."

No sense pretending any longer. The gauntlet had been thrown down. "Don't be sure."

"I am sure. It's time to end you."

"Many have tried."

"True. But I'm not many. And I will get you."

"I look forward to the fight."

"As do I."

"I am a formidable adversary."

"So am I."

She turned and left the terrace.

He stayed in the chair, blanket warming his legs, but suddenly grew cold with something he hadn't experienced for a long time.

Not since that horrible day.

Fear.

Stephanie had connected the dots. So far Stein and Simmons were both dead. Good. Their granddaughters? Alive but not a threat. Luke Daniels? Obviously alive and functioning. Simmons's house? Burned to the ground. Had anything noteworthy been found there? Probably not. All of that had happened for a reason. Moving toward the single remaining unknown that would end this matter. Nothing could be allowed to interfere with that.

He slipped his right hand into his pant pocket.

And found his phone.

40.

LUKE REALIZED THEY NEEDED A PLACE TO LIE LOW, REGROUP, AND make a concerted effort to finally understand what they'd gotten themselves into. Following Sue's instructions, they walked to Spencer Marina and asked for Laird, mentioning Sue's name, and he'd been only too happy to help. He offered them food, drink, and an air-conditioned break room where they waited while a pair of his employees rounded up some fresh clothes, then fetched their Bronco from its parking spot near Ken's, making sure no one was watching or following. Once at the marina, Luke thoroughly checked for tracking devices.

They then drove north to Highway 70 and followed it to Lafayette, where they found a motel whose décor had never outgrown the 1960s. However it was clean, accepted cash, and had air-conditioning so they took a room at the back. He parked the Bronco a few blocks away.

Jillian showered first, then he enjoyed some soap and hot water. He emerged from the bathroom to find her resting on one of the twin beds. He found his phone and checked the screen. He'd managed to charge it back at the Simmons cabin while they'd eaten dinner last night. Despite the dunking it still functioned, as Billet phones were totally water- and shock-resistant. He saw a voice mail had come in from Marcia, which indicated she had some new information. Before returning the call he dialed the number for Ken's Convenience in Hackberry and put it on speaker.

"Ken's," a male voice said.

"I'm looking for Robbie," he said.

"Hold on."

"Robbie speaking."

Sue's voice.

"How's the weather down there?"

"Hot, but not sweltering. You two make it out safe?"

"We did. How about you?"

"Crusoe needs a bath, but otherwise fine. There's something you should know." Her voice cracked. "They burned down the cabin. All the way to the ground. There's nothing left."

"We're so sorry, Sue," Jillian said.

"I'd sure feel better if I knew why."

"You'll be the first, once we know," he said.

"Fair enough. And one other thing."

"I know. Make 'em pay for what they did. We shall."

He ended the call.

They sat in silence for a few moments. This was definitely a hard-pitch-fastball game for keeps. Which was okay. As that was the way he liked it.

He called Marcia.

"Our boss has told me this is official now," she said. "And a top priority."

"Good to hear. Tell me what you found out."

"The harvest email addresses is a dead end. It's a truly unique address. A Googlewhack extraordinaire."

"You sound impressed."

"Most of the tech issues I deal with are pretty simple."

"For you, maybe."

"This one is a mystery. It's almost like it doesn't exist."

The ziplock, vial, and flash drive were still safe in his pocket. Unaffected by the swim. They all required attention. But Marcia was hundreds of miles away.

So he was on his own.

"I need a laptop," he told Marcia. "Along with some privacy. Especially the latter. I'm in Louisiana. Any suggestions?"

They left Lafayette and drove sixty miles to Baton Rouge, zeroing in on the address Marcia had provided. It led to a shady street of 1950s ranch-style homes. Julie Hopkins was the head archivist for the East Baton Rouge Parish Historical Society. According to Marcia she was smart, clever, thorough, and one of her oldest and dearest friends. Totally trustworthy. A call en route told him that a fresh laptop would be waiting for him to use.

"Pigeon knows the score," Marcia said. "She's at work, if you need her. I'll text her cell number. Otherwise, the house is yours for as long as you need it."

Which seemed like a perfect place to lie low a little while and think.

"There, on the right," Jillian said, pointing.

He pulled into the driveway and shut off the engine. "Marcia says the Pigeon nickname came from raising messenger pigeons with her father. She loves them."

Though relatively certain they'd been neither followed nor tracked, he didn't want to risk turning someone else's life upside down. So it was good Julie Hopkins was out for the day.

"Marcia gave me the door code and WiFi password. I was told we're to make ourselves at home."

41.

LUKE WAS A LITTLE DISAPPOINTED.

Aside from a few figurines in the living room, the house bore no sign of Julie's fondness for pigeons. The interior was comfortable and cozy. Jillian switched on lights and he checked the fridge for something to eat and drink. Marcia had said to make themselves at home.

"She sure loves herring and sauerkraut," he called out from the open refrigerator. "For the life of me I have no idea why."

He checked the freezer and found two packs of frozen lasagna. That and the beer in the fridge would make an excellent early dinner. He joined Jillian on the living room couch.

Time to come clean.

"I've got something else," he said.

And he showed her the vial. "It was hidden in the nylon bag from the safe."

"You're just now mentioning this?"

"We've been a bit preoccupied."

She examined the drive through the clear plastic. "What do you think?"

"Talley burned Simmons's house to the ground, with everything in it, for a reason. But this survived. Which is why we're here. We have to take a look. But first, we need food and beer."

The lasagna took an hour to cook. While they waited he called Stephanie and reported more of what had happened. He'd already provided her some of the details a few hours ago.

"I paid Thomas Rowland a visit," she told him.

"Rattling the cage?"

"You could say that. But he knows we're onto him."

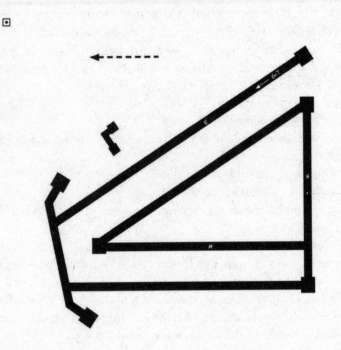

He knew what that meant. The already high pressure would increase. "Hopefully, we're about to learn what this is all about."

"Luke—"

"I know. You'll be the first to know, when I know."

A MacBook Air bearing the stamp for the East Baton Rouge Parish Historical Society had been waiting on the kitchen table. While they both ate and enjoyed the cold beer, he popped in the flash drive from the vial and they studied the screen.

Five files. Not password-protected.

That was all?

One was labeled DIAGRAMS.

He clicked on it and three images appeared.

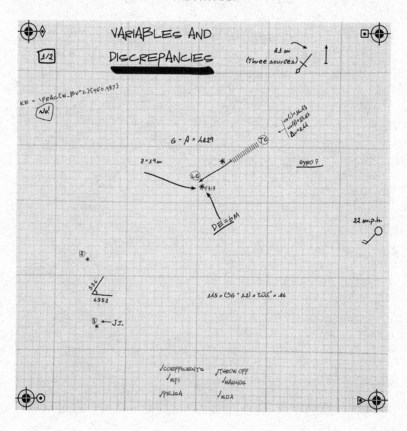

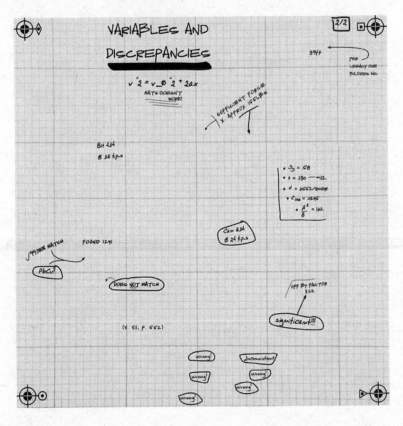

"The first is identical to the one from Benji's lamp," Jillian said.

"And the other two are the same from the pouch."

He returned his attention to the screen and clicked on the file named AUDIO. After a few seconds of silence, a tinny voice on a grainy sound track said—

"*Your name.*"

"*I am Dr. Earl Rose, the Dallas County medical examiner. Who are you?*"

"*Roy Kellerman, special agent in charge of the White House detail of the Secret Service. This is the body of the president of the United States and we are going to take it back to Washington.*"

"That's not the way things are," Rose said. "When there's a homicide in Dallas, we must have an autopsy."

"He's going with us."

"The body stays," Rose declared. "There's a law here. We're going to enforce it."

"The situation is bad," Kellerman said. "Look, there's been an accident, not a murder, so the law can be waived."

Some steel had entered the voice.

In the background a door squeaked open, then shut.

"Let's move," Kellerman said.

A rattling, like wheels on a gurney.

"Get out of the way," Kellerman demanded.

"You are not taking that body," Rose said.

"Either you move or we run over you."

"I'm not moving."

A rustling sound, then the scuffing of shoes.

"Get your hands off me," Rose said.

The wheels again, which faded in the distance.

The recording stopped.

"What did we just hear?" Jillian said.

"That's a really good question."

He was beginning to get a picture, though vague and fuzzy around the edges. But definitely forming. The third file was also an audio, labeled THOUGHTS. He clicked on it and they listened to a gravelly voice they assumed was Ray Simmons.

"Eckstein still has the film. It's in perfectly preserved condition. I've seen it. Amazing stuff. The Canon 814 got it all. He has an engineer's tenacity and has taken the nuggets and spun them into pure gold. He tells me the manuscript is coming along and will be quite revealing. His hypothesis is compelling. The ballistic research has confirmed everything."

"I wonder what kind of an engineer Eckstein is?" he asked.

"And what are the nuggets?"

"Along with the gold," he muttered.

They kept listening.

"David remains hesitant about notoriety. We had the conversation again and he said the same thing. He'll write the book. He's in fact already deep into its creation. But he wants us to take the lead. I've visited him several times. His theory is sound and correct and consistent with all that we've found. I pressed him, asked if his worry was about legal action. He said no. More worried about being wrong. So many people have created so many theories that he did not want to be another joke. He wants us to be right."

"What's that mean?" Jillian said. "Be right?"

Luke had no idea.

He clicked PLAY again.

"So many have thought they had the answer. Just like we do. Are we being arrogant? Brash? Rushing to judgment? I don't think so. We've kept this to ourselves for so long. We've been patient. David says the manuscript is nearly finished, so the time has come to confront Rowland. I worry that I don't have the will or desire to keep going. I'm trying, but I become weaker by the day. My resolve is slowly sinking and I find myself wanting to live less and less. I want to hang on, to be there, but I know all of you can handle it."

"There's a lot of regret there," she said. "The same as Benji had. It's like a suicide note."

They kept listening.

"I'm thinking about trekking up there again, one more time, but I'm getting too damn old for mountains and horses and snow. I'll think about it. Hell, maybe I'll finally beat him at checkers."

"That's the last entry," she said.

"You heard that," he said. "*The time has come to confront Rowland.* There's a link among these four men. And whoever David Eckstein is, he's also got at least one other thing in common with Ray and Benji. They all chose tucked-away places to live. Benji, a small town in Belgium. Ray Simmons, miles from nowhere in the middle of a swamp. And it sounds like Eckstein is high up in some mountains."

"All to stay out of Rowland's way?" she asked.

Maybe.

"Let's see what the fourth file contains."

Labeled COMMISSION, he clicked on it.

42.

The President's trip to Dallas on November 22, 1963 called into play many standard operating procedures of the Secret Service in addition to its preventive intelligence operations. Examination of these procedures show that in most respects they were well conceived and ably executed by the personnel of the Secret Service. Against the background of the critical events of November 22, however, certain shortcomings and lapses from the high standards which the Commission believes should prevail in the field of Presidential protection are evident:

Conduct of Secret Service agents in Fort Worth on November 22—In the early morning hours on November 22, 1963, in Fort Worth, there occurred a breach of discipline by some members of the Secret Service who were officially traveling with the President. After the President had retired at his hotel, nine agents who were off duty went to the nearby Fort Worth Press Club at midnight or slightly thereafter, expecting to obtain food, they had had little opportunity to eat during the day. No food was available at the Press Club. All of the agents stayed for a drink of beer, or in several cases, a mixed drink. According to their affidavits, the drinking in no case amounted to more than three glasses of beer or 1½ mixed drinks, and others who were present say that no agent was inebriated or acted improperly. The statements of the agents involved are supported by statements of members of the Fort Worth press who accompanied or observed them and by a Secret Service investigation.

According to their statements, the agents remained at the Press Club for periods varying from 30 minutes to an hour and a half, and the last agent left the Press Club by 2 a.m. Two of the nine agents returned to their rooms. The seven others proceeded to an establishment called the Cellar Coffee House, described by some as a beatnik place and by its manager as "a unique show place with continuous light entertainment all night [serving] only coffee, fruit juices, and no hard liquors or beer." There is no indication that any of the agents who visited the Cellar Coffee House had any intoxicating drink at that establishment. Most of the agents were there from about 1:30 or 1:45 a.m. to about 2:45 or 3 a.m. One agent was there from 2 until 5 a.m.

The lobby of the hotel and the areas adjacent to the quarters of the President were guarded during the night by members of the midnight to 8 a.m. shift of the White House detail. These agents were each relieved for a half hour break during the night. Three members of this shift separately took this opportunity to visit the Cellar Coffee House. Only one stayed as long as a half hour, and none had any beverage there. Chief Rowley testified that agents on duty in such a situation usually stay within the building during their relief, but that their visits to the Cellar were "neither consistent nor inconsistent with their duty."

Each of the agents who visited the Press Club or the Cellar Coffee House (apart from the three members of the midnight shift) had duty assignments beginning no later than 8 a.m. that morning. President Kennedy was scheduled to speak across the street from his hotel in Fort Worth at 8:30 a.m., and then at a breakfast, after which the entourage would proceed to Dallas. In Dallas, one of the nine agents was assigned to assist in security measures at Love Field, and four had protective assignments at the Trade Mart. The remaining four had key responsibilities as members of the complement of the follow-up car in the motorcade. Three of these agents occupied positions on the running boards of the car, and the fourth was seated in the car.

The supervisor of each of the off-duty agents who visited the Press Club or the Cellar Coffee House advised, in the course of the Secret Service investigation of these events, that each agent reported for duty on time, with full possession of his mental and physical capabilities and entirely ready for the performance of his assigned duties. Chief Rowley testified that, as a result of the investigation he ordered, he was satisfied that each of the agents performed his duties in an entirely satisfactory manner, and that their conduct the night before did not impede their actions on duty or in the slightest way prevent them from taking any action that might have averted the tragedy. However, Chief Rowley did not condone the action of the off-duty agents, particularly since it violated a regulation of the Secret Service, which strictly prohibits the use of liquor while on travel assignment status. The regulations provide further that "violation or slight disregard" of these provisions will be cause for removal from the Service.

Chief Rowley testified that under ordinary circumstances he would have taken disciplinary action against those agents who had been drinking in clear violation of the regulation. However, he felt that any disciplinary action might have given rise to an inference that the violation of the regulation had contributed to the tragic events of November 22. Since he was convinced that this was not the case, he believed that it would be unfair to the agents and their families to take explicit disciplinary measures. He felt that each agent recognized the seriousness of the infraction and that there was no danger of a repetition.

The Commission recognizes that the responsibilities of members of the White House detail of the Secret Service are arduous. They work long, hard hours, under very great strain, and must travel frequently. It might seem harsh to circumscribe their opportunities for relaxation. Yet their role of protecting the President is so important to the well being of the country that it is reasonable to expect them to meet very high standards of personal conduct, so that nothing can interfere with their bringing to their task the finest qualities and maximum resources of mind and body. This is the salutary goal to which the Secret Service regulation is directed, when it absolutely forbids drinking by any agent accompanying the President on a trip. Nor is this goal served when agents remain out until early morning hours, and lose the opportunity to get a reasonable amount of sleep. It is conceivable that those men who had little sleep, and who had consumed alcoholic beverages, even in limited quantities, might have been more alert in the Dallas motorcade if they had retired promptly in Fort Worth. However, there is no evidence that these men failed to take any action in Dallas within their power that would have averted the tragedy. As will be seen, the instantaneous and heroic response to the assassination by some of the agents concerned was in the finest tradition of Government service.

43.

LUKE POSSESSED A LANDSLIDE OF QUESTIONS.

Finally, some clarity was forming.

Repeat and recycle.

The best way to learn anything.

He read back over the COMMISSION file and knew exactly what it was. An excerpt from the Warren Commission Report.

Seven days after the assassination, Lyndon Johnson appointed six men to investigate the death of John Kennedy. A senator, three members of the House, a former CIA director, and a former president of the World Bank, all led by the chief justice of the United States, Earl Warren. They worked for the next ten months, listening to the testimony of 552 witnesses and amassing thirty-one hundred exhibits. In September 1964 they published an 888-page report that concluded Kennedy was assassinated by Lee Harvey Oswald and that Oswald acted entirely alone. It also concluded that Jack Ruby acted alone when he killed Oswald two days later. Far from quelling controversy, though, the commission's report had been a lightning rod for criticism.

Which had not abated in the ensuing decades.

His phone chimed. Marcia.

He welcomed the break.

"I've put together a biography for Ray Simmons. It's all public archive stuff, but it covers his FBI years pretty well. You should have it in your inbox now."

He checked. "It's here. You're the best, Marcia."

"Tell me something I don't know."

"A group of rhinoceroses is known as a crash."

"Is that true?"

"'Night, Marcia."

He disconnected, then opened the attached bio file and started reading about Simmons. From 1959 until 1964 he worked in the Dallas FBI field office. And, as Sue explained, he was a trained marksman and gunsmith. He also participated in firing tests on Oswald's rifle, conducted by the Warren Commission. No mention was made of the subsequent test conducted by CBS News. But that was understandable given it was a nongovernment action.

He had some answers.

But he also had new questions. Who was David Eckstein?

He clicked on the fifth file from the drive marked PERSONAL NOTES AS PROVIDED TO DE.

—Had an established reputation as a gunsmith, ballistic expert, and marksman.

—Test happened in 1967 at H. P. White Ballistics Laboratory in Maryland.

—H. P. was the largest independent weapons tester in the country. Had numerous indoor and outdoor ranges. Conducted controlled tests for firearms companies and law enforcement.

—Test conducted in basement range.

—Had a rifle there identical to Oswald's, equipped with a sling and four-power scope mounted slightly off center to the left.

—Idea was to ascertain if the make and model of rifle could fire three times within 5.6 seconds and strike the target.

—Familiar with the rifle. A true antique from World War II. Unwieldy. The bolt action stiff and hard to operate. Requires the user to slam the bolt hard with the heel of your hand in order to drive a shell into the chamber.

—CBS News sponsored the test. My name was suggested as I participated in the Warren Commission test firings of 1964. Three marksmen fired at a fixed, non-movable target. I was the only one of the three to actually fire off three shots, within 5.6 seconds. None of us scored more than two hits on the target.

—Oswald was no marksman, yet managed to fire three shots and score two direct hits. Idea to see if trained marksmen can duplicate that.

—Eleven marksmen were brought in. Three H. P. White employees, three Maryland state police officers, a ballistic technician, two sportsmen, an ex-paratrooper just back from Vietnam, and me. None of us were told beforehand what we were doing so we would not practice. None of us were paid.

—Test started in basement range. Three shots to a target 150 feet away. Lighting terrible, targets riddled with bullet holes. No way to tell if we hit. Told not to be concerned. This was just a quick, controlled practice.

—They built a mock-up of Dealey Plaza complete with a 60-foot tower to replicate Oswald's perch. Beneath stretched several hundred feet of railroad track down a slight grade similar to Elm Street. A small vehicle ran the rails with a silhouette target of a head and shoulders. Atop the perch was a plank that replicated the window sill Oswald used to rest the rifle. Quite a realistic test, all filmed by TV cameras.

—Difficult to make the shots in the few seconds allowed since once fired, the empty cartridge had to be manually ejected and a new round injected with a stiff bolt mechanism which caused the sights to lose the target, which had to be re-acquired.

—I was the only one of the eleven to hit the targeted head three times in 4.8 seconds, .8 of a second better than Oswald. Two others equaled Oswald's actions of two hits.

—Test showed the rifle could be fired quick and accurate.

—All of which gave credibility to the Warren Commissions lone-gunman finding and dispelled any other explanation.

steel~myth~barrel
depth~signature~language
computer~height~artisan
product~town~hat
news~chocolate~theory
Lancer

The notes were explainable—Simmons recounting his experiences—but the last part seemed out of place.

What was it?

He returned to the laptop and typed, finding an online complete text of the Warren Commission report. He opened the file to the report's index at the back. He found the *R*'s and scanned until he saw the entry.

Rowland, Thomas.

He scrolled back to the page indicated and found the relevant words in the report. Jillian was reading over his shoulder.

Incredible.

"Thomas Rowland was one of the agents, on the ground, in the motorcade," he said. "He was there. In Dallas. That day. Riding in the rear seat of the trail car."

He could see the same question form in her mind as it was in his.

Three of these agents occupied positions on the running boards of the car, and the fourth was seated in the car.

That's what the report had said about the agents who'd stayed out late the night before drinking.

Was the one seated in the car Rowland?

He worked the keyboard again to learn more about the murder weapon.

God bless the internet.

He recalled some, but not enough, as the Kennedy assassination had always held a fascination for him. The Oswald rifle was an Italian Fucile di Fanteria, an infantry weapon, Modello 91/38, manufactured at the Royal Arms Factory in Terni, Italy, sometime in 1940. The stamp of the royal crown and Terni, along with its serial number, had clearly identified it. A poorly made World War II surplus gun. Nothing state-of-the-art about it. It remained stored in a secure location within the National Archives and Records Administration Building in College Park, Maryland. The Warren Commission concluded that Kennedy was killed by a single bullet fired from that rifle. But other theories had blossomed through the years. The so-called grassy knoll shooter, the Badge Man, an individual wearing a police uniform and sporting a rifle, Umbrella Man, along with a hundred other possibilities. None of which had ever borne any fruit. Despite being repeatedly investigated by both the government and private individuals.

Was what Benji, Ray, and Eckstein were doing more of the same?

Something told him it wasn't.

"Thomas Rowland is not a reactionary," he said. "He's moving on this because it presents a clear and immediate threat. Why? I have no idea. But it's scaring the hell out of him."

"So what do we do?"

"We keep going."

She smiled. "I was hoping you were going to say that."

44.

WITH JILLIAN AT THE WHEEL, LUKE SPENT THE ENTIRETY OF THE six-hour drive west staring at the laptop screen and muttering to himself. Pigeon had been good about allowing them to keep the computer on a promise that it either be returned or replaced. She'd also offered them the use of the house for the night, opting to stay with a friend. Thankfully, they were not far from Dallas, Texas, and he'd decided, with Jillian agreeing, that a firsthand look was in order.

When they reached downtown he asked her to find the closest parking spot, which turned out to be an underground garage beside a castle-like redbrick building. The day was bright, warm, and dry. They walked west to a street shaded by massive oaks then stopped before a rectangular reflecting pool. Aligned down its center a trio of fountains rippled the water's surface. Aside from an elderly man in a Cowboys ball cap feeding the birds they were alone. It was Sunday, just after the church hour, and the business district around them was lightly traveled. They took seats on a low stone wall.

"I came here once, in high school," he said. "I pestered my dad until he brought me. I took so many pictures and asked so many questions, people were staring at us. On November 22, 1963, this whole area was packed with hundreds of people. It was unseasonably warm and sunny, a lot like today, but windy, coming from the west-southwest at twenty-two miles per hour."

They both stared out at Dealey Plaza.

"It's so small," Jillian said. "Compact. Like a choke point."

He'd been thinking the same thing. A perfect place to corral your target where the advantage was all with the shooter. Oswald had chosen his spot with care.

"Come on," he said. "Let's walk. It'll be easier to picture if we're standing on the spot."

They headed down the sidewalk toward the intersection of Houston and Main. At the corner they waited until the pedestrian signal changed to green then crossed, turning left into a triangular expanse of lush grass. He led Jillian to the other side and stopped at the curb.

"This is Elm Street. Do you see the painted white X out in the street? That's where Kennedy was fatally shot. They're scrupulous about maintaining it."

"A bit much, isn't it?"

"It's history. To our right is the corner of Houston and Elm. At the time, that tall brick building was the Texas School Book Depository. On the sixth floor, about sixty feet up, in the southeast corner window, Lee Harvey Oswald was waiting with his Italian-made bolt-action rifle. The time was 12:29 P.M."

"You know your stuff."

"On this subject I do. I read a lot about it over the years. It's still fascinating how it all happened."

Kennedy's motorcade drove down Houston Street traveling about fifteen miles per hour. Crowds were heavy, six deep from the curb. There were two cars in the procession. President Kennedy and First Lady Jackie were riding in the back seat of an open-top convertible. Forward of them sat Texas governor John Connally and his wife, Nellie. In the front seat were two Secret Service agents, Roy Kellerman on the passenger side and William Greer, driving. Flanking the limousine were two Dallas cops on motorcycles, James Chaney and Bobby Hargis. Six feet behind Kennedy's limousine was the trail car. According to the Warren Commission Report, nine men occupied it. Secret Service agents Emory Roberts, Samuel Kinney, John Ready, Clinton Hill, William McIntyre, Paul Landis, Glen Bennett, Thomas Rowland, and George Hickey. As they turned left onto Elm Street, the trail car fell behind a bit. It picked up speed and closed the gap and quickly resumed its designated distance to Kennedy's limousine. Both cars were now traveling at about eleven miles per hour. Kennedy's limousine then moved into Elm Street's center lane.

On the sixth floor of the Texas Book Depository, Lee Harvey Oswald was hunched over his rifle peering through the scope, watching as the vehicles made the turn onto Elm. Below, the Kennedys were waving to the people who'd come to watch the motorcade pass on its way to the Trade Mart, where the president was scheduled to speak. Sixty feet away on the grassy knoll, Abraham Zapruder, a clothing manufacturer, and his secretary Marilyn Sitzman, had also come to witness the motorcade. Zapruder was filming the event with his new camera, an 8mm Bell & Howell Model 414. Over the next few moments Zapruder would capture about twenty-six seconds, or 486 frames, of the actual assassination. Zapruder, who suffered from vertigo, was standing on a concrete plinth about four feet off the ground, his secretary steadying him.

When Kennedy's limousine was 265 feet from the book depository, Oswald fired his first shot. The bullet penetrated Kennedy's upper back and exited his throat. Instinctively Kennedy's hands came up to cover the wound. At this point no one realized he'd been shot.

But Jackie was startled.

She knew her husband was in distress.

According to the Warren Report, after the bullet exited Kennedy's neck, it punched through Governor Connally's seat, pierced his chest, came out the other side, and struck his wrist before embedding itself in his right thigh. This bullet was later found on Connally's gurney at Parkland Memorial Hospital.

Zapruder's camera captured the initial gunshot at around frame 180. Sensing something was wrong, Agent Greer, the driver, tapped the brakes. The limousine slowed. The trail car reacted accordingly. At the wheel Agent Roberts also braked, but harder.

The limousine lurched forward momentarily.

A few seconds later, at the now infamous Frame 313 of the

Zapruder film, a second gunshot was fired, slamming into the back of Kennedy's skull and blasting out of his forehead.

In the trail car Secret Service agent Clint Hill saw the second shot. He jumped off the running board and ran toward Kennedy's limousine, where Jackie had climbed onto the trunk. Some reports said she was trying to help Hill into the car. Others said she was trying to retrieve a chunk of her husband's skull ripped free by the second shot.

In the driver's seat Agent Greer now knew they'd come under fire. He punched the gas pedal. Instantly the limousine accelerated to fifteen miles per hour. Clint Hill, now sprinting, managed to mount the car's bumper. He threw himself atop Kennedy and Jackie, hoping to shield them from further gunfire. The president was slumped forward in his seat, already technically dead, Jackie's pink dress covered in his blood.

Horrified onlookers panicked and scattered. Dealey Plaza's layout made it a natural sound amplifier. Some bystanders, thinking the shots had come from the area of the grassy knoll, headed in that direction. Others simply scrambled for cover. Kennedy's limousine and the trail car accelerated toward the triple underpass at the bottom of Elm Street.

What happened next remains in dispute.

A third shot rang out.

Witness James Tague, a car salesman, who'd stopped to watch the motorcade, was standing five hundred feet from Oswald's perch, near an abutment at the triple underpass. He heard the gunshots but thought someone had let off firecrackers. The third shot missed Kennedy's limousine and ricocheted off the curb. Tague caught a fragment of the bullet in the cheek, only later realizing this had occurred.

It all happened in 5.6 seconds.

Inside the book depository, Oswald dropped his rifle and fled downstairs to the ground floor, making a hasty exit.

On Elm Street, Kennedy's motorcade raced past the triple underpass and sped toward Parkland Memorial Hospital, four *miles away. Five minutes later the motorcade reached the hospital. Kennedy and Governor Connally were rushed inside where emergency room doctors and nurses began working to save the president's life.*

But it was too late.

The second gunshot, the head wound, was catastrophic.

He was pronounced dead at 1:00 P.M.

Luke went silent.

After a few moments, Jillian whispered, "You do know this stuff."

"I cheated. Last night, while you slept, I called my boss and she connected me with an expert. He and I emailed back and forth. I supplied him the drawings, the audio recording, and the other notes we found.

"After Kennedy was pronounced dead at Parkland, his remains were quickly transported from Texas to Walter Reed Army Medical Center in DC aboard Air Force One. The president's death was obviously a murder. One that had taken place in Dallas County, Texas. An autopsy needed to be conducted there, in Texas, and the local county coroner's office had jurisdiction. At that time the killing of a president was not a federal crime, so the FBI had no involvement. It was a Texas murder. We know from the audio that the examining room was equipped with a recording device. Not unusual as medical examiners record what they're doing. Secret Service agents forcibly took custody of Kennedy's remains. They were placed in a casket, draped in an American flag, driven to Love Field, and loaded aboard Air Force One. I was told last night that once the body was on Air Force One the Secret Service wanted to leave immediately. They were afraid the medical examiner would show up with police and retake the body. But Lyndon Johnson would not let them leave. He wanted to be sworn in before the plane took off. It was an hour and fifteen minutes before a judge arrived to administer the oath. Then the plane left. No Texas autopsy ever occurred."

He handed Jillian the two diagrams labeled VARIABLES AND DISCREPANCIES, along with the drawing they'd found secreted in Benji's nightstand lamp.

"See those tiny geometric symbols, the square, the triangle," he said. "Look closely at the crosshairs on the diagrams."

Jillian did so. "They're the same symbols on both pages. How did we miss that?"

"Information overload. Plus, it's the way Ray and Benji designed it. Compartmentalization. Without having everything in hand the chances of recognizing the pattern were slim. It's textbook intelligence practice. Now place the diagrams atop one another, then put Benji's drawing on top, but rotate it ninety degrees left."

She followed his directions.

"Now hold the stack up to the sun and align the crosshairs with the geometric symbols."

Jillian gasped. "This is—"

He nodded.

"Dealey Plaza. Right where we're standing."

45.

LUKE POINTED AT THE COMBINED DRAWINGS. "I WORKED A LOT OF this out with the expert last night. He was a wealth of information and managed to electronically merge the three images we have into one."

He showed her on his phone.

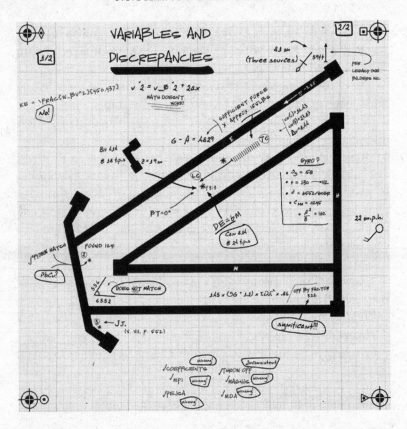

"You see the letters *E*, *M*, and *H* inside the black bars? They represent Elm, Houston, and Main Street. See the Gr -3.15°? That's the grade from Elm Street down to the triple underpass. Minus three point one five degrees. You would need to know that if you want accurate calculations. Add to that the scribbled figures, 22 m.p.h., 59 ft., 81, BH 414, and the rest. That would be the wind speed that day, the height of Oswald's perch, his distance to the motorcade in meters, and Zapruder's camera. A Bell & Howell Zoomatic Director Series Model 414. Check out the tiny stick figure below the 81. You know what that is."

She nodded. "The icon for heavy weapon. But the symbol's not quite right, though."

"I agree. Check out the JT-3 dot near the underpass abutment. That's where James Tague was struck by the third shot ricochet. The Z=19 on the grassy knoll stands for Zapruder's position and distance from Kennedy at the time of the shooting. The F313 in the middle of Elm Street is Frame 313, the moment the kill shot was recorded. That's the white X in the pavement out there." He pointed to the street. "Like I said, that expert was a wealth of knowledge. He told me all this."

"So Ray and Benji were reconstructing President Kennedy's assassination?"

"It certainly seems that way. Along with our mysterious David Eckstein."

He pointed at the phone. "There's a notation, DE=6M, at edge of Elm Street. David Eckstein? Apparently, Eckstein filmed the shooting with a better camera than Zapruder's. He used a Canon 814. We know this from Simmons's notes. I checked. It had a higher frame rate, sharper resolution, zoom, and built-in slow-motion capability."

"So why has no one ever heard of him? That movie would've been sensational."

"The guy I talked to last night told me that, for decades, there's been an urban legend that someone else filmed the assassination, then vanished. The Warren Commission looked. So did the FBI and every conspiratorialist since. But no one was ever found. I'd bet good money that was our DE. There's a problem with that, though. The Canon 814 didn't go on sale until 1967, four years after the assassination."

"That seems a serious inconsistency."

He agreed. "The expert last night pointed out another detail from the Warren Report. A guy named James Dalton was standing about three hundred feet south of the book depository at the corner of Houston and Main. He testified that in the moments following the shooting he watched a man carrying a backpack, running south away from Elm. He crossed Main, then Commerce, to the Union Station parking lot, where he gets into a red Chevrolet Corvair or

Oldsmobile Jetfire and 'tears out like he's late for his own wedding.' The driver was never identified and the tidbit forgotten, just another of a thousand other dead-end leads. There were a lot of frame cameras, plenty, in fact, but none caught the actual shooting. As for movie cameras, only Zapruder. Officially, that is."

He led her across the street, toward the center of the plaza, to the point on the drawing labeled DE6. Traffic remained light and he noticed no one nor anything of concern. "This is where David Eckstein was supposedly standing."

He pointed at the X in the middle of the road.

Not all that far away. Maybe thirty feet.

"What's the calculation below DE's position?" she asked.

"I'm told it's a spin drift equation," he said, referring to how much a bullet drifted according to its weight and barrel rifling. "The expert told me that, according to this, the details are damn compelling."

At first, the expert had been a little aggravated, woken in the middle of the night, sent a bunch of strange drawings, and asked to make sense of nonsense. How many theories had been spit out about how and why John Kennedy died? It seemed a conspiracy that just kept on giving. Never ending. But an hour after receiving everything, the guy had sung a different tune.

Which seemed significant.

He explained to Jillian that the two equations in the upper left-hand corner were for ballistic kinetic energy and muzzle velocity. A bullet's destructive power and how fast it left the muzzle. At the bottom of the diagram was a list of words. *Magnus, MOA, Throw off, MPI, Pejsa.* All ballistic terms noted as wrong.

"*Now focus on Elm Street,*" the expert said. "*Where the actual assassination happened. The black dots numbered 1 and 2 are the shots that strike Kennedy, first in the upper back and then in the head. To the right of those dots are three more equations. They represent how fast the motorcade was traveling at the time and their change in speed after Oswald opened fire.*"

204

"You really know this stuff."

"I've studied it for decades. I'm the FBI's Kennedy assassination person. Every crackpot theory that surfaces nearly every year, I evaluate it. It's not all that known, but the murder remains, to this day, an open investigation."

That he had not known.

"And here's where it got really interesting," he said to Jillian.

"This diagram is fascinating," the expert said. *"It was prepared by people who knew what they were doing. Look at the upper edge of Elm Street. That formula, the one that starts with G, is a measurement of deceleration and gravity. This is the moment the trail car behind Kennedy's car brakes hard. The equation gauges the effect on the occupants of the car. Then go down the street to the note, BT=0°."*

He found it on the drawing.

"That stands for Bullet Trajectory Zero Degrees. Meaning the shooter is in a straight line with his target. Now trace your finger down to the underpass to that angle symbol. See the no? This is another place the math does not match."

"How do you know that?"

"Because whoever created this drawing has the physical evidence to back it up."

"Which is?"

"Straddling that angle symbol are two numbers, 6552 and 556. Put a decimal in the right places and drop in a multiplication sign and they turn into 6.5x52 and 5.56. The first number is the caliber of Oswald's Carcano rifle. The second number is the nomenclature for ammunition used by a Colt AR-15. Above the 556 there's a black dot labeled 2. This is where a bullet fragment from Kennedy's kill shot ended up. There's a notation to the left of the black number 2 dot. PbCu. Those are chemical symbols for lead and copper, the primary makeup of an AR-15 round. Now stick with me. Go back to the asterisk in the middle of Elm Street. That's the second shot's point of origin. The one that took off the top of Kennedy's skull. According to this diagram it didn't

come from the book depository. It came from ground level. From the Secret Service trail car."

Jillian stared at him as he recounted what the expert had told him. And he saw she understood.

"Someone in that trail car may have shot President Kennedy."

46.

LUKE HEARD HIMSELF SAY WHAT HE'D ALREADY CONCLUDED FROM talking to the expert. Of course, he hadn't told the guy any of what was happening. He and Stephanie had decided to keep those details to themselves for now, respecting Rowland's reach within the government, which surely extended to the FBI.

He pointed. "Kennedy's motorcade makes the turn onto Elm. A few seconds later Oswald fires his first shot. The bullet hits the president in the upper back. The lead car brakes. So does the trail car, but the driver stomped on the pedal. That detail is in the Warren Report. The force of the deceleration shoved the car's passengers, one of them an armed Secret Service agent, forward. It's momentary, but enough. In the back seat an agent, crouched high because he's the only one armed with a rifle, falls forward. The barrel of the weapon drops, comes level with Kennedy's limousine, the trigger is accidentally pulled, and the bullet strikes Kennedy in the back of the head."

He kept motioning, re-creating in his mind what could have happened that day, directing Jillian's attention to the street.

"At roughly the same moment that happens Oswald lets off

his second shot, but misses. Now Agent Clint Hill is off his running board and sprinting toward Kennedy's limousine, which is surging forward. Oswald cycles the rifle's bolt and fires his third and final shot. Another miss. The bullet goes downrange, strikes the curb near the abutment, and grazes James Tague. Oswald tries for a fourth shot, but it's too late. The motorcade has disappeared beneath the underpass. Over there."

"So what's his name, this agent with the rifle?"

"Go back to the diagram," the expert said. "Read what's next to the deceleration formula."

He did. Sufficient force. X. Approx 155 lbs.

"That says the braking of the trail car was enough to throw forward a 155-pound man."

So he wanted to know. "Which agents exactly were in that trail car? Who carried the rifle?"

"Jack Ready was on the passenger-side running board directly opposite Clint Hill. In still images he's clearly visible as the limousine heads toward the underpass. So we know exactly what Hill was doing. Emory Roberts was in the trail car's front passenger seat and never moves. Agents Kinney and Landis? Multiple photographs show them pinned to their seats. Same with Powers and O'Donnell, the president's assistants. It was either Hickey—"

"Or the ninth man."

"Correct."

"Thomas Rowland," he said.

"But wouldn't the other agents in the trail car have known if that rifle fired?"

"I asked the same thing and was told that it could have fired and no one in that car knew. Maybe Oswald's third shot and the AR's shot overlapped. An AR-15 round would've crossed the gap to Kennedy's limousine in a tenth of what it takes to blink your eye. Maybe the acoustics distorted the reports. That rifle would have shown no muzzle flash in broad daylight, and in the chaos of the moment all sound would have blurred together. Of course, it is possible those agents knew and were ordered to keep their mouths shut. Imagine the fallout if it's revealed the Secret Service accidentally killed the president. Only three agents were called to testify before the Warren Commission. I learned last night that they were Kellerman and Greer from the lead car and Hill from the trail car. No one else was put under oath."

Which was either suspicious, or another example of the commission's sloppy work. The guy last night had rattled off a whole list of things the commission failed to fully investigate. Was there a cover-up? A rush to judgment that a single bullet from a single assassin did all the damage? Over the past sixty years the Warren Commission's findings had been dissected and reassembled so often it had become a Frankenstein's monster. Not dead, nor alive, but something obscenely in between. But that was not the entirety of the evidence.

There was the audio Simmons preserved.

There's been an accident, not a murder, so the law can be waived.

An odd choice of words.

Was it the pressure of the moment? A slip of the tongue? Or just a lie told to justify the taking of the body?

He stared around at Dealey Plaza.

Traffic was picking up as Dallas adjusted to a Sunday morning. No one was shooting or chasing them, but danger was out there. They were solidly on Thomas Rowland's radar. What about Talley? Had the former Delta soldier truly switched mental gears? *Target up, target down.* That was how effective operators thought. Yet whose side was Talley on? He'd killed Persik and his men, then let Luke and Jillian go. But, after that, he'd pursued them into the bayou and burned Ray Simmons's house to the ground. What in the world was happening here?

Now that Luke had finally verbalized the assassination scenario over which his brain had been mulling, the sights and sounds of November 22, 1963, were stuck on a memory loop. He could see in vivid detail Frame 313 of the Zapruder film when Kennedy's head snapped back. Jackie in her pink dress. Blood and brains exploding.

Horrible.

Two gunshots? Three? Four?

One gun? Two?

He couldn't let this end here.

No way.

You might screw up. You might even fail. But never, ever quit.

His drill sergeant on the first day of Ranger school.

It'd taken every shred of evidence they'd so far uncovered to assemble what was largely a circumstantial scenario. A theory. This wasn't the kind of case you dropped on a U.S. attorney's desk with a Post-it note attached to prosecute. Something like this might even be outside the Magellan Billet's sphere of influence. It could also be an inescapable black hole. One that had consumed Ray Simmons and Benjamin Stein.

He steered his mind back on track.

One foot in front of the other, a step at a time.

More good advice.

"We have one play left on the board," he said.

"I know. Let's find David Eckstein."

47.

ROWLAND HAD NEVER BEEN A RELIGIOUS MAN. NO PASTORS OR priests. No churches, mosques, or synagogues. So Sundays had always been just another day of the week. Nothing special. Not even a day of rest. Just business as usual. Today, he was extra apprehensive. A lot was happening.

But at least he had things under control.

In the months before Benjamin Stein was eliminated there'd only been a few emails, all asking for the same thing. Instead of replying he'd bided his time, then silenced Stein permanently when the time was right. Ray Simmons? Conveniently, Simmons had taken care of himself. Which had been appreciated. That first email had been a shocker. It had been a long time since this subject had been broached. A long time since the Warren Commission submitted its report. Three other subsequent government investigations agreed with the conclusion that two shots struck Kennedy *from the rear*. But the 1978–79 House Select Committee on Assassinations boldly determined that Oswald assassinated Kennedy, *most likely as the result of a conspiracy*.

Whatever that meant.

Its evidence had been shaky. The committee concluded that Oswald fired shots one, two, and four, and that an unknown assassin fired shot number three, but missed, from a point above and to Kennedy's right front, on the famed grassy knoll. All of that had been based on supposed newly examined acoustical evidence. But was it trustworthy? Nobody knew. And nobody took the findings seriously. He'd been grateful, though, as the whole thing had deferred attention onto mysterious unknown others. On the grassy knoll. Which had become a euphemism for *who the hell knows*.

Dammit. It all should be forgotten.

But it wasn't.

People would not let it go.

Dear Mr. Rowland,

We are in the process of writing a book on the death of President John F. Kennedy. Our thesis is that the bullet that struck the president in the head was not fired by Lee Harvey Oswald. Rather, we believe, the bullet came from the AR-15 rifle in the Secret Service follow-up car. It is our belief that the rifle was accidentally fired by you when you leveled the weapon in response to Oswald's shots and fell backwards.

Our thesis is based on a sifting of the available ballistic, medical, and other evidence. It is premised, among other things, on our contention that the behavior of the bullet in the president's skull was much more consistent with that of a bullet fired from an AR-15 rifle than from a Mannlicher-Carcano rifle such as the one used by Oswald, and on an analysis of the trajectory of the bullet, as well as on a number of other factors.

I want to emphasize that we are by no means accusing you of any wrongdoing. The shot was a tragic accident and President Kennedy may well have died from one of the shots fired by Oswald, even if the bullet in question had not hit the president in the head.

It is important that we speak on this subject. We recognize, for obvious reasons, that you have never done such in the past. We would gladly make any and all arrangements, at our expense, to speak with you. We would also record that interview and provide you with a copy of the recording.

Any information in any form that you are willing and able to provide that would shed light one way or the other on the validity of our thesis would be appreciated. Please know that we will carefully consider anything you have to say.

The assassination of John F. Kennedy has never been a happy subject, but it has remained a lively subject. The liveliness has been increased with the release of countless books, movies, and television shows. The world has been racked by numerous conspiracy theories. We have compiled a book that may, at long last, lead to the truth of what happened in Dallas and to the extinction of so many false accusations and conspiracies. Since your actions are an integral part of our thesis, we would not be

comfortable going to press without making a determined
effort to hear what you have to say. You may contact me
directly at the above email.

The email had been sent to his office a few weeks ago by Stein
and Simmons, forwarded on by one of his assistants.

Through the decades his quest for anonymity had been aided by
so many conspiratorialists. A supposed sniper behind the stockade
fence on the grassy knoll. The Umbrella Man in the black trench
coat who shot Kennedy with a super-secret spy pistol. Cuban
exiles, who killed him out of revenge for the Bay of Pigs. The mob,
who shot him for a double cross by his father Joseph Kennedy
or because some godfather didn't want to share Marilyn Monroe.
Lyndon Johnson, who put out a hit because he wanted to be
president.

Take your pick.

But there's a problem with digging up the past. Sometimes you
find ghosts who aren't so happy about being disturbed.

Like him.

He'd hired a private investigative firm to look into both
Benjamin Stein and Ray Simmons. He'd not used his own
people since he did not want to stir anyone's curiosity. It was
important he remained aloof, strong, and unaffected to each
and every one of them. He'd thought about trying to reason
with Simmons and Stein. Or buy them off? Or threaten them
with legal action. But the pair had already decided confrontation
was the best course, no matter how much of a sugarcoating
they'd applied. That course was obviously fortified by evidence.
They would be asking him questions to which they already had
answers.

And that was never a good thing.

Thankfully, he had one factor working in his favor.

The rationalizations people made when they believed themselves in charge.

That everything was in their favor and all would be right.

Now both Stein and Simmons were dead. Simmons's house burned to ashes. No word yet as to whether Daniels and Stein's granddaughter were dead. But Talley had assured him that would happen. Everything was winding down. Finally. Soon, there would be nothing left for Stephanie Nelle to find.

Except for one thing.

David Eckstein.

Patience, he told himself.

That problem too shall pass.

48.

LUKE LED THE WAY AS THEY ENTERED THE ADOLPHUS HOTEL, A downtown Dallas landmark. Incredibly, there was a room available, one of their deluxe, with plush, pillow-top mattresses, an oversized desk, and, most important, high-speed WiFi. Rich leather and wood accents and a spa-like bathroom with marble and a rainfall shower suggested the promise of a few hours of comfort and rest. They both showered and cleaned up, donning the hotel's signature robes, then ordered room service for a late lunch, or early dinner depending on how you kept time.

"I get that this is now your job," she said to him. "But I want Rowland for my own reasons."

"And I get that too."

"You do realize," she said, "all we have is a hunch that this Eckstein might have been there that day, might have filmed what happened, and might live in the mountains somewhere."

"Where it snows a lot," he added.

"We don't even know if he's in the United States."

"He is," Luke said. "Or in Canada."

"What makes you so sure?"

He powered up the laptop and inserted the flash drive, reading again what Ray Simmons had written. *I'm thinking about trekking up there again, but I'm getting too damn old for mountains and horses and snow.* "That's not the language you use if you're talking about overseas. Maybe Canada. But I doubt it. To Ray, *up* meant north of Louisiana."

"I can buy that," she said. "But it still doesn't get us any closer. Obviously, Ray knew where to go, but he didn't write it down on anything we're privy to."

A knock at the door signaled their food had arrived.

They enjoyed the offerings and decided a little sleep would be great. He was especially tired, as he'd been awake most of the previous night dealing with the FBI's expert. The man was on standby, awaiting more information.

As the guy said, *You definitely intrigued me.*

Luke woke and immediately checked the bedside clock.

8:45 P.M.

He'd been out almost three hours.

Jillian was awake, planted in front of the laptop. "That stuff at the end of Simmons's notes has been nagging at me."

He recalled the five lines.

steel~myth~barrel
depth~signature~language
computer~height~artisan
product~town~hat
news~chocolate~theory

"They're similar to the email addresses," he said, "separated by tildes."

"I'm impressed you know the symbol's name."

"I'm not completely stupid."

She smiled. "The email addresses with ~sun~river. Our supposition was that Benji and Ray were using them as a coded contact system. That means one of them had to set it up. I have access to Benji's iCloud account so I checked. He was a subscriber to an app called Find3Points. It's owned by a company that specializes in geotech surveys. Satellite stuff. Apparently Find3Points was a lark, something the founders thought would be cool to try. It divides the earth into five-foot by five-foot grids. Every grid gets a specific, randomly generated, three-word identifier separated by a tilde sign. For example, this room might be labeled FISH~CHURCH~EDITOR."

"Like the email addresses."

She nodded. "I have no idea if Simmons was a subscriber, but he specifically left those five lines of words, all separated by tildes. That can't be coincidence."

"So let me ask the $64,000 question. Did you run those five lines through the app?"

"I bought it half an hour ago."

"And what did they reveal?"

"All five are within a three-mile radius of one another in the northwest corner of Wyoming. A remote location."

"Seems par for this course."

She turned from the laptop. "We can head there in the morning. I'm assuming, with all your connections, you can get us there fast."

"I'll see what I can do."

"Maybe this David Eckstein can fill in the blanks," she said. "I would sure like to know what Benji had to die for."

They both still wore the hotel's terry-cloth robes. His belly was full, he was reasonably rested from the nap, and it looked like they knew where to head next.

Good thing.

As it was all they had.

STEVE BERRY AND GRANT BLACKWOOD

"I have been noticing something else, also," she said.

He was all ears.

"Where'd the good little Boy Scout come from?"

He was puzzled.

"The Ranger I knew in Hawaii would have already made a move on me. But this new-and-improved Luke Daniels. He's like a perfect gentleman. A monk in a cave."

"You just lost your grandfather."

"I did. And I appreciate the respect you've shown." She paused and tossed him a grin. "But enough is enough."

He wondered if either of them had the bandwidth to go there at the moment. Maybe once all this was over? But he was also never one to walk away from an offered opportunity. Why would he?

Besides, they were both grown adults.

So he smiled and said, "What did you have in mind?"

49.

Cody, Wyoming
Monday — March 30 — 10:15 a.m.

Luke buttoned his coat and steadied himself against a stiff north wind. They were on the final leg of an eighteen-hundred-mile journey northwest from Dallas. Stephanie had arranged for another DOJ jet and a Ford F-150 pickup waiting on the ground when they landed. They had what they believed to be valid Find3Points, but for all five grid locations Google Earth imagery showed nothing but ragged peaks, thick pine forests, and plunging, glacier-carved valleys. An internet check of the area revealed zero hits on the name David Eckstein. Nothing in the local property records either, which were all online.

Lingering in the back of his mind was the possibility they were on a wild goose chase. But Ray Simmons had left those locators for a reason. He could have just as easily taken them to his grave. While they matched the LEAD~SEA~PROFIT format and were mountainous and remote, which Ray mentioned in his notes, thousands of places fit that description. But it was all they had to work with and it was better than sitting on their hands and waiting for Talley to come find them.

At Cody they'd stopped at an outfitter's shop and bought hiking boots, jackets, backpacks, multiple layers of clothing, dehydrated meals, a trail stove, fire-making tools, a GPS unit, compasses and maps, headlamps, knives and hatchets, a tent, a pair of sleeping bags, flashlights, a first-aid kit, and extra ammunition for the Berettas.

Everything they might need.

The only thing the outfitter couldn't offer them was a solution for their biggest challenge. Access. While Highway 14, the only paved and reliable road in this part of Wyoming, eventually reached Yellowstone National Park, where he and Jillian were headed there wasn't so much as a gravel tract within three thousand square miles.

They needed horses.

According to the outfitter their best option for that was a Shoshone rancher named Hedow who lived near Wapiti, home to 165 people, a post office, and the oldest forest service ranger station in the United States. It'd be their last bit of civilization between Highway 14 and Highway 26 some eighty miles to the south.

"The snow is starting," Jillian said, peering through the truck's windshield.

"Coming in fast, too. Some of those peaks out there sit at around twelve thousand feet. It's only a few months a year their tops aren't white."

When they'd left Cody the temperature had been twenty-three degrees. The air now trickling through the F-150's dysfunctional air vents felt much colder than that. The laptop, flash drive, and other papers were safely tucked within a waterproof backpack lying on the truck's rear seat.

His phone, which Jillian held, dinged.

"The address is coming up," she said. "I'm amazed we still have coverage."

"Let's enjoy it while we can."

"Turn right here."

He turned off and followed the dirt road half a mile to a clearing surrounded by a meadow and backed by dun-colored hills. Standing on the front step of a long, ranch-style log house was a tall bearded man wearing a red parka and beanie in bright hunter's orange. Luke stopped the truck and shut off the engine.

They climbed out.

"Are you Luke and Jillian?" he called out.

The outfitter in Cody had promised to let Hedow know they were coming.

"That'd be us," Luke said, extending his hand.

"Kinda surprised to get Owen's call. It's a little early in the season for backcountry camping. You two know what you're doing? Lot of bears out there."

"We won't bother 'em," he said.

"You got experience at this sorta thing?"

"He was a Ranger," Jillian said. "I was a marine."

"Last time I checked neither of those were real big on horses. How far are you going?"

"Due south, fifteen or twenty miles," Jillian said.

"No offense meant, but I'd hate to lose a couple good animals because, you know—"

"A pair of idiots who've got no business being out here stepped off a mountainside?" Luke said.

"Your words. Like I said, no offense."

"None taken. I get your point."

If the only hurdles before them were terrain and weather Luke would have no trouble promising the safe return of the horses, but he had no idea what awaited them. While they'd seen no trace of Talley and his men since Louisiana, he took nothing for granted.

"I'll give you a telephone number," he said. "If we don't bring those horses back, call it and the woman who answers will make good."

Of course, if they didn't come back it was probably because they were dead, which he did not like to think about it.

"Who is she?"

"She works for the U.S. Justice Department, as do I."

"You some kind of agent?"

"Some kind of," he said.

"This official business?"

He nodded.

Hedow hesitated, taking stock of them, then said, "Okay."

Bargain struck, Hedow led them behind the house to a barn. Inside, tucked into individual stalls, were half a dozen horses. At the sight of Hedow they all began neighing and bobbing their heads.

"You've got fans," Jillian said.

"It's just me and them here. They're good company. You wanna pick or should I?"

"We're in your hands."

Hedow chose a couple of mares, both sorrels, named Peggy and Bluebell.

"Bluebell," Jillian said. "That's adorable. She's definitely yours, Luke."

He stroked the horse's forelock. "How about I call her Blue? Or Bell?"

Hedow replied. "She hates that. She'll buck you off."

Of course she would.

"They're both mild, are good at finding easy routes, and will let you know if there's somethin' dangerous around." Hedow checked his watch. "If you don't wanna wait till morning, we should get moving."

219

* * *

Hedow hitched the trailer to his truck and loaded the horses aboard. With Luke and Jillian following in the F-150, Hedow headed west on Highway 14 for a few miles before pulling into a paved parking lot. A square brown-and-yellow sign on a stacked stone plinth read WAPITI ROADSIDE. Hedow waved for them to ease alongside his truck.

"Normally you'd fill out your backcountry slip and drop it in the box here. It's how people know you're out there. But it looks like there's someone at the Wapiti Ranger Station at the bottom of the driveway. It's a historical landmark. They're doing some preservation work on it. I know all the rangers, so I'll unhitch the trailer here and get the horses saddled. You can drive down, tell them—"

"Is that necessary?" Luke asked.

"Afraid so. I catch hell if I send anybody out there without paperwork. Last year a couple wandered around, got caught in a storm, and died. Nobody knew they'd gone, so nobody knew to look for them."

"We'd prefer anonymity," he said. "We're not amateurs."

"And I'd prefer to keep my guide license. Listen, there's nothing to it. Go down there and tell the ranger you're headed out. How long do you expect to be?"

"How long to cover eighteen miles?" he asked.

"Count on a full day. When you get back, phone me and I'll drive over."

They spent a few minutes picking Hedow's brain on the easiest routes into the backcountry, then helped him unhitch the trailer and prep Peggy and Bluebell, noting their food and water schedules and tucking some feed into their saddlebags. With a wave out his window, Hedow pulled back onto the highway and drove away.

He and Jillian followed the driveway down to the old ranger station. A green pickup truck bearing the USDA Forest Service crest was parked near the station's porch. The building was wooden, brick red, and surrounded by a split-rail fence and lodgepole pines. They mounted the front steps to the half-glass front door. Inside waited a uniformed ranger who said, "Afternoon, folks, come on in. I saw the horse trailer. You heading in-country?"

"As soon as we can," he said. "We're running out of daylight."

"Let's get your paperwork done so you can get outta here. Just the two of you?"

"Correct," Jillian said.

He almost asked a question of his own. *Do you know a David Eckstein?* But decided that would be telegraphing way too much, especially if this guy alerted Eckstein they were coming.

So he kept silent.

The ranger asked, "Are either of you armed?"

"We are," he said. "Two Berettas. Is that a problem?"

"Not at all," the ranger said. "You'd be fools to go up there without a gun. Just a question we gotta ask."

50.

LUKE FOLLOWED HEDOW'S ADVICE AND THEY RODE SOUTH ALONG Green Creek until it emptied into a string of turquoise-green lakes, then up a snow-covered draw to Wapiti Ridge. On the far slope they found Hedow's recommendation for a camping spot, a horseshoe-shaped ravine whose entrance was partially blocked by stunted white pines and bisected by a gurgling creek that had yet to freeze. The weather report indicated that the temperature was expected to drop below zero after nightfall accompanied by heavy gusts. The ravine would provide good shelter for them and the horses. Judging by the rock-ring firepit and stump stools others had camped here too. Surrounding the ravine were brown, scree-covered slopes and crenellated ridges pockmarked by snow. By the time they'd erected the tent the sun was dipping below the peak of what their map called Citadel Mountain.

"Fire or no fire?" Jillian asked.

"Compromise. We'll use the trail stove."

She set up the stove, a truncated cone of stainless steel on fold-out legs into which she fed twigs and sticks. Soon flames were shooting out the top. Luke broke out the cook pot, filled it with snow, and set it to boil. Dinner was beef stroganoff, all the outfit-ter earlier had in hand. Dessert was two mugs of heavily sugared coffee, then they made sure the horses were settled in before retreating to their sleeping bags. Luke lit the candle lantern and hung it from the tent's roof hook. Outside, the wind was picking up. Snow crystals peppered the tent's nylon wall.

"Talley's coming here, isn't he?" she said.

"It's hard to say, but I'm betting Rowland knows about David Eckstein. He seems to know a lot about a lot."

And had apparently rubbed Stephanie Nelle the wrong way. That woman was the measure of calm. Never raising her voice. Never angry. Only matter-of-fact. She was the epitome of never let them see you sweat. Yet something about Thomas Rowland got under her skin.

"I want him," she said. *"Find whatever it is he doesn't want us to find."*

"You owe him one?" he asked.

"More than one. And I always pay my debts."

That he did not doubt.

Hence why he was out in, literally, the middle of nowhere, in the freezing cold. But there was no place he'd rather be. He also realized that they'd left a trail. No way not to. Talley could find his way to Hedow, or some other local, who would lead him to the ranger station, which would verify they were here. Could Talley have already been here? Had Hedow been offered money to set them up?

Possible.

But not likely.

Hedow had not seemed the type to sell out for a few dollars.

But if that was the case, then this whole thing was a trap and David Eckstein was probably already dead.

Luke slept amazingly soundly, he and Jillian alternating standing guard. They skipped breakfast, settling instead for two mugs of sugary coffee. After making sure the horses were fed and watered they set out, keeping a compass bearing on Battlement Mountain. They stuck to the valley bottoms when they could and the gentler slopes where they couldn't. Around noon their GPS unit said they were a mile from the nearest grid location. They found steel~myth~barrel on the side of a sheer cliff. The second location, depth~signature~language, was a mile farther up a barren scree field.

Soon the mountains grew taller and steeper. The valley narrowed until the creek they'd been following turned into a frothing torrent. They kept the reins on their horses loose, confident the animals knew best how to navigate the treacherous trail. Steadily the rock walls closed in around them. The sun dimmed behind the peaks, leaving them in a midday near-twilight. The temperature dropped a solid twenty degrees. Around 3:00 P.M. they crossed a creek that Luke's map labeled ISHAWOOA into a meadow of sprouting grass and patchy snow. On the west side of the meadow he spotted a steep, V-shaped ravine. In the distance they could see structures straddling the creek and rising up the sides of the ravine, corresponding with computer~height~artisan on the app.

"Has to be an old mining camp," he said. "The map shows several scattered around this area. They found gold here in 1842 and the rush lasted until just a few decades back."

"How in the world—"

"There's an infographic on our map. According to the GPS the product~town~hat locator is halfway between us and that camp. The final locator is about a mile to the southeast."

"They made this difficult," she said.

He studied the rugged terrain. "I'm hoping for a good reason."

"For all we know Eckstein is watching us right now."

"I would be, if I were him."

They kept going and soon entered another zigzag valley barely ten feet across. The wind rose, peppering their faces with bits of scree. Heads down and collars up they kept going. Another half an hour brought them to a meadow from whose center rose a teardrop-shaped copse of pines that climbed partway up the western slope.

Luke checked their GPS. "Officially, we're here. The news~chocolate~theory locator sits dead center in those trees."

But there were no cabins or structures.

Only one thing caught his eye. "Past the trees, at the base of that slope. You see it?"

"I do. That's a trail. No doubt about it. Looks like it disappears into the trees."

"It's the closest thing to man-made we have in sight and the coordinates are right. Might as well check it out."

They picked their way through the trees to the far side and dismounted at the trailhead, which was straddled by a pair of hulking boulders. The horses were tethered to nearby saplings.

He started toward the trail.

Then he heard the distinctive sound of a rifle being cocked.

"You two lost?" a male voice called out from the trees.

"We're here on behalf of Benjamin Stein and Ray Simmons," Jillian said.

"Never heard of them."

"They knew you. I was Benji's granddaughter."

"*Was?*"

"He's dead. So is Simmons," Luke said.

Movement came about fifty feet ahead of them and a man appeared, standing just outside the copse. Thin, short, dressed in a sheepskin jacket and cowboy hat. And old. The face weathered and pockmarked, full creases and crevices. The hair was shoulder-length and silver, not gray, a scruffy beard and mustache dusting the cheeks and neck. Spindly hands cradled a .45-70 lever-action rifle. The old man shifted its aim so the muzzle was pointing right at them, finger on the trigger.

Which Luke had the greatest respect for.

No chance to get a jump on him.

"What happened to them?" the old man asked.

"Simmons killed himself," Luke said. "Benji was murdered by Thomas Rowland."

He watched for a reaction.

But none came.

"You're David Eckstein," Jillian tried. "We know what's going on and we need your help."

"You say you're Stein's granddaughter." The old man motioned with the rifle at Luke. "Who's he?"

"A friend. Here to help."

"That's some friend to come all the way up here in this cold. You realize I can shoot you both right now and no one will ever find your bodies."

"Oh, we get that message loud and clear," Luke said. "But if you do that, Thomas Rowland will win and you'll soon be dead."

"How do you figure?"

"There are folks coming here for you."

"Rowland has no idea I exist."

Finally, an admission. "How do you know that?"

"I just do. Only Ray and Benji knew me. That was done on purpose. So I've done just fine, for a long time. Without you."

Eckstein stayed silent, but kept the rifle aimed. Luke imagined the quandary. Was this friend or foe? Truth or lie? Impossible to know.

So he tried, "Lancer."

Recalling the word from Simmons's notes.

It had to be important.

"Where'd you get that?" Eckstein asked.

"Simmons left it. What does it mean?"

The old man tossed him an annoyed look. "It means that I don't have to shoot you. Follow me, and bring your mounts."

He nodded.

"Lead the way."

51.

Talley stared down at the Wapiti Ranger Station.

They'd landed an hour ago in Cody after a charter flight from Louisiana. Two of his team were already here, making the proper arrangements, which had included securing two helicopters that would suit their needs.

"Put us down, right on the highway," he ordered over his headset.

He glanced back out the side window. In the fading afternoon light he saw a Park County Sheriff SUV astride the highway, its roof rack lights strobing, casting the nearby snow-covered hillsides in flashes of blue and red.

He'd done his homework. The Park County Sheriff employed only thirteen deputies to patrol and police some seven thousand square miles and six hundred road-miles of sprawling rough country. On any given day they were spread paper-thin. And now, with night falling and a winter storm approaching, they were dealing with a high-level request for assistance. Which worried him. If these deputies proved uncooperative, he'd have a real problem.

Rowland had provided him the locale information, along with a specific directive. *Capture Eckstein. Retrieve all electronics. Once done, contact me and I'll provide further instruction.*

He changed channels on his headset. "We're setting down. Look alive."

More of his men were aboard, all trusted and battle-tested. The Sikorsky S-92 seated nineteen, so the remaining cargo space had their equipment, ready for rapid deployment.

Was Daniels here?

Time to find out.

The Sikorsky banked left, slowed to a hover over the highway, and then dropped gently to the asphalt. Rotors began spooling down. Through the side window he saw another Park County SUV headed up the ranger station driveway toward them.

Into the headset he said, "The rest of you stay put, until I give the order. Switching to portable radio channel two."

He climbed out the cabin door just as a deputy eased to a stop at the edge of the rotor's wash. He led the uniform down the gravel driveway, until they didn't have to shout over the rotor noise.

"Are you Talley?" the deputy asked.

He nodded.

"We were told to expect you."

"What about the information I requested?"

"The rangers report that Luke Daniels and Jillian Stein registered yesterday, then headed off into the wilderness."

The cover story included that Daniels was a fugitive, on the run with another fugitive who'd helped him escape from a Mississippi prison. They'd come to bring them both in. Rowland had used his FBI connections to give credence to the story, which the local sheriff had accepted. And which had been fine by the sheriff, as he did not possess the manpower to spare for a bounty hunt.

The wind whipped over him with a fury, swirling a light snow-fall, and chapping his ears and lips. Not the kind of weather to be out in the wild. But Daniels was no ordinary tourist. Not by a long shot. At least he had him within his sights, along with a measure of privacy.

Talley had studied the topography and knew that Eckstein's land lay about twenty miles away, ultra-remote, with no access roads. Horseback was the only way in or out, unless you dropped from the sky—which he planned to do.

"What do you know about anyone living up there?" he asked.

"There are a few cabins, some of the land is privately owned. A lot of it is government-controlled. We rarely go up there. Those folks look after themselves."

Good to hear.

"I would recommend waiting," the deputy said. "This is not chopper weather."

No, it was not. The wind whipped in strong gusts and snow filled the air. Daniels and the woman were probably socked in too, and he was anxious to know what had spooked Thomas Rowland.

He could not recall when he transitioned from a respected special forces soldier to a hired mercenary.

But that was precisely what he was.

Sure, he'd been bitter at the military for blaming him for something it did and forcing him out. And that resentment had factored into his decision in first accepting Rowland's job offer. But the longer he stayed, the deeper he dug the hole, until finally conscience and morality were swept away by simple greed.

But there was also something else.

Appreciation.

Rowland had always been complimentary of what he'd done, praising his efforts, relying on him, just as the U.S. Army once had. Everybody needed attaboys. No. He'd actually craved them and Rowland had surely sensed that weakness and exploited it, trans-forming him into a glorified lapdog. Docile. Trained. Obedient.

But that was all over.

He'd had enough.

Today was liberation day.

52.

LUKE KEPT TO THE TRAIL, FOLLOWING ECKSTEIN AS HE AND JILLIAN were led through a gap in the cliff face barely wider than the horses. His senses stayed on high alert, mindful for booby traps. He had to wonder. Were they walking into trouble?

As a rule booby traps were planted in places that people were naturally attracted to, or forced to use. In Afghanistan that had been abandoned houses left standing in a village, which offered shelter. A locked door or drawer, which suggested something of value hidden inside. Roadside vehicles. Anything people would naturally want to see inside like a crate or rucksack or bag. And, like here, natural choke points, which people had to use whether they wanted to or not. They were literally out in the middle of nowhere, miles from the nearest person, a point Eckstein had hammered home.

When they emerged on the opposite side of the trees they found themselves in yet another meadow, this one barely an acre and ringed by tall old-growth trees. In the center of the clearing rose a large, two-story cabin, the first floor constructed of stripped notch-logs and large arched windows. The second floor more a huge gable with a steep-pitched roof.

A small barn stood off to the side, its doors closed.

"This couldn't have been easy to build," Jillian said.

"Three years of hard work and dozens of helicopter airlifts. But worth every penny. There's a sheltered area by the barn the horses can have. Feed and water are there too."

They dealt with the horses and headed for the house, both armed with their pistols. The cabin's first-floor interior was all light wood paneling and matching floors. Southwestern-style rugs lay down the open halls and across a seating area before a massive stone hearth fireplace, whose flagstone chimney disappeared up through the ceiling. Off to one side was a kitchenette, dining nook, and sliding glass doors that led out to a wooden deck.

"Need a roommate?" Luke asked. "This is my idea of home."

Eckstein chuckled. "I had one until recently, a half shepherd, half husky named Rock. He was fifteen when he passed. I buried him under an aspen out back."

"I'm sorry," Jillian said.

The old man headed toward the kitchen.

They followed.

"He had a nice life. I've had my eye on a senior, three-legged basset in a Cody shelter. I'm picking her up next week." He turned. "Do I need to put that on hold?"

"Not if we can help it," Luke said.

"Why are you talking to us?" Jillian asked. "We're perfect strangers."

"Ray Simmons told me that unless he came personally, the person who did come would utter that word. Lancer. So I'm trusting Ray that you people are okay."

"And the significance?" Luke tried again.

"That was the code name the Secret Service gave to John Kennedy. Nixon was Searchlight. Carter was Deacon. Reagan, Rawhide. Kennedy was Lancer."

"Ever heard of Kronos?" Luke asked.

Eckstein shook his head. "Should I have?"

He waved off the question. "Not really. Just checking."

But the lack of that information on Eckstein's part raised another red flag that he told himself to keep an eye on.

Their host made them hot chocolate and heated some left-over huckleberry pie in the microwave. They settled around the nook table.

"How old are you?" Luke asked.

"Eighty-eight."

"I hope I have your energy and life when I get that old," he said.

"Comes from living here, alone, all these years."

"No wife or spouse?" Jillian asked.

"She died a long time ago. That's when I bought this land and moved here. Paid for with lottery money. We hit it one time. Not huge, but enough that I could live where and how I pleased. And I'm sorry about Benji. He was good people."

"Did you meet him?"

"Only by computer."

"You said earlier that Rowland didn't know about you." Jillian said. "How is that possible?"

"Only Benji and Ray connected with me. And only they communicated with Rowland. I don't own anything that translates into an official record. This house is owned by a trust. My utilities and internet accounts are in the same trust. Nothing traces back to me."

Which meant they might finally have a little open space to work within.

"But people know you around here?" Jillian asked.

"They do. But not as David Eckstein."

"That's a lot of paranoia," Luke said.

"Habits of a lifetime."

"How do you power this place?" he asked.

"There are a few cabins up here, all on private lands. But there's a ranger station a few miles away. They got power, so we got power."

"Internet?"

"I have a satellite dish. That's how we stayed in contact."

He'd brought inside his trail pack that contained the laptop they used in Louisiana and Texas, which he opened and used to give a condensed version of the play-by-play assassination presentation he'd given Jillian.

"You figured all this out on your own?" Eckstein asked. "Pretty impressive. Tell me how you got this far."

Jillian handled that inquiry, recounting her and Luke's journey starting in Belgium and ending with their discovery of the Find3Points phone app.

Luke motioned to the combined graphic on the computer. "That's you there, in the center, perpendicular to the motorcade. DE6."

Eckstein nodded. "That was a terrible day. Third worst of my life. What was done to that man. He deserved better."

"Did you go there to see the president?" Luke asked.

"Not exactly. See, my boy was born in 1962. There was a problem with his heart and he needed an operation. We didn't have the money. I was an optical engineer. At the time I was working for Belvor Labs in Fort Worth. We prototyped stuff, did quality assurance, that kind of thing. We had a contract with Canon to pressure-test an experimental camera—"

"Model 814?"

"Yep. Just like it says there on the diagram. Way ahead of its time. I figured it was going to be a big moneymaker. So I dropped a fishing line to Canon's biggest competitor at the time. They were interested. Said that if the 814 was as good as I claimed they'd pay me $10,000 just to borrow it a bit. Not steal. Borrow for a few hours. I assumed they planned to do some reverse engineering. That was a lot of money. More than I had ever known, and it would get my boy the care he needed. November 22 was the day I was supposed to meet them and make the exchange. I get to the meeting early and have some time to kill. I think, what better way to convince my buyers of the camera's quality than to film a presidential motorcade? So I start walking toward Dealey. As I'm crossing Main I see the motorcade coming toward Houston. I run across the grass, plant myself at the Elm Street curb, and start rolling. I catch Kennedy and the First Lady turning the corner onto Elm."

The old man paused and pursed his lips, a glint of tears in his eyes.

"It always chokes me up remembering that day. It all happened so fast, but I stayed focused on the motorcade until it went through the underpass. I saw it all. Then it hits me. I'm not supposed to have that camera. I could go to jail, lose my job, so I panic and start running. Everybody else was running, too, so I hoped nobody would notice me. I found my car and tore outta there, driving until my hands stopped shaking, then I went back to the lab and put the camera in the equipment locker. Nobody ever knew. But I kept the film. For weeks afterward I was a wreck, waiting for the FBI, or the Secret Service, to break down my door. But nobody ever came."

"And you've never been mentioned anywhere in anything?" Jillian asked.

"I had the camera in a backpack that I was holding. You couldn't see it. In the confusion nobody noticed, nor was I photographed. Believe me, I've checked them all as they were published."

"What about your son?" Jillian asked.

"He died three months later."

Though a long time ago every bit of the pain from that loss was clearly still there.

"All over the news they were asking for cameras and pictures, anything folks may have taken that day. But I couldn't come forward. I thought about sending it anonymously, but if it was traced back to me, I was gone. I needed my job more than I needed to help the government. That's when my wife had her fall."

Luke waited for an explanation.

"While I was at work one day she went headfirst down our basement stairs and broke her neck. Accidental, they said."

"Was it?"

He nodded. "It was. A terrible accident. Nobody ever came after me. I was unknown. Which was great. My wife was gone, my son buried, so I left Fort Worth and wandered the country taking jobs where I could. Back then you could still disappear, and I did. Eventually I settled outside Boston and got a job with Kodak."

"How did you and Ray and Benji come together?" Luke asked.

"That was about twenty years ago. We were all part of an on-line chat group that dealt with the assassination. We developed a connection and branched out, communicating only among the three of us. Ray was a ballistics guy and damn good. He also had a link to the rifle Oswald used. Benji, as a military man, had the government clearances to get access to things. For a long time I refused to meet with either of them, but after a while I decided they were trustworthy. That's when Ray came and I showed him the film. After that we three started our own investigation. We became a team. Studying the timeline, the different players involved, the books and articles, dissecting the Warren Commission and the House Select Committee on Assassinations reports. We also ran a lot of ballistic tests. Ray and I did them right out there in the meadow. Between the three of us we figured it out that Thomas Rowland killed John Kennedy."

53.

ROWLAND HAD ALWAYS ADMIRED ABRAHAM LINCOLN. SURE, LINCOLN was remembered for his monumental successes. Elected president twice. Saved the Union. Ended slavery. Won the war.

But he'd always believed that the key to success was failure.

And Lincoln had a long list of those.

In 1832, defeated for election to the Illinois legislature. In 1833, failed in business. In 1835, the woman he loved died. In 1836, had a nervous breakdown. In 1838, denied being the speaker of the Illinois legislature. In 1843, defeated for Congress. In 1848, lost his bid to be reelected. In 1849, rejected for land officer. In 1854, lost the election for the U.S. Senate. In 1856, rejected for nomination as vice president. In 1858, defeated again for the U.S. Senate.

No question. Lincoln failed his way to success.

And the same could be said for himself.

Yet his failure bordered on the unthinkable.

Initially, the Warren Commission had not been interested in him. Of all the Secret Service agents there that day, only three were called to testify. The agency itself had protected its own. Of course, no one had a clue that the AR-15 had been fired and no one had checked the weapon. In the confusion he'd even managed to retrieve the spent cartridge from the limousine's floorboard and change the clip so that, if anyone looked, there would be a full load. Eventually, though, he and the other agents there that day had been required to submit written statements that ultimately appeared in the final report, buried deep among the nearly thousand pages. All of them were general and vague. What happened the night before in Fort Worth had been mentioned in the report, but the agency had downplayed the incident and assured the commission that all of its agents were ready to go on November 22, 1963.

All was good.

Only conspiratorialists persisted.

None of whom, though, had ever involved him until recently.

How could this be happening?

After six decades.

What purpose would be served by exposing all this now? No crime had been committed. Just a tragic mistake. Revealing it would do nothing but stain the Secret Service. Kennedy's legacy too. Instead of being cut down by an assassin, the president of the United States died from an accidental discharge of a government weapon. But Oswald did, actually, try to kill Kennedy, and the accident would not have happened but for his malice. So everything was Oswald's fault, not his.

Right?

The damn Warren Commission report was riddled with flaws and inconsistencies. So many that more questions were raised than answers provided, and the subsequent congressional investigations only made things worse.

Still the truth remained hidden.

"Listen to me, son," his father said to him. "Here's a story I was once told. One day, a farmer's donkey fell into a well. The animal grieved for hours while the farmer tried to do something to save it. Eventually, the farmer decided the donkey was too old and the well had been dry for a long time, so getting the donkey out just wasn't worth it. So he called his neighbors, and each of them took a shovel and began throwing dirt into the well. The donkey, realizing what was happening, started crying and growling even louder. He clearly did not want to be buried alive. But then, to everyone's surprise, the donkey stopped complaining. The farmer looked to the bottom of the well and was amazed at what he saw. With every shovel full of dirt, the donkey was hitting the ground with its hooves and standing on the growing mound. Soon the donkey came to the mouth of the well and trotted out. The moral of the story? Life knocks you down, but we can get out of the deepest pits if we just don't give up. Use what's thrown at you and move forward. Always forward."

His father had been right.

So he'd left the Secret Service, joined the CIA, and made a career for himself. Along the way he became both important and relevant.

And that deep well he'd fallen into was long behind him.

Or was it?

He'd successfully eluded his fate for a long time. But Ray Simmons, Benjamin Stein, and now David Eckstein wanted something different.

Exposure. The truth.

Which could not be allowed to happen.

He had to be sure the past would finally end here.

Today.

Thankfully, he had a way.

54.

LUKE LEANED FORWARD AND WAITED FOR ECKSTEIN TO EXPLAIN. BUT the old man seemed far off, drifting. "It's sad. My friends are gone. I'm the only one left. The only one who knows."

"Can you prove that Rowland did it?" Jillian asked. "Or is this just more wild conspiracy crap? Tell me that my grandfather's death can be avenged with the truth."

"I've spent the past thirty years working this," Eckstein said. "Your grandfather helped me in that endeavor. A lot. He was the one who found Rowland's statement to the Warren Commission. They buried it deep, but Benji hunted it down. He also obtained that recording from the medical examiner's room in Dallas. That one was tough to get. Speaking of which, wait here."

Eckstein left the dining room table and disappeared into another room. Luke and Jillian listened to what sounded like a metal file cabinet drawer being opened. The old man returned with a few sheets of paper in his hand.

"These are copies of Rowland's commission testimony. It's not much, and it's pretty innocent, unless you know some other things."

Eckstein handed the pages to him.

> Friday, November 22, 1963 — Awoke about 7:00 a.m. washed, packed suitcase, checked out of hotel and had breakfast. About 8:30 a.m. Agent Sorrels met Agent Kinney and me outside the hotel and drove to the airport arriving about 9:00 a.m. We went directly to the garage and relieved the police of the security of the cars. Washed and cleaned both cars and checked outside, inside, and underneath for security violations—none found. We drove the cars to the area where the President was to be. Cars were kept under close observation until the arrival of the President, when Agent William Greer of the White House Detail took over control.
>
> The President and his party then proceeded up to the fence holding the crowd back and greeted and shook hands with them. I assisted Agents on the detail to make a path for them and helped Agent Greer keep the cars abreast of the President as he moved along the length of the fence.
>
> After the President and his party were seated in their car, I entered the trail car, as I had been instructed to do by Agent Lawson. I was seated in the rear left side seat. The shift leader, Emory Roberts, had instructed me to take control of the AR-15 rifle. I did this and had the ammunition clip inserted in the rifle and placed the rifle within easy reach.
>
> The motorcade then left the airport and proceeded along the parade route. Just prior to the shooting the Presidential car turned left at the intersection and started down an incline toward an underpass followed by the trail car.
>
> After a very short distance I heard a loud report which sounded like a firecracker. It appeared to

come from the right and rear and seemed to me to be at ground level, I stood up and looked to my right and rear in an attempt to identify it. Nothing caught my attention except people shouting and cheering. A disturbance caused me to look forward toward the President's car. Perhaps 2 or 3 seconds elapsed from the time I looked to the rear and then looked at the President, he was slumped forward and to his left, and was straightening up to an almost erect sitting position as I turned and looked.

At the moment he was almost sitting erect I heard two reports which I thought were shots and that appeared to me completely different in sound than the first report and were in such rapid succession that there seemed to be practically no time element between them. It looked to me as if the President was struck in the right upper rear of his head. The first shot of the second two seemed as if it missed because the hair on the right side of his head flew forward and there didn't seem to be any impact against his head. The last shot seemed to hit his head and cause a noise at the point of impact which made him fall forward and to his left.

At the end of the last report I reached to the bottom of the car and picked up the AR-15 rifle, cocked and loaded it, and turned to the rear. At this point the cars were passing under the overpass and as a result we had left the scene of the shooting. I kept the AR-15 rifle ready as we proceeded at a high rate of speed to the hospital.

A few moments later shift leader Emory Roberts turned to the rest of us in the car and said words to the effect that when we arrive at the hospital some of us would have to give additional protection to the

> Vice President and take him to a place of safety. He
> assigned two of the agents in the car to this duty. I
> was told to have the AR-15 ready for use if needed.

"The problem is," Eckstein said, "most of that statement is a lie. It took us nearly twenty years to prove that, but prove it we did."

He and Jillian listened as Eckstein explained.

First, Rowland made no mention of falling backward, as another witness recalled in their statement. Then there was, *at the end of the last report I reached to the bottom of the car and picked up the AR-15 rifle, cocked and loaded it, and turned to the rear.* The same witness who saw Rowland fall backward also saw him with the gun at the time of the last shot, not after. Another agent's statement noted that when he saw Kennedy's head being struck with a bullet he reached for the rifle *but Rowland had already picked it up.*

"And Rowland's declaration that he cocked and loaded the AR-15 *after* the shots were fired was directly contradicted by his supervisor who testified that the AR-15 was *always ready to go.* That gun was lying in the car cocked, loaded, with the safety on. Ready to fire."

Luke listened more as Eckstein pressed his case.

"Rowland was one of the agents in Fort Worth who was involved with drinking and staying out late the night before. Benji was able to get a list of names, which the Warren Commission did not include. The Secret Service tried hard to minimize that by saying everybody was rested and on their toes, but you have to wonder. Were they really? In the end nine witnesses, including Rowland himself, put the AR-15 in his hands just after the last shot. Two witnesses put the gun in Rowland's hands at the moment the last shot was fired. One witness saw him stand and fall over just as the final shot was fired. And their testimony corroborates the physical evidence I have."

"Which is?" Luke asked.

"The bullet's trajectory. Its fragmentation. The size of the entrance wound in Kennedy's skull. The fact that Rowland was seen to have fallen over. The gunpowder odor that drifted through the plaza. The absence of any cranial debris on bullet fragments supposedly from Kennedy's head wound. The dent in the empty shell found inside the book depository that seems to preclude any third shot from that location. The disappearance of the brain and other tissue samples that could be used to identify the third bullet. It all points to a singular conclusion."

"It's all circumstantial," Luke said.

"But that doesn't mean it's wrong. Then there's my film. This will all make sense once you see it. Only Ray, Benji, and myself have watched it."

Luke glanced at Jillian and read her thoughts.

He agreed.

Damn right, let's see it.

The old man left the kitchen and returned a couple of minutes later with a large manila envelope from which he removed a flash drive. "I digitized the old film when the technology allowed."

"And the original?" Jillian asked.

Eckstein removed a small metal reel case from the envelope. "Safe and sound."

Luke popped the drive into the laptop and opened the video file.

"We'll watch it at regular speed the first time," Eckstein said.

55.

Luke focused on the screen as an image of Elm Street came into view, the camera pointed up the slope toward the book depository, which framed the left side of the screen. From the right

Kennedy's convertible appeared on Houston. It slowed for the turn onto Elm then eased into the center lane. The camera was aimed at the convertible's windshield, not exactly centered.

"I had the unit inside the backpack," Eckstein said. "I pointed the pack in the general direction, just going for the big picture to impress the people who wanted to steal the technology. I was going to let them develop the film to see the quality. So I wasn't trying for details. The camera was sensitive to motion and could adjust its focus. That's what made it special. Along with the image. Unlike Zapruder's film, which is blurry, this one is clean and clear."

Clearly visible were Agents Greer and Kellerman in the front seat, Governor and Mrs. Connally seated behind them. Kennedy and Jackie in the rear seat. Behind them, the trail car accelerated to close a gap that had opened between the two cars.

Exactly as Luke already knew.

The camera's focus pulled back slightly to encompass Kennedy's limousine. The president and First Lady waved to onlookers. The camera panned right and then left to show the crowd. Standing on his concrete plinth Abraham Zapruder briefly appeared, filming, before the camera returned to Kennedy's limousine.

A slight lift occurred.

The image tightened on the trail car, then panned back to the presidential limousine.

Kennedy's hands rose to cover the neck wound Oswald's first bullet had inflicted. Jackie turned toward her husband and reached for him. The camera zoomed and the screen filled with Kennedy and the First Lady.

The limousine drew even with the camera. The frame widened. On the left Kennedy slumped forward, then sideways toward Jackie.

Kennedy's skull exploded in a red mist.

Agent Clint Hill launched himself on the trunk. The limousine surged forward and sped toward the triple underpass. The camera followed for a few seconds then panned right.

The trail car came into view.

Eckstein hit the PAUSE button, freezing the video. "There, do you see him, at the center of the frame, in the trail car?"

Luke and Jillian leaned in close.

A man was pitched forward with one hand braced on the windshield's upper frame, the other clenched around the AR-15's pistol grip. The muzzle hovered a few inches above the windshield, parallel to the car's hood.

"Take it back to where Zapruder appears, then pause on the trail car," Eckstein said.

Luke did so and made a quick head count of the passengers in the trail car.

Nine men.

"Did you catch it?" Eckstein said.

Neither of them knew what he meant.

Eckstein rewound the file to the point where Kennedy's limousine was almost perpendicular to the camera, then hit PLAY. "Watch. Kennedy's hands come up. He slumps against Jackie. The car draws even with me. One second, two seconds, three seconds. Boom. There's the kill shot." Eckstein rewound again. "I'll slow it down. When Kennedy slumps forward and the camera pulls back, keep your eyes on the trail car."

Luke nodded. "Go ahead."

Kennedy slumped, the frame widened. Luke focused on the right side of the screen. Moving in slow motion a figure rose from the back seat of the trail car then tumbled forward. Yes. Definitely. The barrel of the AR-15 was level with Kennedy's limousine.

"That man on the screen," Eckstein said. "Carrying the AR-15. He was on the driver's side, rear seat. You can see him plain as day, falling forward, finger on the trigger, then an instant later Kennedy is hit."

Yes, you could.

"This is the only evidence of that happening?" he asked.

"It is. The only film of its kind. Zapruder's never shows the trail car, only the first limousine. And there are these."

The old man slid a stack of eight-by-ten black-and-white

photographs from the envelope and laid the first one on the table before them. "Love Field, Dallas airport, 11:38 A.M. Kennedy and Jackie arrive for their appearance at the Trade Mart. Here you see the two of them shaking hands and accepting gifts while handlers guide them toward the limousine. Walking behind Kennedy are David Clay and Ken O'Donnell, his assistants."

Another photograph hit the table.

"Kennedy and Jackie seated in their limousine getting ready to leave.

"Next picture, about three minutes later. This is the trail car. Parked, getting ready to go. Kennedy's limousine is just beyond the left side of the frame. How many men do you see?"

"Eight," Jillian said.

Eckstein nodded. "Secret Service agents Emory Roberts, Samuel Kinney, John Ready, Clinton Hill, William McIntyre, Paul Landis, Glen Bennett, and George Hickey." One by one Eckstein tapped the faces in the photo. "Roberts, front seat. Kinney, front seat. Ready, running board. Hill, running board. Landis, seated behind Ready. Bennett on the rear seat. Hickey beside him. What do you see in his hands?"

Luke hesitated and frowned. "Nothing."

"That's right. No AR-15."

A final photograph was displayed showing the trail car as it left Love Field.

"How many men do you see now?" Eckstein asked.

He counted. "Nine."

"That's right and he's sitting beside Bennet and Hickey. Holding the AR-15. A last-minute addition to the detail. He should not have been there."

Eckstein pointed back at the laptop screen and the frozen image of the same man cradling the AR-15.

Pointed at Kennedy.

"That's who provided the kill shot."

Eckstein rapped his knuckle against the face in the photo.

"The ninth man. Thomas Henry Rowland."

56.

Luke wasn't sure if he was amazed or skeptical.

He again found the audio that Ray Simmons had left from the Walter Reed autopsy, which he'd downloaded to the laptop, and played it.

"Benji got this," Eckstein said. "He had people go through the national archives and they located this recording. It's another example of the Warren Commission either ignoring or failing to appreciate the evidence."

There's been an accident, not a murder.

That's what Agent Kellerman said.

"He could have just been trying to offer an explanation to the medical examiner that would allow them to take the body," Jillian said. "A lie that would work."

"That's entirely possible," Eckstein said. "You can hear the aggravation in his voice. He wasn't going to leave there without the body. But, you have to admit, considering what we know now, it's a strange choice of words."

Luke agreed. "Are you saying the Secret Service knew what happened and covered it up?"

"That's impossible to say. But I doubt it. That kind of secret would have been hard to keep, even for that time in history. But the Secret Service did act awfully suspicious. They took the body then, when an autopsy was performed back in DC, it was effectively botched. Some say even tampered with. Little workable information was gleaned. Which is hard to understand, considering the situation. You would think they would have been extra thorough. Most of the documents and photographs from that autopsy remain, to this day, sealed from the public. Why?

It's been over sixty years. There's no logical reason to keep that information sealed. Some say it's to protect the family. But all of them are dead, except for the Kennedys' daughter."

"Unless they were afraid what might be learned from that information," Luke said.

"Exactly."

"I'm skeptical," Jillian said, "of all this. How could that rifle have fired and no one in the trail car heard it?"

"Look again at my film," Eckstein said.

And they viewed it one more time.

Luke noticed that when Rowland stood, he was momentarily out of view, the agents on either side, both in and out of the car, blocking him from the camera.

"What about the people on the overpass?" Luke asked. "They were above the street looking down."

"There's nothing for them to see," Eckstein said. "AR-15s are equipped with flash suppressors at the end of the barrel. Any muzzle flash would have only been visible at night. It was high noon that day with a bright sun."

"Wouldn't someone have heard the shot?" Jillian asked again.

Eckstein nodded. "They did hear it. But nobody to this day has been able to zero in on where the shot came from. Dealey Plaza was a giant echo chamber, flanked by buildings on three sides. Any sound evidence is useless, as the House Select Committee on Assassinations discovered when it tried."

"An AR-15," Luke said, "is one powerful rifle. It has a loud crack, much louder than Oswald's old rifle."

"That it does," Eckstein said. "But all this happened in a matter of seconds. There was a lot of noise coming from all directions, echoing back and forth. If any of the agents in the trail car heard that rifle fire, no one has said a word about it in sixty years. You don't really think they kept that to themselves? Either the rifle didn't fire, or none of them were aware that it did."

This was a lot to take in.

Luke too remained skeptical, but the circumstantial evidence seemed to be mounting. Then there was Rowland's reaction to the whole thing. If it was nothing but fiction, why would he care? Just ignore it.

But that's not what happened.

Benji was killed.

"There is also the ballistic evidence," Eckstein said. "This is what Ray and I worked up. He was an expert on that sort of thing. He told me that an AR-15 round is encased within a thin copper jacket. At impact the bullet disintegrates and causes a lot of damage."

"Like what happened to Kennedy's head?" Luke asked.

"Precisely. That awful image. Oswald's bullet could not have done that. The first round that hit Kennedy from Oswald's rifle did not do that. It left a clean, neat hole in and out. But somehow the third shot explodes? Then there's the testimony from numerous witnesses who were near the limousine who all say they smelled gunpowder. No way that came from Oswald's rifle."

They sat in silence for a moment.

Taking it all in.

Luke played the video over again.

Clearly, Thomas Rowland had the rifle, and fell forward with it in his grasp, finger on the trigger. Did it fire? There was no visual evidence that it had, but an instant after Rowland fell the president's head exploded. Coincidence with Oswald's shot?

Not likely.

"I won't bore you with the angle evidence of the kill round that struck Kennedy," Eckstein said. "Along with the bullet's kinetic energy and velocity, which all point to AR-15. Then there's the height of the two motorcade vehicles, which were different makes and models, relative to the slope of Elm Street that clearly showed that a kill shot from Oswald was virtually impossible, but a shot from Rowland's AR-15 fit the math perfectly. The Warren Commission investigated none of this."

"But you folks did?" Jillian asked.

"Ray had actually fired Oswald's rifle, part of the FBI's testing in 1963. Then he participated in the CBS simulation in 1967. He noted back then that the time it takes for an expert marksman to cycle the bolt, and fire three shots from Oswald's rifle, doesn't match the Zapruder film. We then applied that timeline to my film and it doesn't match either. Oswald fired three times. That we believe to be true. But we also believe that he only hit Kennedy one time. Rowland's rifle fired the kill shot. The wind speed calculations at the time of the shooting all say that Oswald's rapid trio of shots were more likely to miss. And, we believe, two of the three did. And that's assuming Oswald even got off the third shot. Nobody knows."

This man sounded like he knew exactly what he was talking about.

He was not some wild conspiratorialist.

"It's clear from studying what we have on the autopsy," Eckstein said, "and what little photographic evidence exists, that the kill round did not come from above. It came level and from behind. We ran many simulations. Over and over. All came to the same conclusion. Thomas Rowland caused that gun to fire by accident. He stumbled forward and off it went. No conspiracy. Nothing nefarious. Just a young, green Secret Service agent, probably hung over and tired, who had little to no experience with an AR-15 and who had no business being there."

"It is a heavy weapon," Luke said. "In more ways than one."

Eckstein nodded. "That it is. You need training to be able to wield it correctly. And I should know, I fired one many times during our tests."

"Why was Rowland on that detail?" Jillian asked.

"He was only eight months out of the academy. Our guess? Charles Rowland wanted to beef up his son's résumé. Benji investigated the Rowland family and learned that the father, a big shot within the CIA, never wanted the son in the Secret Service. He wanted Thomas for the agency and, in the end, he got his wish."

"What does that mean?" Jillian asked.

"Thomas Rowland's name appears nowhere in the Warren

Commission findings or in any of the FBI reports. Not a word. Only his statement, buried among hundreds of others, is there. By July 1964 Thomas was out of the Secret Service and at Langley, tucked under Daddy's wing, where he stayed for decades."

Luke wanted to know more about Charles Rowland.

So he googled the name.

Eckstein pointed at the screen. "Charles is one of those people you never hear about. On purpose. He was with Wild Bill Donovan when the Office of Strategic Services was founded. In 1947, when Truman turned it into the CIA, Charles's star took off. Name something that stinks during the Cold War and his prints are on it. Bay of Pigs, Hungary, Guatemala, the shah of Iran, Watergate, Lumumba in the Congo, Baby Doc in Haiti, Gulf of Tonkin. And dozens more no one's ever heard about. His whole life was an exercise in sociopathy. People aren't people, but mere marionettes with strings to be pulled. Murder? Torture? Just levers to be worked. Blackmail and extortion are a first resort, not last. Some senator won't do your bidding? Get his daughter hooked on heroin and pimp her out. An attorney general digging into your affairs? Fabricate and plant evidence to incriminate."

"Are those real events?" Jillian asked.

Eckstein nodded. "Benji and Ray sniffed them out. Bankrupt businesses. Steal family fortunes. Railroad innocent people into prison. The father taught the son everything he knew, and Thomas eventually surpassed Charles in every way. Over the years we found people who would talk about the Rowlands, but only from the shadows."

"Is Charles still around?"

"Died in his sleep twenty years ago. Can you believe that? Nice peaceful end. Thomas spent thirty-five years at the CIA, then retired a few years before Charles passed."

Jillian said, "If Thomas is retired—"

"I know what you're thinking. But once outside of Langley, Rowland became more powerful, even more dangerous."

"He killed my grandfather," Jillian said.

"I hate that. I really do," Eckstein said. "Ray and Benji wanted to make contact with him. Our manuscript is ready to go, so we wanted to give him a chance to explain things. But he never replied to their inquiries."

"That was foolish," Jillian said. "Benji got shot thanks to those inquiries."

"I know. And I'm sorry for that. He was my friend. But none of us thought Rowland would resort to violence. The man is in his nineties. We thought the greatest threat would come from lawyers wanting to sue us."

Luke wanted to know, "Why keep your identity secret?"

"I have the film. It's the single most damning piece of evidence. We didn't want anyone to interfere with what we're doing. We three agreed to keep me in the deep background."

"What happened after Ray died?"

"That was unexpected. It really was. It shook me. He was always a quiet man, but I never thought him suicidal. Ray had told me about Benji being sick and time was short. We were trying to move this along so things could happen while Benji was still here."

"Yet you still did not contact my grandfather," Jillian said. "He knew about you, just not how to contact you."

"We stuck to the plan. We all agreed to that. Our work is done. Rowland never answered their inquiries. So I'll be moving forward with publication. That's what they wanted. So that's what I'm going to do. All three names on the cover."

Snow-swollen clouds that had been stacking over the western peaks during their trek were now releasing frozen moisture. While their host prepared a late lunch, Luke and Jillian sat upstairs and watched through the glass doors as the snow coated the outer deck.

"I could get used to this," she said.

"You and me both. This is a wonderful place to live."

"That isolation cuts two ways."

"I hear you. But Eckstein could be right and Rowland has no idea he exists."

He'd already noticed the gun cabinet across the room. Eight shotguns and rifles stood at attention. Some impressive weapons too. Not a lot of spit clean or polish either. These guns had been used. Which he liked. So they had some firepower, if needed.

"Can someone like Thomas Rowland really have that much influence?" Jillian asked, regaining his attention.

"With enough money and power, absolutely. My boss gives him a lot of credit for bad things, and she's not one to exaggerate."

"I never should have called you."

He glanced at her.

"I'm so sorry I got you into this, Luke. This is not your fight."

"I made that choice, not you. And it is my fight now. This is official business."

She smiled. "You just can't help yourself, can you?"

"Part of my east Tennessee upbringing."

Eckstein called from downstairs, "Food's ready."

After eating and washing the dishes they settled around a crackling fireplace. Outside, snow had fully capped the deck railing.

"How much is expected?" Jillian asked.

"Four or five feet by tomorrow. The wind will pile it into drifts. Spring storms here are ugly beasts. It'll just sit over us until a warm front pushes through. You two might be here a few days."

"There are worse things," Luke said.

"I'm curious about something," Jillian said. "The Zapruder film. Why is it not threatening to Rowland?"

"Zapruder focused on Kennedy's car, not the trail car. I guarantee you, if he hadn't been so tight on Kennedy's car that film would have never seen the light of day. Charles Rowland would have done something. And I didn't mean to scare anybody earlier. Take comfort. Thomas Rowland is old and will be dead soon enough."

"What does that do to your book?" Luke asked.

"Nothin', since I doubt that old man is ever going to talk about this to anyone. We made a reasonable effort to contact him. That's all we have to do. So we publish and see what happens."

"I have a problem with him dying and getting away with killing Benji," Luke said. "That is hard to swallow."

Jillian said, "One of Benji's favorite phrases was, *Choose carefully the mountain on which you want to die*. I've chosen mine. I have another kind of justice in mind for Thomas Rowland. More biblical in nature."

He stared at her.

And got it. Deuteronomy 19:21.

You must show no pity. Life for life.

57.

4:15 P.M.

TALLEY STARED UP AT THE LEADEN WYOMING SKY. MORE SNOW was coming from the north. But the question became, was it flyable? He knew the Sikorsky was a good helo with both FLIR— forward-looking infrared radar—and night vision. However, neither of these mattered without a good stick pilot, and Talley had two of the best, former 160th Special Operations Night Stalkers. Still, wind shear in these parts was going to be unpredictable.

The Sikorskys were fueled and ready for his men, who were awaiting his order to lift off. ETA would be thirty minutes, with a headwind. He could see they would have to come in from the south, low and fast. The locale was perfect. Isolated. Private. Plenty of fresh snow to keep the curious and the official away.

"Load up," he called out.

His men climbed into one of the Sikorskys. He was the last to board and slammed the cabin door shut.

The pilot started the engines.

Rotors spun.

Then they lifted off into the afternoon air.

LUKE STOOD ON THE EXTERIOR DECK AND SOAKED IN THE COLD. Snow continued to drift down, but not in a heavy fall. It was midafternoon but from the overcast sky and semi-darkness it seemed more like twilight.

Off toward the barn the horses rustled.

Which they'd been doing for the past few minutes.

"Hear that little rattle in their snort?" Eckstein asked.

"I do," Jillian said.

"There's something spooking them."

Luke focused toward the barn, but saw nothing. "An animal?"

The old man stepped back toward the open terrace doors. "They'd be squealing and stomping more."

His senses came alert.

They all retreated inside.

Eckstein stepped to the gun rack and retrieved a shotgun. "They're all loaded. Extra ammo is in the cabinet beneath."

He and Jillian each grabbed a weapon and some spare shells. They already toted their Berettas. Had Talley found them? Maybe Eckstein was wrong and Rowland knew all about him.

"Could be nothing," Eckstein said. "But secure your information, including those Love Field photos and my flash drive. You need to keep 'em safe."

Luke gathered up his laptop, drawings, and photographs, stuffing them back into the travel bag. He slipped the flash drives into his pocket.

Eckstein had assumed a position at one of the windows.

Luke heard a familiar sound.

The deep basso tones of helicopter rotors.

Far off.

Coming closer.

"Is there a way out of here toward the north?" he asked.

"There's a saddle that drops down to a ravine, which curves north and snakes its way to an old mining camp, the Ishawooa—"

"How far?"

"Not quite a mile. If we can get that far we might have a chance to lose 'em in the storm."

Luke was counting on Talley not having had time to fully reconnoiter the area. Sure, Google Earth could supply some information, but that didn't mean it was right. Maybe Talley had missed the mining camp, or considered it unimportant.

"Here it comes," Jillian said, nodding out the window.

Over the treetops navigation lights skimmed off the valley floor, then the heavy chopper touched down a few hundred yards away.

Men emerged.

Armed.

Then Talley himself.

"I'm guessing you two have more experience with this kinda thing than I do," Eckstein said. "What's our play?"

"To be gone," he said.

"Wouldn't we be better off holding up here? Defensive position and all that?"

"Talley has a lot more shooters. They'll breach this place in no time. Better we make them hunt for us and hope they spread themselves thin. Jillian?"

"I agree. It's our best chance."

The black forms started heading their way.

TALLEY HAD THOUGHT A STEALTH APPROACH MIGHT BE GOOD, THEN decided a more direct course of action better.

Especially for what he had in mind.

His men were now on the ground with him, and another had remained in the helicopter along with the last of this contingent who piloted the craft. A second pilot and man waited miles away with the other chopper.

He twirled his hand.

The chopper's blades roared to full speed.

And the Sikorsky lifted back into the air.

LUKE LED THE WAY AS THEY DESCENDED BACK TO THE GROUND FLOOR and rushed toward the cabin's rear door. Above them came the roar of helicopter rotors. He stepped outside and saw the chopper's outline slide into view. The downwash blew the gathered snow into a tornado. Something flashed orange. A torpedo-shaped object powered downward. Rocket?

"Run," Luke shouted.

They sprinted away.

The house exploded.

Luke felt himself propelled forward from the blast, driven to the ground. His face felt hot. The edges of his vision pulsed red-black.

"Jillian," he shouted.

"I'm here."

A few feet away she groaned and rolled over. Blood trickled from her left ear.

"You hit?"

She shook her head.

"Where's Eckstein?" he called out. "Do you see him?"

In their dash from the house Eckstein had fallen behind. The old man lay spread-eagle on the ground. Luke ran to him. Eckstein's mouth opened and closed like a gasping fish, emitting bloody wheezing gasps. Then he saw it. A bullet hole in the chest. Jillian rushed over.

"He's been shot," Luke said.

Jillian's attention turned to the semi-darkness around them. "That means they're here."

The house burned behind them.

The helicopter had backed off and risen in altitude, but was still within range to do more harm. Cold air and snow swirled around them. The chopper's navigation lights swung back around and headed straight for them.

Automatic weapons fire erupted.

Bullets thudded into the ground.

The helicopter skidded sideways maintaining its perch at about a hundred feet. He waited until he saw the blinking light on the tail rotor, then took aim at the windscreen sending two shotgun bursts upward, stitching buckshot across the bulbous form. He had little chance of bringing down the craft, but his shots had the desired effect. The helo's nose pitched forward and the pilot banked hard left and backed off.

"Move it," he said to her. "I'm right behind you."

He bent down and clasped Eckstein's wrists, dragging him toward the barn. The helicopter rose vertically and moved back toward them. In the open rear door a figure cradled an automatic rifle and started firing.

Bullets peppered the ground, coming closer.

"Keep going," he told her.

He released his grip on Eckstein's wrist, dropped to one knee, and poured shotgun pellets into the helicopter's open door. The figure fell backward out of sight. He then grabbed the old man by the belt and hauled him into the barn.

He spotted another set of doors at the other side. "See if we can get out that way."

Jillian rushed ahead.

The horses were rattled by all the commotion, uneasy in their stalls.

He knelt down. "David, are you with us?"

No response.

He jostled the old man's shoulder. "David, talk to me."

A string of garbled words came out in a gasp.

"We can go this way," Jillian called out.

Eckstein clutched at his sleeve and opened his mouth, but only a whisper emerged.

"We need to go," Jillian cried out.

He leaned closer to Eckstein's mouth. "Say it again."

"NAI."

"One more time."

"N...A...I...316...21."

"What's that mean?"

"Say it back," Eckstein croaked.

He did so.

He glanced back toward the house and, in the fire's glow, saw four armed men advancing his way. One of them cocked his arm and threw something. He caught a fleeting glimpse of its unmistakable shape and silhouette.

Grenade.

"Frag," he shouted.

Then he dove back, deeper into the barn. The grenade bounced off the snowy ground and exploded. He felt the whomp of the concussion and stayed low. But it had only been a flashbang.

Luke rolled onto his knees, found the Beretta, and took aim through the doorway. A man was there, arm cocked for a second throw. He put two rounds in his chest and the guy stumbled from view. Was he wearing a vest? Probably. But that still stung. A few seconds later a grenade detonated outside. He made sure Jillian was okay then crawled to Eckstein, who lay on his back, open eyes staring skyward.

He checked for a pulse. None.

He sprang to his feet and ran toward Jillian. "He's dead."

"And we will be too if we stay here much longer."

"Bravo Two, this is Bravo One," Talley said over the radio. "Status."

He'd ordered the pilot to back off and hold position away from the cabin, but still capable of observing. Eyes in the sky were always appreciated. Despite the Sikorsky's auto-hover feature the storm's crosswinds wildly buffeted the craft, making it hard to hold steady.

"Positive strike," came the reply. "But there is a casualty on the ground. One of ours."

He stood about a hundred yards from the burning building and had heard the gunfire and grenades. "What about the targets?"

"One is down, condition unknown. The other two exited the barn and are heading north into a draw."

"Cut them off," he ordered. "Pin them down."

If Daniels made it to the open Talley and his team would have a devil of a time finding him. Then again, the man was a Ranger, who always had a backup plan, and it wouldn't be something as foolhardy as running headlong into a blizzard. With the temperature plummeting Daniels would be searching for shelter and a defensible position.

So where might that be?

58.

Luke, half stumbling half sliding, started down the saddle into calf-deep snow. The wind had blown the surface into frozen wave crests. He lost his footing and pitched face-first into the fresh powder. A gust of wind knocked him sideways and, burdened by his pack and the shotgun, he began barrel-rolling. Jillian tried to sidestep him, but he cut her off at the knees. She landed atop him with their legs intertwined. Their slide gained momentum, burying their heads and torsos.

Finally, they lurched to a stop.

To the south the helicopter's navigation lights strobed the sky. They burrowed further into a snow drift and went still. The thump of the rotors intensified, passing overhead, then fading off.

"Come on," he said. "We're halfway down."

The closer they crept to the bottom, the narrower the ravine became. Rock walls towered above them and slackened the wind. Beneath their feet the snow thinned until they were no longer trudging, but jogging. The ravine veered left, narrowed more, and leveled out. The helicopter returned and slowed to a hover over the saddle.

A spotlight popped on.

The aircraft slid sideways, the beam tracking toward the ravine.

"They're on us," he said.

TALLEY STEPPED INTO THE BARN. THE AGITATED HORSES STOMPED AND neighed. One of his men stood beside the body on the ground. He approached and crouched down to see an old man with a bullet wound to the chest.

Had to be Eckstein.

He'd told his people to not engage. Rowland had made it clear that Eckstein was to be taken alive. That was critical. Now the old man lay dead. One of his men had gone trigger-happy.

"Bravo One, this is Bravo Two."

He found his radio and stood. "Go ahead."

"We've picked up tracks at the bottom of the draw. Looks like they've slipped into a slot ravine heading north. They can't be more than a couple minutes ahead of us. We're searching it now. So far no joy."

"Stay on it. Our targets are headed somewhere. I want to know where."

"Roger. Beginning search. How large a grid do you want?"

"Whatever it takes."

With snow piling up fast and the thermometer in the single digits Daniels could not cover much ground. One of Talley's men in the helicopter was injured, not seriously, another lay dead outside. More were standing a few feet away.

Ready.

"Who fired the rounds?" he asked his men.

"None of us. We only used the flashbang."

A stray from the helicopter?

Maybe.

Or at least that's what he'd tell Rowland.

LUKE AND JILLIAN SPRINTED TOWARD A SHALLOW DEPRESSION IN THE rock wall and pressed themselves into it. The Sikorsky's spotlight traced a path along the ravine's bottom. In what seemed to Luke like slow motion, the beam glided past their hiding place and disappeared around the bend.

Then the helicopter thumped away.

"They're moving off, but not giving up," Jillian said.

"Talley will run us to ground or die trying."

With no choice they kept going.

Twenty minutes of careful hiking and the ravine made a sharp turn to the south and abruptly ended at a rock ledge. Three times the helo and its searchlight returned, each pass coming from a different direction in the hope of catching them moving out in the open. Below them lay a keyhole meadow with the mining camp Eckstein had mentioned, the buildings mere fuzzy shapes in the dim light and blowing snow. They leaned against the cliff face and caught their breath. In the commotion Luke had forgotten about the horses. As thorough as Talley was he might have shot them rather than let Luke and Jillian use them to escape. With them already gone, hopefully he'd leave them alone.

"At some point," he said, "we're going to need to double back and get the horses."

"We can wait Talley out here," she said. "We're out of the wind and hidden from view."

He disagreed. "They know we came in this way. If he hasn't already, he'll send men down the saddle. And if we keep heading north the storm and the mountains will swallow us. Our best bet is that camp down there. We need to get out of sight."

And not be easy targets for the helicopter.

Especially considering its pilot was surely equipped with night-vision helmets. His Ranger brain was skipping ahead, working through the various scenarios. He and Talley were engaged in a chess match, one where the loser died. Talley's warning ambush at the Francorchamps heliport had reaffirmed the former Delta soldier as a three-dimensional thinker. Talley had them on the run, in a storm, with only one sheltered and defensible position within miles. Once Talley found the camp—and he would, of that Luke was certain—he'd order it under surveillance and wait. That might explain why the helicopter had not returned for a fourth pass.

Talley might be loosening the leash.

Just a bit.

"We have no choice," she said. "We won't survive for long out here."

She was right.

The temperature was still falling, but that was the least of their problems. Avalanches could soon become a real danger. Something else was also on Luke's mind. The inevitable fight coming their way might not be survivable. Since Belgium he'd watched the toll of their journey chip away at Jillian's spirit. Physically she was strong as ever. A seasoned combat vet. But her eyes had lost their shine. Her smile was less frequent and increasingly forced. More and more he'd caught her staring off into space. Having gone from watching helplessly while Benji withered before her eyes to seeing him shot dead she was shell-shocked, and rightly so. He should have seen it sooner, though he wasn't sure it would've made any difference. In excruciating detail she'd relived the horror of that terrible day in Dallas, then listened as Eckstein chronicled Rowland's sixty-year trail of regret. She'd endured Talley's relentless pursuit and the near-constant threat of death. Even if they survived this ordeal, would she ever be the same? His thoughts were neither pity nor patronage, but rather simple concern for a dear friend.

And that she was.

Her end would not come in the middle of the Wyoming wilderness.

Not a chance.

He looked her in the eyes and tried to convey his resolve. "Okay. The camp is where we make our stand."

TALLEY STUDIED THE MAP.

Not an electronic display.

An actual paper map, which he'd acquired yesterday. In the light from the burning house he surveyed the location the helicopter had reported last seeing Daniels at. Nothing but wilderness for miles in every direction.

Then he saw it.

A notation for an old mining facility.

He smiled.

It was like Daniels was sending him an invitation.

Perhaps he was?

He found his radio. "Bravo Three, start your approach on the ground."

59.

LUKE HOPPED OFF THE ROCK LEDGE INTO THIGH-DEEP SNOW. HE still carried the pack, shotgun, and Beretta. As agreed he and Jillian had separated to make themselves harder targets, then they'd each begun their trudge toward the mining camp's closest building, an equipment hut, by the looks of it, whose back walls had collapsed.

Beyond was Ishawooa Camp proper, a collection of structures linked by enclosed walkways. According to the infographic on their map the bigger structures, which dated back to the original 1847 camp, consisted of the ore house, where raw material was stored, and the waterwheel-powered mill building, where ore was processed and separated. Yet another pair of walkways connected the ore house to a lodgepole bunkhouse set against the meadow's southern slope and a mine entrance set into the northern slope. Interspersed amid the main buildings were dozens of freestanding shacks added, he assumed, to accommodate a once expanding workforce. All told the camp occupied roughly three acres and had been overhauled and modernized through the decades until closing twenty years ago. A rat's nest like this was an attacker's worst nightmare. You'd be constantly looking over your shoulders.

Perfect.

Everything was in surprisingly good condition given its age. Life would have been brutal here, especially the winters. But he knew that the lure of gold was so strong that thousands of men and women had endured conditions worse than this to find it. The isolation, unrelenting cold, and backbreaking work must have been soul crushing.

And all just to be rich.

Jillian approached from his right and came close, cradling her shotgun. He motioned and they took it slow and steady, partially for fear of losing sight of each other in the billowing snow and partially because they knew quick movements were easier for watchful eyes to spot.

Something moved ahead.

He raised a fist.

Jillian went still and sat on her haunches, leaving only her head and shoulders visible. He crouched too. A snowshoe hare bounded into view and just as quickly disappeared into the gloom.

False alarm.

They reached the rear wall of the equipment shed where the listing roof formed an alcove of sorts. Luke's thighs were on fire.

"I need more time on the treadmill," he said.

"My own conditioning is pathetic," she added. "What do you think, if they were here wouldn't they have already sprung the trap?"

"Maybe Talley's going to wait for us to get comfortable before tightening the noose."

"Then let's not get comfortable."

He agreed.

Talley had surely studied a map and narrowed the places where'd they run to. His boss, Rowland, had to be concerned with what Eckstein possessed. Surely the same had been true for Simmons, which explained why the house was burned to ashes. Now Eckstein's smoldered. But they had the two flash drives, the movie reel, photos. The whole damn enchilada.

So what was NAI 31621?

Good question.

Would the evidence they'd thus far gathered even scratch Rowland's paint? Would they be labeled conspiracy crackpots, armed with nothing more than ludicrous diagrams and tales about a phantom mistake? And Eckstein's movie? Credible? Or just something for the trolls to tear apart, frame by frame? He washed those thoughts from his brain and refocused on their current circumstances.

Talley would find them soon enough.

"Let's check things out," he said.

They separated again, each circling the shed so they could approach the headframe from different angles. Off to his right a huge mound came into view. Not a natural formation, he decided, but rather a tailings pile left behind long ago by the miners. He wondered how much of the terrain they'd passed was actually tailings that had settled into the earth over the years since the gold rush ended here. The closer he drew into the camp the thinner the snow became until he was moving through powder no deeper than his ankles. So sheltered was this keyhole meadow that snow was mounting here half as quickly as it was out in the open. Jillian reached the headframe a few seconds before him. She gave him a nod then ducked through an opening.

"Clear," she whispered a few seconds later.

He crawled inside.

The interior, which measured roughly forty feet to a side, was dominated by a chain-driven windlass mounted in the peaked roof. A rusty steel cable descended into a shaft in the dirt floor. Luke dropped a rock into the hole and received a metallic *tink* in response a few seconds later.

"Elevator cage," he said.

"How deep do you think it goes?"

"However deep the veins went. Hundreds of feet, probably. These miners went as far as their air vents would allow."

He crawled back outside and peeked around it. The wind had picked up, further decreasing visibility, but he saw no one moving about. Bad odds had been daily life in Afghanistan. This was no different.

No sense splitting up and one of them going for help. It was a long way to civilization and neither of them had any idea which way was best. They started this together, so they'd finish it together.

"He'll come by air," he said.

"I agree. It's fast and the blizzard be damned."

Absolutely.

"We've got lots to do before they get here," he said. "They'll have to split up and search all the nooks and crannies."

"And we'll make them bleed for every inch of it."

The fire in her eyes was good to see.

And he agreed with her.

They would bleed for every inch.

60.

TALLEY WATCHED AS ECKSTEIN'S CABIN BURNED.

His men had ventured inside to see if anything was there to find. The house was not totally engulfed, so the flames would have to be fanned at some point to finish the destruction. He knew where Daniels had gone and would head there shortly.

But first things first.

One of his contingent emerged from the house and trotted his way. The man drew closer and he saw he was holding what looked like a laptop computer. He studied the unit. Charred. Screen shattered. But probably savable.

Aside from capturing Eckstein and killing Daniels and Stein, Rowland had given Talley one other priority. Search for and take personal custody of any device that might be used to store information, especially videos. No one, including Talley himself, was to view anything. On this point Rowland had been adamant, almost rabidly so. What could be that important, he wondered for the umpteenth time.

"Bag it," he ordered. "Who else knows about this?"

"Just me."

"Keep it that way."

In his headset Talley heard a burst of static. "Bravo One, Bravo Two, come in."

"Go ahead."

"We spotted some structures about a mile and a half north of the cabin."

The mining camp.

"Visibility is horrible. Winds coming off the cliffs are shearing like crazy. I sat her down in a meadow nearby. I estimate at least three big buildings, maybe more. Place looked old and abandoned."

"Why not just send a team in? We've got them outnumbered," his man standing next to him said.

He shook his head. "If we commit too soon, he'll chew us to bits. He has the battlefield." He paused. "For now."

He keyed his headset. "Bravo Two, how's your fuel?"

"We're good."

"Then come get us."

LUKE DECIDED THE FIRST ORDER OF BUSINESS WAS TO CHOOSE THEIR last-stand ground. The bunkhouse and its thick walls seemed in the best shape. If they could barricade the front door the millhouse walkway was the only available approach. This would be the fatal funnel into which Talley's men would have to step.

And that would be their opportunity.

He followed their flashlight beams onto the headframe walkway that led to the millhouse, empty save for a few heaps of ore, then he continued on to a connecting walkway to the bunkhouse. The double-decker beds were still there, twelve of them along each wall, two more against the short walls. He saw a potbelly stove that he rolled onto its side, kicking off a pair of its legs, weak from rust. Jillian wedged those into the front door's handle.

"They might get through, but not easily," she said. "What's next?"

"Those beds. Can you move one by yourself?"

She walked over, grabbed one of the stout wood frames, and dragged it a few feet.

"Easy," she said.

Together they shoved four of the beds into the mouth of the walkway, then another four oriented both vertically and diagonally until the walkway resembled a tornado-ravaged jungle gym showroom.

He said, "If you have to abandon your main position, retreat here, then shove the rest of the beds against the mouth of the walkway. For Talley's men to reach you they'll have to climb through that mess."

"Fish in a barrel," she said.

"What's that on the floor?" he asked, pointing at a black ring.

She leaned down and lifted open a hatch, shining her flashlight into the hole. "Some sort of cellar, is my guess. I can't see how far back it goes."

He clicked on his flashlight and dropped into the hole. A tunnel led away from the cellar and exited beneath the bunkhouse's front porch. The dirt floor was dusted with snow that had seeped through gaps in the façade planking. He pressed his palm against the wood.

Which cracked and bulged outward.

He returned to the cellar and climbed out. "It goes under the porch. Might be a good emergency exit. Come on, let's secure the other doors."

They located all of the main building exits and jammed each one shut with lengths of scrap iron. Then they toured the building, choosing hiding places and firing positions. Dilapidated equipment and mine carts formed choke points and blind corners that Talley's men would have no choice but to negotiate. In the ore building they followed the walkway to the boarded-up mine entrance. Somewhere back there would be a connecting shaft to the processing plant.

Another retreat path.

He mentally filed away that detail.

They returned to the millhouse and surveyed the interior, rehearsing their line of retreat to the bunkhouse when, and if, the time came. Dominating the center of the room was the trommel, a massive rotating cylinder mounted on a slanted scaffold, where soil and gravel were dumped for water sifting. Hanging above it was a chute that surely led to the waterwheel outside.

"Here's where one of us will set up," he said. "The only way in here is through the ore building and straight down that walkway. They'll make easy targets. If they manage to fight their way in, this scaffolding will give them no cover."

"I'll take it," she said. "Let's see how they like meeting a marine rifleman behind a fixed position."

He smiled. "I know where I'm putting my bet."

She had a shotgun and a Beretta. Plenty of firepower.

The millhouse's remaining space was occupied by steel rail carts, each of which weighed a couple hundred pounds. These they rolled into position around Jillian's makeshift bunker at the bunkhouse walkway. She'd have solid, layered cover and clear lines of fire. All but two of the carts they left upright. The others they tipped onto their sides and angled to serve as grenade shelters should they be needed. Once Talley's men realized they couldn't overrun her position they would try to blast her out.

"What do you think?" he asked.

"It's defensible, but it's also a bad-guy magnet. But that's the point, isn't it?"

He nodded. "While they're banging their heads against your wall, I'll be doing my best to make their lives hell."

He hoped to use the maze-like layout and exterior shacks to his advantage, sniping from cover then changing positions before

Talley's men could reorient themselves. They'd gained an advantage by arriving first.

She glanced at the ceiling.

He heard it too.

Rotors.

Helo approaching.

The sound grew louder and louder, the engine warbled as though under heavy strain.

"The wind must be hellish out there," he said. "The shape of this ravine makes it an updraft funnel."

After about thirty seconds the chopper pulled off and the engine faded into the distance.

"Our guests have arrived," she said.

TALLEY STOOD BACK OUT IN THE COLD.

"Bravo One this is Bravo Five, come in."

The sentry he'd left back at Eckstein's cabin.

"I've got the intel you wanted," his man said. "The structures are part of an old mining camp called Ishawooa Creek. I found some pics on a hiker's blog. The images aren't great but it looks like it sits on about three acres. Five large buildings and about a dozen smaller outbuildings, connected by covered pathways. I'm sending pics to your sat-phone now."

Luck favors the prepared, he thought.

In the middle of nowhere Luke Daniels had managed to find what was every soldier's nightmare—a complex and unknowable urban landscape. By now he and Stein would have already familiarized themselves with the locale. Not only would Daniels manipulate the interior and the access points to maximum advantage, he'd also remove any advantages available to attackers. Rangers excelled at taking and holding ground.

That left Talley with two choices.

One, a simultaneous attack from all sides. Or two, blast open their own entrance and run an overpowering sweep-and-clear of each building. Either way, Daniels would have already established a last-stand position, a fatal funnel into which his men would have no choice but to step.

Should he have expected anything less?

Not at all.

He'd discovered the depth of Daniels' resourcefulness back in Afghanistan on Celam Kae. He'd been counting on a repeat and had not been disappointed.

Talley's phone beeped. He scrolled through the pictures then asked, "Any details on the mine itself?"

"Best I can tell there's just one entrance beneath a big angular building against the north side cliff."

"I appreciate the intel," he said into his mouthpiece, then signed off.

He turned to his men. "Let's go."

"Eyes or bullets?" one asked.

Did he want them to conduct a visual-only reconnaissance or a reconnaissance-by-fire, essentially firing upon a suspected position in the hope of determining its strength and disposition? A sensible tactical question with only one right answer. Daniels wasn't going to give up his secrets because of a few incoming rounds. Further, he was unsure how any of this was going to play out, so he erred on the side of caution.

"Just eyes," he ordered. "This target is a pro. Fire on my command only."

61.

Luke spent fifteen minutes doing a final tour of the buildings, rehearsing, revising. Here and there he paused to loosen wall planks should they need a quick exit. Jillian was ensconced at her fighting position, so he spent another ten minutes outside, repeatedly trudging between the main buildings and the outbuildings, leaving in his wake the boldest tracks he could manage. Until the snow filled them, these paths would be yet another uncertainty for pursuers. He then retreated back inside.

"I've got movement to the east," Jillian said. "Two men in alpine-white coveralls, about a hundred meters out. Moving slow and coming straight in."

Recon. Definitely.

Sent to generate a reaction.

"Okay. I'm heading out."

He jogged back through the ore building to the millhouse's east wall and knelt before a particularly wide gap in the planks.

"Where are you?" he muttered.

It took thirty seconds but finally the figures emerged from the swirling white veil, dressed head-to-toe in speckled gray-on-white coveralls. Now their rifles were at ready. Methodically, they picked their way forward, staying as low to the snow as possible.

Best guess?

One team from the east, another from the west, Talley in the center. Jillian probably had the pair from the west in her sights. The most Talley could hope to gain from this approach was the camp's rough geometry, which was relatively useless while the interior remained an enigma. Even the most elite soldiers hated stepping into the unknown. Talley was working out his options.

Okay.

Come and get me.

TALLEY STOPPED IN THE SNOW ABOUT FIFTY YARDS SHORT OF THE camp's beginning and tapped his radio. "This is Bravo One. Take it nice and slow. By the book, do you copy?"

"Copy," his men replied.

"I see no lights and no movement," one of the men on the east reported.

For the sake of clarity he'd designated the camp's main buildings one through seven, starting at the shed-like building closest to the meadow's west side and ending with what he assumed was a bunkhouse.

"Same here from the west," the other said. "I've almost reached Building One."

Team East reported, "We're holding behind cover. I've got about fifty meters of open ground to Building Five. Visibility is erratic. Should I proceed?"

"Stay put," Talley ordered. "Hunker down and watch."

"We've reached Building One," Team West said. "I'm moving to the corner for a better view." A few seconds passed. "Okay, I've got a visual on Building Two."

Building Two was the pyramid-shaped structure. He keyed his radio, "Bravo Two, this is Bravo One, make your run. Shake the tree."

"Roger. Heading in now."

Sixty seconds passed.

The helo roared in through the snow, spotlights on, flashbangs deployed, which lit up the camp. Talley gave it a minute then asked on the radio, "Any reaction?"

"Negative. No change."

The helo moved off, standing by.

"Same on our side," Team West said. "No movement, no lights.

I see a hole in the wall of Building Two. Bravo One, are we sure our targets are even here? Scratch that. I'm seeing tracks, recent ones."

"Going where?" Talley asked.

"Among the buildings, both main and the smaller ones."

He smiled. Smart boy Daniels. Create confusion.

Team West added, "The entry into Building Two is about ten meters away. I think I can make it."

"Negative. Stay put. Do you copy?"

Talley received static and a few clipped words in reply. He repeated, "Do not proceed. I say again, do not proceed."

More static.

He squeezed his eyes shut.

No choice.

"All units, this is Bravo One. Engage target."

62.

LUKE WATCHED AS THE MAN LEFT HIS SPOT AT THE CORNER OF the shed and moved across open ground toward the headframe. Clearly the hole in the wall had been too tempting to ignore.

"Aren't we a little go-getter?" he whispered to himself.

The helicopter was gone, the spotlight and flashbangs designed to elicit a reaction. That bait they'd not taken.

No way.

He trotted back through the millhouse, turned right down the headframe walkway, then slowed his pace until he was creeping.

He pressed himself flat against the wall beside the hole, the shotgun barrel hovering a few inches above it. From the other side came the soft scrape of cloth on snow. A shadow passed before the hole, followed by a head, then a torso. When the man was halfway through, Luke rolled him onto his back and pressed the rifle's muzzle into an eye socket.

"Not a word. Not a twitch. Nod if you understand me."

The man complied.

"Are you on comms with someone?" Luke whispered.

Another nod.

"Blink once for voice-activated, twice for press-to-talk."

The man blinked twice.

He ordered him to cross his hands on his chest, then he grasped the collar and dragged the man the rest of the way inside. He rolled his captive onto his belly spread-eagle, frisked him, and tossed the weapons aside.

"How many are you?"

The man said nothing.

"Answer my question or my partner will drop your friend. Is it just the two of you?"

Nothing.

"Is this how it's gonna be? I ask questions and you play the strong silent type?"

"Pretty much."

"That's what I figured."

Luke reversed the rifle and smacked the butt against the back of the man's head. The body went limp. He quickly donned the man's headset. Through the earpiece a voice was saying,

"Do you copy? Do you copy?"

Jack Talley.

Tempting as it was to engage in a bit of psych-ops banter, he resisted the impulse. Static seemed his best weapon. One of Talley's team had just disappeared, cause and disposition unknown. On the battlefield such occurrences gave soldiers serious pause. He was hoping for the same here.

"Anyone have eyes on Bremer?"

A chorus of negatives came in reply.

A long, static-filled pause came before Talley's voice returned. "All units, switch to backup channel. This one is compromised."

Luke removed the headset and stuffed both it and the radio into his pack.

He took a quick inventory.

Another rifle, two frag grenades, and two flashbang grenades. Excellent.

He then bound the man's hands and feet with zip ties retrieved from his captive's vest. These guys came prepared. He had a tentative plan for his prisoner, but only time would tell whether it was feasible. He then returned to Jillian's position and handed over the extra rifle and three grenades, keeping one of the flashbangs for himself.

"How long until Talley makes his move?" she asked.

"A few minutes at most."

"How many men are we talking about?"

"Impossible to say. But we do control the high ground."

"I appreciate your optimism, but aren't you forgetting Mr. Murphy? We're due a visit."

Anything that can go wrong will go wrong. Gospel among soldiers.

But not to him.

In battle he'd seen circumstances turn on a dime, for better and for worse, but he'd yet to see everything go wrong of its own volition. That usually involved some element of mistake or carelessness.

"I prefer my own version," he said. "Luke's Law."

"Let's hear it."

"Be prepared."

"Doesn't quite have the same pithiness, but I get your point."

"You all set here?" he asked.

She nodded and offered what he decided was an indulgent, affectionate smile.

"Don't get yourself killed," he added.

"Same for you."

63.

LUKE LEFT JILLIAN HUNKERED DOWN AND HEADED OUT. ALONG the way he hid the backpack with the laptop and other information, adding the two flash drives from his pocket, leaving only weapons and ammunition in his possession. He then proceeded carefully to the headframe, circling the shaft and dropping to his belly before the hole in the wall. Through the blowing snow he saw more men, each armed with an assault rifle, trudging toward the equipment hut.

One walked with a limp.

Talley.

Allowing them uncontested access to cover seemed a mistake. At this distance he could not make a hit, but he could stop their advance. So he aimed the shotgun and pulled the trigger, sending a wad of buckshot their way. Scattering had been the objective, but the men charged forward. Talley and anyone he'd hire would be combat-tested. Backing down would not be their style. He racked in another shell and sprinted down the walkway just as the men opened fire, shredding the walls around the position he'd just abandoned.

He reached the mill building and ducked around the trommel, sprinting down the next walkway to the ore house where he turned left and knee-slid to a stop before his next firing position, a gap he'd widened in the plank wall. He sighted on the corner of the equipment hut. A head peeked around. He fired, shattering the wood beam beside the man's face and driving him back. From the hut's opposite corner a muzzle flashed. Bullets peppered Luke's wall.

He backed away.

Thankfully, Jillian was sticking to the plan and not firing. He wanted to keep her position unknown to their attackers for as long as possible.

He rushed for the millhouse.

His firing position there was an upturned mine cart wedged into a collapsed section of wall. He ducked behind it just as bullets thudded into the cart's steel. Overhead, the helicopter had returned. The spotlight popped on, casting bright white stripes on the dirt floor. Rapid fire came from above and rounds began chopping away at the roof, showering Luke in splinters. He threw himself into the cart and curled into a ball.

Then he realized.

His prisoner was exposed.

He peeked out and saw the unconscious man lying in the middle of the millhouse floor. An enemy, for sure, but leaving him to die like that wasn't right. The helo's gunner began walking rounds across the room, punching up geysers of dirt. Luke rolled from his shelter and sprinted toward the fallen man. Rock shrapnel peppered his clothes. He reached the man and combat-dragged him back to the overturned cart. The fire slackened briefly, then resumed, now concentrated on the ore room walkway.

"Incoming your way," he shouted, uncertain whether Jillian heard him over the din.

Preparatory fire.

Designed to disorient while others made for the mill building.

The rifle fire intensified but the accuracy decreased, further suggesting the shooters were moving. Bullets sparked on the cart and ricocheted across the room. He waited for a gap in the gunfire then rose to his knees. The two men he'd forced to take cover behind the equipment hut wouldn't stay still for long. The head-frame was the next nearest structure and therefore their likely destination. The helicopter ceased fire and roared away. He knew what that meant. The attackers on the east side were close now and the helo's gunner didn't want to risk hitting his comrades.

"What's happening over there?" he called out.

"Two are still behind cover."

"That won't last long. Let them get inside, then drop them as quick as you can. They don't know where you are."

Though they'd barricaded the millhouse's door, either it wouldn't hold for long or Talley's men would simply find a weak point in the wall and blast through. If Jillian could dispatch them before they reached her walkway, the next wave of attackers wouldn't know where the killing shots had come from.

"That helo will be back," he said.

"Understood."

He headed off and reached the headframe, focusing on the hole in the wall, but he miscalculated his angle at the mine shaft. He spun sideways and managed to avoid the hole, but crashed into the wall and fell on his ass.

A man scrambled through the wall hole.

Luke rolled backward and lifted the shotgun but before he could fire the man was on him. He released his grip on the gun and delivered a thumb-punch to the throat, which elicited an *ugh*. The man sagged sideways, but maintained his grip on Luke's jacket.

Tangled together, they rolled.

Then plummeted down into the mine shaft.

He realized there'd only be seconds. So he spun around on top. They slammed into the elevator grate roof, the guy beneath him taking the lion's share of the impact. The car buckled under the sudden weight, shifted, then gave way and they dropped down into the elevator cage. Which snapped the steel cable and the cage dropped another foot, steadied, dropped again, then started swing-ing. The guy beneath him was stunned, eyes blinking rapidly, but managed to reach into his web harness and unsheathe a knife.

"I wouldn't do that," Luke said.

The man lunged.

Luke tilted his head to one side.

The blade missed his right eye by an inch before striking the cage wall. Luke grabbed the man's wrist, locking the knife hand in place. "You're a special kind of stupid, aren't you? This cage is going to fall any second. Stop moving."

The man didn't reply, but jerked his arm, trying to free his hand. Luke cocked his head back and slammed the crown of his skull into the man's face, shattering his nose.

Blood squirted.

He twisted the guy's wrist and the knife fell away.

The cage dropped again and crashed into the wall, rocking from side to side. He glanced up. The cable was unraveling. As each strand gave way, a *twang* filled the shaft. He tossed himself forward, grasped the man's collar as a handhold, and started crawling toward the wall shaft and a tunnel entrance a few feet away. The man's hand clamped onto his ankle and jerked him backward.

"No, you don't," his adversary wheezed.

The cable popped.

More *twangs* rang into rapid fire.

"Wanna bet?"

He slammed the heel of his boot into the guy's face.

The man let go.

Luke scrambled, hands clawing at the tunnel floor until his fingers found a crack in the rock. He pulled, kicked off the man's head, and slid the rest of the way up and into the tunnel.

With a gunshot-like crack the cable severed.

The cage tipped onto its side and lodged itself between the walls. Luke looked down. The man stretched his arm out for help.

Their fingers touched.

With the grinding of steel against rock the cage rolled onto its side, then slid down the shaft. He caught a final glimpse of the man's terrified face before it was absorbed by the blackness.

64.

LUKE'S CHEST HEAVED.

He rolled onto his back and grabbed hold of himself.

The tunnel was a few feet wide and half his height. He crept back to the edge of the shaft and craned his neck so he could look up into the headframe. The cable had severed near the windlass. No way to reach it. Nor did the shaft walls show any handholds.

He wasn't escaping that way.

He'd heard no more gunfire. Did that mean Talley's men had paused their attack—or had they already overrun Jillian's position? No, she wouldn't have let that happen without expending every last bullet at her disposal. Hopefully she was hiding, waiting, biding her time. He decided to return the favor she'd tossed him back in Louisiana and interrupt their search for her. He found his Beretta, angled its barrel up the shaft, and fired three rounds in quick succession.

He reloaded, then took a moment to survey his surroundings. He wondered if this shaft was merely an old equipment alcove, but a quick check with his headlamp revealed the tunnel extended ten feet into the rock before turning left. It was clearly man-made so it had to have both a purpose and a destination.

Where, though?

His first shots hadn't gotten a reaction. He needed to try something different. With a hand braced against the ceiling he leaned into the shaft, took aim on the windlass at the top, and squeezed the trigger. His bullet struck steel with a satisfying thunk that echoed through the space.

Boots pounded down the walkway.

That's it, come on.

Luke took aim.

A face peered over the side. Luke shot him in the head. The man pitched forward, bounced off the shaft wall, and tumbled into the darkness.

From above, a shout. "Stop. Get back. He's down there."

Another face appeared, but withdrew before Luke could fire.

A whispered voice said, "Twelve feet down on the right."

A moment later from the opposite side of the shaft an arm popped out. Clenched in the fist was a flashbang grenade.

Luke ran.

He reached the tunnel bend and heard the grenade bounce off the floor and clatter toward him. He dropped to his knees, covered his ears, and squeezed shut his eyes.

He felt a *whomp* in his belly.

The tunnel exploded in blinding white light.

He uncovered his ears. Over the residual ringing he heard a muffled voice say "—has to come out somewhere. Find it and cut him off."

He'd gotten his wish. He definitely had their attention.

He started down the tunnel, his headlight beam bouncing off the walls. The route curved left, then right, before straightening again. In his mind he brought up the mining camp's layout and decided he was somewhere between the headframe and the ore building, heading toward the meadow's northern slope.

The tunnel floor angled down.

The air cooled.

In the distance gunfire began again.

He picked up his pace.

Ceiling stanchions appeared along the walls, and stone gave way to rough-hewn planking. The floor now angled upward and came to a stop at a rock wall. Affixed to the face by pitons was a ladder. He placed his boot on the first rung and tested.

It held.

He turned off his headlamp and slowly ascended, one rung at a time.

He emerged in another horizontal shaft, this one wider and taller, at an intersection, judging by the rail tracks disappearing down four smaller side tunnels.

He stood still and listened.

More gunfire.

Still in the distance.

He chose one of the tunnels and started walking. After fifty yards he found himself standing before another rock wall, this one rising into a double-wide shaft. A pair of equally wide ladders bolted to the rock led into the darkness. A gust of cold air poured over his face. There was an opening up there, a big one. Maybe a construction entrance to the old processing plant.

He'd been going in the wrong direction.

He returned to the intersection, closed his eyes for a twenty-count, then opened them again. He spotted a faint speck of green and jogged toward the light. Soon the mine entrance came into view.

The sound of gunfire increased.

He picked up his pace.

Then froze.

A flashlight had clicked on. In its glow he saw a pair of legs standing just outside the entrance.

"Check it," a voice said.

Legs shifted. A torso appeared beneath the lowermost slat followed by a head. The flashlight beam skimmed toward Luke. He backed up and pressed himself into the wall.

"Clear."

The men moved off.

Luke gave them a ten-second head start then crept toward the entrance, stopping five feet short. He went prone. The two men had reached the midpoint between the mine and the ore house.

He refocused on the men in the walkway.

Time to act.

He took aim and shot one of them in the leg.

The other man shouted for help and began dragging his partner to safety. Luke put a round in his hip. Writhing in agony, this man got on the radio and started shouting.

"We're down and taking fire at the mine."

65.

TALLEY HEARD THE REPORT THROUGH HIS HEADSET AND REPLIED, "This is Bravo One, describe your wounds."

"Leg and hip. Single shots."

"Are you still taking fire?"

"No, sir."

Luke had obviously found a route between the shaft he'd fallen into and the mine proper, which begged the question, where else might he pop up unexpectedly?

"Get yourselves to Building Three," he ordered. "All Bravo units, this is Bravo One. Hold on the extraction."

"Come again, Bravo One. I've got wounded."

He knew Daniels was trying to siphon off men. If he'd wanted those two dead, they'd be dead. Which told him something about the strategy. Daniels was staying on the move, acting as the hammer, which meant the Stein woman was the anvil. She'd be lying in wait behind a fixed position.

"You heard me," Talley said. "All units, stay on task. Sweep and clear."

LUKE HEARD ONLY ONE SIDE OF TALLEY'S EXCHANGE WITH HIS wounded men.

But it was enough.

Talley wasn't falling for it.

So he made his way back to where Jillian was ensconced.

"You here?"

"I am." Her voice was a whisper.

He crept over closer. "Talk to me."

"They're taking their time, moving in tight pairs, clearing the attached outbuildings as they go."

"If any retreat this way, take them out."

"Understood."

He left her and made his way back to where the two wounded waited.

"Can you two hear me?" he called out.

"We hear you."

"Leave your weapons, grenades, and radios."

"Go to hell."

He put a round into the floorboards between them. "Guess you didn't hear me. I said, leave your weapons, grenades, and radios."

Each man shrugged off his equipment.

"Keep going and don't look back."

He waited until they left then ran out, collected their gear, and returned to the mine. In the distance he heard a flashbang detonation. Followed by shouts and sporadic gunfire that ceased almost immediately.

He did some quick mental math.

Between dead and wounded he'd removed four from the playing field. Of course, Talley would be keeping his own count. In most soldiers losing over half your number might cause hesitancy, but Talley was no ordinary soldier. Now is when he'd crank up the heat and seize the advantage.

He hustled back Jillian's way with his cache.

"Change of plans," he said to her.

"I'm listening."

"Talley's going to throw what's left into the fray. When they find you, turn that walkway into hell. Don't linger. Pour your ammunition onto them."

He left her with one of the rifles and grenades. He still carried one of the flashbangs and shouldered the other rifle.

"You're sure about this?" she asked.

"When you do, I'll finish them."

TALLEY SPOKE INTO HIS RADIO. "THIS IS BRAVO ONE. GIVE ME AN update on the wounded."

"Stable, but no longer operational," came the reply. "Daniels took their equipment. I suggest we split up and—"

"Negative, stay on mission. Find Stein's position and overrun it. We grab her and Daniels will give up. Once you get the woman, do whatever it takes to get Daniels into the open. Is that clear? No holds barred."

"Understood."

LUKE DIDN'T HAVE TO LOOK UP TO KNOW TALLEY WAS SENDING everyone he had left into the fight. The roar of the Sikorsky's engine converged over the meadow. The overlapping whomp of the rotors echoed and multiplied off the cliff faces until the cacophony filled his head. He kept his eyes fixed on the ore building's west wall and bulldozed through the snowdrifts until what he judged was the last second, then dove headfirst into the powder.

He rolled onto his back and went still.

He would only get one chance to do this, and his window of opportunity would last mere seconds. He'd learned the hard way in Afghanistan that helos are at their most vulnerable when hovering for troop recovery or deployment, which was why most of them came equipped with a door gunner. The trick would be how quickly that gunner pinned down Luke's firing position.

Overhead the Sikorsky swooped into view, banked hard over the millhouse, and stopped in a hover. Given the confines of the meadow, the only landing sites left were on the east and west sides. He readied the automatic rifle and rolled into a prone firing position, sighted on the door, and squeezed the trigger. His first burst went wide so he adjusted the aim and sent the next into the Sikorsky's cabin. The door gunner responded, issuing an orange stream of bullets that ripped into the equipment shed and the headframe building. He centered his fire on the shadowed figure with an automatic rifle.

And fired.

The man fell back.

The gun went silent.

He turned his attention to the cockpit, under no illusion his gunfire would bring down the helo, but a panicked and overcorrecting pilot certainly could.

He sent rounds into the rotor.

The helicopter staggered left, steadied, then began climbing, moving away.

Smoke poured out.

The Sikorsky lurched sideways and banked off. The helo's engine groaned, the rotors clawing at the thin, frigid air for purchase. He watched, half horrified, half fascinated as the Sikorsky rolled fully onto its side and the rotors slammed into the slot ravine's upper edge and shattered. Shrapnel whined overhead and tore into the headframe and the millhouse. Now rotorless, the Sikorsky crashed into the ravine, then tumbled down the cliff and came to rest roof-first in the snow.

Silence overtook the camp.

Then he heard a torrent of rifle fire and the rapid, overlapping thunk of bullets peppering the mine carts.

Jillian.

He desperately wanted to go to her aid but for his new plan to succeed he needed Talley's men focused in a single direction.

Hers.

He started toward the fallen helicopter, gun up and tracking for movement until he reached the cabin's inverted side door. Ignoring the twisted bodies, he climbed inside and started rummaging around. A burst of radio static from the cockpit stopped him short. He leaned through the opening and groped until he touched the pilot's helmet, which he freed and donned.

"Bravo Two, this is Bravo One, do you copy?"

Talley.

He partially covered the microphone with his sleeve and keyed the headset. "Bravo One...wounded...pinned."

"Say again. Who am I talking to, over?"

He rubbed his sleeve over the microphone. "Pinned... tourniquet...slot canyon."

"Hang on. I'll send help. We have an incoming helo."

He removed the headset and dropped it. Whether he'd pulled off the ruse or Talley was playing him Luke didn't know, but it was an opportunity he couldn't afford to pass up. And thank goodness he hadn't. But—

Incoming helo?

Just great.

He ran from the crash site and chose a spot where the snow was particularly deep, then lay flat and half buried himself. From the east came the chop of more rotors. Another Sikorsky swept in fast over the millhouse roof, nosed hard over, then leveled ten feet above the ground with the cabin door facing the crash site. A man leaped from the door, plunged into the snow, and started bulldozing his way to the wreckage. Luke waited until he was almost there then sprang to his feet and ran, hunched over, toward the hovering Sikorsky. The pilot spotted Luke and shouted something. The door gunner's face appeared in the cabin window, then pulled back. Luke dove beneath the helo's skids then rolled onto his back. The door gunner, now armed with a rifle, leaned out and fired three quick shots. Luke pulled the pin on the flashbang he'd been carrying, let the spoon go, then arched it into the Sikorsky's open door.

Smoke gushed from the door.

The Sikorsky dropped straight down. Luke rolled sideways but not quickly enough. The left-side skid graced his shoulder.

Which hurt.

The helo landed and a man emerged from the smoke armed with a rifle, advancing for a point-blank shot. Luke searched for his rifle, which had fallen from his grasp in the chaos. He spotted it and was reaching for it when two shots rang out.

The man's head became engulfed in red mist.

Jillian appeared with her Beretta leveled.

"I appreciate your timeliness," he said.

"You hurt?"

"Just my pride."

She grinned. "It'll survive. What's the plan?"

"Into the mine, then up into the processing plant."

"How do you know we can get in there?"

"I've been there. Trust me. There's only one way in. If they want us they'll have to follow."

She shook her head. "Where have I heard that before?"

66.

LUKE FOUND A WEAK SECTION IN THE ORE HOUSE'S PLANK WALL AND kicked the way through.

Just in time.

Bullets ripped into the wall, showering them with wood chunks. Talley's men had found them.

"Move it," he told Jillian. "Get to the mine. I'm right behind you."

Talley's men were exiting from both the millhouse and the head-frame. He counted three. Then he saw Talley himself, hobbling along, before he followed Jillian. She'd already ducked through the half-boarded entrance.

"Straight back a couple hundred yards," he said.

"You hear that? Radio static."

He dug into his pack, pulled out the radio he'd taken from the first man, and settled the headset on his head.

"Daniels, if you can hear me, come back."

"It's Talley," he said.

He lifted the earpiece slightly so she could listen.

"If you're on this channel, respond."

He stared at her with eyes that asked, *What do you think?*

She shrugged, so he said into the mic, "I hear you."

"Got time for a chat?"

"Say what you're going to say."

"You know how this is going to end. Why delay things?"

"By my count, you've lost a lot of men, plus two helicopters."

"I have reinforcements. You do not."

He glanced at Jillian, who shook her head.

"I know where you're headed," Talley said. "It's a death trap with only one entrance and exit."

"How do you know that?"

"You chose it."

"Hypothetically speaking, what happens if we give up? You let us walk away and Rowland leaves us alone?"

"I'm afraid that road's closed."

Which made him wonder, considering what had happened in Belgium. "Then you're wasting our time. I like our odds. You keep sending your men after us and we'll keep chewing them up."

He removed the headset and tossed it aside.

"He's worried," Jillian said.

"That makes two of us."

For all they knew, Talley wasn't lying about reinforcements. He could even wait them out and let hunger, thirst, and exposure do the work. But that wasn't his way. Reinforcements or not, Talley would press the attack.

"Let's keep moving. It's not far."

They reached the rock wall and Luke went up first, testing the ladder rungs as he climbed. After forty feet the shaft opened onto a platform. An unfinished rock floor stretched out as an expanse of dips and bumps that extended to the far wall. Sixty feet above, through crisscrossing beams and walkways, he saw a massive horizontal slit through which moonlight poured.

The conveyor scaffolding.

Jillian reached the ledge and he helped her to her feet.

She gazed upward.

This high on the cliff face the wind whipped treacherously. Gust-driven snow gushed through the conveyor scaffolding and filled the air with ice crystals that sparkled in their headlamp beams.

"Which way?" she asked.

"Up. This floor won't give us enough cover. Talley's men will flank us in no time. But from those catwalks we might be able to pick away at them."

"Providing they don't collapse under us."

"Yeah, there's that. It's your call."

"High ground is smarter," she said. "If we fall, we fall."

"That's the spirit."

Nearby they found a steel ladder bolted to a vertical beam that led to the lowermost catwalk. Jillian went up first and reached the top, then she tightrope-walked across a crossbeam and leaped on the catwalk.

"It's solid," she called out.

He climbed up to her. At the far end of the catwalk another ladder rose to the second level.

"Shouldn't they have reached those ladders by now?" she asked.

"Probably. But we can't worry about that. Let's find our spot and get sighted in. After you."

They made their way to the end of the catwalk. Jillian started her ascent to the second level. A roar came from the outside. The second helo? Back in the air? Above them, a shadow passed before the conveyor scaffolding then came to a stop at the midpoint of the wall.

Apparently so.

"Drop down," he said.

Automatic weapons fire rained down. The outer wall started disintegrating. Had to be .50-caliber. Each bullet the size of a human thumb and coming in at a rate of ten rounds per second. The wood wall, having borne too many Wyoming winters to count, wilted under the rapid fire. Swaths of wood disappeared, either chewed into sawdust or plummeting down the cliff face. This was why Talley's men hadn't followed them up the shaft. He'd warned them what was coming.

"These walkways won't hold for long," he said. "We gotta get down."

"You first. I'm on your heels."

He began crawling back toward the ladder.

"The wall's half gone," she yelled.

The .50-caliber rounds were now exploding against the upper catwalks. One of them gave way, crashing and bouncing off crossbeams before shattering on the rock floor. Their own catwalk tipped sideways, dropped, then steadied.

Luke kept going.

The ladder was ten feet away.

He glanced over his shoulder. The Sikorsky, sliding sideways, appeared in the obliterated wall. The .50-caliber went silent. The opposite cabin door slid open. That meant only one thing. Rockets. Which needed open rear space for the blowback.

He heard the whoosh as one left the tube.

He extended his arm, wrapped his fist around the ladder rung, then reached back for Jillian. "Grab my hand."

The world exploded.

And he fell.

Slamming into the rock floor.

Hard.

White-hot pain rippled through his torso. Broken rib? Or ribs? Probably. Nothing new. Some of the walkway debris pinned him down. He worked through the pain and pushed himself to his knees, plowing through the debris.

"Jillian."

"Here."

From his left.

He turned that way and kept crawling until he saw her. Standing. Okay.

The Sikorsky backed away.

"Give it up," Talley shouted.

Luke headed in the direction of the voice. The rifle was gone, and so was the Beretta. But he didn't care. He'd had enough. To his right a figure rose from behind the debris. Talley. Twenty feet away. A rifle tucked into his shoulder aimed right at him.

"That's far enough."

Luke kept walking. "You and me, Jack. Time to settle this."

Talley opened fire.

Bullets ricocheted off the rock floor.

He stopped ten feet away and stood his ground. "Call off your men. Stop it now. You and I can settle this between us."

Talley just stared, saying nothing.

"This has to end, Jack. You can't win. The Department of Justice is all over this now. They're going to get Rowland, whether you kill us or not."

Finally, Talley clicked his mic. "All Bravos, this is Bravo One. Stand down. I say again, stand down. Acknowledge." A pause. "Evacuate in the helo. I'll be following."

They stared at each other.

He'd guessed right. Talley wanted privacy. Now he had to learn just exactly what this man was after.

"Jillian," he called out. "Make sure they all leave."

"Got it."

He heard her scramble off.

"Alone at last," he said to Talley. "This was all so senseless."

"I don't disagree. But I had no choice."

"A lot of blood and guts have been spilled here today," he said. "Not to mention Benjamin Stein and David Eckstein."

"Do you know what's at stake here?" Talley asked.

"You don't know?"

"Not a clue."

He decided that honesty was best. "Your boss accidentally killed President Kennedy."

Shock filled Talley's face. "You're kidding? Right?"

"Afraid not."

"Heaven help us."

"He was in the trail car. It braked suddenly and he fell forward holding an AR-15. It fired and the bullet took Kennedy's head off."

"There's proof?"

He nodded. "In living color, on film."

"That's what Eckstein had?"

"I have it now."

"Good. You'll know what to do with it."

In the distance the Sikorsky powered up, then the rotors faded off as it flew away. Talley still toted the rifle, finger on the trigger. It was important to Luke that he talk this situation down. Talley was a man on a mission. He just needed to ascertain what that actually entailed and how he fit in. "What are you after, Jack?"

"Contentment."

A strange reply.

"I'm tired of selling my soul," Talley said. "I'm tired of being the bad guy. I want Tom Rowland to pay. *Before* he dies. If he killed Kennedy, then let's tell the world."

"That's above my pay grade. I'll turn everything I have over to my boss and she'll make that call. But she hates him as much as you do."

"Then I like her already."

"Jack, we need to leave here. Together. And we need to take care of Rowland. Together."

Talley brandished the rifle. "I have a wife and children. They'll be fair game for Rowland. He's attacked families before."

"Using you?"

Talley shook his head. "Persik and his thugs." He gestured with the rifle. "This all has to end. But it's not going to be that simple."

"Tell me why, Jack. With your testimony, Rowland will die in jail."

"And my family will be in the crosshairs. He's a vengeful man with no morals. He can hire it done."

"We can deal with him."

Talley motioned with the rifle. "No. We. Can't. If that were possible, I would have already done it."

Motion came from Luke's left, among the rubble. He was exposed and unarmed. Who was that? Talley whirled to his right at the sound. One of Talley's men appeared with a pistol aimed ahead, steadying himself to take a shot. The man planted his feet. No way Luke could dive for cover in time. Talley angled his rifle toward the man and fired. The round caught the guy in the upper chest, the impact sending the black-clad figure lurching backward off his feet.

Another gunshot echoed.

From behind Luke.

The top of Talley's head exploded in a mass of red mist.

No. It can't be.

Their gaze met and he watched as the life drained from Jack Talley's eyes, which went from surprised to sad to nothing. Talley opened his mouth to speak but nothing came out. Then the body collapsed to the ground.

He spun around.

Jillian was advancing with her Beretta aimed and level, both hands on the weapon.

"For God's sake, why did you do that?" he yelled.

"He had a rifle. He fired."

"He just saved my life."

"That's not the way I saw it."

He was furious.

She lowered her weapon. "There were two of them, with guns, and you looked like you needed help."

"I was talking him down. He shot the other guy to protect me."

"Luke, I saw what I saw and reacted. You would have done the same thing. And let's not forget Talley killed my grandfather."

"No, he did not."

"You believe that bullshit? Talley worked for Rowland. Persik worked for Rowland. They're all the same. He was no innocent."

His anger turned to rage. "You killed him for nothing."

"He came here with an army to take us out. That's not nothing. And that's twice I've saved your hide in the past half hour. You're welcome."

He knew that part of her marine training included high-risk detention, similar to police stop protocol. She was schooled in situations just like this, taught how to handle them and not jump the gun. But bad things happened when volatile situations spun out of control.

"Look," she said, "I get that I may have fired too soon. But I reacted, to save your life."

Let it go, he told himself.

For now.

"The rest are gone," she said.

"How did one of them get by you?"

"I didn't have a list of all the bad guys with guns here. I thought they all left, as Talley ordered. That one over there slipped away. But that might have been planned. He and Talley are now dead. Let's get the evidence and leave. This is over."

"It's gone."

She stared at him, incredulous. "Gone?"

"I was attacked by one of the men. We fell down a shaft. In the commotion I dropped the pack. It's gone."

"Did you look for it?"

"No. I just let it go."

She heard the sarcasm in his voice.

"I looked," he said. "It's gone. Dropped into a deep, black pit."

"So all this was for nothing?"

"I wouldn't say that. You got your revenge."

67.

Luke had been busy.

He and Jillian had made their way back to David Eckstein's property. The house had burned to the foundation, nothing left, and the old man's body remained in the barn, which he examined one last time. They'd retrieved the horses and quickly headed back to the ranger station. There, they'd left the animals for Hedow and contacted Stephanie, who prompted an immediate and dramatic response. A cleanup team was dispatched to deal with the mess and bodies. Thankfully, everything had occurred in a remote location. The National Park Service was brought in to secure the area so the teams could work undisturbed. A private jet had been waiting at Cheyenne Regional that whisked Jillian cross-country. He stayed behind. There were things to do here. Official things that did not concern her. So they said their goodbyes, the relationship chilled to nearly ice. They'd spoken little on the journey out of the wilderness. But on the tarmac before she boarded the plane, they'd made a semi-peace.

"*I know you don't agree with me shooting Talley,*" she said. "*But I thought you were in trouble. I did what I thought best. Just like when I killed the first guy.*"

"*Forget it. It's done.*"

"*I appreciate all you did. I really do. Thank you. What about Rowland?*"

"*That's not my problem. Or yours. My boss will handle him.*"

"*Going to be hard without any evidence.*"

"*She'll figure it out. You can count on that.*"

And he meant it.

Once she was gone he'd contacted Stephanie again. He'd lied to Jillian about the evidence being lost. This was a classified mission and Jillian knew way too much already, so Stephanie had suggested lessening her knowledge.

He'd misled Jillian and not mentioned that everything was safely tucked away at the mining camp. A helicopter returned him to the site and he retrieved his pack. All other tangible items from the shoot-out, including bodies and the helicopter wreckage, had been removed. Eckstein had been buried on his property. Only the barn and ruined foundation remained. What would happen to it? That wasn't the Magellan Billet's responsibility.

Luke, though, had several problems.

"*Tell me what's on your mind?*" Stephanie asked on a secure line.

"*Just a theory.*"

"*Care to explain?*"

"*Never change your hair color from the floor.*"

"*Excuse me?*"

"*Another of my mama's favorite sayings. Translated it means, don't make big decisions when you're at your lowest.*"

"*Is changing hair color a big decision?*"

"*For a southern woman, it is. Or at least it is for my mama.*"

"*I think I'd like your mother.*"

"And the feeling would be mutual. I have to finish this. My way."

"You sound more and more like Cotton every day."

"Is there any reason to insult me?"

"It was a compliment. And you're hedging, 'cause you're unsure."

"Maybe. But I'm going to find out. My way."

"You let me know the second you do."

He'd liked the fact that she was trusting him. Like Malone. To handle the situation as *he* saw fit. No micromanaging. No interference. Just get the damn job done. But she had offered some relevant intel.

"Rowland's home on Starlings Island is well guarded. But he has a second retreat, one he visits often, even at his advanced age. It's called Compass Cay, a private island he owns in the Bahamas. He gets there on his yacht. BreakAway. It's docked in Fort Lauderdale. On the boat and at the cay he's vulnerable, as he purposefully does not maintain a large security presence. He feels secure there since he surely has lots of friends in the Bahamian government. With Persik and Talley both gone, and with the right pressure, he might choose its isolation for a little while, outside of the United States."

He'd nearly smiled.

She was reading his mind.

But he took her assessment to heart and made a few calls, putting his plan into action. Now, after three days, he was ready to move.

But first he made one more call.

To James "Fancy" Detmer, an honored resident of Blount County, Tennessee, who answered with his trademarked "Yo."

"How we lookin'?" Luke asked.

"The fish are bitin'."

"Glad to hear it. And our target?"

"I'm starin' right at the thing. And for a while those fellas were staring right back at me. I'm a quarter mile away and it still made 'em nervous."

"Remember what I told you. Step carefully. These are the kind of people you don't want interested in you. Got it?"

"I hear ya."

"Stick to the schedule I gave you. Change boats, clothes, times you fish, never take the same route twice to the marina—"

"I ain't stupid."

Fancy, whom Luke had met on their first day of middle school, was one of his oldest friends. Together they'd hunted, fished, and explored every square inch of Blount County. They'd chased girls, gotten their driver's licenses, gone to keg parties, and caused more than their fair share of general mischief. While Luke had joined the army in the hope of exploring the world, Fancy had chosen to bury his roots even deeper into the Tennessee soil. He'd married his high school sweetheart and had two kids with plans for more.

"You didn't mention that this guy owned the *Titanic*?" Fancy said.

"That big, huh?"

"And fancy. Which I should know."

Fancy's nickname harked back to high school when someone had teased him for wearing overalls to class every day, to which he'd responded, "So what? These are my fancy overalls."

What he was now doing came under the heading of an off-the-book exercise. Nothing official at all. So he'd turned not to a fellow Magellan Billet agent, but to the person he trusted the most in the world.

And sent him to Fort Lauderdale, Florida.

To bird-dog Rowland's yacht.

"You keep watchin'," he said. "He'll be coming your way soon. Let me know the moment he does."

"Gotcha."

68.

LUKE WAS BACK INSIDE HIS MUSTANG. A WONDERFULLY RESTORED 1967 first-generation model that he'd bought as a gift to himself while in the army. Silver with black stripes—not a scratch on it—he stored it in a garage adjacent to his apartment building in DC. He didn't own a lot of things, but his car was special. Thirteen smiles per gallon, he liked to say. He'd wrecked it bad during a previous assignment, but thankfully it had been repaired. Good as new. Or as good as a nearly sixty-year-old car could be.

He'd driven from Washington into Maryland, finding the driveway and easing up to what Stephanie had described as *the guard shack*. While the structure's size fit the image of a shack, the mostly glass architecture did not. Nevertheless, a man in uniform emerged as he braked to a stop. The guard asked for his name and his point of contact, then checked his driver's license against an iPad screen.

"You'll be met in the lobby. Visitor parking is on the right, a couple hundred yards down," he was told.

He followed the curved, tree-lined lane until the parking lot appeared. It was only half full so he had no trouble finding a spot near the main entrance. Like the guard shack, the main building was all sleek and modern with a white-concrete façade and great swaths of shimmering glass.

As promised, Victoria Sandberg, one of the senior curators, met him in the sun-filled lobby. She was an older woman, with cascading silver hair and a broad smile. He expressed his thanks for her taking the time to meet with him.

"We get a lot of requests that generally relate to yours," she told him. "But nothing quite this specific. You've really piqued my curiosity."

It had been several days since David Eckstein breathed his final words.

NAI 31621.

His initial Google search for the acronym NAI had turned up dozens upon dozens of hits ranging from the inane—New and Improved—to the puzzling—NATO Analog Interface—and everything in between. The number sequence 31621, aside from apparently being the model number for a popular toilet, was so commonplace Luke gave up his hunt after only a few minutes.

So he'd backtracked and started with the question, what was David Eckstein's role in his partnership with Benji Stein and Ray Simmons?

The answer came immediately.

Researcher.

And where were materials and artifacts from the Kennedy assassination stored? The national archives. And how are those items cataloged? NAI. Shorthand for "National Archives Identifier." 31621? An item number within the National Archives and Records Administration database.

From there his job got easier.

In addition to the building in Washington, DC, which was the national archives' public face, there were eighteen other records centers but only one of those, the College Park campus, dealt specifically with the assassination of President John Fitzgerald Kennedy.

He said to Victoria Sandberg, "I imagine curiosity is a prerequisite for your job."

"Absolutely. But this particular subject is a specialty of mine. Hence, why you have me today. I've set you up at a space on the fifth floor, inside the Still Pictures Research Room."

He followed her to a bank of elevators. When the doors closed behind them he said, "You have an entire floor dedicated to pictures?"

"We store about fifteen million hard-copy artifacts, including negatives, slides, and transparencies. On top of that we've got about fifty thousand large-format graphics and another three million digital images."

"That's a staggering amount," he said.

"Only if you have to dust them all," she said, with a grin. "Sorry. Archivist humor. If you don't mind me asking, what's your interest in this subject?"

Truth was, he had no idea what he was about to see, but as it had been David Eckstein's final utterance it was a thread worth chasing.

And Stephanie had agreed.

"It's official business, if you get my drift."

"I thought as much."

"Has there been any requests to see these items before?" he asked.

"We get a lot of requests related to the assassination. Most of them come from amateur enthusiasts."

Not exactly an answer, but he knew what that meant. "Conspiracy nuts?"

She gave him a sheepish grin. "Don't misunderstand, they're perfectly nice people but how many times can you stare at a frame from the Zapruder film until you're satisfied a picket fence is just a picket fence?"

"I hear you," he said.

"I had one gentleman who was convinced the Umbrella Man was in fact Lady Bird Johnson in disguise."

He grinned.

The elevator doors parted to reveal a softly lit space with gray carpet and rows of white laminate tables. The walls were lined with small computer workstations, storage cabinets, and copying machines. Only a few of the desks were occupied.

She led him to a small conference room near the floor's rear. "I'll be right back."

She returned a few minutes later with a black cardboard archivist box and placed it before him. "The specific item you requested is in sleeve 14 near the bottom. Do you want some background or would you prefer to dive in?"

"You're familiar with this?"

"When a researcher makes an appointment we make it a point to offer a bit of context. Some folks like it, some not so much."

He gestured to the opposite chair. "I like it."

She closed the door and sat.

"Identifier 31621 are black-and-white hard-copy photos taken with a Beirette Junior II 35mm camera by a young lady named Pearl Yates. On November 22, 1963, she was thirteen years old and had just won an essay contest sponsored by the Texas State Board of Education. The topic was, My Personal Ambition. Pearl's was to be a doctor. As the contest winner she was able to choose a hospital where she would shadow the staff for a day. She chose Parkland in Dallas."

"Fate," Luke said.

"You could say that."

"Pearl was returning from a lunch break when the presidential motorcade arrived carrying President Kennedy and Governor Connally. Of course, the emergency room was cleared of all unnecessary personnel, so Pearl was left outside. On a whim she started shooting pictures with the new camera her father bought her a month earlier. She took a total of twenty-one photos, eighteen of which were displayed as part of a temporary Smithsonian exhibit to mark the Kennedy assassination's fiftieth anniversary."

He opened the box and found the sleeves.

Each of the photos was encased in a laminate. With Victoria's help he spread them in a grid across the table's surface. Number 31621, the tenth photo in the series, was on the bottom row.

He felt the hair on his neck bristle.

The image, taken from a shallow angle, showed a car's rear chrome bumper, black trunk, and bat-ear taillight. Having lived and breathed the grittiest of details surrounding the Kennedy assassination, he immediately recognized the vehicle. A 1956 Cadillac Fleetwood 75 convertible known as the Queen Mary II by the White House press corps, and 679X by the Secret Service. The trail car from where Thomas Rowland had accidentally shot John Kennedy.

The car was parked, and clustered around the Cadillac's trunk were four men in dark suits. Two of them stood in profile while the third man's back was turned toward the camera. The fourth man, blocked by the others from the waist up, leaned against the trunk, his knees slightly buckled. Dangling from his right hand was a Colt AR-15. But it wasn't Rowland. No. Another man, older, held the rifle.

Rowland stood off to one side.

"What made Pearl's photos extraordinary," she said, "is what they don't show. The primary characters of that day's events are nowhere to be seen. The images Pearl captured were police, nurses, doctors, Secret Service agents, all of whom, still in shock, were waiting to see if their president was dead or alive."

"What do you know about this specific photo?" he asked.

"It shows four of the Secret Service agents who were there in the motorcade. You can almost feel the anguish in their body language."

Yes, he could.

"Pearl didn't come forward with these until July 1964," Victoria said. "She told the FBI she was worried she might get into trouble."

"Did she?"

"Not at all. The FBI examined the collection for several months then returned them to her with a thank-you letter from J. Edgar Hoover. These are copies, which the FBI deposited here in 1965."

He studied the rest of the photos. In style they were similar, but only two other images caught the trail car in frame. Both were either blurry or cut off.

"You said there were twenty-one photos in the series? But there are only eighteen here."

"Three went missing long ago. We have no idea what happened to them."

"Isn't that a bit unusual?"

She shook her head. "Not really. It happens."

"Any idea what these three images showed?"

"Unfortunately, no."

His request to view these specific items had come officially from the Department of Justice, through Stephanie. So this woman knew he was government, not a conspiratorialist.

Time to play his hand.

"Like I said, I'm here on official business. People have died in the past week, and all of those deaths related to these photos."

"That's horrible," she said.

He pointed at the pictures. "I was led straight to these by someone with knowledge. I'm going to give you some names and I need to know if any of them ever came here to see these."

"We have a record of every visitor."

"Benjamin Stein, Ray Simmons, David Eckstein."

69.

LUKE CAUGHT THE MOMENT OF RECOGNITION WHEN HE MENTIONED Eckstein. This woman was good, but not that good.

"You knew him?" he asked.

"I didn't say that."

"You didn't have to."

"What did you mean *knew* Eckstein?"

"He's dead."

Shock filled her face.

"So are Stein and Simmons. Thomas Rowland killed Stein and Eckstein. Simmons killed himself."

"Oh, my God." Her eyes watered and she began to cry.

He was hoping the truth might prove productive. Then he realized something. NAI 31621 was Eckstein's way of sending him to her. A name would have been meaningless, and it had taken all the old man had to even say the identifier.

"Did you know David?" he asked.

She nodded. "We became friends after his many visits here. When the request came to view this particular portfolio, it caught my attention. Only David has looked at these in the past decade. How did you know him?"

"I became involved in the investigation he, Simmons, and Stein were conducting into the assassination. With his dying breath, David pointed me here."

"I was afraid Thomas Rowland wasn't going to take their accusations lightly," she said. "David supplied me with a pretty good bio on Rowland that he said Benji composed. Rowland had a long history with the CIA, like his father before him. They were trying to see if Rowland would talk with them. I never thought he would, but the publisher said they had to try before submitting the manuscript."

"What do you know about the proposed book?"

"I wrote it."

He was shocked.

"None of the men had the skills to put it together," she said through her tears. "I did. So over the course of the last three years I wrote the manuscript, using David's, Benji's, and Ray's research."

"Who knew that?"

"Only David. I never met Ray or Benji. David handled all that."

"Is it finished?"

She nodded. "It's in my office."

Okay. Things just escalated.

"You don't know me at all," he said. "But I'm going to ask you to trust me. I have David's film, some drawings, and notes. All of which he gave me. What I don't have is their complete research. I'm assuming all that is laid out in the manuscript. To get Rowland I'm going to need that manuscript."

She stared at him, still crying.

He found his phone and dialed Stephanie, placing the call on speaker.

"I'm here with Victoria Sandberg. Ms. Sandberg, this is Stephanie Nelle, head of the Magellan Billet, a unit of the Department of Justice."

He and Stephanie had already discussed contingencies before he came.

"We're going to need that firepower," he said.

"Sit tight," Stephanie said. "I'll be back to you."

He ended the call.

"I never thought Rowland was a violent man," Victoria said. "But we all thought he'd guard his reputation through legal action. David actually welcomed being sued. He said he had the evidence to make his case."

"I've seen the film. It's pretty powerful."

"It is. But there is plenty of science to back up what you saw, along with witness testimony. It's all detailed in the manuscript."

"Which I'm going to need. But I wouldn't expect you to just hand it over, and I would never take it."

His phone buzzed.

He answered and accepted the special video link. The small screen split into thirds. One part held Stephanie. The other two the faces of the U.S. attorney general and the director of the national archives. He saw that Victoria recognized both.

"Ms. Sandberg," the director said. "We've never met, but I've been told that you have served the archives faithfully for a long time. I need your cooperation here. I understand you are privy to some information that could change history."

"I am. We've been working on this for a long time."

"That's what we've come to know," the attorney general said. "Sadly, all of your partners are now dead. Only Thomas Rowland remains. We need to arrest him. Can you help us right this wrong?"

The tears had abated.

Victoria Sandberg was focused on the moment.

And in her eyes he saw resolve.

"I can do that," she declared.

"Then we need you to work with Luke," Stephanie said to her. "You can trust him with your life. We want Thomas Rowland. What he did in November 1963 was a tragic accident. What he's done here is multiple homicides."

"You can count on me," Victoria said.

The call ended.

"I came prepared," he said to her, "in case I met any resistance. I did not expect to find you."

"I haven't heard from David in a few days. Which was unusual. When did it happen?"

"Tuesday. I was there." He pointed at the picture with the AR-15. "In this picture Rowland does not hold the weapon."

She seemed to grab hold of her emotions. "That's true. And that bothered David too. But there's something else. I lied to you earlier. Forgive me, but I had no idea who you are or why you're here."

"About the three missing pictures?"

She nodded. "We were going to obtain those next week."

"You know where they are?"

"I found Pearl Yates. After a lot of digging, I finally managed to reach her daughter-in-law."

"Why are they so important?"

"They can't be denied."

He got the message.

Important.

"I need those pictures," he said.

She bit her lip, then said, "Wait here. Let me make a call."

He waited until the door to the room had closed and she'd left before he made a call of his own. To Marcia Pooler.

"What do you think?" he asked her. "Is it doable?"

He'd supplied her with some information a few hours ago.

"Just about everything's doable, Lukey. But this is a bell you can't un-ring, you know that, right?"

"I do. What I'm asking, is can you do it anonymously so we don't get any blowback?"

"That's the easy part."

"How much more time do you need?"

"None. I've identified twenty-four hundred of the biggest influencers on the net who are most likely to run with this. I'm talking blogs, TikTok, Facebook, Twitter, Instagram, the whole shebang. Among them they've got hundreds of millions of followers. Once we pull the trigger, it will explode."

"Release it when I give you the word."

"I am here to serve. It shall be done."

"You're the best, Marcia."

He ended the call just as the door opened and Victoria Sandberg returned with a small piece of paper in her hand.

"Here's the address. They are expecting you."

70.

GREENSBORO, NORTH CAROLINA
5:00 P.M.

LUKE MADE THE 250-MILE DRIVE IN THREE AND A HALF HOURS, finally pulling to a stop in front of a white stucco two-story house fronted by a vine-covered picket fence. On the front lawn a lone sprinkler hissed and sputtered. The front door opened, revealing a middle-aged Black woman with close-cropped hair who waved at him. He waved back and climbed out of the car.

"Miss Kathleen?"

"Victoria said you were a polite southern boy. I can see she was right. Come on up."

He opened the fence gate, waited for a gap in the sprinkler's stream, then dashed up the walk to the porch without getting wet.

"Come in, come in, we're having sweet tea on the back patio. We've got something a little harder too, if that's your preference."

"Sweet tea sounds good."

She led him through the living room and kitchen to a sliding glass door overlooking the patio. "Now, one thing you should know," she said in a conspiratorial whisper. "I got the cancer six months ago—"

"I'm sorry."

"Kind of you, but that's not it. I'm in remission right now. See, when I was about to go through chemo and radiation, I had one of those head-shaving parties. My mama, Pearl, came to watch, or so I thought. Next thing I know, she's under the clippers. But she went even further. Had them shave her bald. She says she'll keep doing it until I'm cancer-free."

"Sounds like a remarkable woman."

"You got that right. Just don't lie to her. She'll know, and shut down on you in a heartbeat."

"Understood."

They stepped outside and Kathleen made the introductions. Pearl Yates sat in a cushioned outdoor rattan chair. Victoria had told him she was nearing eighty, but she looked a decade or more younger. Beneath her bald pate were a pair of sparkling, astute eyes crinkled by laugh lines. They sat for a while sipping tea and exchanging pleasantries until finally Pearl said, "I like this one, Kathleen. He's okay. You go inside and get working on supper. Me and Luke are gonna talk."

Kathleen smiled. "Sure thing, Mama."

When they were alone he asked, "Did you ever make it to medical school?"

"I found out after high school that all that studyin' just wasn't for me. I never became a doctor, but I was one damn fine nurse. I worked fifty-four years before retirin'."

"Good for you."

"You're wonderin' about those three missin' pictures?"

"Yes, ma'am, I am curious. I'm trying to right a wrong. A big wrong. If you don't mind, let me turn the tables on you."

"If you can, my boy," Pearl said. "Give it a try."

"I think you're a private person, but that's not all there is to it. I think after your Parkland photos you and your family got some attention. The kind of attention that gives you goose bumps."

Her gaze grew more penetrating.

"I'm betting some men came sniffing around and you were smart enough to stay out of their way."

Pearl blinked at him, let out a sigh. "Boy, that sounds a little spooky."

"I've met those men," he said. "Not the same ones that came looking for you, of course, but I know the type."

"Even after sixty years, it's a memory I don't like reliving. See, back when I submitted that essay we were living in a town called Bethlehem about two hours east of Dallas. We had this little enclave, I guess you'd call it, just outside of town. All Black families that looked after one another. Black-owned businesses, private schools, all that. Back then some parts of Texas weren't kind to folks like us, if you get my meanin'."

"I do."

"Still a lot of issues there to this day. And everywhere else too."

He agreed.

"We had ourselves a tight-knit, family-oriented safe place. When these two men came lookin' for me it was early '64, about a month after I turned my pictures over to the FBI. We knew it wasn't no coincidence.

"They tried hard to be discreet, but they stuck out like rat droppings in a bowl of rice. They had badges of some kind, though nobody got a good look at 'em. For days they drove around askin' where I could be found. They didn't get anywhere, of course, but it didn't stop 'em from coming back. All through that year and a bit into the next. Sometimes it was the same men, other times different ones.

"See, I was born dirt-poor in my mama's bed. No hospital records, no birth certificate, didn't get a Social Security number until I got married. As far as the government was concerned, I didn't exist."

"Your good luck," he said.

"I think so too. Anyway, after a while they stopped comin' around. So we tucked those pictures away and never talked about them again."

"That was smart," Luke replied. "A lot of other people weren't so smart."

"Folks that are no longer with us, I presume?"

He nodded. "Recently departed."

"Is this a government thing?"

"No, just one man. On his own."

"Does this have somethin' to do with what happened that day?"

"Most definitely."

"And my pictures show somethin' worrying?"

"Maybe," he said. "Those kind of men tend to err on the side of caution when it comes to threats."

"That's a terrible way to be."

"They're terrible people."

"Is there any chance they'll come looking for me again?"

He shook his head. "Not if I have my way."

"What would you do if I told you I destroyed the pictures and negatives a long time ago?"

"I'd thank you for your time and the delicious sweet tea, then be on my way."

"You're a nice boy, Luke."

"And you're a lovely lady."

"I have the photos," she said. "And the negatives. Victoria says you're the man to trust. I can now say I agree with her. I'd be grateful if you took the whole lot off my hands. Could you do that for me?"

He smiled. "Happy to help, Miss Pearl."

After dinner he and Kathleen retreated to the basement office, where the photo collection waited on a fold-out metal table. The collection was in pristine condition, the photos protected by archivist-quality sleeves. Similarly, the negatives were sealed in hermetic cannisters.

"Miss Victoria," Kathleen said, "made sure they were all tucked away nice and safe. She's a good person."

One by one he compared each of Pearl's photos against his memory of the ones he'd seen at College Park NARA until he'd picked out the three that weren't there. Which he carried back upstairs, along with the one with Rowland in it he'd already seen.

Pearl waited at the dining room table sipping a cup of coffee. "Made one for you, Luke. You look like you could use a little boost."

"Thank you. Would you be up to answering a few questions?"

"Fire away."

He laid a photo on the table. "This is the one I saw at the national archives."

"I remember it. In fact, I remember everything from that day like it's a movie in my head. Sometimes wish I didn't."

"Sorry for bringing it all back."

"You're taking them away. That's a kindness. What else do you want to know?"

"These other three photos are the missing ones. And now I know why they're gone."

"You want to explain it to me?"

"Do you really want to know?"

"I kinda do."

He laid the three other photos out on the table before her. All three showed the same Cadillac limousine. The trail car. And the same men. But from different angles.

"What made you focus on them in the first place?" he asked.

"Everyone in that parking lot was anxious, scared. Those four were too, but their body language was different. That gun drew my attention. Somebody told me they were the president's bodyguards. So ten minutes earlier they'd seen a man get his head shot off."

"How far apart were these pictures taken?" asked Luke.

"The first two about a minute or so. The other two about five minutes after that."

"And you took only four photos of these men?"

Pearl nodded. "Right after I took the fourth picture, they moved off, talked for a while longer, then they went inside the hospital."

He studied each of the missing three images.

The first showed the car as it came to a stop at the hospital. He counted. Eight men. One had fled the trail car and hopped into Kennedy's limousine during the shooting. Rowland was there, among the others. The second image was snapped a minute or so later. The agents were out of the car. Six in the frame. And there he was, Thomas Rowland, exiting the vehicle holding the AR-15. The third image showed more of the surroundings with the car still in the frame, but other vehicles and people were also visible. In the final image, the one he'd seen back in Maryland, four of the agents were at the car, only now the rifle was no longer in Rowland's possession.

"It's strange," Pearl said. "I haven't looked at these in a long time. I now realize my memory's been stuck at thirteen years old, if that makes sense."

"What do you mean?"

"At the time I was just a kid. What did I know about how adults act during a crisis? But now, after seven decades on this planet, and fifty inside a hospital, I see it different. I look at those four

315

men, particularly the one with the rifle, and they just give me the willies."

The older woman paused a moment.

Then stared straight at him and asked, "What does it all mean?"

71.

LUKE LEFT NORTH CAROLINA AND HEADED BACK TO HIS APARTMENT in DC. He leased near Georgetown in an ivy-veined brick building brimming with tenants in their seventies. He liked the quiet and appreciated the fact that everyone seemed to mind their own business. He spent only a few days there each month, between assignments, mostly on the downtime Stephanie Nelle required all of her Magellan Billet agents to take.

He hadn't been able to answer Pearl's question, *What does it all mean?*

Simply because he wasn't sure.

Not yet.

Victoria Sandberg had turned over her manuscript. Both a word processing file and a hard copy that she kept as a backup. She told him that a publishing contract had been secured and they were readying the book for a final submittal. But no one outside of her, Ray, Benji, and Eckstein had seen the manuscript. All that remained was contact with Rowland and the securing of all the pictures that would appear in the book. He'd promptly emailed the file to Stephanie, who told him she'd be reviewing the manuscript while he headed back to DC.

On arriving home, his phone rang.

Stephanie.

He reported what he'd located, the three missing images now in his possession.

"This book is explosive," she said. "And persuasive."

"Just Rowland's actions alone give the whole thing total credibility."

She agreed. "I'm sending someone to get the hard copy and everything else you have," she said. "It all needs to be safeguarded. The good part is Rowland thinks it's under control."

She provided him the proper code words to use to ensure the courier was legit.

"I'll be here until the time is right to leave," he told her.

"You sure about all this?" she asked.

"I'm afraid I am. It has to be dealt with."

"I have the info you wanted on Rowland's yacht and Compass Cay."

She told him that the *BreakAway*'s captain was a qualified master, but the rest of the crew, six in all, were ex-military. She'd even been able to obtain blueprints of the yacht along with a map of Compass Cay, all of which the courier would deliver to him.

"It's time to flush the ducks," he told her.

As a kid, hunting with his father and brothers, their golden retrievers had never failed to shake the tall grass and scare the birds into the air.

Where you could take a shot.

"Keep in mind," she said, "we don't have a lot of direct evidence here. It's all circumstantial. In a criminal case, before a jury can rely on circumstantial evidence, they have to be convinced that the only reasonable conclusion supported by that evidence is that the defendant is guilty. If you can draw two or more reasonable conclusions, then it all fails. I've gone through the manuscript. I've watched Eckstein's film, and now we have three photos."

"And lots of bodies," he added.

"That's right. So I think we can make this stick. But, you know, in the court of public opinion, we don't really have to prove a thing. All we have to do is say it, then keep on saying it, and never, ever stop saying it."

Exactly his thought too.

He ended the call and texted Marcia, forwarding her e-images of all four photos. Nothing like a little show to further make your point. Then he added a simple instruction.

Do it. Now.

Five minutes later a reply came.

Package sent along with agreed-upon hashtags. I'm tracking on my end. Will keep you posted.

He was woken early the next morning by another text from Marcia.

Hashtag Rowland_CIA_blunderer trending strong across all platforms. Of 2400 packages sent, 90% response rate. Expecting regional TV station coverage by day's end, national not far behind.

He then called Fancy. "You someplace safe?"

"Sittin' down the shore a bit. If that yacht leaves, it'll have to pass me."

"Expect some action soon."

"I'll keep you posted."

Around 1:00 P.M. Marcia texted again.

Fox News, MSNBC, CNN all running chyrons with hashtags. AP and Reuters putting out feelers. CIA press office declining to make comment. Google searches for Thomas Henry Rowland up by 900%

He turned on the TV and flipped between news stations until he heard a CNN anchor reporting what he had so far and saying, "Our sources are confirming that a Thomas Henry Rowland was at one time an employee of the Central Intelligence Agency, but in what capacity we don't know. We have contacted the CIA's Office of Public Affairs but have not yet received a response."

He switched to Fox News, then MSNBC and the network's streaming services. All were mentioning the information and showing the photographs. Nothing major. Just more content to fill in the twenty-four hours they broadcasted each day. He continued monitoring things through the evening, taking in Marcia's increasingly frequent updates, switching between TV stations, checking news websites, and spot-checking social media for trends. Around 3:00 P.M. the courier had arrived and they switched parcels. Near midnight, he called it quits and went to bed only to be woken three hours later by a call from Fancy.

"She's preppin' to leave."

"You're sure?"

"I'm directly across from the marina. They're untying those big ropes at the front and back. I see smoke coming from the exhaust and the crew's scrambling around like they've got firecrackers in their drawers."

"Pull up stakes and go—"

"Wait, hold on. A SUV just pulled up to the dock. Two guys gettin' out. One of 'em's holding open the back door. Now an old dude is gettin' out. That your guy?"

"That's him. Anybody else?"

"Yep."

He listened to the full report, then said, "Fancy, your job's done. I owe you one. Now get outta there and back to your family."

"You got it, brother."

He hung up and started another countdown in his head. Five to six hours, depending on speed. The time *BreakAway* would take to reach Compass Cay. Rowland was using the cover of darkness to slip away, thinking himself safe.

Not this time.

72.

LUKE HAD NEVER VISITED THE BAHAMAS BEFORE. SO HE'D ASSUMED reaching its largest city, Nassau, ahead of Rowland was his biggest hurdle. When in truth, George Town, the nearest settlement to Compass Cay, lay 120 miles to the south.

He'd flown commercial out of Dulles and already settled on a plan before leaving the States, using Airbnb to find a shabby beach bungalow called Pine's Rest nestled in a palm grove just south of George Town. The reviews for the bungalow were horrible and it had apparently gone a year without a renter. Pulling up on his rented scooter he could see why. The roof was missing a quarter of its shingles, the plank walls were warped, and the front porch had a twenty-degree slant.

Perfect.

Pine's Rest met his two primary requirements. One, it had an unobstructed view of Compass Cay, about half a mile offshore, and two, it was a short walk from Jester's Pub, which, according to the intel Stephanie had provided, was where Lewis Peters, *BreakAway*'s chief engineer and former 10th Mountain Division soldier, liked to drink Red Bull gins and talk Seattle Mariners baseball with anyone who'd listen. In height, weight, and hair color Peters was a fair match for Luke's own features. Not perfect, but close enough he hoped.

He'd also learned from the Coast Guard that *BreakAway* was cruising straight for him at a leisurely pace.

No hurry at all.

Double perfect.

* * *

He drove south through George Town to Michelson a few miles down the coast then meandered the mostly signless streets before heading to Manny's Fandango on Old Airport Road beside a soccer field overtaken by weeds. He sauntered inside, took a stool, and ordered a beer. When the bartender returned with it he said, "I'm looking for Lionel."

The bartender pointed toward a pool table in the back where a tall, rangy Black man was lazily ricocheting a cue ball across the green baize surface. He walked over and smacked a $100 bill on the table.

Lionel stared at the bill then squinted at Luke.

"Do you want the money or not?"

"Depends. What's it for?"

"A gun."

"That's illegal."

He dropped another hundred on the table. "Now?"

"What kind of gun?"

"What kind you got?"

Lionel asked, "How'd you find me?"

"Does it matter?"

"Does to me."

"I think we have a friend in common. Stephanie."

"Doesn't sound familiar."

"She's a couple inches shorter than me, short grayish hair, and carries a really big stick."

The face broke into a grin. "Oh, that Stephanie."

Lionel signaled to the bartender, who retrieved a key ring from a drawer and tossed it across the room. Lionel snatched it from the air. "Follow me."

He led Luke out the rear exit and across a dirt path to a freestanding garage. Lionel lifted the big door, revealing an interior crowded with cardboard boxes, dilapidated bikes, and a partially disassembled dune buggy. He followed him through a short maze of boxes to a paint-spattered workbench.

Lionel said, "Pistol, rifle, or shotgun?"

"Pistol, small-frame semi-automatic, 9mm."

"That I don't have. I can sell you a .22."

"Show me."

Lionel unlocked one of the workbench drawers and pulled out an older-model Taurus with half its grip missing. "Serial numbers are gone. Sixteen-round capacity, four-inch barrel. Three hundred U.S. dollars. I'll throw in the bullets and an extra magazine for another fifty. As a favor to Stephanie."

He handed over the cash and left.

After a brief stop at a grocery store for canned beans, bread, two gallon jugs of water, some toiletries, and a few other needed items, he returned to Pine's Rest and mentally rehearsed things. Would Rowland stay aboard? Stephanie had told him that, of late, the old man preferred the comfort of the ship. So he needed to internalize the yacht's layout right down to its doorknobs. In a perfect world he'd want to know where and when the crew slept, how many remained on duty at night, where they were stationed, a weapons inventory, and the location of communications devices.

But his intel was spotty.

And it was all he had to work with.

So he whittled his plan down to the essentials. What was under his control and what wasn't. Speed and surprise would be his greatest advantages. But the crew element still troubled him. The crisp white uniforms and polished shoes were a façade. These were armed, trained soldiers. Which just might work to his advantage.

He was as ready as he was going to be.

His course set.

His plan would either work or it wouldn't.

Shortly before 11:00 A.M., *BreakAway* glided into Exuma Harbor, then turned down the mile-wide channel separating George Town and Stocking Island. The water was shallower there, the shoals more unforgiving. By the time it zigzagged its way around

Crab Cay the captain slowed her to a walking pace, just enough to maintain steerageway. Finally, just before noon, the yacht made its final turn and snugged itself into Compass Cay's horseshoe anchorage, about a hundred yards offshore. Through the binoculars Luke watched the anchor splash into the turquoise water.

He then tucked the Taurus into his belt, slid the extra magazine into the side pocket of his shorts, and set out for Jester's Pub.

73.

IT WAS A FEW HOURS BEFORE LEWIS PETERS SHOWED UP. LUKE HAD taken a stool at the bar's center, nursing a Red Bull and gin he'd ordered upon walking into the pub. Peters, still wearing his dress white uniform, called to a few locals he apparently knew, then shook hands with the bartender and took a seat four stools away.

"You know what I want, Timmy," Peters said.

"Red Bull and gin it is."

Luke said, "I thought I was the only one."

"What's that?" Peters said.

Luke raised his glass. "Red Bull G. You're the first person I've run into that likes these things."

"It's an acquired taste, that's for sure."

"But once you start, you can't stop, am I right?"

"Damn straight."

Peters grabbed his drink and raised it in Luke's direction. "Prost."

"Salud."

They drank in silence for a while. When Peters had downed his third Red Bull G, Luke bought him another. Peters returned the favor, then took the stool beside Luke. "You mind?"

"No, suit yourself."

"I'm Lewis."

"Tom," he said.

"You American?"

He nodded. "I just broke up with my girlfriend. I needed to get away."

"That sucks, man. Where're you from?"

"Tacoma."

"No kidding? I'm Seattle."

"Native or transplant?"

"When I was in the army I did some training up in the Cascades. I fell in love with the place so when I got out I made the move from Phoenix."

"Gorgeous country, if you don't mind the rain," he said. "Only one thing wrong with it."

"What's that?"

"Not enough Red Bull G lovers."

Peters laughed. "Maybe we should start a support group."

"We got the core membership right here."

The evening wore on. Luke continued buying Peters' drinks while nursing his own. He'd gradually learned that Peters' boss was a hard-ass, resented by the crew, who liked to cruise from Florida, stay awhile at anchor, then cruise back. This time, though, they'd been told he might stay awhile. By 10:00 P.M. Peters was wobbly on his stool and slurring his words.

"No, I'm telling ya, the Mariners bullpen is stronger than it's been in ten years."

"I hear you," Luke said, "but do we have any strong finishers? That's what we need if you ask me."

"Fair point, fair point. Man, I'm blasted."

"Yeah, me too. I should call it a night. Where're you staying?"

"On that big white yacht that came in earlier."

"How do you get out there, swim?"

"Nah, man, the dinghy. It's tied up on the beach. Five-minute ride and I'm in my bunk."

Peters pushed himself off the stool, then lost his balance and stumbled sideways. Luke caught him. "Whoa, buddy. You don't have your land legs yet."

"Guess not."

"Come on, Ahab, I'll get you down to your dinghy."

"Ahab," Peters barked in a loud voice. "I love it. My new nickname. Ahab."

With Peters' arm draped over his shoulder, Luke led him outside then started down the road toward Pine's Rest.

"You remember any good marching songs from the army?" Luke asked.

Peters broke into a tuneless babble interspersed with shouts of "Left, left, right, left."

When they were a hundred yards from Luke's bungalow, Peters stopped suddenly and looked around. "Is this the right way?"

"Yep. Almost there."

"Nah, you missed it. It's back that—"

Luke pulled the Taurus from his waistband and coldcocked Peters behind the ear. The body slumped to the ground and Luke ducked and hefted Peters over his shoulder. Thirty seconds later he was through the bungalow's front door. He dumped Peters facedown on the bed, stripped off his clothes, then bound his hands and ankles with some of the duct tape bought earlier.

Luke donned Peters' uniform. Everything fit reasonably well save the shoes, which were half a size too small, so he wore his own. He half untucked his shirt to conceal the Taurus then slipped the spare magazine into his back pocket. He then stepped out onto the porch, locked the front door, and headed down the road.

The dinghy's motor was an underpowered trolling model so the journey across the inlet to *BreakAway*'s anchorage took longer than he'd estimated. Twenty minutes after leaving the beach he looped around Compass Cay's sandbar and into the horseshoe inlet. The yacht loomed dark except for a few yellow-lit cabin windows near the bow. He cruised to within twenty feet of the stern's platform and a crewman in a white uniform appeared at the aft railing. A pump-action shotgun was slung over his shoulder.

"Come on, Lewis, do you know what time it is?"

He mumbled a reply, keeping his head down and the peaked cap pulled low on his forehead.

"I can smell you from here. You trying to get your ass fired?"

When the dinghy's rubber bow bounced off the platform, Luke intentionally fell forward slightly. "Get the line, huh? I can't reach it."

"You're pathetic, dude."

When the man's arm came into view Luke grasped the wrist and jerked the guy into the dinghy.

"What the—"

He slammed his open palm into the man's nose once, then again, grabbed the shotgun, and twisted hard, looping the sling around the man's throat until his face turned purple and he went limp. He then untangled the shotgun and climbed out onto the stern platform.

He heard the rapid clicking of shoes on the wooden deck. "Is everything okay—"

Another crewman skidded to stop at the aft railing. He spotted Luke, stiffened slightly, then reached for a hip holster. Luke found the Taurus and aimed it level with the guy's chest.

"That would not be smart. Draw that pistol, with two fingers, and toss it overboard."

The man did so.

"Step down here."

The man joined Luke on the stern platform. He jammed the gun under his chin. "I'm here for the big man down below. You know who I'm talking about?"

A nod.

This next part was tricky. But everything depended on it.

"Is he paying you enough to die for him?"

No reply.

"I know him and I know how he operates," Luke said. "After tonight you won't have to worry about him anymore. Have you seen the press coverage on him?"

The man nodded. "Some of our wives sent us the information."

"You still want to die for him? Or go to jail? I assure you, soon there will be federal agents everywhere. Your choice."

"What do you want?"

"How many men on duty right now?"

"Just me."

"How many more crew aboard?"

"Three. The captain's ashore."

"Doing what?"

"He's got a girlfriend here."

"The others are asleep in their cabins?" Luke asked. "Are they armed?"

"Yes to both."

"I'm going to give you all the same deal. Die here, or get arrested trying to defend that piece of crap you work for. Or hit the beach and find a second chance. What do you think, am I wasting my time?"

"I really don't know."

"What's your choice?"

"To hell with Rowland. He's an asshole."

"That's what I hear. Let's go wake up your friends." He gave the Taurus an extra push, tilting the man's head backward. "Just so we're clear, if you or anyone else puts a toe out of line, you'll be the first to go. Do you believe me?"

"I believe you."

He kept the gun pressed against the man's spine as they walked forward through the main salon, then down the companionway to the second-deck passageway. LED lights embedded in the base-boards cast a soft glow. There were two polished walnut doors on each side of the passage.

He halted his captive with a hand on his shoulder.

"Bring your friends out."

He tapped on the doors.

Three men appeared in gym shorts and T-shirts. Luke kept the gun close to his captive. "I have no quarrel with any of you. And by now you know what your boss is. I'm a federal agent, the advance guard, and this boat is about to be overrun with badges. I'm ex-army, like all of you, a military guy. We can part company right now and you go find better lives to lead. That's option one. Option two is you get either killed or arrested. Hold up the finger of your preferred option."

All four men raised an index finger.

"Then get up on deck and use that dinghy to get the hell out of here."

74.

LUKE WAITED UNTIL THE CREW DISAPPEARED INTO THE DARKNESS, puttering away. He'd even told them where to find Lewis Peters. To be sure, he searched all the crew cabins and found them empty, then crept to the end of an upper-deck passageway, Rowland's cabin according to the plans, and pressed his ear to the door.

He heard nothing. But lights were on past the door.

For this to work he had to go in unarmed. Foolish? Maybe. But it was his only chance. So he laid the gun on the floor and knocked softly.

"Enter."

He turned the knob, pushed the door open, and stepped through.

Rowland was seated behind a polished kidney-shaped desk in an elegant on-the-water bedchamber that doubled as an office.

"Luke Daniels," the old man said. "I've been waiting."

"Good to know you expected me. I thought it was time we met face-to-face."

Rowland glared. "What happened to my crew?"

"They're halfway to the beach by now. As it turns out, not a single one of them wanted to die for you. It's just a hunch, but it might have something to do with your poor interpersonal skills."

"The reports on you were correct. You are a smug son of a bitch."

Rowland sat, one hand on the leather desk blotter, the other in his lap. Which surely held a weapon with the safety off. Especially considering he'd been expected.

"I'm unarmed," Luke said.

Rowland's hand came up into view.

Yep. Gun.

"I'm not."

"Where is she?" he asked.

A door to his left opened and Jillian stepped out.

"I told you, my dear," Rowland said. "He knew all about you."

He'd hoped he was wrong. But that was not the case.

"Why?" he asked.

"Money. What else?"

She also held a 9mm, finger on the trigger.

He was seriously outgunned.

But he had to play this out.

"When did you know?" she asked.

"For sure? After you shot Eckstein."

"Who says I did?"

"Everybody else there had high-powered rounds. Your Beretta, though? It would leave a nice neat hole. So unless you're like Rowland, and accidentally pulled the trigger, you shot him dead on purpose."

She shrugged. "That was the right opportunity. I didn't think you'd be so observant."

"Or did you think me too stupid to notice?"

"Both."

"Your protests of a mistake and jumping the gun with Talley didn't ring right either. You were trained to handle those kinds of situations, not pull the trigger at the first opportunity. Unless, of course, you intended to kill Talley, which you did." He asked what he really wanted to know. "Who the hell are you?"

"Not that good little marine you once knew, that's for sure. I grew up. In the real world. Where money rules and power gets things done."

He faced Rowland. "The perfect person for you."

"I do appreciate a negotiable individual. So much can be accomplished when everyone is in need."

"You do realize that you're done," Luke said.

"You underestimate me," Rowland said.

"I think you're the one doing the underestimating. What did she tell you? That all of Eckstein's stuff was lost? Surely you know that was a lie."

"Of course. So either Stephanie Nelle was coming with a warrant to arrest me, or you were coming with perhaps something else on your mind. Let's be real here. There's no proof of anything."

"You see the news coverage yesterday?"

"Superficial. Which spoke volumes. Rumor. Innuendo. If you wanted me, you would have gotten me. No, Mr. Daniels. You were sending a message. Thankfully, I listened and have a lizard skin."

"No. You don't. Otherwise none of this would have happened. You would have left it alone. Instead, you care how you're to be remembered. So much so that people were murdered to protect your reputation. In fact, that is what the entire thing was about."

"My legacy is fine. You apparently did not share your supposed proof with Stephanie Nelle."

"Some of Talley's men survived Wyoming."

"I am aware," Rowland said. "But they will be dealt with."

"I survived," Luke noted.

Rowland grinned. "And here we are, dealing with each other, face-to-face, and you unarmed."

"Did you like the little taste I gave you yesterday?" Luke asked.

"Sensationalism never lasts."

"Eckstein's film is pretty damning," Luke said.

"Except it doesn't show the gun firing," Jillian added. "And that's a big problem."

"Did you kill Benji?" he quickly asked.

"I did. Right before you made your grand entrance. I told Rowland you'd take those guys down, and you did."

He recalled how the van driver had killed two of the intruders. "Those men dying. All a show. Just to get me involved."

She nodded. "You had to have a purpose. Superheroes like you always have to have a purpose. So we created one."

"You took a big chance on Talley or Persik not killing us both."

"Not really. Persik was kept in the dark. He was after us and the mythical rifle. Just doing his job."

"Which is why you confessed about the rifle in the hangar?"

"I was just doing what you told me to do," she said. "*Tell the truth*. It tied it all together rather nicely, I thought. The problem came with Talley, who was sent to Belgium to watch Persik. Instead, he shot them all dead, which shocked the hell out of me. He could have taken us down in that old hangar too. But he didn't. He had his own agenda, and he was counting on you to make it happen. What he didn't know about was me."

"I kept our arrangement," Rowland said, "just between the two of us. I sent Jack to Belgium and Louisiana to spur you along. His betrayal was definitely a surprise. Thankfully, it was dealt with and turned to an advantage."

"And I did save your ass," Jillian said. "That guy at the helo, in the mining camp, would have killed you."

"That wasn't because you cared. You needed what I had. Keeping me alive was the only way to get it."

"The chase from the museum in Brussels," Rowland said,

"almost caused an issue. Persik's men were just supposed to spook you, not engage, but they were never good at following orders. That drew police attention. But, thankfully, Mr. Daniels, you managed to escape. The two men inside Benjamin Stein's house were sent by Persik to find the rifle. They too were part of the show. For your benefit."

"Which Wonder Woman here handled."

"I thought I did a good job kicking that idiot through the stairwell," Jillian said.

"So Ray and Benji made contact with you," Luke said to Rowland. "They wanted your comments on their theory, on their book. You, of course, declined, but investigated them, learning somebody else was involved. You just didn't know who?"

"Actually," Jillian said. "I found out about David Eckstein. Benji was quite the talker. Unfortunately, he had no idea where Eckstein lived, and Ray Simmons was dead."

"The email you supposedly sent asking about Kronos?" he asked.

Jillian grinned. "All fake. Sounded great, didn't it?"

"It actually did."

"The codes, though," she said, "were real. Benji and Ray were careful with their communications. Paranoid, I assume."

"With good reason, considering what happened. I led you right to Eckstein."

And got the man killed.

But, unfortunately, he hadn't figured it out before Eckstein died. Which was why he'd kept what the old man said to himself. Just in case his suspicions turned correct. And they had. The good part, though? These two don't know a thing about Pearl Yates or Victoria Sandberg.

Willful ignorance.

The Achilles' heel for every self-absorbed psychopath.

75.

Rowland had dealt with many confrontational situations. In fact they were his specialty. He adhered to what Andrew Jackson said. *I was born for the storm, a calm does not suit me.* But this was the first time where he was the storm. And it made things different. But he showed none of his anxiety. Luke Daniels had come here, unarmed, for a reason.

Find out why.

"Do you plan to have me arrested?" he asked Daniels.

"Stephanie definitely wants to. But tying you to those murders is going to be tough without Talley, me, or your lying accomplice over there."

"Do you enjoy insulting me?" she asked.

"I do, actually." He was curious. "Was the sex in Dallas part of the show? Taking one for the team?"

"That was purely for myself, but it did keep you moving forward."

"Ms. Nelle may find it hard to have me arrested," Rowland said, interrupting the moment. "It's why I came here, to the Bahamas. I own a lot of friends here."

"Curious way to put it."

"Perhaps. But accurate. More than enough to block any international extradition."

"What was the purpose of the press and social media coverage yesterday? As I said, it seemed spotty and misinformed."

"Stephanie wanted something out there, so she went with what I gave her. Which wasn't much. Unlike you, she actually believed me when I told her the information had been lost in the mine. I was hoping, though, that it might get your attention."

"It did."

Jillian Stein had assured him Daniels would appear, and come he did. She'd also made clear that she could handle him.

But he wasn't so sure.

"How did you two connect?" Daniels asked Stein.

"One of those fortuitous events," Rowland said. "For us both."

"Benji called," Jillian said. "After all the years, all the negativity, he finally needed me. He and I hadn't spoken in years. He despised me for quitting the army. He wanted it to be my career. Like him. Me? Not so much. Too little pay for too many risks. So I got out and he disowned me. I needed his help a few years ago, and he told me to stick it. But when he was dying, and there was nobody else, the old fool called me. I was all the family he had left."

"Lucky for him," Daniels added.

"Lucky for me, actually," she said. "At least that's the way I looked at it. When I got to him, he was pretty apologetic. He wanted to make amends. He told me all about what he and Simmons were doing. What they'd discovered. What they were planning with a book that had been sold to a publisher. He told me about Eckstein and Thomas Rowland. I called some friends still in the military, who made some calls, who found out that Mr. Rowland was an important man. I figured he might be interested in what was coming his way."

"And I was," Rowland said. "Most interested. By then Stein and Simmons had made contact with me for a comment on their book. When Ms. Stein found me, I was able to cultivate a friend on the inside."

"But only Simmons knew where to find Eckstein. That missing link out there had to be closed."

"Quite right. And we used you to help make that happen," Rowland pointed out.

"I have to admit," Jillian said. "You've changed from back in Hawaii. I thought you were still that happy-go-lucky Ranger who managed to land a job in the intelligence business thanks to your president-uncle. But you're different. More focused. More intense."

"And you're not the same person I knew in Hawaii. Pathological. Psychotic. A murderer. I grossly underestimated your fallacies. I apologize."

"Always the perfect gentleman. Seems I'm the one who got the better of you."

"If that's the way you see it."

She smirked. "Care to enlighten me?"

Daniels pointed Rowland's way. "You never figured Jack Talley would turn on you, did you?"

"I was genuinely surprised by that, and it changed things drastically. Thankfully, with Ms. Stein in place, Jack's duplicity was not a problem. She ended his employment. Permanently. And, as you know, she also took down David Eckstein."

"But you both missed the most important part."

Really? "Do tell," Rowland said.

"There's a book. A completed manuscript. A nice neat package with everything in one place. Eckstein told us about it."

"I must admit," Rowland said, "I would have preferred to have that in my possession. If it surfaces, my lawyers will deal with it. Even if the book makes it to publication, it will be shelved with the hundreds of others that all have postulated the so-called truth behind the Kennedy assassination. Yes, there will be a momentary blip in public relations. But it will pass and be forgotten as unproven speculation. The kind of thing you might see on the Discovery Channel for entertainment. Not in the history books as fact."

"With a little disinformation campaign thrown in to discredit all involved. Right?" Daniels asked.

"Of course. That always helps. People today love to believe the worst about others. Such a sad state of affairs."

"The problem," Daniels said, "is this is not like all those other theories. Far from it, in fact. That book has some solid forensics to go along with the science and math, which all point straight at you. So does the photographic evidence. Straight to you."

"There are no photos," Rowland said.

"But there are. You know three photos are missing from the national archives. I suspect you, or your father, had them purged long ago. But I found the originals. Less than two days ago I was sitting at a kitchen table, talking to the person who took them. A person who vividly remembers that day. I have those three photos."

"You're a liar."

Daniels slowly reached back, found his phone, and tapped. The younger man then displayed the screen for him to see.

Oh, God. They did still exist.

"What did it feel like?" Daniels asked. "To have killed the president of the United States through pure carelessness. You had no business being in that car that day. You were a late addition. Daddy make it possible? Called in a favor? Being in a presidential motorcade protection detail is a big deal. Great career booster. But what did you do? Stayed out the night before, drinking. Got little sleep. Woke up hung over and decided to wing it. But when the shots were fired all you did was stumble forward and pull the trigger. The only good thing was nobody heard or noticed. And you would have gotten away with it but for David Eckstein's film."

"Which proves nothing."

"Except that the barrel of your weapon was pointed straight toward Kennedy at the moment his head was blown off."

76.

LUKE WAS PRESSING HARD. HE HAD TO. NO CHOICE. LIKE Malone always said, you got to jostle the barrel to see what spills out.

He turned his attention back to Jillian. "What else do you get out of this, besides money?"

"Talley's job."

"I figured as much."

"It pays well. Much more than I was making. I consider the whole thing a win-win."

"Why pick me? You're bound to have other people you know. Somebody else you could have used."

"And miss the fun of watching you figure all this out? No way. I knew you worked with the Magellan Billet. Mr. Rowland said that would be perfect, considering how your boss feels about him. And we needed someone on board who could help us jump through a few hoops. He managed to learn that you were in London. So close. If you'd been farther away, our little show would have been delayed until you arrived. As it was, you got there quick. Coming to my rescue."

"I knew Stephanie Nelle hated me, and with good reason," Rowland said. "I recently tried hard to have her and the Magellan Billet eliminated. It was a certainty that once she realized I was involved, she'd do whatever she had to do. And she did. Predictability is a definite liability in her business."

"I assume I was not supposed to survive?"

She nodded. "I could have taken you out right after I shot Talley, but I'd already sensed you knew something you weren't telling me. Something Eckstein may have told you right before he died. I saw how intense you and he were. We needed to find out what. And now we know."

"You really are a psychopath," he said.

"Just an enterprising woman taking advantage of all her opportunities. I am curious, though, what tipped you off, besides Eckstein's bullet hole and my eagerness with Talley?"

"It was a combination of things. It started early. Why would anyone have geotagged my rental car in Belgium? After I thought about it, the whole thing seemed a bit much, considering they didn't know who I was. Or, maybe they did? Of course, you were the one who told them everything. Where we were, where we were headed, but the tracker was a nice touch. Added an element of confusion."

"I instructed Persik to do it," Rowland said.

"Which diverted attention away from me," Jillian added.

"It wasn't until we got to Ray Simmons's house that my radar went to high alert," he said. "He had a lot of books on the assassination. Yet Benji had none. Then there was the diagram you found in the lamp. Just a little too convenient. Your idea?"

"Believe it or not, that's where Benji actually hid his stuff. There was more there, which I destroyed, leaving only the one innocuous diagram as bait. I went to that storage facility in Luxembourg weeks ago. The rifle case was already there. Empty. Benji told me that he'd bought an old AR-15 a few years ago, which was sent to Simmons in Louisiana. He kept the case. So Mr. Rowland bought another old AR-15, which I planted there with no serial numbers."

"More bait?" he asked. "For me?"

"Not entirely," she said. "We needed something for Persik and Talley to be after too. On the off chance they might find the storage unit we made sure there was a rifle. That homemade alarm system was all Benji. But with him gone it was useless. How would you put it? A good bird dog likes the scent?" She tossed him a smirk. "That storage unit was filled with stuff relating to the assassination. Books, papers, all kinds of stuff. I destroyed all of it, and I purged the house clean. We didn't actually want you to figure things out so quickly."

"So you could use me to find Eckstein?" he asked.

"That was the plan. The lockbox was Benji's and the receipt for the storage unit real. I added the piece of paper with the Googlewhack email address. All made up to justify my calling you. There is no Kronos. I came up with the email address after seeing the ones Benji and Simmons used. We just made everything consistent."

"I chose the name Kronos," Rowland said. "The Titan lord of the universe. The god of time, harvest, fate, and justice."

"That was another thing," he said. "The Googlewhack. And what Marcia Pooler said to me. *Almost like it doesn't exist.* That got me thinking too. Maybe it didn't."

"Mr. Daniels," Rowland said. "What happened that day in Dallas was a terrible accident. Nothing more."

"So what did happen?" Luke asked. "Since you two played me like a fiddle, at least tell me the story."

Rowland did not immediately answer, but he could see the old man was definitely considering some old memories. Sixty-plus years he'd held all this inside him. Even for an amoral asshole that takes a toll.

"The first shot was fired," Rowland said. "Which we now know hit the street. I heard it, turned completely around, and saw Oswald on the sixth floor of the School Book Depository building. There's even a photograph of me looking that way from the trail car. I turned back and reached for the AR-15, released the safety, and began to lift the gun. The second shot was fired. This one hit Kennedy and Connally. That's when the president's car, and our car, sped up. It was sudden. Quick. I was standing on the cushion of the rear seat, not the floorboard, so I was unstable. As the car sped up, I fell forward. When I did, I pulled the trigger. Incredibly, at that precise moment, the gun was pointed right at Kennedy and the round struck him in the back of the head. It all happened in a matter of a few seconds. Everybody watches that damn Zapruder film in slow motion, thinking it clicked by in slow motion. That's not how it happened."

"Why not just come clean then?" Luke asked.

"I wanted to. But my father refused to allow it. He said nothing good would come from that. He would ask, do you want to be remembered as the man who inadvertently killed John Kennedy? Of course not. Thankfully, no one else knew. So he did what he could to sanitize things, which was actually quite easy considering the mess the Warren Commission made of the whole thing. Now here we are decades later, this is ancient history that matters not anymore. It should be forgotten, but three men made it their life's work to make sure that it wasn't. Thankfully, they are now gone." Rowland pointed. "Only you remain, Mr. Daniels."

"You don't really think I came here alone," he tried.

"I think that's exactly what you did, considering you utilized an old friend, outside the government, to watch my yacht for the past few days," Rowland said. "We allowed that, so you'd come this way."

Good. They understood one another. "Then you know this is not official Billet business."

Luke was keeping a close watch on Rowland and Jillian. Both were armed and as unpredictable as two sharks in the water. The old man's reflexes were probably slow, but Jillian's would be lightning-fast.

"My lawyers will quash any book before it's published," Rowland said. "They have already contacted the news networks who ran the little bit of bait you dangled yesterday, threatening action. The internet? The attention span there is measured in microseconds. No. You are the only real problem that still exists."

"How do I get in on this?" he asked.

"You don't," Jillian made clear.

"Why not? You got in." He faced Rowland. "You had Persik and Talley before on your payroll. Why not Stein and Daniels now? I can see an opportunity too."

"I thought you didn't come here alone," Rowland said.

"I lied. You were right. This is all me, as you already know. And, you're right, without me, there's nothing but a bunch of unsubstantiated mumbo jumbo."

He was hoping that a narcissistic asshole, like Rowland, would think everyone was purchasable. He'd also noticed something else about the organization. No women. A male bastion. So he was hoping his offer might be well received.

"I want what she's getting, plus 50 percent," he said. "The extra is for my silence. In return you get psycho-girl here and me to look after things for you. Since she obviously has no issues with killing people, she'll make a great replacement for Persik. I'll take Talley's job. She does the dirty work, I do the rest."

"Can you deliver the manuscript, Eckstein's film, and the photos?" Rowland asked.

"You're not seriously considering this?" Jillian asked.

"For twice what she gets," Luke said. "Consider it done."

"You have it all in your possession?"

"Damn right. Screw Stephanie Nelle. I agree with what was said earlier. Too little pay for too many risks."

"And if you double-cross me?"

"Then I'm sure you'll send her"—and he pointed at Jillian— "to kill me."

He glanced her way and saw she wasn't happy with his offer. But he'd guessed right. Rowland was a tried-and-true misogynist, working with a woman only out of necessity, not choice. Old school all the way.

A bang disturbed the silence.

His head jerked left.

Rowland's gun had fired at Jillian.

The bullet caught her in the chest. She tried to react and return fire, but Rowland sent two more rounds her way, both of which found flesh. Her focus had all been on Luke, not Rowland, so the old man had caught her unawares. She staggered back, off balance, hit the wall, then slid down to the floor, the neck craned to one side, blood pouring from the wounds.

"You may consider that we have a deal," Rowland said.

"You didn't have to do that."

"We both know that I did. She was not really a team player. You would have eventually killed her yourself."

He stepped over to her and checked for a pulse.

None. Dammit.

He freed the gun from her hand.

"When can you deliver the items?" Rowland asked.

"Couple of days. It won't be a problem."

"You can start to work then. Talley said you were resourceful. A man not to be taken lightly."

He continued to stare at Jillian. How was this going to play out? He'd had no idea. He'd been improvising. Making it up as he went. And he'd been hoping this moment would not come. The idea had been to spur some conflict, where things could be ended in the heat of battle. Like in combat. You never thought about what you were doing, you just did it. Thinking about it took too much time, and time was a commodity in short supply on the battlefield and in the intelligence business. How many people *had* he killed? He really did not know. But there was one thing about every one of those kills that was the same. None were ever in cold blood. Each was a matter of survival. Kill or be killed. No third choice. Here, there was no heat of battle. Just him and an old man who'd spent his life dealing out misery to others. And all for favor or profit. Jack Talley had been a good man. A little lost at the end, but still good. Jillian murdered him, as she had David Eckstein and her grandfather. Had she reaped what she'd sown?

Afraid so.

True, this could play out through the media and the internet with the book, the photos, the film, and all the other assorted sundries. But none of that would offer justice for the men who'd died. Their lives would have little to no meaning, as Rowland fought the truth through lawyers until the world tired of the spectacle and moved on to the next. Which would not take long. Stephanie had told him to handle the situation as he deemed best.

"*Sometimes you're going to have to do things you might not like,*" Malone once told him.

"*How do you know if you're right?*"

"*You don't. You just do it.*"

So he stood, turned, and fired.

The 9mm round struck the old man square in the chest and sent him reeling back in the chair, eyes wide, mouth agape. The gun dropped from Rowland's grasp. Breath wheezed. Luke shot him again, this time in the head. All sound and movement ceased. He lowered the weapon. Was that murder?

No. That was justice.

He still held his phone. Right before he found the pictures to show Rowland he'd hit the RECORD button. Most everything had been memorialized.

Including Thomas Rowland's confession.

77.

College Park, Maryland
Tuesday — April 7 — 10:40 a.m.

LUKE ENTERED THE SECURED STORAGE FACILITY LOCATED WITHIN THE National Archives and Records Administration Building. This was the place where some of the most valuable national artifacts were stored under lock and key and high security.

He'd left the Bahamas Sunday night. Rowland's and Jillian's bodies were not found until Monday afternoon when officials boarded the anchored yacht, after having been tipped off to a disturbance. He imagined that Thomas Rowland had far more enemies than friends, and that even the friends were tenuous as most had been bought or coerced. Few would mourn his passing. Jillian either. As far as he knew her only family had been Benji, and he now knew what she'd thought of him. She would be buried in an unmarked pauper's grave somewhere in the Bahamas, no one even bothering to claim the body. A part of him was sad at that reality, but another recalled Deuteronomy 19:21.

You must show no pity. Life for life.

Stephanie had not questioned what happened. She merely listened to his report and nodded when he finished, asking, "You did what was necessary in the situation to protect yourself?"

He nodded.

"That's good enough for me."

He'd returned to Maryland to see Victoria Sandberg. There were a couple of details that still needed fleshing out. And he hated loose ends.

"You ready for me?" he asked her.

"Everything is out."

Stephanie had made all the arrangements with the head of the national archives, obtaining the necessary permissions. Victoria led him to a second-floor conference room where two large wooden cases lay atop a wooden table. She opened one of them to display a rifle. But not just any rifle. An Italian Fucile di Fanteria, an infantry weapon, Modello 91/38, manufactured at the Royal Arms Factory in Terni, Italy, sometime in 1940. Lee Harvey Oswald's rifle.

He stared at the weapon.

"Not many people get to see this," she said. "This gun has quite a history."

He was listening.

"The FBI kept it from November 1963 to November 1966, except for a short while when it was loaned to the Warren Commission and test-fired. Then in late 1964, Oswald's widow, Marina, sold whatever rights she had to the rifle. The buyer, a Denver oilman and gun collector, sued in court for possession. But Oswald had used fictitious names when purchasing the weapon, in violation of the Federal Firearms Act of 1938, which allowed the government to seize the rifle. The buyer then sued the government for damages of $5 million for the taking of the weapon, but his claim was rejected by the courts."

He never knew any of that.

"It's an interesting opinion," she said. "The court said the whole thing was unconscionable, and it was. That $5 million figure was based on some projected market value that could only have been acquired from exhibiting the gun on a profit basis. Which was hideous to think about."

He agreed.

"Since 1966, it has stayed here, under lock and key," she said. "Why did you want to see it?"

"Curiosity more than anything else. Kind of a once-in-a-lifetime thing. But it's the other weapon that really interests me."

She opened the second case to reveal a military-style semi-automatic Colt AR-15. A civilian version of the M16. And old. First or second generation. From the early to mid-1960s.

"The provenance on this one is equally clear," she told him. "This particular model was issued in 1959 to the 1st Special Forces Group in Nha Trang, where the first Vietnamese Army troops were trained. Then it made its way to Laos with a mobile training team. In 1962 it returned stateside. Sometime in early 1963 the rifle was issued to the Treasury Department, specifically to the United States Secret Service. On November 22, 1963, Thomas Rowland carried this weapon in the trail car."

"There's no way to do any ballistics on this, is there?" he asked.

"Ray and David looked at that in great detail. Benji even managed to buy one quite similar. But the rounds this gun fires disintegrate on impact for maximum killing effect. No way to match a thing. But they did perform experiments and fired the one Benji found from the same distance, at the same angle, as that day and it obliterated the target."

He would have expected no less.

"All that is detailed in the manuscript, with photos."

He stared down at the two weapons, both of which contributed to the death of the thirty-fifth president of the United States. Finally, the truth. No great conspiracy existed. The whole thing was a tragic, fateful accident. Would Oswald's first shot through Kennedy's neck have resulted in death? That was hard to say. But there was no doubt that the third shot was absolutely fatal.

"Everything we have is going to be returned to you," he said. "Including an audio recording where Rowland confesses to the whole thing."

She was amazed.

"So you have some edits to make in that book. We assume you still plan to publish?"

She nodded. "That's what David, Benji, and Ray wanted. They will be the named authors. I was always supposed to be a ghost-writer."

They talked for a little while longer, then he said goodbye, wishing her well.

He was still sad about Jillian. Sure, she'd used him.

But he hadn't wanted her to die.

Shooting Rowland? His first cold kill? Or first murder, depending on how you viewed it? He had no qualms or reservations in the least about pulling that trigger, either time. Some people just needed to die and Thomas Henry Rowland was, without question, one of those.

But like Cotton Malone would say—

Killing people ain't easy. So don't get used to it.

WRITERS' NOTE

(FROM STEVE BERRY)

I've wanted for a long time to give Luke Daniels a book of his own. He's a fun character, a free spirit, a younger more error-prone version of Cotton Malone. But tough and determined. Finally, that dream has become reality. But writing two books a year is impossible for me. A Cotton Malone story takes a full eighteen months from start to finish to complete and consumes all my thoughts. So I was grateful when the incomparable Grant Blackwood agreed to co-write with me.

Ours was a true collaboration. I conceived the basic idea, then together Grant and I worked through the plot. Grant then produced the first draft. After that, I created the second draft. Back and forth we went on edits. I've never written a full-length novel with someone before. The experience was different, interesting, and satisfying. So much so that there will be two more Luke Daniels adventures coming in 2024 and 2025.

Time now to separate fact from fiction.

The locales generally all exist. Most of the towns and cities are faithfully described. Of course Benjamin Stein's house, Ray Simmons's compound, David Eckstein's cabin, and the mining camp are our inventions. The KOPASSUS Red Beret Corps (chapter 2) exists in Indonesia and does indeed have a horrible record of human rights violations.

Two actual rifles take center stage. The first is the AR-15 used by the Secret Service in 1963. As to the precise rifle carried that day in Dallas, we could not determine if it had been preserved and, if so, where it was stored. The second rifle was the one used by

Lee Harvey Oswald, an Italian Fucile di Fanteria, Modello 91/38, manufactured at the Royal Arms Factory in Terni, Italy, sometime in 1940. The stamp of the royal crown and Terni, along with its serial number, identified it clearly. A poorly made World War II surplus gun. Nothing state-of-the-art about it. That weapon remains stored in a secure location within the National Archives and Records Administration Building in College Park, Maryland.

The Warren Commission Report figures prominently into this story. Excerpts that appear throughout are from the actual report. The statement quoted in chapter 54 is nearly verbatim from one offered to the commission by Secret Service agent George Hickey (see more below), who was riding in the trail car. The part quoted in chapter 42 about agents staying out late the night before and drinking in Fort Worth is another verbatim account. Only Thomas Rowland's addition is our invention. The Secret Service at the time denied that any of those agents were compromised by fatigue or alcohol. But the commission expressed reservations regarding the Secret Service, declaring (chapter 42) *against the background of the critical events of November 22, 1963, certain shortcomings and lapses from the high standards which the Commission believes should prevail in the field of presidential protection are evident.*

The event on which this book's plot is centered, the death of John F. Kennedy, not only is ingrained in the history of the United States, but has also sparked an enduring fascination for millions of people around the world.

Grant and I count ourselves among that number.

Countless books, thousands of articles, and a lot of movies and documentaries have sprung from November 22, 1963. Many facts seem indisputable, but many more are topics for spirited debate. Countless timelines of various lengths have been assembled. Still images have been scrutinized down to the pixel. The most famous image taken that day, the Zapruder film, though only seconds in duration, has seared itself into our minds. Ideas about what truly happened that fateful day, and the roles played by its participants, are abundant. Consequently, in constructing this albeit fictional account we knew a balance between offering an accurate recounting and weaving an entertaining tale was paramount. Some readers might recognize materials from which we drew the threads of our narrative. We cast no judgment on those sources or their authors. All are deserving of attention. In the process of our work we relied on sources of varying credibility, from independently verified eyewitness statements, exacting forensic details, and government-sanctioned reports to compelling yet unrealistic hypotheses.

Somewhere amid all this information lies the truth.

Many people have made up their minds. Others are open to new ideas. Still more believe the truth will never be known, either because opaqueness naturally follows the passage of time, or because of crafted obfuscation. Regarding the real-life characters that appear in the story, many of whom behaved admirably under daunting circumstances, we've left their names and actions relatively unchanged. But this is a novel, designed to entertain, so changes had to be made, albeit we kept those to a minimum (which mainly center on the addition of Thomas Rowland to the historical events).

The basic premise that Kennedy was accidentally killed by an errant shot from a Secret Service rifle is not ours. It comes from *Mortal Error: The Shot That Killed JFK*, a 1992 nonfiction book by Bonar Menninger who detailed the theory, as postulated by sharpshooter, gunsmith, and ballistics expert Howard Donahue.

Like Ray Simmons in our story, Donahue became interested in the assassination of John F. Kennedy after participating in a 1967 re-creation of the shooting sponsored by CBS News (chapters 31 and 43). He was the only one of eleven marksmen to fire three shots faster than the 5.6-second window Oswald utilized. During that experience Donahue discovered that the Warren Commission Report was inexplicably devoid of ballistics testimony. Few to no tests were run. Why? It seemed ballistics would have been the most crucial of evidence to investigate. Yet little to nothing had been done.

So he conducted his own ballistics investigation.

Donahue eventually decided that the bullet that struck Kennedy in the head had in fact been accidentally fired by Secret Service agent George Warren Hickey Jr. from an AR-15 rifle carried in the trail car immediately following the president's limousine.

Controversial to say the least.

Donahue further believed that Oswald's second shot, which penetrated Kennedy's neck, may have already killed the president before the third shot was fired. He also concluded (from reconstructions) that the trajectories of the rounds that struck Kennedy and Connally supported the single-bullet theory for the second shot. Oswald's shot. There was no shooter on the grassy knoll or otherwise. According to Donahue there were only three shots. Two fired by Oswald. The first missed and the second struck the president in the neck. The third shot came from Hickey's AR-15. Further backing up this conclusion was witness testimony, findings from Kennedy's autopsy, and the math and science as applied to that day under the conditions that existed. All of it pointed to George Hickey and the AR-15 in his charge.

But is any of it worthy of belief?

When *Mortal Error* was released in 1992 few noticed the book and no one gave it much credence. Donahue himself was surprised that the work aroused so little interest. He died in 1999. Prior to publication, both the publisher and the authors repeatedly contacted Hickey to offer him a chance to address the allegations. They even visited his home to no avail. The letter noted in chapter 47 is nearly word for word from the one sent to Hickey in 1991. Hickey did not respond to any of the overtures and took no legal action until 1995, when he sued St. Martin's Press over the claims. That suit was dismissed in 1997 on the grounds that Hickey had waited too long after the book's initial publication to file his action.

Which is puzzling in and of itself.

Why did he wait four years to finally defend himself?

Hickey refiled his suit when the paperback edition of *Mortal Error* was published, and later settled with St. Martin's Press in 1998 on undisclosed terms. But the book was not withdrawn or ever amended. Not a word was changed. Nor was there any public legal finding of libel, slander, or falsity. Hickey died in 2011, never publicly addressing the substantiative allegations with anything other than a wholesale denial.

A docudrama, *JFK: The Smoking Gun*, aired in 2013 on the Discovery Channel, part of a series of shows commemorating the fiftieth anniversary of the assassination. It was based on a book by the same name, penned by Colin McLaren, an Australian police detective. McLaren essentially agreed with Donahue and, based on some additional research conducted by him, he confirmed Donahue's conclusion that the third shot came from the AR-15. No legal action from the Hickey heirs ever sprang from the broadcast of this show.

So is any of this true?

We will never know.

But it sure is tasty food for thought.

ABOUT THE AUTHORS

Steve Berry is the *New York Times* and #1 internationally bestselling author of seventeen Cotton Malone novels, five stand-alone thrillers, and several works of short fiction. He has twenty-six million books in print, translated into more than forty languages. With his wife, Elizabeth, he is the founder of History Matters, an organization dedicated to historical preservation. He serves as an emeritus member of the Smithsonian Libraries Advisory Board and was a founding member of International Thriller Writers, formerly serving as its co-president.

Grant Blackwood is the *New York Times* bestselling author of the Briggs Tanner series (*The End of Enemies, The Wall of Night*, and *An Echo of War*), the co-author of the Fargo Adventure series (*Spartan Gold, Lost Empire*, and *The Kingdom*) with Clive Cussler, as well as the co-author of the #1 *New York Times* bestseller *Dead or Alive* with Tom Clancy. A U.S. Navy veteran, Grant spent three years aboard a guided-missile frigate as an operations specialist and a pilot rescue swimmer. He lives in Colorado and is at work on a stand-alone series with a new hero.

Cotton Malone returns in *New York Times* bestselling author Steve Berry's next page-turning adventure, in which Malone must unravel a mystery from World War II involving a legendary lost treasure worth billions.

THE ATLAS MANEUVER

Available February 2024

Please turn the page for a preview.

PROLOGUE

General Tomoyuki Yamashita group for the final time. A hundred and seventy-five men stood before him in the dimly lit underground chamber. All engineers. Specially selected. Each having accomplished his task to perfection. One hiding place created per man. They'd performed so well and so fast that he'd ordered a celebration. Fried brown rice, boiled eggs, grilled sweet potatoes, and dried cow's meat. All washed down with copious amounts of sake. For the past two hours they'd sung patriotic songs and shouted *banzai*, long life, until they were hoarse. All the harshness of war had been set aside for a few precious hours.

He'd been reassigned to the islands last October, charged with stopping the rapidly advancing American forces. Prior to that he'd led the Imperial Army during the invasion of Malaya and the Battle of Singapore. Both resounding victories. He took pride in how Churchill had described the fall of Singapore. *The worst disaster and largest capitulation in British military history.*

But everything here had gone wrong.

Now he was doing nothing more than delaying the inevitable. The war was lost. MacArthur had returned. Japan was isolated. And he was trapped in the mountains north of Manila, low on supplies, with the Americans rapidly closing in. For the past few months he'd been less a military commander and more a miner. And banker. Taking deposits. Building vaults. Securing their presence for future withdrawals.

"For you," he said to the engineers, his metal cup held high. "And a job well done. *Banzai.*"

They echoed his good wishes.

The underground chamber around him was the largest they'd

constructed, perhaps as big as twenty meters square, illuminated by battery-powered bulbs. Rectangular bronze boxes, filled with gold bars, were stacked eight high against the walls, each bar around seventy-five kilograms and individually marked by weight and purity. A little under thirty-seven million total kilograms.

An enormous amount of wealth.

With this being just one of a 175 buried vaults, each of the others containing a similar hoard of treasure. All plundered from Asian countries, starting with China in 1937. More came from Korea, Thailand, Myanmar, Vietnam, Cambodia, Malaysia, Hong Kong, Timor, Indonesia, and New Guinea. National treasuries, banks, religious shrines, private estates, museums, factories, homes, galleries. Anything and everything had been looted. A grand larceny of wealth that had been accumulated by its owners for thousands of years. A lot of it had already made it toward Japan, over land, through Korea. The rest was to go by sea, through the Philippines. But the Americans had stopped that redistribution with a submarine blockade. No way now to ship anything, much less something as heavy and bulky as gold.

So another way had been conceived.

Hide it all in the mountains of Luzon and come back for it after the war.

The plan had been formulated at the highest level, all the way to Emperor Hirohito himself. Several of the lesser royal princes had headed teams of thieves that had fanned out across the conquered territories, but the emperor's charming and cultivated brother, Prince Chichibu, had supervised the overall plunder, along with its secreting away, naming the entire scheme *kin no yuri*, Golden Lily, after a poem the emperor had written.

"To each of you," Prince Chichibu said, his metal cup raised. "The emperor extends his thanks for your dedicated work. He wishes great blessings to you all."

The engineers returned the toast and offered long life and blessings to the emperor. Many of their eyes were watering with emotion. None of them had ever been this close to someone of the royal house. Nearly all Japanese, Yamashita included, spent their whole lives in awe of the imperial family. The emperor controlled the entire sovereign state, commanded the armed forces, headed the national religion, and was believed to be a living god.

Chichibu stepped close to Yamashita and whispered, "Is all ready?"

He nodded.

Months ago, Prince Chichibu had moved his headquarters from Singapore to Manila and ordered all plunder still on the Asian mainland to be brought to the islands. Thousands of slave laborers and prisoners of war had spent the past few months digging tunnels and fortifying caves with concrete. Each site had to withstand earthquakes, aerial bombing, flooding, and, most of all, time. So the vaults had been constructed like military bunkers. As each was completed the prince had come to personally inspect, like tonight, so there was nothing unusual about his presence.

The men continued to enjoy the revelry, their job completed. The last of the 175 vaults—this one, Tunnel 8—had been finished three days ago. All of the architectural drawings, inventories, instruments, and tools had been crated and removed. With each vault's completion the prisoners-of-war laborers had been shot, their bodies sealed inside. Also, Japanese soldiers had been included with the doomed so that their spirits would help guard the treasure in the years ahead. Which sounded good, but it only masked the real purpose, which was to limit the number of eyewitnesses.

"Is the map secure?" the prince asked him.

"In your car, awaiting your departure."

Everything had been sped up after MacArthur landed at Leyte. Two hundred thousand enemy troops were gaining ground every day, the Japanese forces slowly retreating ever higher into the mountains. A submarine awaited Prince Chichibu to take him back to Japan, along with the map that led to each of the vaults. Natural markers that worked as pointers had been left across the lush landscape. Subtle. Hard to decipher. Part of the jungle. All of it in an ancient code called Chako. The map would be returned to the emperor, who would hold it until the time for retrieval arrived. They might lose the war militarily, but Japan had no intention of losing financially. The idea was to hold the Philippines through a negotiated peace so they could return and retrieve the gold. How much wealth had they hidden? More than anyone could have ever imagined. Somewhere around fifty million kilograms of precious metals.

For the glory of the emperor.

"Time for us to leave," he whispered to the prince. Then he turned his attention back to the engineers. "Enjoy the food and the drink. You have earned it. It is private, quiet, and safe here. We shall see you in the morning when we evacuate."

The group offered him a collective *banzai*, which he returned, noticing the smiles all around from the men. Then he and the prince left the chamber and made their way to a crude elevator that led back up seventy meters to ground level. Along the way he noticed the dynamite that had been set in the shaft while the celebration had been ongoing. A separate access tunnel had also been rigged to explode, the charges spaced far enough apart to seal the passage, but not close enough to totally destroy the path.

He and the prince left the elevator and emerged out into the steamy tropical night. Three demolition experts waited for them. Once the shaft and tunnel were blown the last remnants of human consciousness, the one hundred and seventy-five engineers, who knew the precise location of the caches, would be dead. Most would suffocate, but some would surely commit ritual suicide in service to their emperor.

He turned to one of the soldiers and nodded.

The charges were ignited.

Explosions rumbled and the ground shook, the charges detonating in a predetermined sequence, each one bringing down a portion of the excavation. The final charge obliterated the main entrance in a cascade of dirt and rock. Before dawn it would be smoothed and dressed, and within a few weeks, the jungle would replace the lost foliage, completing the camouflage.

They walked toward a waiting vehicle.

"What of these soldiers?" Chichibu asked of the demolition team.

"They will be dead by morning."

Which should end the killing. And with 7,107 islands in the Philippines, even if the enemy knew what had been done, searching for those 175 caches would take decades.

But he had to wonder?

"What of me?" he asked the prince. "Am I to die as well?"

"You are a high-ranking general in the Imperial Army," the prince said. "Sworn by oath to allegiance with the emperor."

They reached the car.

The prince opened the rear door and retrieved a leather satchel. From inside he withdrew a Japanese battle flag. A red disc atop a white background, with sixteen rays emanating from it, symbolizing the rising sun.

Chichibu laid it out flat across the hood. "I thought you might be apprehensive. Let us be frank. The war is over. All is lost. It is time now to prepare for the future. I have to return to Japan and work with my brother to secure that future. You have to stay here and hold the Americans at bay for as long as possible."

Which made sense.

The younger man withdrew a small ceremonial blade from the satchel and pricked the tip of his little finger. Yamashita knew what was expected. He took the knife and punctured his own little finger. Together, they dripped blood onto the flag in a ritual that dated back centuries, one that supposedly bound the participants together in a blood oath.

"We are one," Chichibu said.

He suddenly felt the same pride that those engineers had experienced. "I will do honor to the trust you have shown in me."

"You will be needed," the prince said, "once this war ends and we return to retrieve what is ours. And we will, Tomoyuki. We will be back. Japan will survive. The emperor will survive. In the meantime stay safe, and I will see you then."

Chichibu climbed into the vehicle. The driver was already behind the wheel. The engine coughed to life and the transport drove off down the narrow, rutted road. One of the demolition experts approached, stood at attention, and saluted. He knew what the man wanted to hear. "Set the traps. Secure the site."

Every one of the caches had been rigged with explosives and a variety of other lethal, defensive measures. If anyone dared to breach the vaults they would pay a heavy price.

In the distance he heard gunfire and mortars.

It would not be long before the enemy controlled the islands.

Thankfully, though, Golden Lily was finished.

PRESENT DAY

CHAPTER 1

COTTON MALONE COULD NOT DECIDE IF THE THREAT WAS REAL OR imaginary. He'd been sent to assess the situation, keep an eye on the target, and intervene. But only if necessary.

Did this qualify?

The streets of Basel were busy. Not surprising given this city of two hundred thousand had been a commercial hub and cultural center since the Renaissance. Six hundred years ago it was one of Europe's great cities. Location helped, strategically placed where Switzerland, France, and Germany converged, the Rhine River divided downtown into two distinct sections. One from the past, the other rooted in today. Its old town filled two hills that rose against the river's southern bank. A place full of ivy-clad half-timber houses, which cast the last traces of a long-ago medieval town, the cobbled paths a mix of pedestrian-only and light-traffic streets.

He stood, bathed in sunshine, beside one of the more congested traffic routes and enjoyed a bag of roasted chestnuts purchased from a nearby vendor. His target was inside a small boutique on the other side of the street, about two hundred feet away, where she'd been for the past thirty minutes. Windows of fashionable stores and shops drew a continuous stream of patrons. Lots of cafés, shops, jewelers, designer clothing, and, his personal favorite, antique bookstores. Plenty of them too. Each reminiscent of his own bookshop back in Copenhagen. He'd owned it now for several years, the store modest in size, tastefully appointed, and well stocked. He catered not only to bibliophiles, but also to the countless tourists who visited Copenhagen. He'd netted a profit every year, though he spent more time away from the shop than he liked. He was also the current secretary of the Danish Antiquarian Booksellers Association, a first for him as he was not much of a joiner.

But what the hell?

He loved books. They loved books.

People moved steadily in every direction, his brain attentive to the slightest detail that had always signaled trouble in his former profession. No one stared or lingered too long. Nothing at all out of sync, except for one car. A dark-colored Saab. Parked thirty yards away among other vehicles nestled to the curb. All of the others were empty. But not the Saab. It contained two people whose forms he could make out through the lightly tinted windshield. The driver and another in the backseat. None of which, in and of itself, should spark any suspicions to most people.

But he wasn't most people.

He was a trained intelligence officer who'd worked a dozen years for the Magellan Billet, a covert investigative unit of the United States Justice Department. He'd been one of the first people recruited by his old friend Stephanie Nelle, who both created and continued to run the unit. She'd recently found some trouble with the new American president, Warner Fox, but all that had been resolved and now she was back in command. And though he'd been retired from the Billet for a while now, he continued to work freelance for Stephanie whenever she managed to entice him away from his bookshop. He liked that he was still needed, so he rarely refused her. Sure, there'd come a day when she would ask less frequently and he would become only a bookseller. But thankfully, for now, he still had his uses, though he wasn't here for Stephanie. This favor was for another friend, whom he'd encountered a few months back in Germany.

Derrick Koger.

Recently promoted European station chief for the Central Intelligence Agency. Who'd piqued his curiosity with an amazing tale.

Toward the end of World War II billions of dollars in plundered gold, silver, and platinum had been systematically hidden underground by the Japanese across the Philippine Islands, mainly in the mountains north of Manila. General Tomoyuki Yamashita, who'd commanded the final defense of the islands, supervised its secretion. Yamashita surrendered to the Allies in September 1945, then was quickly tried and convicted of war crimes in December 1945. Two months later Yamashita was hanged.

Why so fast?

Simple.

The Office of Strategic Services, precursor to the CIA, had learned about 175 buried vaults. Yamashita flatly refused to cooperate with locating them and the last thing the Americans wanted was him still alive, able to tell the world about the gold.

So they hanged him.

Once that loose end had been eliminated, and the island of Luzon militarily secured, the OSS moved in and managed to retrieve several of the larger caches, tons of unaccounted-for gold, which was shipped off to repositories in forty-two countries across the world. All done with the full knowledge and blessing of both General Douglas MacArthur and President Harry Truman.

Why was it taken?

Three reasons.

First, if the recovery of such a huge mass of stolen gold had become known, thousands of people would have come forward to claim it, many of them fraudulently, and governments would have been bogged down for decades resolving ownership.

Second, the sheer volume of the gold, if dumped back on the open market, would have devalued the price. At the time most countries linked their currencies to the US dollar, and the dollar was tied to gold, so an unexpected plummet in price would have caused a worldwide financial disaster.

And finally, once Hitler and Japan had been defeated, the greatest threat to world security now came from the Soviet Union. Communism had to be stopped. At all costs. And hundreds of millions of dollars in unaccounted for wealth could certainly be channeled into that purpose.

So, slowly, over time, the retrieved gold was consolidated to one location under the control of what came to be known as the Black Eagle Trust. Where was it centralized? The Bank of St. George in Luxembourg. And there that wealth had sat since 1949, safe behind a wall of secrecy that had only, according to Koger, in the past few months fallen.

The whole thing was fascinating.

The car with the two occupants cranked to life.

Cotton's attention shifted from the vehicle to the boutique.

His target had appeared, stepping from the front doorway and turning onto the busy sidewalk. Had the car cranking been just coincidence?

Doubtful.

He'd only seen one photo of Kelly Austin, who was employed by the Bank of St. George. Her job? He had no idea. All he'd been told was to look after her and intervene only if absolutely required. Koger had been emphatic on that last detail. Which was why he'd positioned himself across the street, among people walking here and there, oblivious to anything around them outside of their own concerns.

Kelly Austin walked away from the Saab, which swung from its parking place and crept forward in the street. No cars were behind it, but one was ahead. The one in front accelerated and headed off past Cotton. The Saab though never changed speed.

No question. This was a threat.

Austin kept walking his way, on the other side of the street. No head turns. No looking around. No hesitation. Just one step after another with a shopping bag dangling from one hand, a purse slung over the other shoulder.

Oblivious.

He tossed the chestnuts into the waste can beside him and stepped from the curb, zigzagging against the lanes of traffic to the pedestrian bay at the center. There, at the first break in the cars, he crossed, fifty feet ahead of Austin. People passed by, heading in the opposite direction. The Saab kept coming, moving a little faster, now nearly parallel with Austin.

The rear window descended.

A gun barrel came into view.

No time existed to get closer to Austin. Too far away. So he reached back beneath his jacket and found the Beretta. Magellan Billet issued. Which he'd been allowed to keep after retiring out early. The appearance of the weapon sent a panic through some of the pedestrians. No way to keep the gun out of view.

He told himself to focus.

In his mind the all-pervasive background noise common to cities around the world ground to a halt. Silence dominated his thoughts and his eyes assumed command of the rest of his senses. He leveled the gun and fired two shots into the open rear window. The Saab immediately accelerated, tires grabbing the pavement as the car squealed past. The danger from return fire seemed great. So he sent another bullet into the open window.

People scattered. Many hit the ground.

The Saab raced away.

He focused on the license plate and etched the letters and numbers into his eidetic memory. The car came to the next intersection, then disappeared around the corner. He quickly stuffed the gun back under his jacket and looked around.

His lungs inflated in short, quick breaths.

Kelly Austin was nowhere to be seen.